RED
AS
FLAME

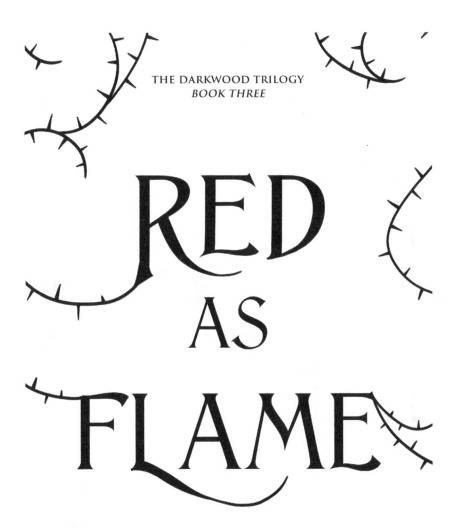

THE DARKWOOD TRILOGY
BOOK THREE

RED
AS
FLAME

USA TODAY BESTSELLING AUTHOR
ANTHEA SHARP

Cover by Mulan Jiang. Map by Sarah Kellington. Professional editing by LHTemple and Editing720.

Fiddlehead Press
63 Via Pico Plaza #234
San Clemente, CA 92672

ISBN 9781680131499 (hardcover)

Subjects: Siblings - Young Adult Fiction / Fairy Tale & Folklore Adaptations - Young Adult Fiction / Royalty - Young Adult Fiction / Coming of Age Fantasy - Fiction

Visit www.antheasharp.com and join her newsletter for a FREE STORY, plus find out about upcoming releases and reader perks.

QUALITY CONTROL
We care about producing error-free books. If you discover a typo or formatting issue, please contact antheasharp@hotmail so that it may be corrected.

Don't miss the previous Darkwood-set books, ELFHAME, HAWTHORNE, and RAINE, available in print and ebook at all online booksellers.

DEDICATION

This one's for Laurie -
with many thanks for your fabulous editorial eye and friendship throughout the
years.

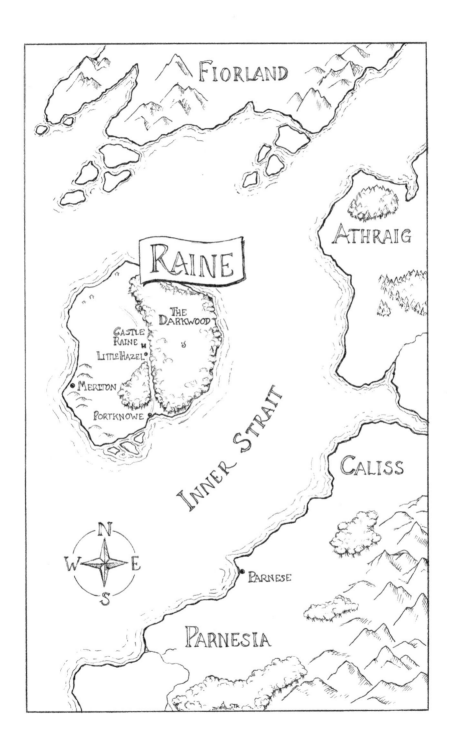

PART I

CHAPTER 1

The red priests are coming to Raine. All night, the terrifying knowledge had haunted my sleep. I dreamed of fire—how could I not—and woke restlessly in the dark with the prickle of imagined flames racing over my skin.

Worse yet, the king had commanded me to accompany him to Portknowe to meet the ship bearing the leader of the priests, Warder Galtus Celcio. No one knew precisely why the warder was coming, or why he'd demanded a meeting with Lord Raine. Was the warder's visit the precursor to an invasion? Stars knew the red priests had brought their fearsome fire sorcery to bear upon their closer neighbors, charring and conquering without mercy.

I'd believed—naively, it seemed—that the island kingdom of Raine was safe from the priests of the Twin Gods.

I turned beneath the covers, my mind whirling with dread, until Trisk, the cat, mewed with sleepy impatience from her place by my feet. With a sigh, I rose and went to my window seat. Settling on the cushions, I pushed the curtains aside, though the sun was still hours from rising. My hair stuck to the back of my neck with sweat, curling tendrils escaping from my braid.

Outside the castle wall, the quarter moon rode low over the black trees of the Darkwood. I leaned my forehead against the glass, trying to absorb its coolness.

I desperately wished Thorne was there with me—the Dark Elf guardian of the forest, and the keeper of my heart. Yearning for him twisted in my chest with every breath I took.

Unfortunately, he was not in the mortal world at all, but across the gateway in the realm of Elfhame, tending to my sister, Neeve. He wouldn't return before I had to depart Castle Raine for Portknowe.

This is your fault. My little voice, ever-present goad and critic, spoke the knowledge I'd been trying hard to deny. I squeezed my eyes shut, blocking out the sight of the evergreens, the scattering of stars faded by the moon.

I hated to admit it, but the truth was a hard stone in my belly. It *was* my fault.

The leader of the red priests was coming in answer to my newly awakened fire sorcery. It was the only explanation. In the past, Thorne had explained that magic could seek out other magic. Indeed, it was part of his duties to make sure the Darkwood and its secrets were well warded against such arcane searching.

But until very recently, I'd no knowledge of my own power, let alone how to shield and contain it. For anyone looking for such things, as the red priests were known to do, my magic must have blazed like a bonfire in the sorcerous ether.

And so. In three days, Galtus Celcio would arrive in Portknowe. And the king, my mother, and I would be there to meet him.

❀

"LADY ROSE."

The soft voice woke me, and I blinked in the light of morning, my neck sore from sleeping awkwardly propped up in my window seat.

My maid, Sorche, stood before me with a cup of tea and a worried expression.

"Oh." I sat up, grimacing, and gratefully accepted the tea. "Good morning."

Though, of course, it wasn't.

"The king would like you to attend him and the queen at break-fast," she said. "Which dress would you like to wear?"

"Something bright, I suppose." It was a vain hope that the color of my gown would lighten my mood, but I could try. And it never hurt to face Mama with a bit of extra armor, even though I knew I'd never fully win her approval.

Sorche went to my wardrobe and picked out a pale yellow dress edged with green brocade. I quickly finished my tea, then let her lace me up.

I settled at my dressing table and began undoing my braid. Facing the king and my mother alone wasn't an enticing prospect, especially without Neeve and Kian beside me. I missed my companions acutely, but my sister was in the realm of the Dark Elves, and Kian had left for Fiorland only a few days before.

"Is it only to be the three of us at breakfast?" I asked.

"I believe so." My maid picked up the silver-handled hairbrush and began taming my red hair.

I let out a breath and tried not to wince as she brushed out the tangles. Despite being constrained in a braid all night, the frizzy curls always got loose. Not for the first time, I considered chopping it all off and wearing a cap. But princesses did not do such things.

Neeve would, if her hair was as much of an untamed riot as mine was. But my stepsister was blessed with a silky fall of hair as black as a raven's wing. In the Nightshade Court of Elfhame, she'd taken to braiding it intricately as the elves did—a style that looked elegant on her, and foolish on me.

Luckily, Sorche didn't attempt such an elaborate coiffure. Instead, she simply twisted and coiled my hair up, securing it with ties and hair-pins until I looked presentable. At least for the next hour or so, until the curls began escaping again.

"Your crown?" she asked, lifting the golden circlet the king had given me on my seventeenth birthday.

"At breakfast?" I frowned.

"I think the king would like to see you wear it," she said.

"Very well." With a sigh, I let her place it upon my head.

Sorche knew the mood of the castle better than I, having served there for almost a decade—despite the fact she was barely a handful of years older than I. I'd only been in Raine five years. Long enough to discover its secrets, but not enough time to fully understand all the swirling undercurrents.

To please my mother, I swiped a bit of color across my lips and cheeks, then stood. It was time to face the king and queen.

"Thank you," I said to Sorche.

She smiled and bobbed her head. "It's a pleasure, Lady Rose."

"Just Rose," I said, though I knew she would persist in addressing me formally. In the past, I'd been Miss Rose, if that. But now I was of age, and a recognized princess of Raine—although Neeve was the rightful holder of that title. I was just the stepsister.

But Neeve isn't the only girl here with magic, I reminded myself. Since my flames had burst forth, I was no longer second best.

I left my rooms and walked alone through the stone-walled corridors of the castle. It was strange. Since the moment I'd arrived in Raine, Neeve and I had gone almost everywhere together. Her absence was a hollowness at my side, an emptiness echoing with every footstep.

How was she faring in the Nightshade Court? Were the healers successfully beating back the hereditary Dark Elf sickness that had lodged in her blood?

Thorne would tell me, when he returned.

And I would have stories of my own, of meeting the leader of the red priests and returning unscathed to Castle Raine. I clung to the thought, despite the fear squeezing my lungs at the reminder of what lay ahead.

First, however, there was breakfast.

I descended the staircase leading from the private rooms of the castle to the main floor, where the dining room was located. The guard before the door gave me a half bow.

"Lord Raine is expecting you," he said, waving for me to enter.

I lifted my chin and went into the room, where the king was already seated at the end of the long table. My mother sat at his right hand, with the gruff captain of the guard, Sir Durum, across from her. At least I had company, though Sir Durum wasn't a particularly warm ally. Above all else, he served his king.

"Your majesties." I halted at the far end of the table and gave them my best court curtsey.

"Come, darling." Mama beckoned me to the chair at her side. "We must discuss our departure tomorrow."

Although still very beautiful, my mother looked drawn. Her fair skin seemed almost translucent, a far cry from my own coppery complexion, and her smile, though as gracious as ever, had a brittle quality visible to those who knew her well.

Which meant only I could see it.

When I was thirteen, she'd married King Tobin of Raine after only a short acquaintance, then announced we would be moving to the kingdom of Raine. I'd been shocked, and very unhappy to leave the sunlit streets of Parnese for the cloudy skies of Raine. But I'd had no choice in the matter.

Now I was of age, but still had few choices of my own. The most important ones, though, I would battle fiercely for. Including the fact that I'd pledged my love to Thorne, the *Galadhir* of the Darkwood.

The king and Mama didn't know about that yet. They still believed me a pawn upon the chessboard of the kingdom, a bit piece that could be moved and married to advantage.

But pawns didn't possess power, let alone untamed fire sorcery. I would make my own choices, whether the rulers liked it or not.

I settled beside my mother, and one of the waiting servants brought me a tray filled with pastries. I picked out one of the huge sweet-rolls the cook was known for, and nodded when another servant offered me tea.

"We depart for Portknowe after breakfast tomorrow morning," Lord Raine said, giving me a stern look.

I hastily took a sip of tea to wash down my bite of sticky pastry and the lump in my throat caused by his words.

"I'll be ready," I said after a moment. As ready as I could be, I supposed, despite a sudden, overpowering urge to run away into the Darkwood.

I'd already spent days wandering lost in an enchanted forest, however, and wasn't terribly thrilled at the thought of repeating the experience. Besides, the king would send his soldiers after me and haul me back to the castle, where I'd have even less standing than I did now. There was no escape from the journey looming ahead.

"How long will we be in Portknowe?" my mother asked, a slight tremble in her voice.

Like me, she was coming to the port town under duress. Both of us were justified in our fear. After all, we'd seen her friend Ser Pietro incinerated before our eyes by the very man the king insisted we must go meet. Warder Galtus Celcio.

The leader of the red priests had also pursued us through the harborside alleys of Parnese, attempting to stop us from fleeing the city. My recollection, hazy as it was, featured a huge fireball flung at our little rowboat as we battled the waves to escape.

At the time, I hadn't understood how I'd managed to seize control of that pulsing flame and thrust it deep beneath the sea. But two days ago—how had it been so short a time?—Mistress Ainya, the herbwife, had determined that I had the unheard-of ability to siphon magic from sources outside myself.

She'd also taught me the mirror shield, both to hide my sorcery and to keep my power from questing outward. I'd driven myself hard, practicing that spell, though now I was nearly out of time.

"May I go to Mistress Ainya's today?" I asked, twisting my napkin between my fingers.

The linen slipped over the stub of pinky on my left hand and polished the wine-red garnet ring on my right, the depths shimmering with captured stars. It was a reminder of the vows I'd almost made, and the weight of the connection binding me to the Nightshade Court of the Dark Elves.

"You may visit the herbwife, with a guard," the king said. "Don't stay long."

I bowed my head, which wasn't the same thing as agreeing. I'd take however much time I needed at the herbwife's cottage, and not a moment less. The more magical training I could stuff into my brain before facing Galtus Celcio, the better.

CHAPTER 2

"**D**on't lose focus," Mistress Ainya said to me while her power pushed at my shield.

I squeezed my hands into fists, trying to repel the jabs of her magic while summoning my own sorcery. It was like balancing on one foot while pouring a heavy jug of water into a tiny glass, without spilling a drop.

Inevitably, I failed. The mirror shield broke, my wavering power fled, and the *cailleach's* spell pricked me like a dozen needles to the chest.

I winced and rubbed my palm over my heart. "I'm sorry."

The scent of drying herbs and mint tea filled Mistress Ainya's cozy kitchen, and the sound of bees in the garden drifted through the open window. I inhaled deeply, trying to regain my sense of control.

"It was better than the first time," the herbwife said.

"Not much." I frowned. "What if the red priests try to probe my magic?"

"Oh, they will, of a certainty." She smiled at me, the lines around her bright blue eyes crinkling in her wizened face. "But your shield is strong enough that they will not see all of your power."

If she was right, that was a relief. I didn't know what the priests might do with me. In Parnese, anyone with fire sorcery was either forced to join the sect of the Twin Gods or was put to the stake and burned alive.

I couldn't imagine Lord Raine allowing either of those fates for me. Still, the less the priests knew of my abilities, the better.

"Will they be able to tell that I can siphon power?" I asked, wrapping my hands around the earthenware mug of tea on the table before me.

Mistress Ainya shook her head. "They can't possibly suspect such a thing, unless they witness you doing it. Which you must never, ever do. They would either try to incinerate you on the spot, or twist your powers to their own uses."

"I'll be careful." I took a swallow of tea, trying to ease the fear tightening my throat.

Despite my lack of control, I couldn't imagine any circumstance in which I'd use my magic around the red priests. Unless, of course, that was the reason they were coming to Raine.

"Will they test me for sorcery?"

She gave me a steady look. "We both know the priests are coming to Raine in answer to your power, Rose. Why else do you think Lord Raine is bringing you to Portknowe to meet them?"

"But..." I forced myself to breathe, so the rest of my words wouldn't come out tight with panic. "Once they confirm I have the power, then what? Will they force me to go to Parnese with them?"

"The king won't allow them to steal you away." She gave me a considering look. "They might use you as an excuse to leave a priest in Raine, however. Someone to tutor you—and spy upon the kingdom."

I caught my lower lip between my teeth. Despite the sunshine spilling over the flagstone floor, a chill moved up my spine.

"They can't," I said. "What if they discover the doorway to Elfhame?"

The gateway to the magical realm of the Dark Elves was the kingdom's most closely guarded secret. If the red priests discovered it, they'd certainly try to invade, battle their way to the center of the Darkwood, and attempt to open the doorway by force. The priests were hungry for magic and power—and Elfhame held both in abundance.

The warrior mages of the Dark Elves would be able to fight the fire sorcery of the red priests, but not, I suspected, without great cost.

"The king will do what is necessary to protect the kingdom," she said calmly. "And you."

I wasn't certain I believed her, though I supposed I had little choice.

"I'm ready again," I said, pushing my mug away. "Let's keep working on the mirror shield."

The *cailleach* nodded, then stabbed at me with her power so quickly I was barely able to raise the mirrored bubble around myself.

Reflect, I thought fiercely. *There's nothing much here. Only traces of magic.*

Mistress Ainya continued to prod and poke, but I thought of Thorne, and my sister trapped in Elfhame, and steadfastly kept the shield in place.

"Excellent," she said after several minutes. "I doubt the priests will give you a sustained examination—and even if they do, you've just proven yourself able to withstand it."

I blew out a breath, suddenly aware of the weariness settling over me. A broken night's sleep and a grueling magic tutorial were taking their toll.

"Give yourself a rest," Mistress Ainya said. "But keep practicing."

"At least I won't have to worry about trying to hold the shield and using my sorcery at the same time," I said. It would be foolish indeed to try practicing magic in the presence of the Twin Gods' priests—and especially in front of the warder.

"When you return, we'll work on teaching your sorcery how to draw from within." Her expression grew serious. "It's very strange that your magic would try to use outside sources instead of the power inside you."

"Why do you think it's doing that?" I asked.

"I can only guess it's because of your late onset. Such a strong ability should have manifested years ago." She tilted her head at me.

"And perhaps it was attempting to emerge, when we consider the strange happenings in your past. Most unusual, at any rate."

I let out a quiet sigh and rubbed at the pinky stub on my left hand. It had started aching, probably because I'd been clenching my hands so hard in concentration. Once again, I'd proven myself flawed.

Would things ever be easy for me? I was so weary of struggling for every scrap.

You have Thorne, I reminded myself, and the knowledge flooded me with warmth. We belonged to each other now, though we'd spoken no formal vows. But despite the uncertainty in our future, I knew we'd face it together.

A knock came at the cottage door, followed by the voice of the guard who'd accompanied me to Mistress Ainya's.

"Lady Rose, it's time to leave."

"Give me a moment," I called, then looked across the table at the herbwife. "Well. I suppose I'm ready."

She reached over and took my hand. "You are, child. Trust yourself and the choices you make."

I blinked at her. "What do you mean?"

The words were an eerie echo of what the Oracles had said to me in Elfhame. Choices and consequences. I'd thought the price they'd referred to had already been paid when I faced the Nightshade Lord in his throne room.

But maybe I'd been wrong.

"Fate isn't done with you yet," Mistress Ainya said. "I sense it still hovering at your shoulder."

Wonderful.

"What can I do?" I tried to keep my voice firm, though the question trembled through me.

"Walk the path before your feet." She squeezed my hand, then let go. "I have faith in you."

"Lady Rose," the guard called again.

"Coming!" I scraped back my chair and stood. "Thank you, Mistress Ainya. For everything."

She shook her head at me, her gaze bright beneath the white thistledown of her hair. "Don't thank me yet. Travel safely."

Well—that was slightly ominous. At least the herbwife wasn't as opaque as the Oracles, though she still spoke in half riddles.

"I will. I'll be back soon."

Her expression as I stepped out the door made me uneasy. It wasn't the look of someone who expected to see me the next week.

The guard helped me mount Sterling, the gray mare I was accustomed to riding, then swung up on his own mount. As we turned down the grassy lane leading away from the *cailleach's* cottage, I turned in the saddle to give the clearing one final look.

It was peaceful: the profusion of herbs and flowers growing about the whitewashed walls, the curl of smoke ascending from the chimney above the faded gold of the thatched roof. Still, I couldn't shake the premonition that I wouldn't see it again for some time.

Foolishness, surely. I straightened and followed my escort down the lane.

We wound through the village of Little Hazel, a cheerful place, despite the fact it abutted a fearsome enchanted forest. The few people we passed raised their hands in greeting, but most of the villagers were working, either at the castle or in the fields, or tending to their homes.

Lively chatter and the sound of glasses clinking came from Geary's Alehouse as we rode past. I glanced at the angle of the sun, realizing with mild surprise that the afternoon was nearly gone.

Another day closer to facing the red priests. Despite the warmth of the summer sun, I shivered.

As soon as we returned to the castle, I went to my rooms, unsurprised to find Sorche packing my travel trunk.

"Surely I won't need that many gowns," I said, glancing at the stack of a half-dozen carefully folded garments upon my bed. "Three are enough."

"I can't send you off unprepared," she said, pulling yet another dress from my wardrobe. "What if you're delayed, or spill something on your sleeve? It's better to have too many than too few, I'm thinking. And there's certainly room."

"Maybe we can find a smaller trunk," I said, half in jest, glancing at the wooden container. If she really wanted to, Sorche could probably cram my entire wardrobe into the voluminous space.

The maid gave me a reproachful look. "You're a princess. If anything, you should be traveling with *more* luggage."

"We'll only be gone a few days."

I pressed my lips together, calculating. One day to travel to Portknowe; one to wait for Galtus Celcio's ship to arrive. A day, perhaps two, for the king to meet with the red priests and then send them on their way. One more to travel back to the castle. Less than a week.

But Sorche had made it clear that arguing with her was futile. I left her to sort out my attire and retreated to my small sitting room. The empty hearth smelled faintly of old ashes, and I couldn't help remembering all the times Neeve, Kian, and I had sat there, talking and arguing and drinking spiced tea.

I'd write to my sister again, after we returned from Portknowe, and tell her all about the red priests. I should write to Kian, too, though a letter would take longer to reach Fiorland by boat than by simply handing it to Thorne to carry between the realms.

Once more, yearning for Thorne twisted through me, a bittersweet wrench of emotions that made me want to smile and cry at the same time.

But he'd be returning to the mortal world soon after I was back at the castle. I could wait that long, especially with the fearful trip looming ahead to distract me. It was the only good thing about the arrival of the red priests, though I'd far prefer a boring stretch of days at Castle Raine to the stomach-churning prospect of coming face to face with Galtus Celcio.

CHAPTER 3

The air smelled of salt as we came into Portknowe. My mother and I occupied the lead coach, along with her lady's maid, a quiet woman named Briddy, who spent most of the long day's journey bent over her knitting.

I'd brought a novel, but found it difficult to read as we jolted down the road. For the most part, I stared out the window at the wall of evergreens passing by and thought of Thorne.

"Try to say nothing when we meet the priests," Mama finally said as we crested the rise leading down to Portknowe. She'd been pale and silent the whole way, alternately frowning and pretending to nap.

"I don't plan to say anything." I twisted the Nightshade Lord's red ring on my finger. The less notice they paid me, the better.

"And keep your hood up, if possible."

I nodded, smoothing the blue wool cloak folded about me. It was a vain hope that Galtus Celcio wouldn't recognize me as the bearer of the sorcery he'd surely sensed, but I'd feel better hiding my face.

The road turned to cobblestones as we entered the port town. As we clattered our way to the best inn, I smelled roasting meat, and my stomach tightened with hunger. Lunch had been hours ago. We'd eaten in the coach and, in a mark of true distraction, Mama hadn't even scolded me for scattering crumbs on the floor. Not that there had been many, but she was a fastidious eater.

The coach rocked to a stop in front of The Whistling Dolphin, which was located in the town square. We'd taken a meal there, once, but never spent the night. I was certain the accommodations wouldn't meet Mama's standards, but given her current state, perhaps she wouldn't notice.

I'd never seen my mother so withdrawn and tense—almost as if *she* were the one in danger of being burned alive, not me.

The memory of Ser Pietro's death by fire shivered down my spine. Though Mama had kept me from seeing the worst of it, I still recalled his cries of anguish, the feel of fierce heat against the side of my face.

The priests wouldn't do any such thing on Rainish soil, I reminded myself. It would be a true act of war. Even if they managed to overwhelm the soldiers and capture or kill Lord Raine, his heir, Princess Neeve, was safely tucked beyond their reach.

Besides, according to the king's spy, only Galtus Celcio and two other priests were aboard the small ship on its way from Parnese. That didn't seem like an invasion force, no matter how powerful the warder was. And Sir Durum had sent for an extra garrison of soldiers from the city of Meriton to help keep Portknowe, and us, safe.

The coach door opened, and the king stepped forward, holding out his hand to assist Mama from the vehicle. He and Sir Durum had chosen to travel on horseback instead of being cooped up all day. I didn't blame them, though so many hours in the saddle would have exhausted my rudimentary riding skills.

I alighted after my mother. The fresh wind off the sea lifted my hair as dozens of soldiers milled around us. Some of them would be taking the remainder of the rooms at The Whistling Dolphin, keeping guard over us. The others would be stationed at the harbor and about the town, along with the Meriton soldiers, whose tents were pitched like pale mushrooms in the meadows outside Portknowe.

Curious faces peeked from windows in the upper stories of the businesses that surrounded the square, though only a small contingent of townspeople had come to meet us. The mayor, I guessed, and her council members.

A figure in a dark cloak drifted up to the king, and I recognized the spy who'd brought word that the priests were coming.

"Tomorrow afternoon," she said to Lord Raine, so softly I scarcely heard the words.

"Come," my mother said, taking my arm and turning me away from the king. "I am utterly weary. Let us find our rooms."

I wanted to stay and see if I could glean anything more, but Mama's grip was tight as she hauled me away, and I didn't want to make a scene in front of everyone.

I'd heard enough, though. The priests would arrive tomorrow.

The inn was pleasant inside, with plastered walls, a staircase opposite the large fireplace, and several tables scattered about the common room. It smelled somewhat comfortingly of ale and wood smoke. We didn't linger, however, as the innkeeper bustled forward to show us to our rooms. Briddy trailed us up the stairs, followed by soldiers bearing our luggage.

"Here you are, your majesty," the innkeeper said, opening the door of a large suite near the end of the hall. "Our best rooms, for you and the king. I hope they'll suit."

Mama gave a cursory glance about the carpeted sitting area and turned to the man with a vague smile. "They'll do."

"Excellent." He bobbed her a bow. "I'll have some tea sent up while you settle. And my wife bakes wonderful scones. They'll tide you over while we finish cooking your dinner."

My mother nodded and stepped into the room without a backward glance.

She doesn't care what becomes of you, my little voice said with a vicious edge.

She's only distracted, I replied. Mama had never been a particularly warm parent, but I had to admit I was disappointed at her lack of concern. What if the red priests struck me down on the spot tomorrow? What if Galtus Celcio kidnapped me and forced me to go to Parnese? Ignoring her daughter didn't seem particularly kind.

I blew out a sigh and stood back from the door as the lady's maid and baggage-laden soldiers followed Mama into the suite.

"Princess Rose," the innkeeper said with a deferential nod, "you're here, just across the hall."

He opened the door, and I stepped into a room containing a bed, a stone-fronted hearth, a small wardrobe, and a writing desk and chair. The single window looked away from the harbor and toward the last fringes of the Darkwood before it met the coast. I was glad of the sight.

"Thank you," I said. "I'll be quite comfortable, I'm sure."

As comfortable as anyone could be with the threat of fiery death hanging over them.

He smiled at me from the doorway. "Good, good. We'll let you know when dinner is ready."

A pair of soldiers came in with my trunk. They deposited it next to the wardrobe, bowed, then left, closing the door behind them. No doubt they would be taking positions outside, guarding my door. I might be barely a princess, but I was still part of the royal family.

What was Neeve doing that moment in the Nightshade Court? I stepped to the window, looking out the slightly rippled glass toward the heart of the forest. I could imagine my sister there, elegantly garbed in a Dark Elf gown of ruby red, gems sparkling in her hair.

No doubt she was learning everything she could about her heritage from her uncle, the forbidding Nightshade Lord. Perhaps she was casting illusions in the dim gardens, beneath the double moons of Elfhame. Perhaps she was learning battle magics, to go with her already-honed swordsmanship.

I hoped she would write back to me, but even if she did not, I'd keep penning letters to her. It was strange, to think that well over a week had sped by in the mortal world since I'd last seen her, while for her it had barely been a single day.

There was no time for her to miss me yet, I supposed. Though maybe she yearned for Kian, whom she'd promised to marry. I hoped so, though my sister wasn't the pining type. Still, it was clear that she and the Fiorland prince had developed a deep bond. One that would only grow stronger through the years—provided the healers were able to cure the Dark Elf sickness in her blood.

They would, I staunchly told myself.

As for Kian, he'd certainly arrived in Fiorland by now, reassuring his parents he hadn't been murdered in the Darkwood. I missed him, too, though my feelings for him had cooled to something more like sisterly love.

The brightest flame in my heart, as ever, belonged to Thorne.

And to myself, I supposed. Carrying fire sorcery wasn't comfortable, but it gave me more options than I'd ever had before.

Which reminded me that I needed to practice the mirror shield. I'd tried, in the coach, but it had been difficult to concentrate. I thought I'd succeeded in strengthening the outer reflections, but it was impossible to know without Mistress Ainya there to test me.

My rooms were quiet enough that I could attempt to hold the shield and call upon my power. And then try to bury it deep inside me, so the red priests would sense nothing more than quiet embers.

Ignoring my waiting trunk, I took off my cloak and went to sit on the side of the bed.

Come, I thought, closing my eyes and holding out my hand. *Esfera.*

I'd gotten that word from the red book I'd discovered hidden in the library—a book I'd recently began studying again, with the king's permission. It was, on the surface, a strange collection of recipes, but buried in the pages was a long-ago spy's account of infiltrating the warder sect of the Twin Gods.

Unfortunately, many of the hidden pages had been glued too tightly against the innocuous recipes concealing them, and it had proven impossible to pry them open without permanent damage. As a result, the book still held many undiscovered secrets.

The book had remained at Castle Raine, though I'd memorized the chant for calling fire: *Esfera to quera, firenda des almar.*

When I returned to Castle Raine, I vowed to spend more time trying to steam the pages loose. Perhaps Mistress Ainya, or even Miss Groves, would have some tricks to loosen the stubborn glue.

For now, though, I had the words of the chant—though I was afraid to speak all of it. The memory of the Nightshade throne blazing to ashes in mere seconds made me wary. My power was strong, and I couldn't fully control it.

But I could coax it to me.

"*Esfera,*" I said softly, cupping my palm. Inviting the fire to nestle there, in my hand.

Faint warmth tickled my skin, and I opened my eyes to see the barest flicker of orange and yellow dancing on my palm.

Joy swept through me at the sight—but as quickly as the flames had come, they snuffed out. I stretched, reaching after them, but my power folded itself away, turning its back on me.

Though I tried for another hour to coax the flames to life again, they never came. I told myself it was for the best. I'd succeeded in stifling my power, and wasn't that what I wanted?

⚜️

A COLD WIND whipped off the sea, despite the fact it was midsummer. I shivered and wrapped my cloak more tightly around me, tasting salt and fear. We stood on the main dock in Portknowe's harbor: the king, Sir Durum, Mama, and me, surrounded by guards. The mayor hovered warily behind us, and more soldiers were clustered at intervals along the shore and up into the town.

They were spaced apart just in case Galtus Celcio started flinging fireballs ashore. Even if one group fell, the rest could come running to our aid. Half the Meriton garrison waited north of Portknowe, as well. Just in case.

The white sails of the small ship bearing the warder and his priests seemed altogether too innocent as the boat sailed across the blue waters. In my imagination, the boat bearing the red priests should be made of charred and blackened timbers, the sails tattered and smeared with ash.

We watched silently as the ship entered the curving harbor, tacking back and forth across the sun-tipped waves. Not long now. I closed my eyes and imagined the outer surface of my mirror shield polished to brightness. Reflecting everything, revealing nothing.

Beside me, Mama was very pale. Her gloved fingers were laced tightly together, and I could see her hands trembling. I wasn't in much better condition—but there was nothing to be done except face the arriving priests with as much courage as I could muster.

Imagine you're Neeve, I told myself. *Show no fear.*

My sister would greet her enemies calmly, although she never could control the fierce color that rose in her cheeks whenever she was upset. It made me love her more, that she was not always a collected statue of a girl.

As the ship approached the dock, a handful of Portknowe's sailors sidled past us, preparing to help guide the vessel into its berth. I could make out figures on the deck now, and my breath froze at the sight of the red-cloaked trio standing at the bow.

Warder Galtus Celcio's hood was thrown back, revealing hawklike features and hair a darker auburn than my own. Flanking him were a thin-faced older man with gray-threaded hair and a plump young woman whose rounded features seemed familiar. The wind combed through her wavy brown tresses, and I leaned forward, eyes narrowed.

That couldn't be... Was it my old childhood friend, Paulette?

Surely not.

My concentration faltered, and I felt a tickling sensation at the edges of my shield. Quickly, I focused on imagining the protective sphere around me, reflecting back any seeking probes. I couldn't afford to be distracted at that moment. Even if the young woman in the scarlet cloak *was* Paulette Dominas.

The sails lowered, flapping in the wind. Gulls circled the ship, crying, while the sailors on the dock shouted instructions. Ropes were tossed down, and slowly the ship was drawn snugly into its berth. The sailors onboard pushed out the gangway, and it, too, was quickly secured.

The trio of priests appeared at the top of the ramp, and for a moment the restless wind paused. So did my breathing and the muttering of the soldiers around us. The stub of my pinky prickled with a sudden ache.

At least the warder hadn't lobbed fire at us from the ship then turned and fled—which had been one possibility.

But as the priests descended, the hair on the back of my neck rose. I could feel the warder's power rising off him like a heat mirage. Galtus Celcio had no need to shelter his magic or try to hide it within a mirror shield. He strode forward confidently, scanning the waiting crowd. I shrank behind Mama, pulling my hood forward.

The king stepped forward, his guards close about him. As soon as the priests set foot on the dock, Lord Raine spoke.

"Greetings, warder." It was not a particularly warm welcome.

"Your majesty." Galtus Celcio dipped his head. His voice was rich and deep, like dark honey. "Thank you for allowing us to land."

The king's cool demeanor didn't change. "What brings you to our shore?"

Well. Lord Raine certainly wasn't wasting any time with polite formalities. Then again, why should he welcome a potential enemy into the kingdom?

One of the warder's auburn brows twitched up. "No offer of a cup of ale at the hearth first? No pleasantries before we discuss more weighty matters?"

"No." The wind picked up again, whipping Lord Raine's cloak around him.

An ironic smile lifted Galtus Celcio's lips. "I'd heard you Rainish folk were blunt, and I see the rumors are true. Do you really want to proceed in this manner?"

"I do." The king's voice was hard. "Whatever you have to say, I prefer you speak it out in the open."

Beside me, Mama let out a little whimper and reached for my hand. Her grip was tight on mine, and I didn't pull away, much as I wished to. What did she fear so greatly?

"Well then." The warder paused, once again looking over the people assembled on the dock. When he spied my mother, his gaze sharpened.

Then he looked at me, and I froze like a rabbit beneath the shadow of a hawk. Our eyes met, and with a shock I realized his were the same slate-blue color as my own. Lightning prickled around my shield, and I clenched my fists, trying to keep the mirrored sphere from collapsing. Trying to keep the knowledge of who he was at bay, even while the truth settled like ice in my bones.

Galtus Celcio gave a sharp, satisfied nod, then turned back to the king.

"I am here," he said, his voice heavy with gratification, "to retrieve my daughter."

CHAPTER 4

M ama gasped, like a woman stabbed through the heart. I scarcely felt her grip squeezing the blood from my hand. All my attention was on the red-haired man standing before us.

Warder Galtus Celcio, fire sorcerer, leader of the red priests.

My father.

So many questions slid into answers, with a velocity that made me dizzy. Foremost among them was the puzzling truth of my fire sorcery —which, suddenly, was no mystery at all.

"You have no kin here," Lord Raine said in a hard voice, as if denying it would make it true.

"On the contrary." Galtus Celcio smiled, sharp and exultant, then looked at my mother. "Tell him, Arabelle. Tell him the truth of your past."

The king turned to look at my mother, his dark brows lowering in a frown.

"What is this?" he demanded.

"I..." Mama faltered, swaying.

I stepped up beside her. Not in true support, but because I, too, was desperate to hear her answer—and if she fainted on the pier, it would only postpone the inevitable.

"Is it true?" I asked her in a tight voice. "Is the warder really..."

I couldn't speak the words aloud, though they thundered through me. *My father.*

How could she have kept such a secret from me? I wanted to shake her, to rail at her, to yell my confusion to the blank blue sky.

"I was young...and foolish," Mama said, the words barely audible above the screaming of the seagulls.

"Not that young." The warder's voice was hard. "Not that blameless, either. How could you conceal my own child from me?"

"I had no choice." My mother straightened, strength returning to her voice. "I could not give Rose up, nor consign her to a life in the temple, to become nothing more than a handmaiden of fire."

The young woman behind Galtus Celcio twitched. I shot her a glance—it *was* Paulette, as I'd thought. I could only muster dim surprise at the fact. All my horrified attention was taken up by the revelation of my parentage.

"Rosaline." Galtus Celcio looked at me. "Let me see your face."

I could scarcely refuse. The time for hiding was over.

With trembling fingers, I pulled down the hood of my cloak. The wind caught my curls, and I brushed them impatiently out of my face. I'd neglected to wear my crown, and perhaps I should have, but now I wasn't sure if I was even a princess of Raine any longer.

The warder's gaze met mine. Though our eyes were the same color, his coppery skin was a few shades darker, his hair a richer auburn than my own.

But there was no denying the resemblance.

"Rose," he said softly. "Daughter. I felt your fire calling to me. I'm here to bring you home."

I swallowed, conflicting emotions trembling through me. At my side stood my mother, who had never loved me. Before me stood one of the most powerful men in the world, who had come in search of me. Because I was his daughter, his blood.

My mirror shield slipped, and I scrambled to hold it, even as my emotions spiraled, unmoored. Galtus Celcio gave me a sharp look tinged with satisfaction.

"She doesn't belong to you." Mama caught my arm, her fingers digging in through the thick wool of my cloak. "Rose has another father, and a life here."

Not that Lord Raine had been particularly paternal toward me, though he'd treated me kindly enough.

The warder looked at Mama, his expression cooling. I shivered at the hardness in his eyes.

"You would rob her of her birthright," he said. "Deny the power that runs through her veins, try to hide her in some backwater kingdom rather than see her rise as princess of a new empire."

His words resonated deep inside me, like a blacksmith pounding at heated metal. Each blow of the hammer, every word Galtus Celcio spoke, struck sparks, hardened me at the core of my being.

My mother had lied, and lied, and lied. I turned to her, rage and misery tangling in my heart.

"How could you?" I asked.

"My darling, I had no choice." Tears shimmered in her eyes. "I couldn't let you become like him."

"I loved you, Arabelle," Galtus Celcio said tightly. "I never understood why you turned me away."

"You know nothing of love." Mama lifted her chin. "You only ever wanted power."

A faint, bitter smile touched his lips. "At heart, aren't they the same thing?"

No, I wanted to say, thinking of Thorne, of Neeve. Love was sacrifice. Love was doing what you must, no matter the cost.

Lord Raine took a step, coming to stand beside my mother.

"The past is gone," he said, a harsh note in his voice. "And my stepdaughter is not yours to claim. She is of age and can make her own decisions."

One of the warder's auburn brows tilted up. "Then if she chooses to come with me, I'll have no arguments?"

"I'm not coming with you." The words were automatic, though I spoke them without much conviction.

"Are you quite sure?" There was velvet-covered violence in Galtus Celcio's voice.

A gust of wind whipped off the water, and Mama shivered.

"Let us remove to the inn to discuss this further," the king said, a heavy frown on his face. "Your companions will remain aboard the ship."

Behind him, Sir Durum nodded, one hand on his sword.

"I think not." The warder glanced to the man at his right. "Castin, you may return to the boat and keep watch. But you, Paulette"—he turned to my childhood friend—"you will come with us."

"I don't think that's necessary," the king began, but Galtus Celcio cut him off with an abrupt gesture.

"I believe you recall Sera Dominas," he said, drawing Paulette forward to stand before me.

"Paulette," I said, my mind racing with questions. "Why are you here?"

She smiled at me, her expression open. "I'm here because I'm lucky enough to belong to the red priests of the Twin Gods. And because the warder requested my presence."

"But are you... Do you have fire sorcery?"

"I do." Her eyes narrowed in concentration, and she lifted her hand, turning the palm up toward the sky. "*Firenda,*" she said, and a tongue of flame appeared in her hand.

Mama let out a little gasp and shrank away, but I leaned forward, staring intently at the fire. It glowed sullenly, dimmer than the bright yellow and orange flames I'd been able to summon, though clearly Paulette had more control over her sorcery than I.

The brisk breeze lifted her rust-colored cloak, and the flame snuffed out. She closed her hand quickly, as if she'd chosen to extinguish her fire, but I sensed it hadn't been a voluntary quenching.

Galtus Celcio had been watching closely, his eyes hooded, and he nodded in approval.

"You see, Rose," he said, "there is much you'll be able to learn. Paulette has walked the path of the red priests and can tell you anything you wish to know."

"Gladly," she said, giving him a look bordering on adoration. Clearly, she was a willing member of the Twin Gods' sect.

I tightened my mouth and poured more strength into my shield, vowing to keep my own abilities hidden. If Galtus Celcio discovered the strength of my fire sorcery, there was no telling what he might do. Force me to come with him, probably, using threats I didn't want to contemplate.

"Very well," the king said tightly. "Sera Dominas may accompany us."

He turned and strode down the dock, and the soldiers closed around us. The man the warder had called Castin went back up the gangway, and I was relieved. Even though my own magic was tightly leashed, I sensed that he wielded greater power than Paulette.

No one, however, blazed as brightly in my senses as Warder Galtus Celcio.

Go with him, my little voice urged. *Your mother never wanted you. You belong at your father's side.*

Hush, I told it, disliking how true the words seemed.

I couldn't leave Raine, for that would mean leaving Thorne. Now that we'd finally been honest about the fact we loved one another, it would break both our hearts if I left.

He leaves you, all the time, my voice said. *And he will for the rest of your life.*

I bit the side of my cheek and gave no answer.

The wind pushed us off the dock and up the street to the town square. Soldiers watched intently from their posts, and I was glad of their presence. Even though it didn't seem Galtus Celcio was there to attack.

Provided he got what he wanted.

Me.

I shivered at the knowledge that, once more, the fate of Raine—and, by extension, Elfhame—rested on my shoulders. If the Oracles had been able to come to the mortal world, no doubt they would be making some opaque pronouncements at that very moment about my place in the weave of the future. As it was, the weight of the present was heavy enough.

Inside the deserted common room of the inn, which had been kept cleared in case of such a meeting, the innkeeper gestured us to the largest table, a wide slab of polished wood with benches drawn up on either side. The king took his place on one bench, and Galtus Celcio settled across from him. Mama quickly skittered to her husband's side, and Sir Durum hovered, hand still on his weapon, behind his liege.

Paulette sat next to the warder, then patted the bench next to her. "Come sit by me, Rose."

I hesitated, hating to admit that, despite my fear, my curiosity was nearly brimming over. How had Paulette come to the attention of the red priests? What was her life like in the Temple of the Twin Gods? How had she learned to master her sorcery?

And, perhaps most importantly, what was my father like? Galtus Celcio exuded power and confidence—and there had been a warmth in his eyes when he looked at me, an acceptance I'd never seen in my mother's gaze.

I couldn't ask those questions, of course. Not immediately. But if I sat beside Paulette, perhaps I might be able to glean a few answers. Yet —would doing so be a signal of my willingness to go to Parnese?

As I hesitated at the end of the table, the innkeeper arrived bearing a tray with pints of clear amber ale. He served everyone at the table, then turned to me, holding the last glass up.

"Lady Rose?" he asked, clearly wondering where to set it.

My mother sent me a piteous glance, and that decided me. With a lift of my chin, I rounded the table and settled beside Paulette.

Sir Durum grunted in disapproval, and the king frowned. I didn't look at Mama, knowing I'd see the hurt of betrayal in her eyes.

"Welcome," Paulette said softly, a smug curve to her lips.

"It doesn't mean anything," I said quietly in return.

To keep from having to look across the table, I stripped off my gloves and reached for my glass. The red ring on my hand glinted, seeming to throw off sparks, and Galtus Celcio leaned forward in sudden interest.

"What an unusual ring," he said. "I don't think I've ever seen its like. Where did you get it?"

I hastily snatched my hand back into my lap and tried to steady my suddenly racing heart.

Could the warder sense the magic of Elfhame imbuing the ring? Blast it—I should have thought to remove it before meeting the red priests. And yet taking off the ring would undoubtedly weaken my anchor connection to the gate. Since returning to the human world, I'd worn the piece of jewelry constantly. I couldn't risk removing it, and cursed myself for not asking the Oracles more questions about its properties.

"It was a gift," I said. "From a friend."

True enough, on the surface. Though the Nightshade Lord wasn't exactly my *friend*.

Galtus Celcio smiled at me. "You have discerning companions. Speaking of which, I hope you and Sera Dominas can renew your acquaintance. I understand you were close as children."

"That was some time ago," I said tightly.

At that, the warder threw back his head and laughed—a warm, full-throated sound. Even though he was chuckling at my words, I felt welcomed into his amusement, not shut out on the other side.

"You are not so very old as that," he said, smiling at me. "Even though it's clear you're mature enough to make your own decisions."

I knew what he wanted that decision to be. Biting my lip, I rubbed the Nightshade Lord's ring with the tip of my thumb, still keeping my hand concealed under the table.

"Rose can't go with you," my mother said, her voice wavering. "Your sect is perilous."

"Only to those outside it," he said, his amusement shading to something darker. "Rose is welcome among the red priests. She would be in no danger."

Unless she crossed us. I wondered if anyone else heard the unspoken threat. My mother paled further, and the king's eyes narrowed.

"Princess Rose has a place in Raine," he said.

"Well then." Galtus Celcio bared his teeth. "Do you admit she possesses fire sorcery?"

Lord Raine gave a terse nod.

"And are you willing to take the risk of her untrained power rampaging through your castle?" The warder glanced out the window. "Through your forests?"

I couldn't help but shiver. It was the very thing I feared most—my flames slipping free to burn anything they could.

"She hasn't ignited anything yet," the king said coldly. "And there are those here who will help train her."

Galtus Celcio leaned forward, his gaze sharpening. "Who, pray tell, might those people be?"

"He means the herbwife, Mistress Ainya," I said hastily. The priests couldn't be allowed to learn about the Dark Elves, and I wondered that the king would even veer toward such dangerous territory.

"An herbwife?" The warder turned to me, his expression mild. "Believe me, Rose, tisanes and poultices are no way to harness fire."

"And there's the bard, Master Fawkes," I added.

One of Galtus Celcio's red brows twitched up. "I've heard of these Rainish bards. They can create weak illusions using song, I understand. Hardly the same thing as controlling flame."

I lowered my gaze. He was right. Put that way, there was no one in Raine who could give me adequate training. That he knew of.

"Raine will care for its own," the king said, though he gave me a wary glance that said the warder's warning had hit its mark. What if I *did* burn the castle down after all?

Across the table, Mama's expression was pleading, but I couldn't tell what she wanted. To keep me in Raine? To let me go? Or simply for me to forgive her, which I couldn't imagine ever doing.

"In that case, I'll leave my lieutenant, Ser Castin Naldi, behind to train Rose in the ways of her sorcery." Galtus Celcio bared his teeth again in a warmthless smile.

My heartbeat lurched with dismay. Under no circumstances could the power-hungry red priests be allowed any further into Raine. I was already uncomfortable with how much we'd revealed. Given a little time, I'd no doubt Ser Naldi could ferret out the Darkwood's secrets and discover the doorway hidden in the center of the forest.

The king frowned, and my breath caught as I realized he was actually considering the idea. Did he want to use me as a pawn that badly, that he'd let a red priest into Castle Raine? Perhaps he thought that having a trained fire sorcerer of his own was worth the risk.

"What assurances can you give us that your man won't be a threat to our kingdom?" Lord Raine asked.

None, I wanted to scream.

Ser Naldi was a sorcerer, and powerful enough to feel the wards surrounding the Darkwood the moment he set foot in the forest. I stiffened, recalling what happened the first time I'd come to Raine. Sensing my potential for fire magic, the Darkwood had tried to strangle me.

The warder's lieutenant was a far greater menace than I'd ever been. If the forest attacked him—which it surely would—Ser Naldi would fight back with all the flame-filled power at his command. Whether the result was his death, or a forest burned to the ground, Raine would be plunged into war with the red priests.

My mouth went dry with panic, and I stared at the king, willing him to see the imminent danger.

Now that it was too late, I realized I should have run away into Elfhame instead of coming to meet the red priests. The Dark Elves were powerful enough to keep me, and Neeve, safe.

But that would have left Raine, and the Darkwood, at the mercy of the priests. My mind raced, trying to see a way out of the terrible maze we'd stumbled into.

Every possible outcome led to Galtus Celcio forcing his way through the kingdom and deep into the forest. He would leave a charred and ruined country behind. Whatever protections the *Galadhir* had in place, the priests were powerful—especially my father.

And fire was the Darkwood's worst enemy.

"I give you my word," Galtus Celcio said smoothly, "as warder of the red priests, that Ser Naldi will do nothing to harm you or your kingdom. His only task will be to ensure that my daughter's power is properly trained, so that she doesn't pose a danger to herself and everything around her."

I could see Lord Raine weighing his options. He didn't understand the power of the forest, and how it would immediately betray us the moment it detected the threat of Ser Naldi's presence. No matter what the warder might say, I knew his lieutenant was our enemy, and would enter Castle Raine intending the kingdom's downfall.

If only Thorne were with us! The *Galadhir* would have been able to explain to the king what a disaster it would be for the red priest to set foot in the Darkwood.

"My lord," Sir Durum said in a low voice, "I don't feel this is wise. Perhaps we should send Princess Rose away."

"He's right," I said, without thinking.

The words rippled into stillness, and I could feel everyone turn to look at me.

A cold knot formed in my belly, made half of fear of what I must do, half of anguish at the thought of leaving Thorne. Once again, the fate of the kingdom was in my hands.

There was only one option, of course. Galtus Celcio and his priests were a threat to Raine, to everyone I held dear, and the only way to remove that danger was to go with them. To let them leave the kingdom with what they'd come for.

Me.

I drew in a deep breath and straightened my shoulders, then turned to Galtus Celcio.

"I'll go with you," I said steadily, though my heart quailed at the thought. "I'll go to Parnese and learn how to use my fire sorcery."

"No," Mama said, though there was no strength in her protest. I could see from the desolation on her face that she knew she'd lost me.

"Good." Triumph sparked in the warder's eyes, though he kept his expression mild. "I'm so pleased to hear it, Rose. You have much to learn from the red priests, and I welcome the chance to get to know you as a daughter."

Paulette nodded vigorously, a smile lighting her pretty face. "It's truly the right choice, Rose. You'll be so happy with us! I can hardly wait to help get you settled."

"Are you certain?" The king glowered at me, and I could tell he wished to forbid it. Yet after all his words about my free choice, he could hardly do so.

At his shoulder, Sir Durum sent me a look, approval in his eyes. I'd made the choice any good soldier would—give my life to defend king and country.

Or *Galadhir* and Darkwood, as the case might be.

It won't be so bad, I told myself. I'd learn how to control my fire, then find a way to return to Raine.

My little voice scoffed. *Once you're in Galtus Celcio's clutches, do you think you can escape so easily?*

Well, no. Not if I were honest with myself. But I had to cling to that hope, otherwise my heart would break in two.

I'm so sorry, Thorne. I'll come back to you. I promise.

"I suppose you'd like a little time to prepare," the warder said. "We'll accompany you back to the castle while our ship waits at harbor."

"That won't be necessary," I said hastily. Under no circumstances could the warder and his people be allowed any closer to the Darkwood. "I have everything I need."

Except a handsome Dark Elf, a sardonic sister, and a loyal friend.

But I wore the jewelry binding me to Elfhame—Neeve's pendant hidden under my dress and the Nightshade Lord's ring encircling my finger.

As for my clothing, I had enough to travel with packed in the trunk upstairs. Once I reached Parnese I'd need to expand my wardrobe, but such concerns were tiny compared to the enormity of leaving Raine.

All my other possessions I could leave behind. Even the little red book. I'd no need of it if I were being escorted into the Temple of the Twin Gods by Warder Galtus Celcio himself.

"Indeed?" He gave me an appraising look. "Then we'll sail at dawn."

CHAPTER 5

T he warder and Paulette took their leave, surrounded by
guards, and I was left to face Mama and the king.

"Be careful," Lord Raine said, his voice stern.

I knew he meant I should guard Raine's secrets closely, not that he
was expressing concern over my safety. Mama, however, was frightened
for me, as was clear from the stark expression in her eyes.

"My darling." She stood and rounded the table, then draped herself
over me in a disconsolate embrace. "Please, don't go."

The scent of her perfume was smothering. I patted her arm and
tried to lean away without letting her fall against the bench.

"She must go," the king said. "She said she would, and a princess of
Raine does not break her word."

"Don't worry, Mama," I said, finally managing to scoot out from
under her embrace. "It's the right choice. And don't you think it's
better that I learn to control the power I was born with?" My voice
hardened on the last words, reminding her of the truth she'd concealed
from me.

She sniffed and straightened, giving me space to breathe. "At least
write to me."

"I will." *Sometimes.*

Of course, I fully intended to send letters to Thorne and Neeve—though I'd have to be clever in my wording. I wasn't so naïve to think that Galtus Celcio wouldn't read all my correspondence. In fact, I'd tell him that my mother would be expecting to hear from me at regular intervals, just to make sure the letters got through. In both directions.

This was my last night in Raine. My last chance to write openly to Thorne, though my heart clenched at the thought. How could I possibly tell him I was leaving?

Our words of love to each other felt like centuries ago, not mere days. The bright, beautiful future I'd envisioned for us was crumbling before my eyes. I wanted to sob, to rage, to pick up my glass of ale and dash it to the stone floor.

Instead, I rose and smoothed my skirts.

"I need to prepare," I said to Lord Raine. "Thank you for letting me make my own choices."

His mouth twisted. "My kingdom is suddenly plagued by a lack of princesses. I must admit I'm not happy at the fact. Do what you must, Rose. But try not to stay away too long."

I wasn't sure I had any choice in the matter, but I nodded. "If Neeve... If anything happens, please send for me."

My throat tightened at the thought of losing my sister. I'd tried to ignore the fact that the worst outcome wasn't Neeve being trapped in Elfhame. It was that the healers wouldn't be able to cure her at all.

The king's expression was shadowed. "I will."

I curtsied, then went up to my room with a heavy heart.

My trunk held my journal and a pen, as I'd planned to write down my impressions of the red priests. Now, though, I wouldn't need to—I'd be experiencing their world firsthand.

I ripped a few pages out of the journal and sat down on my bed to write to Thorne. After several false starts and chewing the end of the pen for minutes, I still couldn't find the words. Exhaling with frustration, I decided to write to Neeve instead. Perhaps that would help me work up to telling Thorne I was leaving.

DEAR NEEVE,

Just when you thought I couldn't get into any more trouble, it seems I've landed in a heap of it. Warder Galtus Celcio, the leader of the red priests, has arrived in Raine and—well, it turns out he's my father.

My father!

I am so very angry at Mama for hiding this from me. It explains my power, of course. I wonder if she suspected I'd develop fire sorcery and that's why she married your father and swooped me off to Raine, hoping to delay the inevitable.

EVEN AS I wrote the words, it seemed obvious that my mother had indeed been trying to escape the consequences of her actions. And I'd been the one to pay the price.

It was strange—I'd all but forgotten my childhood with Jake and Paulette, but seeing her face brought the memories rushing to the fore. We used to splash in the blue-tiled fountains and race each other through the squares of Parnese. The loser had to buy everyone oranges, a cheap indulgence in that sunny land.

And now it turned out Paulette had joined the red priests. That might have been my fate, too, had I remained in Parnese. But I hadn't, and ultimately, I was glad.

AT LEAST COMING to Raine meant that I met you—and Thorne, of course. And didn't get burned alive, I suppose. But the presence of the priests here in Raine means danger for all of us. You, especially, and Elfhame as well.

The warder has already noticed the ring Nightshade gave me, and I'm terrified the red priests will either trigger the Darkwood's defenses or sense the power of the gateway. Or both. They must leave Raine right away.

Which is why I'm going with them first thing tomorrow, bound for Parnese.

I can hardly bear it—but it's the only way to make them go. At least this way I'll get proper training in the use of my power.

I'll do my best to return once that's done. I don't know...

.   .   .

I SAT BACK, trying not to let a sense of doom overwhelm me. Part of me wanted to write a hopeful end to the letter, full of reassurances that I'd be back in Raine in no time, that the sect of the Twin Gods wouldn't trap me in Parnese forever, swallowing me up within their ranks.

But Neeve was never one for platitudes. She knew that the world was difficult, and preferred the truth to sweetly frosted lies. I closed my eyes briefly, then continued the letter.

I DON'T KNOW if I'll be able to come back, or if I'll ever see you again. Or Thorne.

Be well, sister.
All my love,
Rose

BLINKING BACK TEARS, I gently folded the paper and set it to the side. I must write Thorne next—but not yet, or the page would be splotched with my grief. He'd know how desolated I was, but I wanted to put up a brave front for him. To be strong, no matter what.

One of the inn's maids knocked on my door, calling that supper was about to be served. I had no appetite, but with the journey ahead, I should keep up my strength.

Not that a summer sea crossing to Parnesia was hard, but I'd no idea what awaited me on the other side. Maybe the priests of the Twin Gods made new arrivals live on nothing but bread and water for a month, or something of the sort.

And it was the last time I'd have a meal with Mama. As angry as I was with her, a part of me was still a lost child who wished for her mother. Even a mother as distant and selfish as Mama.

I stood, shoved a few stray curls behind my ears, and splashed water on my face from the basin in my room. The earthenware bowl and pitcher were nothing like the opulent arrangements of the water alcove in my room at the Nightshade Court, and I felt a momentary pang.

What if I'd stayed in Elfhame, wed the Nightshade Lord, and never returned to the human world?

The Oracles ejected you from the realm, my little voice reminded me. I hadn't had the option of staying—not when the Nightshade Palace was nearly incinerated by the force of my uncontrolled fire.

At least the red priests would know how to manage that power. I wondered if there were buckets of sand and water scattered about the Temple of the Twin Gods, in case of sorcery gone awry. Or was I a special case?

Paulette had seemed to struggle to summon a pale wisp of flame upon her palm. And the warder had said he sensed the flare of my awakening fire all the way from Parnese, which seemed to indicate I had more power than most. I prayed he hadn't also sensed the gateway to Elfhame, or the subtler magic of the Darkwood.

He hadn't given any indication of it, though, and seemed pleased enough at the prospect of whisking me off to Parnesia. Thorne and the Dark Elves were safe.

For now.

Yet I must be constantly wary during my time with the priests. Despite the ring on my finger, I had to give no indication that any such gateway, or people, existed.

Subdued, I went down to the inn's common room.

The king and Sir Durum were seated at one side of the table we'd occupied earlier, in deep conversation. They nodded to me when I arrived, then went back to their discussion, which involved how best to strengthen the military presence in Portknowe. A good idea, I thought. One could never be sure with the red priests.

The innkeeper came over and quietly asked if I'd like ale.

"Just water," I said. I wasn't sure I'd be able to stomach anything stronger, not with the clamp of nerves in my belly.

Tomorrow, my life would change again. Perhaps irrevocably.

Mama descended the stairs a few minutes later, looking pale and ethereal in a gown of sky blue. Despite the situation—or perhaps because of it—she'd dressed elaborately for dinner. Her hair was caught up in a net of silver and sapphires, and more of the blue gems sparkled about her throat and on her fingers.

Lord Raine and Sir Durum rose, and the king bowed over her hand, then led her around the table and seated her at my side.

"Our last meal together," she said to me, a catch in her voice as she leaned forward to cup my cheek.

"Surely not," I said staunchly, though her words echoed my thoughts.

Mama shook her head sadly. "I shudder to think what those terrible priests will do to you."

Her melodramatic pronouncements had the effect of steadying me, of steering my mind from that same tendency and back onto a more sensible path.

"Paulette seemed happy enough," I said. "And I've no doubt my *father* will see I'm well cared for."

I leaned into the word, gratified to see my mother wince. She didn't have the right to swoon and sigh with despair for me. Not after concealing the truth of my parentage for so long.

The servants brought out our meal, a simple dinner of roast meat and vegetables, bread, and another round of ale. I took a piece of bread and slowly tore it into pieces. Some of those pieces even went into my mouth, though most ended up scattered over my plate.

The king and his captain satisfactorily settled the question of which troops were moving where, and were eating heartily.

"We should send a guard with Rose," Sir Durum said, between bites of meat.

Thorne! For a moment my pulse leaped. He could cast an illusion over himself, and accompany me...

But then reality settled in. He was in Elfhame, for one thing, looking after Neeve. And for another, he was *Galadhir* of the Darkwood. Even if he wanted to come with me, I couldn't ask him to leave the responsibilities that defined him.

Besides, the Nightshade Lord would never approve of such a thing, and ultimately Thorne answered to his liege. I sighed and ripped off another bite of bread, letting it crumble under my fingers.

"A good idea," the king said. "Who would you recommend?"

"I was thinking of Lem," the arms master said.

I glanced at him in surprise. Lem was second-in-command of the king's soldiers. It was a mark of honor and respect that Sir Durum would suggest he accompany me.

Lord Raine's mouth tightened, and he regarded me for a long moment. Finally, he shook his head. "Parnese is too far away, and it's foolish to send your second so openly into enemy territory. He knows too much of the inner workings of the castle guard and our defenses. Though I'm sure he's circumspect, I don't trust Galtus Celcio or any of his people."

The light of warning in the king's eyes made it clear that he considered me a liability to Raine as well. I couldn't blame him, but I could do my best to reassure him.

"I know how to guard secrets," I said, lifting my chin. "You don't have to fear that I'll say anything to the red priests."

"Perhaps not. But I'd prefer not to send two points of vulnerability into the world." Lord Raine glanced at Sir Durum. "How about one of the newer recruits?"

The captain nodded slowly. "Enough training to be of use, but not so much knowledge that they're a liability. A good thought."

"Have you anyone in mind?" the king asked.

"Donal, I think. He's a bit green, but I suppose the posting will toughen him up."

I didn't know any of the soldiers well—that had been Kian's forte.

If only the Fiorland prince were still in Raine. I knew he'd come with me in a heartbeat, as he'd done before. There was no one I trusted more, after Neeve and Thorne. But Kian was in his homeland now, some distance from Raine, and even farther from Parnesia.

"Then it's settled." The king drained his glass then stood. "Tell Donal to make ready for the journey. Meanwhile, I recommend the rest of us seek our rest. Dawn comes early."

Too early. But I knew I wouldn't be able to sleep—not with the abyss of the future gaping open before me.

CHAPTER 6

I paced the small bedroom, the inn's floorboards creaking slightly under my steps. Back and forth, from the washstand holding the pitcher and basin to the narrow iron-framed bed, while I tried to compose a letter to Thorne.

How could I tell him I was leaving?

I halted several times, picking up my journal and attempting to write.

~~THORNE,~~
~~It breaks my heart to have to tell you this~~

~~DEAREST THORNE,~~
~~I have to leave. Please try to understand~~

IT WAS NO USE. The anguish crashed over me each time, and I curled over, breathing softly with despair. I couldn't do it—I couldn't leave Thorne. Yet I had no choice.

Pace. Write. Pace again.

The night wore on, the sounds of Portknowe slowly quieting, until I could hear the wash of the sea in the harbor. Tomorrow it would carry me away from Raine.

I never thought I'd be so heartbroken at the thought of returning to Parnese.

The mirror mounted over the washbasin showed my wavering reflection each time I turned back to it—my eyes wide with panic, my hair a frizz of unkempt red curls. I marched toward myself, then away, over and over.

Until the moment my image blurred, then re-formed to show the sharp, elegant features of Thorne's face staring out at me.

"Thorne!" I rushed to the wall, bracing my hands on either side of the mirror and putting my face as close to the glass as possible.

"Rose," he said softly. "Can you meet me at the forest's edge?"

"Of course. Where are you? In Raine?"

He nodded. "Just northeast of Portknowe—but I can't come any closer. My wards are stretched as far as possible, and if I can sense the red priests, then they can sense me."

"I'll be there as soon as I can." My breath misted the mirror.

"Be careful." He raised his hand.

I set my palm to his, though I felt only cold glass and not the warmth of his skin. "I will."

His reflection faded, and I whirled to don my cloak.

It had been some time since I'd drawn upon my old skullduggery lessons, but I still recalled enough to keep to the edges of the stairs and move as silently as a shadow. In the darkened common room, I paused, thinking.

Soldiers were posted at the doors, and they would prevent me from going out into the night. My best option would be to try easing a window open along the side of the building and slip out that way.

I went to one of the tables positioned under a diamond-paned casement and carefully climbed onto the tabletop. The window was locked, of course, but I was lucky enough to be on the inside. I drew back the bolt, pausing every time it scraped, until I'd pulled it free.

Then, holding my breath, I pushed the window open a crack,

hoping there were no nearby lanterns to send a telltale glint off the moving panes. There was no moon, and the sky was skimmed over with clouds, lending a faint pearly glow to the sleeping town.

I watched for several moments but saw no guards making their rounds. Likely they thought the side of the inn safe enough, locked up tight for the night. Which it was—from the outside.

Carefully, I opened the window wide and inched over the sill. A flower box of geraniums provided a slight obstacle, but I managed to navigate over it with only a little damage to the flowers. The spicy smell of their broken stalks clung to my cloak as I dropped to the grass beneath.

I listened, heartbeat pounding, alert for any outcry. None came, to my immense relief. I pushed the window closed, making sure it didn't latch, then, the sea at my back, skulked my way out of Portknowe.

Groups of soldiers patrolled the streets. Though they carried shielded lanterns, I was able to avoid them and keep to the darker patches beside the buildings. The guards had their attention focused on the red priests' ship and the harbor area, after all, alert for undue activity there and unconcerned about the quiet town.

When I left the last building of Portknowe behind, I breathed a sigh of relief. I crept behind the stone walls and hedges lining the main road, then struck off to the east as soon as I saw the first trees of the Darkwood rising blackly against the sky.

As soon as I set foot beneath the cedars, Thorne stepped forward and enfolded me in his embrace.

I leaned against him and hugged him back fiercely, wishing I could imprint the feel of him against me forever. Our lips met, and I wished the moment would never end. Wished we never had to speak of parting.

At least we had this farewell, no matter how bittersweet.

Finally, reluctantly, the kiss ended, though we still stood twined in each other's arms.

I inhaled, tasting the scent of loam and herbs, and the blue flame of Dark Elf magic.

"You're here." My voice nearly cracked on the words. I'd feared I would never see him again.

"Rose—what is happening?" His voice was tight with worry. "I felt the red priests' fire sorcery the moment they set foot in Raine, and came as soon as I could."

"You sensed them, even in Elfhame?"

He nodded. "As *Galadhir*, I can feel any threat to the Darkwood in the human realm. And the priests are no small danger."

"It's not just any priests," I said, swallowing back my fear. "Their leader, Warder Galtus Celcio, is here. And..."

I didn't know how to say the next words. What would Thorne think when he discovered I shared blood with the forest's worst enemy?

"Tell me." He searched my face, his expression intent.

"Galtus Celcio is my father."

"Ah." I felt the knowledge shiver through him, and he rocked back slightly on his heels.

Still, he didn't release me from his embrace. I held tightly to his strength. If there was any way through this tangle, we would find it, together.

"That explains much," he said after a long moment.

"It does. And the worst part is...I've agreed to go to Parnese with them." I couldn't keep the misery from my voice. "Tomorrow."

"No." He stared down at me, his dark eyes alight with amber sparks. "It's too dangerous."

"It's too dangerous if I stay." I held his gaze. "You've said the priests can sense you if you get too close. They must leave Raine—but they won't go without me."

"The king can force them." His voice was tight. "He should have already."

"And risk a deluge of fire on Portknowe, or worse?" I shook my head. "Lord Raine's responsibility is to all his people, not just me. He has allowed me to make this choice." Though really, there was none. This was the only way.

Thorne dipped his head, resting his cheek on my hair, and let out a long breath.

The night breeze rustled the treetops overhead, and I closed my eyes, holding on to Thorne, trying to hold on to the moment that was passing so quickly.

"The worst part is leaving you," I said softly into the folds of his cloak. "I hope you know that. It isn't a choice I'm making lightly." But I had to make it—to protect him, to protect all of Raine. And Elfhame.

"You've given too much already," he said.

I looked up at him with a bleak smile. "It seems more is required. I'll write, when I can, and send letters to the castle for you, and for Neeve."

"And I will scry to you."

My heart leaped at the thought, but I wrestled it back down. Much as I hoped he would use his magic to contact me, it seemed unwise.

"What if the priests see you, or sense you?"

"I will only scry when it's safe." He let go of me, then bent and rummaged in the thick needles beneath one of the trees.

After a moment he straightened, two small gray stones in his palm. He closed his other hand over them and murmured a series of Elvish words. Faint blue light shone between his fingers. When it faded, he opened his cupped hands. The stones seemed unchanged, but I knew better.

"Take this." He handed one to me. "They are linked now. If you speak the rune for light, mine will glow. I'll scry to you then, if I'm able."

I closed my hand over the stone—so unremarkable. So precious.

"If you're in Raine," I said. I knew that even the *Galadhir* couldn't scry between the worlds.

He nodded. "I will try to spend as much of the summer as I can in the Darkwood."

"Can you leave Elfhame for that long? How is Neeve? I have a letter for you to give her."

Some of the stark worry eased from his expression. "She's improving. Slowly, but unmistakably. The healers are pleased."

"Thank the stars." At least one thing was going right in this awful tangle of a summer. "Do you think she'll be able to step through the gateway soon?"

His lips tightened. "Not that soon—at least not in human time. A year, perhaps? I cannot say."

Disappointed, I gave a heavy nod. I supposed it was just as well that my sister was tucked away in the realm of the Dark Elves for now, where the priests couldn't find her, though my heart broke for her and Kian. And for me and Thorne, too.

The four of us were about to be scattered, to the Nightshade Court and Fiorland, to Elfhame and Parnese—seeds cast adrift on the wind.

I reached into my cloak pocket and took out the letter for Neeve. "Will you give this to her?" I asked, handing it to Thorne.

"I have one for you, in return," he said, pulling a sealed piece of paper from his tunic.

"Neeve wrote to me?" I was surprised, and pleased.

"I don't believe it's very long." He gave me a wry look.

"Still." I pressed it against my chest, then slid it into my pocket to read later.

He glanced at the sky. "Dawn is coming. You must return before the king discovers you're missing."

No, my heart cried, but I knew he was right.

"Be very careful until the priests are far from Raine's shore," I said.

"You must take care, too," he said solemnly. "Keep your mirror shield strong. I wish we'd been able to teach you how to ward your rooms."

We'd run out of time, little knowing how close danger had been. I sighed.

"I'll try to glean what I can of such things—if human magic is even able to cast that kind of protection."

"Mistress Ainya's cottage is warded, so it is possible," he said.

I nodded, my heart giving a pang for all I was about to lose. For the future I was about to step into. It wasn't what I'd envisioned, but it was the one that had overtaken me all the same.

Thorne opened his arms, and I moved into his embrace, blinking back tears.

"I love you," I whispered. So sweet and bitter, to be able to speak the words freely even as we were about to be parted.

"I wish I could come with you," he said. The branches around us rustled, the trees groaning ominously.

"No." I glanced apprehensively at the dark cedars. "Your place is here. The Darkwood knows you'll never abandon it."

"This is true," he said, and the forest quieted. "But when you go, you take my heart with you."

"And I leave mine behind." My voice caught. "I'll come back as soon as I can, Thorne. I promise."

Neither of us mentioned that I might not come back at all.

CHAPTER 7

With a heavy heart, I returned to the streets of Portknowe. Thorne was right—the first light of the rising sun was turning the eastern sky pale. In another hour, I'd be setting foot on the red priest's ship, and I shivered at the inevitability of it.

There were fewer shadows between the buildings, and I wasn't taking as much care to stay within them. I was still a few blocks from the inn when a guard patrol spotted me.

"Stop!" one of them cried.

I halted immediately, too sad to be afraid, and pushed back the hood of my cloak.

"It's me, Princess Rose," I said wearily.

The lead soldier looked confused. "What are you doing wandering the streets, milady?"

"I had a bad dream and needed some air. Will you escort me back to the inn, please?"

He could scarcely argue with that. He offered his arm and, with the other soldiers trailing behind, took me to The Whistling Dolphin.

The guards at the inn's front door were startled to see me, but held their tongues when the soldier presented me to them, along with a stern word about allowing me to go out alone. Better to be thought negligent, I supposed, than to admit they hadn't even known I was gone.

Inside, the common room was full of soldiers partaking of a hasty breakfast. They looked up at me, mildly curious, but continued eating. All except one, the guard chosen by the king to come with me to Parnese, whom I'd been hastily introduced to after last night's supper.

"Lady Rose," Donal said, intercepting me at the bottom of the stairs. His brow was creased with consternation beneath his curling brown hair. "Why are you not safely upstairs?"

I tilted my head at him, realizing I had a bit of leverage. "Weren't you supposed to be guarding me?"

"Well, I..." He glanced about guiltily. "Not until we boarded for Parnese, I thought."

"Are you quite certain you're up for this assignment?" I gave him my haughtiest expression, pretending I was Neeve.

He straightened, setting one hand to his sword. "Of course I am."

"Good. I'd hate to have to speak to the king about it."

"You won't need to, milady."

I gave a sharp nod. "Once our journey begins, I'll expect you to answer to me. Now, you may escort me to my room."

"Very good, milady." He bowed, then gestured for me to precede him upstairs.

Once I reached the solitude of my room, I locked the door behind me then settled on the bed. There was no use trying to get any sleep—we'd be leaving the inn soon. At least I was already dressed, my trunk packed and ready.

I did, however, have a letter to read. I cracked the seal—dark purple wax imprinted with a nightshade flower—and unfolded the heavy parchment. I thought of my letter to Neeve, scrawled on torn notebook paper, and shook my head. The Dark Elves could be very formal about certain things, though I knew it wouldn't matter to my sister.

Though the letter was short, as Thorne had said, I read it eagerly.

· · ·

Rose,

I'm glad to hear that you and Thorne have finally come to your senses. I would say I told you so, but I think there's no need.

WHICH WAS, I thought, as good as her saying so outright. I could almost hear her voice—her astringent tone overlaid with a hint of fondness—and it made me smile slightly.

NOTHING IS HAPPENING HERE. Of course, scarcely more than a day has passed since your dramatic exit. No doubt Mistress Ainya's instruction will be helpful, and before long you won't be accidentally burning things down.

I LET OUT A WRY LAUGH, shaking my head. Ah, I missed her.

I HOPE to see you soon.
        Neeve

SO MUCH WAS PACKED into that final short sentence, though I was one of the very few who'd be able to tell. Determination, certainly, a promise to get better, and warm affection. It would never be like my sister to write effusively, but I knew what she meant, and it was enough.

I'd leave the letter with the king. It would be foolish to bring yet another artifact with me from the Dark Elves' world for the red priests to discover. And even though Neeve's words weren't for her father, I knew he'd be glad to read them.

A knock came at my door.

"Lady Rose? Do you need help in dressing?" Mama's lady's maid called.

Mama, of course, hadn't bothered to visit me. She knew I would never forgive her for her lies.

I tucked the letter away, then went to let Briddy in. At the very least, she could braid my hair back from my face, though I knew from experience that an hour at sea would unravel even the best efforts at containing my unruly curls.

She stepped briskly in and nodded at me. "The king would like you to wear your crown."

Of course he would—and I supposed it was a good reminder to the priests that I was still a princess of Raine.

I went to the trunk and fished out the golden circlet. Sorche had packed it in among my few dresses, along with a small bit of jewelry and a satchel of cosmetics.

"Speaking of Lord Raine," the maid continued, "he's directed me to put three bags of coin into your trunk. Do you have a hidden compartment?"

"I don't know." For all my curiosity, it had never once occurred to me to investigate my trunk, and I inwardly scolded myself.

"Well, let's fix your hair, and then we'll check."

She directed me to sit at the small dressing table and went to work. The brush caught in my hair, and I bit the side of my cheek, trying not to yelp as she worked the tangles out. Sorche was much gentler—but slower, too, and I supposed we didn't have any time to spare.

Coiffed and crowned, I let the maid inspect my trunk.

"One place, here," she said, pressing along the bottom. "There's a small compartment, see?"

I blinked in surprise. "I never knew that was there."

"Not much will fit—but I'll put one pouch of coin here and pack the others among your clothes." She closed the little compartment with a click.

"Thank you." With some coin of my own, I'd be able to provide for myself if Galtus Celcio proved stingy. It was a relief to know I wouldn't be entirely dependent upon the red priests.

I thought briefly of tucking my enchanted stone into the compart-ment, but was reluctant to let go of it. It would be safe in my pocket.

Mama opened my door without knocking. "Rose, my dear, we must go down to breakfast. Are you ready?"

No.

"Yes."

She looked me over, mouth pursing slightly. "You look well enough —though you could do with a bit more color in your cheeks."

"The sea breeze will accomplish that soon enough," I replied, wishing for a hint of warmth from her.

Her remorse from the day before seemed to have evaporated, and she was back to regarding me from a distance, as though I were a strange object she'd unexpectedly come across. A dangerous one, now.

I let out a silent breath and followed her to the common room, where the king and Sir Durum sat, along with Donal. The guard looked a bit overawed to be dining in such company.

The innkeeper served us fresh-baked bread, eggs, and sausage, along with mugs of strong tea. I made myself eat as the light outside the window grew stronger. As we broke our fast, two guards carried my trunk down and out of the inn. I hoped Mama's maid had tucked the pouches of coin inside, as promised.

"Time to go," Sir Durum said, rising. "I'll check on our escort."

He departed, and I handed Neeve's letter to the king. "Would you keep this for me? It's from Neeve. You can read it if you like."

He took it gravely. "Thank you."

Mama gave me a curious look, but neither she nor the king asked me how I'd come to receive a letter from my sister. They probably guessed—but my farewells to the man I loved were none of their business.

There was no more delaying. We stepped out of the inn, and I inhaled deeply of the moist, salty air. It clogged my lungs with grief. Despite myself, I glanced toward the distant shadow of the trees.

A semicircle of soldiers closed about us as we walked down the cobbled streets to the harbor. I forced my sorrow aside. Now was no time for weakness. I must concentrate on making sure my mirror shield was securely in place.

The sky was far too beautiful for such a troubled morning. The clouds were brilliant banners across the pale blue sky, the sea reflecting pink and gold as if there was nothing to worry about in the whole wide world. The red priests' ship had one of its sails up, the white cloth billowing softly in the breeze.

A few fishing boats were heading out to sea, dark specks on the shallow bay. Unlike myself, they'd be returning to safe harbor for the night.

I hated leaving Thorne, I was afraid of the red priests...and yet, as we stepped onto the pier where their ship was docked, I couldn't help feeling my mood lift the tiniest bit. Parnese awaited, as well as the chance to master my fire sorcery.

And get to know my father, who already seemed fonder of me than my mother ever had.

Galtus Celcio waited at the bottom of the gangway, his hair a rich auburn touched by the rising sun, his scarlet cloak flapping in the breeze. As we approached, he smiled at me. Unlike Mama's beautifully composed smiles, this one reached his eyes, crinkling the corners.

"Good morning," he said, his voice resonant. "It's a fine day for a journey."

"It is," I said, ignoring my mother's little noise of distress.

The king stepped forward, motioning Donal to join him. "This soldier, Donal Murphy, will be accompanying Rose," he said. "He will look after her and ensure her safety."

One of the warder's brows tilted up. "Do you think I would treat my own blood so poorly? Never fear—Rose will be well cared for."

"Nonetheless," the king said, "Donal goes with her."

"If you insist." Galtus Celcio shrugged slightly. "But if you expect regular reports from your spy, I fear you'll be disappointed."

"I'm not a spy," the guard said tightly, but the warder's look of skeptical amusement didn't waver.

"I'll be writing to Rose regularly," Mama said, a spark of defiance in her voice. "And she, of course, will respond to each of my letters."

Galtus Celcio gave her a look. "Of course, Arabelle. We all know how much you consider Rose's wellbeing."

Not at all, his tone implied.

Mama paled. "I've cared for Rose better than you will ever know."

I doubted that. Her actions spoke far louder than her words.

"I'm ready to go," I said, stepping forward.

The warder nodded. "I'll escort you aboard. I'm so pleased you've decided to come to Parnese, where you belong."

I turned and curtseyed to the king. "Thank you, your majesty, for everything you've done for me."

"Safe travels, Rose," he said, and I thought I saw a hint of softness in his stern expression.

Reluctantly, I embraced Mama. She clung to me tightly.

"Be careful," she whispered in my ear. "The priests are not to be trusted. I fear for you, my darling."

"I'll miss you too," I said, pulling back.

Her eyes filled with tears, but I had no stomach to stand there and watch her weep. Instead, I set my hand on Galtus Celcio's outstretched arm and let him lead me up the gangway. Donal trailed behind. For a moment, I wondered what the guard was leaving behind. Did he have a true love that he must part from, too?

As soon as we reached the deck, sailors scurried to stow the ramp. Overhead, more sails were being hoisted, flapping in the fresh breeze off the water. The sun had cleared the horizon, tipping the waves with sparks.

Paulette and the other fire sorcerer stood by the railing. Galtus Celcio led me over to them, Donal a shadow at our heels.

"Castin Naldi," the warder said, gesturing at his lieutenant, "allow me to formally introduce my daughter, Rose Valrois."

The acknowledgement warmed me, and I nodded to the priest. "Pleased to meet you."

"Likewise." Ser Naldi regarded me with an austere expression. "Perhaps you should consider taking your father's last name, Sera Valrois. It carries much weight in Parnese."

Beside him, Paulette nodded eagerly. "What a fine idea."

Maybe. And maybe not.

"I wouldn't want to impose," I said. And, much as I wanted a father, I knew that the name Celcio was feared and reviled by much of the Continent.

It was difficult to reconcile the knowledge that the man beside me, who so far had treated me with nothing but kindness, had also mercilessly burned entire villages to the ground when they would not yield to him.

Galtus Celcio glanced at me with a faint smile. "You are free to go by whatever name you please, Rose. Castin is correct, however. As my daughter, Sera Celcio is appropriate."

I caught my lower lip between my teeth. I was just Rose. I didn't want to appropriate a place I wasn't even sure I wanted. Especially as I wasn't planning to remain in Parnese forever, no matter what plans the red priests might have for me.

"Thank you," I said. "I'll consider it."

"You and Sera Dominas will be sharing a cabin," my father said. "Whenever you're ready, she'll help you get settled."

"As soon as we're out to sea," I said. I couldn't turn my back on Raine that quickly, though later I knew I'd welcome the distraction from the pain of leaving.

"Weigh anchor!" the captain cried.

I went to the railing next to Paulette and wrapped my hands around the polished wood. Leaning forward, I could see where Mama and the king still stood on the dock, surrounded by their retinue of guards. I glimpsed Sir Durum behind them, and spared a thought for my newfound ability not to trip over my own feet during weapons training.

Perhaps I would have been good with swords, after all—but now we'd never know. I brushed my fingers over the short dagger at my waist, reassured that Galtus Celcio hadn't taken the weapon from me. Not that the small blade was very imposing, despite my ability to fling it with speed and accuracy.

I wished I'd brought my throwing knives, but they remained in my rooms at Castle Raine. *I won't need them anyway,* I told myself.

Are you really that naïve? my inner voice replied.

I ignored it, lifting my hand in farewell as the ship's sails filled and we pulled away from shore. The king put his arm around Mama's shoulders, and I imagined I could hear her sob of dismay as she clasped her hands at her heart.

Now both of them had lost their daughters. I hoped they could find some solace in one another—even though neither of them were particularly good at giving comfort.

Galtus Celcio came to stand beside me, setting one hand on my shoulder. It was partially a gesture of affection, partially a proprietary grip, but I didn't move away or ask him to let go. At least he wanted me with him.

"Will you miss Raine?" he asked as the figures on the dock grew smaller.

"A little," I said, trying to keep any hint of longing from my voice.

My eyes went to the fringe of trees behind the town.

Thorne was there, hidden in the margins of the cedars, watching me sail away. I felt his presence in my heart. Were it not for the warder of the red priests hovering over me, I would have raised my arm and waved wildly at the forest. I yearned to be there in the Darkwood, safe in Thorne's embrace as we watched the ship bearing the red priests sail away.

Instead, I was going with them.

"Parnese will welcome you home," Galtus Celcio said. "There is a place for you among the priests. You will be happy."

"I look forward to it," I said, not really meaning the words.

For now, my gaze was fixed behind us, on the receding shoreline.

He squeezed my shoulder, then let go. "I must consult with the captain, but tell me if you have need of anything. Your luggage has been taken below, and, as I said, Paulette will show you about the ship."

"Thank you." I looked up at him, searching his face for traces of my own features.

We didn't look that alike, except for our eyes. And my red hair, of course, which seemed too bright in comparison with his deep auburn locks.

"I'll see you at supper," he said, then stepped away, nodding at the older priest to accompany him.

I turned my attention back to Raine. Portknowe seemed a tiny collection of buildings compared to the weight of the Darkwood carpeting the land behind it. The sight reminded me of everything that held Thorne there, and I let out a sigh.

Too bad I'd be sharing a cabin with Paulette. I'd have to wait until we reached Parnese to try to scry him—provided I had my own room. Were new inductees to the sect of the Twin Gods afforded such luxuries? If not, I'd have to ask my father for an exception.

The light-imbued stone lay safely in my pocket, but once we reached shore, I wanted to find some way to keep it even closer. A small silken pouch, perhaps, that I could wear about my neck.

"Well." Paulette turned to me, smiling. "Here we are again, after all these years."

"I never imagined it." I gave her a curious look. "Did you?"

She tilted her head, the breeze pulling at her wavy brown hair. "The Twin Gods work in mysterious ways. I don't think it's a coincidence that we were childhood friends, and then I joined the red priests. Our paths were meant to cross."

"How did the priests find you, anyway?" I didn't ask why they hadn't burned her to a crisp.

Unlike Mama's friend Ser Pietro, younger people were taken as aspirants to join the priesthood. Older ones, too, as long they didn't resist. Pietro had resisted, and the memory of his burning had left a char mark on my soul.

Never forget who the red priests truly are, my little voice reminded me.

"The priests sensed my fire sorcery, of course," Paulette said, a bit smugly. "I was glad to leave my parents' shoemaking business for a life in the temple. I'm one of the stewards of the relics, you know."

"Ah." I had no idea what that meant—but no doubt I'd find out. "And what of Jack? Do you know what became of him?"

"Of course! He's one of the temple guards, though sadly he has not a touch of power. We can't all be so lucky." She gave me an encouraging look. "Don't worry, Rose—I'm sure with training you, too, will be able to summon the flames the warder senses within you."

It wasn't a question of summoning them, but of being able to control the raging inferno when they came. Paulette didn't need to know that, however, so I simply nodded.

She patted my shoulder, then glanced behind me with a teasing look. "But who is this good-looking guard following you about? Have you a name, sir?"

"Donal, milady," my guard said, stepping forward and making her a brief bow. "Honored to meet you."

"The pleasure is all mine." Paulette gave him a coy smile. "I am Sera

Dominas. But I must ask, why are you coming along to Parnese? Not that I mind in the least having such a handsome soldier aboard."

He reddened slightly. "My duty is to guard Princess Rose."

I hadn't recalled Paulette being such a flirt—but then again, I'd only been thirteen when I left Parnese. Clearly, she'd grown into the tendency later.

"Princess Rose." Paulette's attention shifted back to me, her gaze flicking to the crown on my head. "Things will be different for you in the temple, of course. There are no servants there to wait on you hand and foot."

"I'll manage," I said dryly.

"I hope so," she said. "The aspirants' dormitory will be quite a step down for you—unless, of course, you have enough power to become an initiate right away. Galtus Celcio seems to think you do."

She leaned forward, and I felt a sudden, clumsy seeking thrust toward me. It slid off the smooth sides of my mirror shield, and Paulette frowned. I pretended not to notice anything amiss and turned to watch Raine fading in the distance.

It already looked so small—just a little island set across the Strait from the bulk of the Continent. Unimposing. Holding no great secrets.

And yet I knew better. Knew that it held everything.

Thorne. I sent my yearning back across the water, hoping he could feel it. Hoping he knew that, as soon as I mastered my sorcery, I would return to him.

No matter what.

PART II

CHAPTER 8

The crossing to Parnese took three days, but at least the weather, though lacking wind at times, was pleasant enough.

Not so pleasant was the constant scrutiny of the red priests. Paulette was harmless, I'd decided, but Castin Naldi watched me whenever I was in his presence. His attempts to probe my power were much subtler than Paulette's had been, but I still felt them, and held my mirror shield steady.

My father, however, seemed unconcerned about the strength of my sorcery. He'd told me he felt my power all the way from Parnese, and that seemed to suffice. I only hoped he was right, and that I'd be able to gain full control over my flames.

The cabin I shared with Paulette was adequate for one person but cramped with two. After a somewhat restless night, I slipped down from the upper bunk, quietly dressed, and left her to her slumber.

I'd made the crossing over the Strait enough times that my sea legs returned quickly. The smell of food led me to the galley, where the cook fetched me a mug of tea and a piece of buttered bread. I sipped enough tea so the liquid wouldn't slosh over the sides, then made my way above to enjoy my meal on the deck.

The sea stretched around us in all directions, lazy blue under the morning sun. Despite our being far from land, several gulls squawked and soared about the masts. I took my breakfast over to a coil of ropes near the bow and settled, finding a spot where the errant wind wouldn't blow my hair into my mouth as I ate.

It was peaceful—a welcome interlude between the pain of leaving Thorne and the worry of what was to come. Had I made the right choice? Well, it was too late to change it now, so I must walk the path ahead.

Straight into the Temple of the Twin Gods.

"Good morning," Galtus Celcio said, striding over to where I sat. "Did you sleep well?"

"Well enough, thank you."

"May I join you?" He nodded at the coiled ropes that were my current perch.

I nodded and scooted over to make room for him, trying not to compare his easy manner with Mama's brittleness whenever I was in her presence.

"What will happen," I asked, "when we reach Parnese?"

"Once we're at the temple, you'll be placed with the other aspirants."

"Oh." I frowned. Maybe my power wasn't as special as I'd thought.

He gave me a sympathetic smile. "Never fear—we'll have you out of the dormitory in no time. It's more to satisfy the formalities than anything. I believe I only spent one night there before passing the test to become an initiate."

"You started as an aspirant?" I wasn't sure why the knowledge surprised me so much.

He laughed heartily. "I didn't spring full-grown from the brow of the Twin Gods, I assure you. No, I came to the temple like all of the priests do—as a hopeful supplicant who'd shown the beginnings of fire sorcery."

"How old were you?" I thought of my string of birthdays, of my constant yearning to manifest a shred of power, denied each time. Until, of course, raging flames had erupted from me when I turned eighteen.

"The night before my thirteenth birthday, I dreamed of fire. The next day, I went to the temple."

"So, the priests didn't scoop you off the streets?"

"Most aspirants come to us," he said. "It's only the ones who try to hide—or whose parents attempt to conceal their abilities—that we must search out."

I didn't mention the purge that had taken place when I was seven, where all those with fire magic were rounded up. Those who refused to pledge to the Twin Gods, or those they caught trying to escape the city, had been burned alive.

By Galtus Celcio.

The morning seemed colder, and I suddenly wished I hadn't agreed that he could sit with me.

"Don't worry," he said, misinterpreting my sudden withdrawal. "You'll pass the test easily."

"What does it consist of?"

Smiling, he shook his head. "I cannot tell you. Some among the priesthood will believe I'm showing you undue favor because you're my daughter. You must prove you can advance on your own. Though I've no doubt you can."

A soft warmth pressed against my mind, and belatedly I realized it was Galtus Celcio's seeking. Hastily, I strengthened my mirror shield. My fire, which had been quiet since we boarded, stirred sleepily, as if called by the warder's power.

Hush, I told it. *We are surrounded by water. There is nothing you can do here.*

"With a little training, Rose, you'll be formidable," he said. "You'll be able to sense the fire within you and summon it at will. Indeed, I wonder..."

He regarded me intently, and I tried not to shift guiltily. What was he looking for?

"What do you wonder?" I asked after the silence had stretched out uncomfortably.

"With the strength of your power, I'm surprised it didn't manifest before you were eighteen."

"Maybe I was too far from Parnese," I said, not willing to admit I'd often wondered the same. "Also, Raine is a very damp country." That seemed a weak excuse, but I had no other to give.

"Perhaps." His mouth firmed, and he didn't seem convinced.

I couldn't blame him—but they were the only explanations I'd been able to come up with. Other than the fact I'd been in the enchanted realm of the Dark Elves when my power manifested, and that perhaps the presence of their magic had, finally, triggered my own. That speculation, however, was certainly one I couldn't share with the warder.

I picked at the coiled rope, thinking. As usual, I had a thousand questions buzzing through my brain. And Galtus Celcio seemed inclined to answer them—at least for the moment.

"So," I said, "if I understand correctly, weaker talents take longer to appear? Does anyone manifest fire sorcery late in life?"

"The oldest aspirant we ever had was a young man who'd just turned twenty, but most are in their early teens. If no fire ability manifests before reaching full adulthood, then it was never there to begin with."

I tilted my head. "How old was Paulette?"

"Fifteen." A faint smile ghosted over his face. "I believe she pities you for manifesting so late—but your power far outshines hers."

That still remained to be seen, of course. If it were true, I hoped she wouldn't begin to hate me once I started my training. Of course, a strong talent for fire sorcery meant nothing without the ability to control it.

"I must go," he said, standing. "Thank you for allowing me to join you, Rose."

"Thank you for answering my questions."

"If more arise during our journey, don't hesitate to ask. But I'm afraid I'll be quite busy once we return to Parnese."

My heart twisted. I'd hoped he'd take me under his wing, be the attentive father I'd never had. I'd been foolish to think the warder of the red priests would spend his time leading me by the hand about the temple.

"Will I see you at all?" I asked.

"Of course you'll see me." His expression was warm. "I'll be paying close attention to your progress."

I nodded. "I'll do my best."

"Then you will do very well indeed."

He tipped his head in farewell and left, the sunlight turning his cloak to blazing crimson as he strode away.

⚜

THE REST of the journey passed uneventfully, and on the third day, the coast of Parnesia emerged from the blue. First it was a dark line on the horizon, growing wider by the hour until, finally, I could make out the cliffs and crags along the shore.

Little villages with red-roofed houses clustered here and there as we approached Parnese, until at last the wide arc of the bay opened before us. I watched eagerly from the prow as the city came into view, having many good memories here before the bad ones overshadowed everything. My guard, Donal, joined me, of course. He was a near-silent shadow at my heels, and it took effort not to tell him to go occupy himself elsewhere. I was the reason he was on the journey, after all.

Still, he didn't need to track my every move. I wondered what he'd do when we reached the Temple of the Twin Gods. No doubt the priests would separate us—unless he decided to become an aspirant, which I thought highly unlikely.

Ranks of white-walled houses with tiled roofs rose, with a glimpse of blue mosaic or pointed turret between. The streets wound back and forth up the hill the city was built upon until they reached the royal palace. The palace looked like an ornate cake perched atop Parnese, or a very fancy hat. I smiled at the thought, then sobered as I recalled that the current monarchs and their families were under house arrest. The government was now run by the red priests.

Beside me, Donal shaded his eyes with his hand and surveyed the city. "Big place, isn't it?" There was a note of wonder in his voice.

I glanced at him. "Where are you from?"

"A village outside Meriton, milady. I thought that city was large. But this..." He shook his head. "I feel lost just looking at it."

"You'll find your way around it soon enough. When in doubt,

follow the streets up and you'll reach the Temple of the Twin Gods." I pointed to the high golden dome shining below the walls of the palace. "Mid-city are the marketplace squares and residences. And lower town has inns and the type of establishments I'm sure Sir Durum wouldn't want you to frequent."

"Oh, I wouldn't do that." He gave me a solemn look. "I take my responsibilities seriously."

I let out a sigh. "You can take a day off now and then, you know. I'm under the protection of one of the most powerful men on the Continent."

Donal's hand went to his sword. "That's why I must be vigilant," he said darkly.

"I do appreciate it. But maybe Sera Dominas would be able to show you about the city."

If anyone could pry Donal from my side, it would be Paulette. She'd continued flirting shamelessly with my guard for the entire sea voyage, and he didn't seem immune to her charms.

His cheeks reddened slightly, but he didn't argue. I returned to watching Parnese grow ever closer. The chime of bells drifted across the water, marking the hour. The familiar sound made me feel as if I were home.

As did the dry air and the faint scent of orange blossoms as we drew near the shore. That delicate fragrance was soon overcome by the smell of fish, however, and my joy in returning to Parnese dimmed as I considered what lay ahead.

I must navigate the world of the red priests without revealing any of Raine's secrets, or making enemies along the way. I had to pass tests that I knew nothing about and learn to control my magic—though I supposed I didn't need to keep the strength of my power hidden any longer. My former fear that Galtus Celcio would snatch me away to join the red priests hardly mattered, now that I'd chosen of my own free will to walk into their clutches.

And finally, I must keep my heart from breaking every time I thought of Thorne.

I clung to the knowledge that he could scry me whenever he was in the mortal world, but there was so much danger involved, I didn't know when I might be able to summon him. Or if I should even try.

All too soon, the ship docked. Amid a swirl of seabirds and shouts, the sailors set the gangway. I noted a large carriage waiting nearby, painted a deep scarlet. It came as no surprise to see the porters carrying my trunk to it, along with several other pieces of luggage. Only the warder of the red priests would travel in such a coach.

Galtus Celcio, Paulette, and Ser Naldi gathered at the top of the ramp, and my father nodded for me to join them. A little apprehensively, I did so. Once I set foot on shore, the path ahead would feel inevitable.

It already is, my little voice said. *What else will you do? Fling yourself melodramatically into the sea?*

I lifted my chin and stepped forward. This was my choice, after all.

CHAPTER 9

T he scarlet coach came to a stop in the plaza fronting the Temple of the Twin Gods. I suspected there was a back entrance, but we weren't using it, as Galtus Celcio's return was an important public spectacle. As we'd traversed the streets of Parnese, I saw the attention of the crowds turn toward us and a subsequent surge of people hurrying up to the temple.

Did the citizens of Parnese esteem the warder so much, or was it fear that drove them? Two years ago, a heavy sense of oppression had hung over the city. Now, though, scarlet banners were draped from the windows and the cheers sounded genuine.

I understood it, a little. Galtus Celcio had done terrible things, including burning an innocent man to a cinder before my eyes. Yet the warder had charisma enough that it was easy to separate the man from his actions—especially when in his presence. Even though I knew better, it was difficult not to be lulled into a sense of complacency.

Besides, he was my father.

That doesn't matter, my little voice whispered. *After all, look at how little your own mother cares for you. All she's ever done is lie to you.*

I had no proof Galtus Celcio would be any different—yet he'd

come all the way to Raine to find me. Surely that counted for
something.

We disembarked in front of the temple. I squinted up at the huge,
gilded dome, which shone bright enough to rival the sun. Gray-robed
priests lined the way from the street to the temple, keeping the crowds
back from the steps.

I'd been to the temple plaza before, on a dare with Paulette and
Jack. We'd crept about the edges of the open cobblestoned space, too
afraid to come any closer to the blood-colored walls.

And now Paulette lived there, an initiate of the red priests. I
glanced at her as we walked toward the hewn red blocks.

"Do you remember it?" she asked me.

"A little."

"You'll come to know it much better." She smiled at me. "I'm so
glad you're finally home, Rose."

I didn't answer. I doubted the imposing temple would ever feel like
home—and besides, I didn't want it to. The home of my heart was in
the Darkwood.

As our entourage strode up the stairs, the spectators bowed and
made the sign of the Twin Gods: two fingers of their right hands
pressed into the upraised palms of their left. Galtus Celcio nodded,
and I was glad to see that the priests weren't required to return the
gesture. I supposed they didn't have to prove their own piety. Their
scarlet cloaks spoke volumes.

At the top of the steps, beneath a long portico, stood two huge
arched doorways. Over each door was a recessed niche holding a life-
sized statue. The left-hand one depicted a young man with curly red
hair, wearing a crimson robe embroidered with an orange and yellow
pattern of fire. He stared remotely out over the plaza, a carved golden
flame cupped in his right hand.

The other statue was, presumably, his twin. She had the same
embroidered red robe and curling hair, though hers fell midway down
her back. I frowned as I realized it was painted the exact same shade
as my own. Instead of a flame, however, she held a sword made of some
dark stone that seemed to absorb the light, the tip pointed toward
the sky.

The Twin Gods. They did not look particularly pleasant.

Black-robed priests stood beside the doors, presumably there to keep out the riffraff. They inclined their heads to the warder and stepped aside so we could enter the temple. Galtus Celcio and Ser Naldi moved to the left-hand door. I made to follow, but Paulette snagged my elbow and steered me beneath the sword-wielding twin.

I shot her a questioning look. "Does it matter which door we use?"

"Not really—but since you match the Sister, it seemed fitting for your first entry."

Clearly, I wasn't the only one who'd noticed the similarities. I didn't much welcome the comparison.

With Paulette at my side, I stepped into the cool, cavernous interior of the Temple of the Twin Gods. As I crossed the threshold, my shoulders tightened and I scanned the arched hallways lining either side of the huge room. Nothing moved in the shadows there—no invisible fire lashing out to flay my senses, no prickle of sorcery sliding over my tensely held mirror shield.

Flickering lamps mounted on the walls illuminated the main part of the temple, which held dozens of rows of wooden benches facing a crimson-draped altar. There, a live flame burned in a golden bowl and a black sword was mounted upright, pointing to the domed ceiling high overhead. An enormous painting of the Twin Gods dominated the space behind the altar. Their cold eyes looked out over the pews, seeming to focus on me.

Foolishness, I told myself. It was just a painted image. Nothing to be afraid of.

Galtus Celcio strode down the aisle between the benches, followed by his lieutenant. Paulette and I fell in behind, then came two more priests, insulating us from the flood of worshippers streaming in from the plaza.

Echoing whispers gave way to a low babble of excitement as the benches filled. Ser Naldi opened the low railing separating the pews from the altar space, then stood back to let Galtus Celcio precede him. The warder halted behind the altar, and Paulette guided us to stand a few paces to his right. My throat was dry from thirst. And fear. I desperately hoped Galtus Celcio wasn't about to incinerate some poor soul on the spot.

Soft light filtered in through the high windows set just under the dome, and I could make out two smaller sanctuaries branching off on either side of the main room. They were lit with hundreds of votive candles, the light playing over the severe features of the Brother on the left-hand side and the Sister on the right.

"Welcome," the warder said, raising his voice to fill the echoing space.

The crowd quieted, the last empty spaces on the benches filled. Those who hadn't arrived in time to find a seat stood massed in the back. There were hundreds of people in the temple, and I had a momentary, panicked notion that between their breathing and the copious candles, all the air was being sucked out of the room.

"I am glad to be home again," Galtus Celcio continued. "My absence was necessary, however, as I have returned with a prize."

As he spoke, anxiety mounted inside me, twisting in my chest. Surely he wasn't about to—

"I'm most pleased to introduce my daughter, Princess Rosaline Valrois Celcio!" He turned and beckoned to me.

I stood frozen for a moment, until Paulette gave me a little shove. With leaden steps, I moved to stand beside my father. After all his talk of choices, of the decision of what name to use here in Parnese, he'd taken that option from me. And named me a princess into the bargain!

He's using you, my little voice said.

No, he's just proud of me, I tried to argue, but the protest felt hollow.

Galtus Celcio took my hand in his and raised it as the worshippers let out a cheer.

"Smile, Rose," he said under his breath.

I forced my lips to curve. I'd been naïve to think I'd enter the temple as a simple aspirant, as unnoticed as some peasant girl from the countryside. No, I was a symbol, proof of my father's humanity, proof that the power of the red priests could not be denied.

"Rose has come to Parnese to learn the way of the flame and the blade," he said, projecting his voice once again. "The fire burns brightly within her, as you are about to see."

What? I glanced at him, wide-eyed. "I can't—"

"You will." He lowered our linked hands and turned me to face him, then released his grip. "Cup your palms before you."

Slowly, I did as he asked. My hands trembled, and the crowd grew breathlessly still.

"Now, call the flames," he said. "Concentrate on the fire within you and speak these words—*firenda des almar.*"

The second half of the chant I'd memorized from the little red book. Pulse fluttering wildly at the base of my throat, I wet my lips, then did as he asked.

"*Firenda des almar.*"

My sleeping magic roared awake. A column of fire leaped from my hands, and the crowd gasped in wonder. The people seated closest to the altar shrank back, shielding their eyes from the bright, gold-tinged flames.

Heat wrapped around me like a blanket, heavy and stifling. My forehead grew damp with sweat; my legs trembled. Galtus Celcio watched me with a triumphant light in his eyes. He didn't seem worried that I'd burn the temple down.

Calma, I thought desperately at my fire, trying to pull the flames back. *Calma.*

If anything, they pulsed higher, as if seeking to touch the dome high overhead. Now my arms were shaking, too.

"Enough." Galtus Celcio brought his hands over mine, snuffing out the fire as easily as extinguishing a candle.

I swayed, spent. In a heartbeat Paulette was at my elbow, supporting me as she guided me back to my place. Awe shone in her eyes.

"He was right," she whispered. "You are worthy of the temple."

Suddenly, I wanted to be anywhere but the Temple of the Twin Gods.

I stood there, sweaty and shaking, fearing that I'd stepped into a situation I had no control over. My assurances to Thorne and the King of Raine seemed foolish now. Though I couldn't reliably harness it, I had a great deal of power. Power that my father, clearly, would use for his own purposes.

Galtus Celcio turned back to his worshippers.

"Spread the word," he said. "The Temple of the Twin Gods is stronger than ever. The red priests are here to guide Parnese to greatness."

His words sparked a cheer that resounded through the temple. With a nod, he turned, sweeping his scarlet cloak behind him, and strode toward the huge painting of the Twin Gods behind the altar.

There was a door there, I realized, set just beside the painting in a filigreed panel of red and gold. The warder touched the side, and it swung open. He ducked inside, Paulette pulled me after him, and Ser Naldi followed at our heels.

A moment later, the door closed, shutting out the noise of the temple and leaving us in a short hall dimly lit by a single sconce. I let out a breath and wiped the perspiration from my forehead with my sleeve, then shuffled after Galtus Celcio.

He opened the door on the other end of the corridor, and we stepped out into a medium-sized room lined with arches along one side. Like the rest of the temple, it was made of polished red granite. As we walked through, I glimpsed a small altar on the far side of the room, partially hidden behind the arches.

"That went well," he said, a smile in his voice. "The common folk needed a demonstration of our power, a reminder of why their allegiance belongs to the temple."

It's not your power, I wanted to argue. *It's mine.*

Even if I didn't know how to control it. Yet I was already gaining the knowledge I'd hoped to find in Parnese. Including the fact that, apparently, I'd been using the wrong part of the chant to summon my fire. I felt like a fool for not realizing it earlier.

"As you say, Warder," Ser Naldi said. "Still, Rose must have proper training. It's not wise to invoke untamed power in so public a display."

"Are you questioning me?" my father asked, his voice deceptively mild. "Understand, Castin, that you serve at my pleasure. There are other priests worthy of becoming my lieutenant."

"My apologies." Ser Naldi's voice was low with contrition. "I spoke out of turn."

"See that you consider your words more carefully next time."

Galtus Celcio glanced over his shoulder. "Especially when in the presence of my daughter."

"Yes, Warder," Ser Naldi said.

I looked at Paulette, wondering if I needed to worry about the political undercurrents, and if she'd tell me anything useful.

"Rose," my father said, halting at a branching corridor, "I'm afraid I must leave you now. Paulette will take you to the aspirants' dormitory and see that you're settled."

"She's not to have an initiate's room?" Paulette glanced at him. "I thought, after what we saw in the temple..."

Galtus Celcio gave her an indulgent look. "It's important to follow the protocols, but we all know that Rose won't be an aspirant for long. As soon as I tend to a few matters, I'll set the testing day."

I made a little noise in the back of my throat, and his gaze shifted to me.

"There's no need to worry. You'll have the guidance of proctors, who will help prepare you. Meanwhile, get to know the temple—but I ask that you not leave the grounds."

"I'm trapped here?" I stared at him.

"Of course not." He set his hand on my shoulder. "But until you have more training, it's not safe for you to go into Parnese without an escort."

Not safe for me, or for the city? The temple was built of solid stone, but the lower quarters of Parnese were much more flammable.

"Very well." I didn't like it, but I'd do as he asked—for the time being.

"I'll see you again, soon." My father smiled at me. "I'm so glad you're here, Rose. Where you belong."

I kept my doubts to myself as he and Ser Naldi strode away.

"The dormitory is very plain, but don't worry," Paulette said, leading me down the featureless red hallway. "As the warder said, you won't be staying there long."

"How many other aspirants are there?"

"It depends. Sometimes there are only one or two, sometimes nearly a dozen. They stay until they pass the test. Or fail it."

A sudden coldness gripped me. "What happens to the ones who fail?"

"They are returned to their homes, of course." She gave me an open smile.

"Ah." I didn't press the matter.

In some ways, Paulette seemed quite innocent. It didn't seem to have occurred to her that anyone with inside experience of the temple or the ways of the red priests, however rudimentary, would potentially be put to death if they failed, rather than set free with that knowledge.

She was so enamored of the sect of the Twin Gods, and of my charismatic father, that perhaps she couldn't even contemplate the fact that the warder had done—and continued to do—terrible things. It was a problem I understood completely. I, too, wanted to love my father wholeheartedly. And yet...

"What happens at the test?" I asked.

She shook her head. "I can't tell you—but you, of all people, certainly won't fail it."

"I've failed at plenty of other things in my life," I said, with a touch of bitterness.

"I don't believe that! You're Galtus Celcio's daughter, after all."

"I didn't even know I was until a week ago."

"Still." She looked me up and down. "You're powerful, and beautiful, and a princess into the bargain."

I blinked at her. I'd certainly never thought of myself in that light. Besides, those were all things that were external to me, not who I *was* inside.

And who are you? my little voice asked.

Impulsive, though no longer a child. Determined not to be used as a pawn, though fate seemed intent on pushing me about. Curious, always.

Overlaid atop all that was the tarnished silver of my longing for Thorne and the cool shadows of the Darkwood. My heart twisted with yearning and the fear that I might never see him again.

That was who I was. Just Rose, trying to make my way forward in a tumultuous world. No matter what, I must remain true to myself—and hope that, eventually, everything would come out right.

CHAPTER 10

The aspirants' dormitory was, as Paulette had warned me, very spare. It was located in a high-ceilinged room containing rows of beds with a small chest at the foot of each, divided in half by a wall that didn't reach the roof.

"That's the boys' side," Paulette said, pointing to an opening set in the dividing wall. "And this is Matris Vella, who oversees the aspirants."

A woman in a light gray robe rose from her desk near the door. Her white-threaded hair was twisted into a bun at the back of her head, and she gave me a disinterested look as she pulled a piece of parchment and charcoal pencil from a drawer.

"Name?" she asked.

"Rose Valrois..." I hesitated a moment, then added, "Celcio."

Her head jerked up, her gaze sharpening. "Ah. So you're the one he went to find."

"I suppose." I shifted uncomfortably.

"Don't expect any special treatment from me, miss." There was a touch of hostility in her tone. "You're a simple aspirant as far as I'm concerned."

Paulette drew in an indignant breath. I held out a hand to keep her from saying anything and nodded at the matron. "Of course."

"Rose won't be here long, anyway," Paulette couldn't help saying.

Matris Vella's eyes narrowed. "We'll see about that. You'll be in bed four." She pointed with her pencil to one of the cots in the middle of the row. "Mealtimes are at seven, eleven, and four. Don't be late. Paulette can show you where."

"How many are in the dormitory right now?" Paulette asked.

"Three—including Shamsan."

"Still?" Paulette shook her head.

"Is that a bad thing?" I asked.

"Not particularly, but he's been here for months now. Every time he's up for testing, something happens. He gets ill, or breaks his leg, or the adjudicator is called away."

"Nothing but a beggar," the matron said. "He's running out of time. And of the two girls, only one of them will pass."

"How do you know?" I asked.

Matris Vella shrugged. "I've been here long enough to tell. Never wrong, except that once."

She gave Paulette a pointed look.

"Which proves you don't know everything." Paulette twitched her red cloak. "I'll show Rose where the bathing room and refectory are." She turned back through the door, gesturing me to follow.

As soon as we were out of earshot, she let out a sigh. "Matris Vella never changes, I'm sorry to say. But you won't have to bear with her for long."

I gave her a curious look. "She thought you'd fail the test?"

"I wasn't a terribly strong aspirant." Paulette smiled ruefully. "But Galtus Celcio himself selected me, so I had to prove I was worthy."

She opened a door across the hall, and I was glad to see it led out to an enclosed courtyard. I'd been starting to feel like I was trapped in a maze of hard red stone. The sweetly scented air of Parnese wrapped around me as we went outside, and I pulled in a deep breath. A large fountain played in the middle of the brick terrace, and benches were set along the side walls, where one could find shade in either the morning or the afternoon.

The sky overhead was a brilliant, cloudless blue. High over the city a hawk floated, spiraling lazily in the updraft from the harbor.

"The refectory is straight across here," Paulette said, leading me past the splashing fountain. "To keep the aspirants from too much contact with the initiates and priests, your mealtimes are before the regular hours."

"I noticed," I said dryly.

Early rising was not one of my strengths, sadly. I wondered if I might skip breakfast and instead smuggle out a bit of lunch or dinner to keep for the next day. Probably not, considering how strict Matris Vella seemed to be.

Yet another reason to pass the test as quickly as possible.

We went through wide double doors propped open to the courtyard, and I was glad to discover that the dining room was bright and cozy, in contrast to the featureless granite halls of the main temple complex. A few pink geraniums bloomed in pots beneath the windows, and the wooden tables were polished to a golden shine. The smell of cumin and onions filled the air, and I sniffed appreciatively.

"The cooks are very skilled," Paulette said. "That's another good thing about living in the temple—though it makes it hard to stay trim. If only the desserts weren't so delicious." She patted her round belly ruefully.

We passed a sideboard where a pitcher of water stood, sliced lemons floating on top, along with a plate of the anise cookies particular to Parnesia. Paulette snagged a cookie and nodded to me.

"There's always something set out, in case you get hungry. Though the aspirants aren't supposed to come into the refectory except at mealtimes. Now, the bathing rooms are this way."

She turned the corner to the right, and we were back to another smooth red hallway lit by flickering wall sconces. Midway down, she gestured to a pair of doors on the left.

"First one is the men's room, second is the women's."

"Do the initiates use them too?" I asked.

"Oh, no—we have our own suites." She waved her half-eaten cookie at me. "Very nice, too. In fact, the one next to mine is currently empty. Wouldn't it be grand if they put you in there?"

"I'd like that." It would make me feel less alone to have Paulette right next door.

We turned another corner to the right, and I realized we'd returned to the corridor leading to the dormitory. Matris Vella barely glanced up from her desk as we stepped inside and Paulette led me to bed number four.

"Your aspirant's robe is here," she said, lifting the lid of the chest. "And a nightgown, washcloth, and towel."

"Where's my trunk?" I glanced about the plain room.

Not that I had many possessions to begin with, but I didn't want to be deprived of the few items I'd brought from Raine. Thank goodness I'd been keeping Thorne's scrying stone in my pocket.

"In storage," Paulette said. "Once you pass the test, your things will be moved to your new rooms. The aspirants are required to shed all traces of their station in life while under consideration for the priesthood."

My hand went to the necklace hidden beneath my dress. It was Neeve's, a delicate Dark Elf design of silver leaves and thorns, set with sparks of rubies. In turn, she wore mine, a matching necklace made of gold, with blue drops of sapphire.

No matter what the temple might dictate, I wasn't going to set the necklace aside. Nor the scarlet ring on my right hand, nor the enchanted stone tucked in my pocket. I hoped the aspirant's robes had someplace to conceal it. Leaving it in the bottom of the chest wouldn't do, as I'd no doubt Matris Vella would check for any personal items and confiscate them.

"I'll leave you to get changed." Paulette gave me a sympathetic look. "And I'm afraid I won't see much of you until you pass the test. I wish I was suited to be a proctor, but only the older priests are given the responsibility of working with the aspirants. After lunch, you'll begin attending the training sessions with the others."

The other aspirants: long-in-residence Shamsan and the two girls. At least I'd have company.

I nodded at Paulette. "Thank you for showing me around."

"Of course—I only wish we could move you into your rooms right now." She let out a little sigh. "Oh well. Soon enough. Goodbye for now, Rose."

Once she was gone, the dormitory seemed cold and empty. I turned my back on Matris Vella and quickly changed into the plain brown aspirant's robe, glad to find that the neck was cut high enough to conceal all traces of my necklace. The sleeves were short, leaving my tattooed arm bare, but there was a coarse wrap that I draped over myself.

I was relieved to discover the robe had pockets, and surreptitiously transferred Thorne's stone, wishing I could call upon him that instant. But there was no place I'd seen that would be safe and secluded enough. Another incentive—not that I needed one—to pass the aspirant test as quickly as possible and move into my own private room.

"Fold your clothing into the trunk," Matris Vella called. "Then wash up—it's almost lunch."

I did as she asked, glad to step out on my own into the red corridors. I hadn't been truly alone since the night I'd snuck out to see Thorne.

Missing him was an ache deep inside, echoed by thoughts of Neeve. Being with my sister was almost like spending time with my own shadow—a dark yet undemanding presence. Except, of course, when she chose to be difficult.

The temple most likely wouldn't allow aspirants to write letters, but as soon as I could, I'd pen a vague yet cheerful note to her. And one to Mama, too, I supposed, assuring her I'd arrived safely and that the red priests hadn't incinerated me in my sleep.

Yet, anyway.

After washing my hands and face, I decided to go to the courtyard to wait for the summons to lunch. The sunshine and open air were far preferable to the watchful stare of Matris Vella in the dormitory. I chose a bench in the shade and sat.

A pot of twining jasmine bloomed sweetly in the near corner, and the fountain splashed, murmuring softly to itself. For a moment I was reminded of the mud maidens I'd encountered in the Erynvorn. But this was Parnese. No strange, enchanted creatures would emerge from the water or move, flickering silver, through a dense thicket of trees.

Here, there was only flame.

My fingers closed around the stone in my pocket, and with effort I kept myself from drawing it out. I could not risk revealing any of Raine's secrets.

A moment later, my caution was rewarded as two girls in the brown robes of aspirants stepped into the courtyard. One of them was tall with a long nose, her light brown hair plaited over her shoulder, the other was short with a cap of shiny black hair and bright eyes that made me think of a sparrow.

"There she is," the tall one said in a loud whisper, shooting me a sideways glance.

I stood. "Hello. I'm Rose."

The shorter girl cocked her head at me, then came forward. "I'm Lena." She gestured to her companion. "And that's Jenni. We've heard about you."

Wonderful.

"Nice to meet you," I said, despite the fact the tall girl was glaring at me.

One of these aspirants will fail. It was knowledge I wished I didn't have, especially meeting them for the first time.

From over the walls, the ringing of the city's bells filled the air, chiming the hour. It was the sound of my childhood, and I couldn't help smiling.

"Lunchtime," the tall one—Jenni—said, walking around me and through the open doors of the refectory.

"Don't worry about her," Lena said. "She's from up north, near Caliss. They're a shy folk."

I raised my brows. *Shy* wasn't the word I'd use.

"Lena!" A boy with a frizz of dark hair and the deep brown skin of the southlands hurried into the courtyard. "Did you know that the warder's daughter—" Catching sight of me, he broke off. "Oh."

"Shamsan." Lena gave him a warning look. "This is Rose. Our newest *aspirant*." She stressed the last word.

"Right, yes, of course." Shamsan nodded vigorously at me. "We're all just aspirants here. Starving ones, too. Let's go in. Where's Jenni?"

Lena glanced at the refectory. "Halfway through her soup by now."

"She's a cold one," Shamsan said, then grinned at me. "Must be that northern blood."

"Where are you from?" I asked him as Lena led the way into the dining room.

"Down by the Ypteg border, where the white Elin flows." He spoke the words like something out of a poem. "And Lena's from a village near here. Oh look, broth and bread again. Joy."

He scooped up one of the three trays set on a counter beside a door that probably led to the kitchen. Lena took the next, and I picked up the last one. As Shamsan had said, it contained a bowl of soup and a hunk of bread, along with an orange and a tumbler of water.

"The aspirants eat very simply," Lena said, going to the wide table where Jenni sat.

The tall girl did little more than glance up as we joined her. I wondered if her hostility was a result of her own fear, and if she was the one who'd struggle with the test when the time came. I had to admit I wouldn't mind seeing her go, instead of bright-eyed Lena.

"What happens after lunch?" I asked as I spooned up a bite of the thin, but thankfully well-spiced, soup.

"More training." Shamsan dunked his bread into his bowl and bit off a hunk. "It's endless."

"For you, maybe," Jenni said.

He sent her a warmthless smile, white teeth flashing. "Just wait."

"You'll be with me and Jenni," Lena said, giving me an encouraging look. "Sham has his own proctor, since he's been here a little longer."

Jenni's lips curled. "More than a *little*. I don't think you'll be wriggling out of this next testing, though." She stood, clearing her dishes, and left without even saying goodbye.

"She's just nervous," Lena told me, but Shamsan shook his head.

"She's an utter prig, and we both know it. It would be worth failing the test just so I won't have to become an initiate with her."

Lena reached across the table and patted Shamsan's hand. "We'll all pass—don't worry."

I didn't say a word, only followed along as we took our empty trays to the counter, then waved to Sham and followed Lena when we stepped back into the temple hallways. Despite their monotony, they did stay pleasantly cool while the heat of midday pressed down over Parnese.

"What does the training consist of?" I asked as Lena led me deeper into the building.

"How to access your fire sorcery," she said. "And the different chants to channel it."

Well, those would certainly be helpful—especially as it seemed I'd been using the wrong ones. The red priests' approach seemed similar to the Dark Elves' use of spoken runes, and I glanced at Lena.

"Is it possible to control your power without the chants?" As I thought over my past encounters with magic, it seemed to me I'd accessed my fire sorcery without using the proper words.

She looked back at me, wide-eyed. "I wouldn't think so. You could ask Proctor Tal, I suppose."

"I will." *Maybe.*

Or maybe all I needed to do in Parnese was learn the red priests' chants, and I'd be in full command of my power. My chest squeezed with hope that it would be that simple. Learn the chants before the autumn storms even touched the Strait, let alone closed it. And then return to Raine, to Thorne.

It won't be that easy, my little voice said.

Of course not. It never was.

CHAPTER 11

Proctor Tal was a thin, dour-faced man who looked me up and down and then gestured me to sit in the middle of the three chairs arranged in front of him.

Jenni already occupied the one on my right, and Lena took the one on my left. Other than the chairs, there was nothing in the red-walled room besides us and the proctor.

"It's so nothing catches fire," Lena whispered to me, noting my survey of our classroom.

I nodded, pushing away the memory of hungry flames consuming the Nightshade Lord's throne, burning the tapestries to ash in a heart-beat. It was a wise precaution on the part of the priests.

"So," the proctor said, "the first chant. Jenni, stand up and demonstrate for our new aspirant."

Jenni did, tossing her plait behind her shoulder, then lifting her cupped hands. "*Firenda des almar,*" she intoned.

A tongue of red fire lit in her palm. I felt my own power stir in response.

"Very good," the proctor said.

With a smug smile, Jenni took her seat again.

"Fire of the soul." He gave me a steady look. "A lucky few are born with it, born to serve the will of the Twin Gods. Here at the temple, we develop that power and put it to the use of the divine."

The light of faith shone in his eyes. I wondered if the will of the Twin Gods really was to conquer all of the Continent—or if that was the desire of men who craved power.

Men like Galtus Celcio, whose magic was strong enough to bend kingdoms to his will.

Raine is safe, I reassured myself. My father had gotten what he went there for. Besides, while the red priests had annexed Caliss and parts of Ypteg, they hadn't pushed farther. The Athraig were a formidable force to the north, and the southern deserts were full of nothing but sand and nomadic tribes.

"Repeat after me," Proctor Tal said. "*Firenda.*"

I did, mimicking the way he rolled the *r* slightly. Lena spoke the word too, and with an impatient toss of her head, Jenni joined us.

"*Des almar,*" the priest said.

We echoed him.

"Say it alone." He nodded at me. I hesitated, and he gave me an impatient look. "They are simply words, until you put the weight of your power behind them. Do you think every urchin who yells out *firenda des almar* in the streets is gifted with flame? Now stand up and say the chant."

Despite his scoffing, the memory of what had happened earlier in the temple pulsed inside me. I had spoken the words, and my fire raged forth, uncontrollable until Galtus Celcio snuffed the flames.

I pulled in a breath, strengthened my mirror shield, then hurriedly said the chant.

The power inside me stirred again, but didn't rise to the surface. I didn't know whether I was disappointed or relieved by the fact.

The priest narrowed his eyes. "Slow down and try to reach the spark inside you. Imagine you are blowing softly on an ember, coaxing it to flare into flame."

Flare into flame? That was the last thing I wanted. Did I dare drop my mirror shield and let my power flow freely?

"How do you extinguish it, though?" I asked. "Just in case."

"I hardly think you need to worry about that," Proctor Tal said.

"Your pardon, proctor." Lena raised a hesitant hand. "I heard that Rose summoned a huge pillar of fire before the altar earlier today. What if she does—"

"That was Galtus Celcio's power," the priest said condescendingly. "He wanted to impress the worshippers."

I opened my mouth to argue hotly that no, it had been *my* magic, then reconsidered. What if he were right? What if my father had somehow channeled his sorcery through me? The flame had come so effortlessly, and he'd extinguished it so readily.

Doubt seeded itself in my heart.

"Is that possible?" Lena asked. "For a priest to lend their power to another?"

"For the warder, anything is possible if the Twin Gods will it," Proctor Tal said.

"I knew it." Jenni sniffed. "So you're saying our newest aspirant doesn't actually have power of her own. She's just here because of who her father is."

"No." The proctor frowned at Jenni. "Galtus Celcio would not have brought her to the temple if she were entirely lacking in sorcerous ability. It is my job, however, to draw out the latent talent within all of you." He swiveled to me. "Now, try again. Hold your hand cupped before you, say the chant, and try to reach the fire sleeping inside."

I straightened my shoulders and lifted the palm of my right hand. The scarlet ring sparkled faintly in the light from the wall sconces.

"*Firenda des almar.*" This time, I spoke the words clearly, determined to prove Jenni and her skepticism wrong.

My power roused, as if hearing its name being called. I felt it gather itself, and I stared at my empty palm, willing a flame to appear.

"*Firenda des almar.*" I clenched my teeth.

For a moment, a faint shimmer of orange shone in my hand. Proctor Tal leaned forward with interest—and then it was gone, as if doused by his attention. Drat it! I closed my hand into a frustrated fist.

"Hm," the priest said. "Almost. We will let you rest. Lena?"

With a wobbly smile, Lena stood, and I sank back down into my chair. Lena thrust her cupped hands in front of her.

"*Firenda des almar,*" she said, a pleading note in her voice.

Nothing at all happened. Not even the faintest pulse of light shone within her palm. Proctor Tal let out a sigh. "Again."

She nodded quickly, then spoke the chant once more. I leaned forward, trying to will the fire into her hands, but again, nothing was there.

"Lena," the priest said, "you must try."

"I *am* trying." Her voice was thick with tears. "I know it's there. I can feel the power, I swear it."

His lips set in a grim line, Proctor Tal stepped forward and took her wrists. "Do you want to go back home a failure? *Reach*, girl." He gave her a little shake then let go.

"*Firenda...*" Her voice wobbled, and she swallowed then tried again. "*Firenda des almar.*"

Something twisted inside me. She was so desperate. Thinking of what the priest claimed my father had done, I closed my eyes and imagined pushing my power toward Lena.

She let out a little gasp. "Look! There it is!"

I opened my eyes in time to see a pale yellow glow against her cupped palm. Quick as a breath, it was gone, but the relief in her eyes didn't fade.

Had I helped her, or was it her own power? I had no way of telling.

"Finally," Jenni said. "At least I'm not entirely surrounded by failures."

"It is not your place to speak," the priest said sternly to her, then turned back to Lena. "Aspirant, I'm glad you've finally touched your power. It bodes well for the upcoming test."

"The day has been set?" Jenni leaned forward. "I'm so ready."

Proctor Tal glanced at her. "Tomorrow afternoon, two members of the inner circle of the red priests will conduct the testing to move from aspirant to initiate."

"Will the warder be included?" Jenni sent me a look. "Because I wouldn't want there to be any cheating."

I narrowed my eyes in return. "There won't be."

"Galtus Celcio will observe," the priest said, "but he will not be the one judging the aspirants. As you say, there must be no bias."

I nodded, though I didn't believe my father would elevate me without cause. But would summoning a faint glow be enough to pass the test? If not, both Lena and I were in trouble.

"We will move to the second chant," Proctor Tal said, going back to stand before us. "*Quera quemar*. Repeat."

We chorused the words, though I wished I knew what they meant. After a short time, the priest gestured for us to stop.

"Jenni, demonstrate," he said, standing aside.

Jenni stood, held her palm up toward the back wall, and spoke the words: "*Quera quemar*."

As soon as the last syllable left her lips, a small gout of fire spurted from her hand. I understood why the priest had moved out of the way, though Jenni's fire would only have singed the edge of his robes, if that.

"Excellent," he said. "Lena."

Jenni took her seat with a look of triumph as Lena rose.

"*Quera quemar*," Lena said, holding out her hand almost as an afterthought.

To no one's surprise, there was no resulting spark or flame.

"Again." Proctor Tal sounded resigned.

Lena tried three more times, her shoulders slumping a bit lower with each failure. I curled my fingers into my palms and leaned forward, trying to channel my power toward her. This time, without apparent success.

"Sit," the priest finally said with a dismissive wave.

Lena nodded and folded back into her chair.

Proctor Tal gave me a cool look. "Rose. Are you ready to attempt it?"

I stood and held my hand out—my left hand this time, moved by a notion that perhaps the magical ring of Elfhame encircling my finger was interfering with the sorcery.

"*Quera quemar*," I said loudly as I turned my palm toward the far wall.

Flame shot from my hand. Lena let out a squeak, and the priest jumped out of the way. A curl of smoke rose from his sleeve, where my fire had grazed it.

Serves him right for doubting you, my little voice said, and I couldn't help but agree.

As quickly as it had come, the flame was gone. Despite the sudden ache in my pinky stub, I'd clearly exceeded expectations. I couldn't help shooting a smug look at Jenni, who stared back at me, wide-eyed.

"Well." Proctor Tal brushed at his robe and gave me a thoughtful look. "It seems the warder was correct. You carry the blessing of the Twin Gods after all."

Now I must keep channeling it, and do everything I could to pass the aspirant test.

CHAPTER 12

T hat night, I couldn't sleep. The dormitory was lit with the city's glow filtering in through the high windows, along with the noises of Parnese: random laughter and shouts, the thud of wood on stone, a distant bell.

The sheets were rougher against my skin than the fine linens of Castle Raine. I twisted and turned, trying to find a comfortable spot. When I finally did, I lay there clutching Thorne's stone beneath my pillow and wishing with all my might that I could summon him to scry with me. My heart beat hollowly with yearning. I squeezed my eyes closed, sending my longing across the sea and hoping he could somehow feel me thinking of him.

Two beds away, Jenni snored softly. I sighed and turned over again to see Lena awake in her bed, staring up at the shadowed ceiling high overhead.

"Are you worried about the test tomorrow?" I whispered. "I am."

She turned to look at me. "You don't have anything to worry about —unlike me."

"We'll both do fine," I said, wishing it were true.

"Maybe." She went back to gazing at the ceiling. "But at least it will be over. One way or the other."

I'll help you, I wanted to tell her, though I truly had no idea if I could. Or if that would be considered cheating. But Lena had manifested a little power that afternoon. Surely it would be enough to keep the red priests from tossing her out on the streets.

Or worse.

"What about Shamsan?" I asked.

She smiled ruefully. "I think he'll finally get a chance to pass. Poor boy."

I didn't know his full history but hoped he'd be able to earn his place on the morrow. I hoped we *all* would.

"Would you two be quiet?" Jenni called irritably. "Some of us are trying to sleep."

"Sorry," Lena called back, then looked over at me once more. "Good night, Rose."

"Good night," I replied softly.

I forced myself to lie still, despite the whirling of my thoughts. At least I'd proven my ability to call fire. After I passed the test, I'd have my own room, and with it, the privacy to contact Thorne at last. I clung to that thought, along with the stone, and finally drifted off to sleep.

⚜

THE MORNING BELLS WOKE ME. I blinked groggily, wishing I could burrow under the covers and go back to sleep. I still held the stone, and brought it to my heart in a gesture of promise. If all went well at the testing, then later that very day I'd be able to scry with Thorne.

That prospect got me to sit up, albeit reluctantly, and look about the dormitory. Jenni's bed was neatly made and she was already gone, which I found unsurprising. Lena was dressed and putting on her shoes. When she saw I was awake, she smiled at me.

"I wasn't sure if I'd have to shake you out of bed or not," she said. "Breakfast time."

"Mm," I managed to say. I hoped there would be strong tea.

I pulled on my aspirant's robe, turning my back so neither she nor Matris Vella could see my necklace, then groggily followed Lena to the refectory. As we crossed the patio, I paused a moment, breathing in the dry air and sun-warmed smell of the bricks.

"There you are," Jenni said irritably when we joined her and Shamsan at the aspirants' usual table. "How can you sleep late today, of all days?"

I ignored her and took a swallow of my tea—the smoky blend imported from Ypteg that was so pervasive in Parnese and barely known in Raine.

"I've been up since dawn," Shamsan said with a broad grin. "No ill proctors, no broken legs. If the Twins allow me to make it through this afternoon unscathed, I'll gladly serve them for the rest of my life."

"There's the meditation to get through first," Lena said, shooting him a look.

"What's that?" I asked, wishing I'd had more time to get to know the ways of the temple. I'd scarcely arrived, and the testing was already upon me.

Jenni gave me a scathing look. "You hardly know anything. I can't believe Galtus Celcio took the trouble to go find you."

"She's as gifted as you are," Lena said mildly.

"I can hardly wait to see!" Shamsan turned to me, enthusiastically brandishing his raisin-studded spice bun.

At dinner the previous night, Lena had told him of my success with the fire-throwing chant, and I'd chimed in that Lena was able to summon flame. Jenni had looked on disapprovingly, saying that aspirants weren't supposed to compare notes—though clearly she was just jealous.

I blinked at Shamsan. "We're tested all together?"

"Of course," Jenni said. "That way it's clear who is worthy of being accepted as an initiate. And who is *not*." She gave me a pointed look.

"We are all worthy," Shamsan proclaimed, flinging his arms open.

I noted that Lena had hunched into herself, and I gave her an encouraging pat on the shoulder. But with Jenni there, I didn't want to do anything overt, like assure her I'd try to help. Besides, I didn't even know if I could.

"So, what happens next?" I asked, mindful that my previous question had gone unanswered.

"We spend the morning in the temple," Lena said, "praying and thinking on our service to the Twin Gods, until we're called for the testing."

"So you'd best fill your belly. There's no lunch." Shamsan suited action to words, and stuffed his mouth with a hunk of butter-slathered bun.

"We only have one meal beforehand to preserve clarity of mind," Jenni said, a note of disapproval in her voice. "It's supposed to be meager."

I noted she'd only eaten half an orange and one slice of creamy white cheese. With a defiant glance, I grabbed a second bun and two pieces of cheese off the plate.

"I imagine a rumbling belly would be more distracting, personally," I said. "But it's your choice."

She curled her lip. "Mind over body."

"I'm certain squabbling doesn't contribute to a productive meditation," Lena said. "We're supposed to focus our thoughts inward and connect with our fire, remember?"

To me, it seemed that quiet emotions were *less* conducive to calling my flame. Then again, as Jenni was fond of pointing out, I was unversed in the ways of the red priests. As usual, I was probably going about things entirely backward.

The bells rang, signaling the end of our breakfast. Shamsan rose, snagged one last roll, then waggled his brows at us. "Good luck, girls. Victory awaits!"

After he'd cleared his tray, Lena shook her head. "He's always so dramatic."

"At least he has power." Jenni stood and whisked her empty dishes away. She didn't bother wishing us luck before she left the room, back straight, brown braid swinging behind her.

"Well." I finished the last swallow of my tea, then gave Lena an encouraging look. "To the temple?"

She nodded, and I glimpsed the worry shadowing her eyes.

We deposited our trays on the counter, and I followed her through the maze of red corridors. Our footfalls echoed softly, and I tried to calm my pounding heart. I didn't like being there, entrapped within the walls of the Temple of the Twin Gods—but my circumstances would be changing soon enough.

Even though I'd scarcely had a day to learn the chants! But I'd been able to summon my power, and I felt fairly confident that I'd be able to pass the testing without too much trouble.

"I suppose they don't want us to practice the day of," I said as we turned yet another corner.

Lena nodded, her short black hair bobbing with the motion. "We must preserve our power for the examinations."

It made sense, despite the itching in my fingers to keep working to control my fire.

The sibilant sound of whispered prayers floated through the air, and I guessed we were almost at the main temple. Lena paused before a door and fumbled with the handle. Despite her calm demeanor, I could see her fingers trembling.

We slipped through the door into the cavernous main room. A black-robed priest standing guard turned to look at us as we emerged, then dipped his head when he saw it was just aspirants, and went back to placidly watching the worshippers.

There were quite a lot, and I hesitated a moment, looking for a space among the packed benches.

"Not there," Lena said softly, tugging at the sleeve of my robe.

Keeping close to the wall, she led me to one of the side rooms—the Brother's, which made sense, as he was the Twin with a flame in his hand. An intricate grillwork had been pulled across the entire opening, again guarded by a dark-robed priest, though this one was female.

She silently swung open the small door in the wrought metal barrier, and Lena and I stepped through into the sub-chapel of the Brother. The other two aspirants were already there, seated on a backless bench facing the statue of the male Twin God.

Lena and I slipped onto the bench behind them. Shamsan glanced over his shoulder and winked at me, but Jenni sat rigidly, giving no sign she was aware of our presence. I wiggled, trying to get comfortable on the plain wooden bench. There were no cushions. I wasn't looking forward to spending hours perched there, contemplating the hard-faced visage of the Brother.

Although maybe I'd gain some sudden insight, my connection to my sorcery opening like a flower.

Unbidden, I recalled the glowing *nirwen* blossom Neeve and I had seen in a vision, when she first demonstrated her scrying powers to me in the Darkwood. That flower had certainly played a pivotal role in my life, though it had nothing to do with my fire sorcery.

What about the rest of the scrying? my little voice prodded. *The part where you and Neeve were facing one another in battle, fire at your fingertips, a blade in her hand. Remember that?*

Just because I'd seen a thing didn't make it true, I told myself. And at any rate, I was in Parnese and Neeve was in Elfhame. The prospect of a flame-and-sword fight between us seemed far distant, at best.

If it ever happened at all.

I bit my lip, trying not to worry, and turned my attention back to my present surroundings. Shamsan and Jenni sat very still on the front bench. Beside me, Lena was gazing up at the Brother, seeming wholly absorbed in her meditation.

Trying to be a good aspirant, I laced my fingers together and inhaled deeply. The air smelled of sweet incense and candle wax.

For a time, I pondered the statue, counting the different shades of crimson used for the Brother's hair and robes. At least eight different colors, I decided, ranging from rust to deep ruby. The fire pattern embroidered on his robes twisted and twined, the stylized flames picked out in gold and orange thread.

When I grew tired of studying the Brother, I surreptitiously stretched, flexing my legs and arms, twisting a little until the priest let out a sharp cough of warning.

Very well. I made myself sit still again and turned my attention to the flickering fire of the votive candles...

Lena's elbow jabbed me in the ribs, and I woke with a start. No one else had seemed to notice I'd nodded off, but clearly I needed something to occupy my thoughts. Composing letters in my head would provide a reasonable distraction, and hopefully keep me awake. I took a breath and thought of my sister.

· · ·

DEAR NEEVE,

Here I am in the Temple of the Twin Gods, if you can believe it. I certainly can't. It's every bit as strange as you might think, and I'm still half afraid I'll end up a cinder—either from my own power running amok or a red priest catching me doing something I shouldn't.

LIKE SCRYING THORNE. Or trying to help Lena through the testing.

I'VE ALREADY LEARNED some important things about summoning and controlling my fire sorcery, though—like the fact I was using the wrong words! So that's been valuable, at the very least.

Today is the test to pass from aspirant to initiate, and after that, my training will begin in earnest. I'm hopeful that I'll be able to master my magic sooner rather than later.

AND THEN, somehow, depart Parnese, though I knew my father wouldn't like the idea of losing me. A momentary clutch of fear squeezed my lungs as I admitted it wouldn't be as easy as simply walking out of the temple. Galtus Celcio liked to hold on to power, and that would include me, especially if I were able to channel what he'd called my *formidable sorcery.*

But I'd tackle that problem when the time came. After all, I'd escaped the city once. There were ways, even if I was the daughter of the warder of the red priests.

I blew out a sigh, and Lena shot me a warning glance. We weren't supposed to make a single sound, apparently. I smiled briefly back at her, then returned to my imaginary correspondence.

I KNOW that not much time has passed in Elfhame, but I hope you're recovering. If Thorne is there with you, tell him he must do everything he can to hurry the healers along. Maybe by the time I'm able to leave Parnese, you'll be back in Raine.

I miss you.
Love,
Your sister, Rose

THORNE WAS HARDER, of course. Part of me wanted to throw all caution away and speak the Dark Elf rune for light over the stone tucked in my pocket, so that I might see his face, hear his voice. But that was utter foolishness. So instead, I thought of all the times we'd spent in the Darkwood, beneath the hushed branches of the cedar trees.

Closing my eyes, I could almost smell the dark loam, feel the moist air against my skin. Thorne would be waiting there, at the verge of meadow where the forest began, still as a shadow in his green cloak, his dark hair braided intricately back from his face.

I remembered the first time I'd seen those slightly inhuman features—the sharply angled cheekbones, the tips of pointed ears visible through the black waterfall of his hair—and wondered who, and what, this guardian of the Darkwood might be.

That was not the first time we'd met, however, as I later learned.

No, the very first time I'd traveled through the forest, the wards sensed a threat in me. Even now my heart hammered at the memory of the Darkwood's magic wrapping around my throat, cutting off the air to my lungs. I'd lain on the crushed bracken fern at the side of the road, dazed and dying—

Until an enormous bear leaped from the woods and stood over me, breaking the spell. Its dark eyes were flecked with amber, like a sprinkling of gold dust in a deep stream.

I shook my head at myself for not recognizing those eyes when I first met the *Galadhir*, Thorne. But who would've expected such a thing? A man who could transform into a creature of the wild? The only magic I'd known then was the fire sorcery of the red priests of Parnese.

And now I was about to become one of them.

The forest, as it turned out, had been right about me all along, though I would never turn my fire against it. I was bound to it, after all, by magic and by blood. The leaf and vine inscribed on my left elbow was physical proof of that connection.

Which I must keep hidden from Galtus Celcio at all costs.

THORNE,

I miss you with all my heart, my breath, my every thought. I wish I could be there at your side, helping strengthen the Darkwood's wards, helping Neeve heal, helping you shoulder all the burdens you carry without complaint.

You once told me I burn so brightly—but the flame within me shines for you. Be well, be strong, know that I think of you always...

I BLINKED BACK my tears of longing. That wouldn't do.

With effort, I turned my attention to the temple: the ebb and flow of sound behind me as worshippers came and went, their murmured prayers and footsteps like the surge of a quiet sea. The smell of melting wax from the votive candles flickering in their red glasses on the altar before me. The glint of light off the gold-leafed flame held aloft in the Brother's cupped palm.

Who had been the first warder of the red priests? How had they learned to claim and control the sorcery within them?

Perhaps it was written in some well-guarded annals of the priesthood, passed down through the centuries. Secrets I would probably never see, but I was happy to let the deeper mysteries of the temple alone, as long as I could return to the Darkwood.

Which meant passing the test. I worried the scarlet-spark ring on my right hand and pulled in a deep breath. *Firenda des almar,* I thought. *Quera quemar.*

There were more chants than those, I was certain. I'd seen Galtus Celcio summon a huge ball of flame, and despite Proctor Tal's dismissal, there must be a way to extinguish the fire.

I'd learn what I could, and then smuggle myself back to Raine. Could I do so before the winter storms closed the Strait? I bit my lip, calculating.

The languid heat of summer still spread over Parnese, though soon the light would slant into autumn. But I had time. Once I became an initiate, I'd concentrate everything on mastering my sorcery. I prayed it wouldn't take too long. Otherwise, I'd be trapped in the temple until the spring weather reopened the waters between the Continent and Raine.

And who knew what might happen during those long months?

CHAPTER 13

F inally, after my backside had gone numb from perching on the hard bench all morning, a red-robed priest came to take us to the testing. I exchanged an apprehensive look with Lena, but none of the aspirants spoke as we filed after the priest. It seemed to me that the whispers in the temple grew more sibilant as we passed, the scent of candle wax and incense thicker, hazing the air.

The priest led us to the altar, then past it and to the door beside the immense portrait of the Twin Gods. I wondered if any of the other aspirants had passed through the dim red corridor to the room beyond before. Another of the dubious advantages of being Galtus Celcio's daughter, I supposed.

We didn't linger in the archway-lined room, however, nor pause at the mysterious far altar.

"Here," the priest said, pulling open a door embossed with a huge scarlet flame.

As we stepped in, I blinked, trying to accustom my eyes to the lack of light. Wall sconces with reddish flames cast a faint, ruddy glow over a room somewhat smaller than the training room we'd been using. A stone slab in the center of the room served as an altar. Upon it stood four unlit white candles and a golden bowl.

At the far end of the room, two red priests—one male, one female —sat facing us at a narrow table. In the corner, arms folded, stood my father.

He met my gaze and nodded slowly. Jenni let out a sniff of displeasure.

Shamsan nudged me and nodded to the wall on our right. Squinting, I could see black scorch marks upon the stone, black streaks against the red granite.

"Line up," our escort said, prodding us to stand before the altar. "Show your respect to the Twin Gods."

Shamsan stepped forward, then Jenni, then Lena. I was at the end of the line. Despite my rising worry, I concentrated on keeping my breathing steady.

What if I didn't pass the test?

You're the warder's daughter, I reminded myself. I'd pass, and then receive the training I'd come to Parnese for.

As one, the other aspirants held up their hands, bringing two fingers to the center of their palms in the sign of the Twins. Belatedly, I followed, aware of Galtus Celcio's gaze upon me.

"Aspirants," the female priest said, "you are here today to demonstrate your worthiness to become an initiate of the red priests, and to devote your life in service to the Twin Gods."

I tried not to twitch in denial. I had no intention of spending the rest of my years trapped in the sect of the red priests.

"To that end," her companion said, "we will be asking you to show proof of the divine fire burning within you. The proctors have assured us that each one of you has demonstrated enough promise to face this test."

Lena inhaled raggedly, and I resisted the urge to reach out and pat her shoulder.

"However," the female priest said sternly, "no matter what aptitude you have displayed during your practice sessions, *this* is the test. An aspirant must show mastery over their fire when called upon to do so. If you fail here, our decision is final, and you will be promptly escorted from the temple."

She didn't say that the unlucky aspirants would be returned to their homes, and again I couldn't help my dark suspicions. What truly happened to those deemed unworthy of the priesthood?

I glanced at my father, but he was watching the other priests intently.

"You each have three tests to pass," the priest continued. "Summon fire into the bowl, light a candle, and cast flame against the wall." She gestured to the scorch-marked stone on our left.

"Shamsan Zaine," the male priest said, "invoke the power granted to you by the gods. Call your fire to the bowl."

It was good that Shamsan was going first. The rest of us could see what we were supposed to do, and his confidence would help carry us forward. I hoped.

Eyes bright under his mop of unruly black curls, Shamsan glanced at the bowl, then raised his cupped hands.

"*Firenda des almar,*" he said, his voice strong.

A bright red tongue of flame flickered to life above his palms. In my belly, my own fire roused, embers glowing with heat.

"Send it to the vessel of the Brother," the male priest urged. "Beg Him to show you the path."

Shamsan nodded once, then spoke the fire calling again. I held my breath and leaned forward. The golden curve of the bowl was suddenly illuminated, red and orange fire dancing within it.

"Excellent," the priest said. "The Brother has shown you favor. Extinguish your fire."

"*Calma,*" Shamsan murmured, and the bowl went dark.

"Now," the red-robed woman said, "call upon the Sister and light your candle."

I frowned slightly. There hadn't been any instruction in how to do such a thing during our training. Was it one of those simple chants I'd somehow missed learning? I leaned forward, my attention focused on Shamsan.

"*Arder,*" he said softly, flicking his fingers toward the right-hand candle. The wick lit, shining with a steady yellow flame.

Arder. I filed the word away for when it was my turn.

"Good." The woman nodded to him. "The Sister shows you favor.

Leave the candle burning and call upon the Twins together to cast your fire against the wall. Other aspirants, step back."

We quickly shuffled against the wall to make room for Shamsan's flame. I briefly wondered how many times priests and initiates suffered burns during the course of their training.

Shamsan easily called his fire, then flung it against the wall. A new mark blackened the granite, and I bit my tongue on a cheer. He'd done it! And made it look so simple into the bargain.

I glanced at Lena, whose shoulders had slumped. Not that Shamsan's success meant she would fail. I tried to give her an encouraging look, but she wouldn't meet my eyes.

"Very good," the female priest said, a faint trace of warmth in her voice. "By the divinity of the Twin Gods and the authority of our sect, I declare you, Shamsan Zaine, a formal initiate of the red priests. Welcome. Join us."

She beckoned for him to move forward. Grinning, he winked at the rest of us, then took his place on the other side of the altar. Galtus Celcio raised his hand in greeting and approval, and Shamsan's grin widened. At last, he'd passed the test and joined the ranks of the initiates. I was glad for him.

"Jenni Hardager," the other priest said, "step forward and be tested by the holy power of the Twin Gods."

Tossing her braid behind her shoulder, Jenni advanced to the altar. She held her hands out, palms cupped to the ceiling, and spoke the chant to summon fire. Immediately, an orange flame flickered to life in her hands.

"Call upon the Brother," the priest said. "Set your flame within his vessel."

Jenni nodded tightly. "*Firenda des almar,*" she said.

For a heartbeat, nothing happened, and then fire glowed in the golden bowl.

"Good," the priest said. "The Brother has accepted you onto the path."

"Invoke the Sister," the female priest said. "Light your candle."

Jenni lifter her hand and spoke the same word Shamsan had, and light sprang to life atop the second candle. Then, as instructed by the priests, she faced the wall and summoned her flame.

"*Quera quemar!*" she cried, thrusting her hand forward.

Another black mark joined Shamsan's upon the red stone. Head high, Jenni was welcomed into the ranks of initiates, and went to stand beside Shamsan. My father greeted her, too, and she nodded as though it was only her due.

My fire flicked through me, restless.

"Lena Pecheur."

"Good luck," I whispered as Lena stepped forward.

She gave no sign that she'd heard me. Her fingers were twisted tightly together, and it took her a moment to untangle them and cup her palms in the proper gesture.

"Call upon the Brother," the male priest said. "Let him grant you his power."

"*Firenda des almar,*" Lena said. Her voice wobbled on the words.

I held my breath and stared at her hands, willing a flame, a glow of any kind, to appear.

Nothing.

"*Firenda des almar.*"

Pale flames rose in the golden bowl, flickering faintly, and I let out a breath of relief.

"Satisfactory," the priest said. "The Brother welcomes you on his path."

"Beseech the Sister," his companion said. "Your candle awaits."

Biting her lip, Lena turned to the row of candles, two lit, two unlit. She raised her hand.

"*Arder,*" she said softly.

Come, Lena, I thought, leaning forward. *You can do it.*

"*Arder,*" she said again. Her candle remained cold and lifeless.

"One more attempt," the woman said. "If you cannot summon a flame on the third try, you fail the test."

I swallowed. No one had mentioned this particular rule before. *Rise,* I urged the fire within me. *Help Lena.*

She pulled in a ragged breath.

"*Arder.*"

I echoed the word silently along with her and *pushed*, as if my power could lend itself to hers. Something twisted inside me, a sudden twinge of pain, as though I'd sprained a muscle in my ribcage, and I winced.

Flame roared to life atop the candle, the wax melting and running down the sides. Lena gasped and stepped back. I could see the flame reflected in her eyes.

"Astonishing," the female priest said. "The Sister has answered your call."

I glanced at the table where the priests sat and caught my father's gaze. He was staring at me intently, a considering look in his slate-blue eyes. Had he sensed what I'd just done?

"Invoke the Twins," the other priest said. "Summon your fire."

Lena dazedly turned toward the right-hand wall. I nodded at her in encouragement, but she scarcely seemed to notice me.

"*Firenda des almar*," she said.

Orange flame flickered to life in her hand. She looked down at it, then up at the sooty wall. Uncertainty shone in her expression.

Don't fail now, I thought. Just one last summoning. I reached for my fire.

"*Quera quemar*," Lena called, flinging her hand forward.

As before, I echoed the word, thrusting my own power toward her.

Although the resultant scorch wasn't incredibly strong, her flames managed to reach the wall before sputtering out.

"Adequate," the male priest said, then welcomed Lena into the ranks of the initiates.

She joined them, her face shiny with perspiration. Shamsan patted her arm, and even Jenni unbent enough to give her a grudging nod. Still, I noticed my father watching her, his eyes narrowed. Clearly he'd sensed that something had happened. Did he know it had been me?

I was the last aspirant left. The three candles upon the altar flickered, Lena's still sending out a blaze of heat I could feel against my face.

"Rose Valrois Celcio," the priest said, putting emphasis on the final name.

Squaring my shoulders, I stepped forward.

"The Brother awaits," he said. "Call upon him and show us your power."

I looked at the golden bowl, empty and waiting, then cupped my hands.

"*Firenda des almar.*" I spoke the chant strongly, concentrating on reaching the fire within me and directing it toward the bowl.

The only response was a sluggish stirring deep inside, an empty ache. No flames lit in my palm. Had I spent too much of my magic helping Lena?

Squinting with effort, I tried again.

"*Firenda des almar.*" *Come, fire of the soul. Nestle in my hands. Show yourself.*

Not even the barest sensation of warmth. My palms cupped empty air, nothing more.

It was too much like my struggles at Mistress Ainya's cottage, when I knew my power was there, but couldn't reach it. It felt as though we were separated again, as if my sorcery was a thing outside me, or buried deep within, that I had no access to—a caged animal staring at me from behind impenetrable bars.

A flicker of scarlet as Galtus Celcio leaned forward, his expression set. The prospect of failure flooded me. I swallowed and, reluctantly, thought of the hard-faced Twin Gods.

I knew the priests believed their magic came from that divine source, but I'd seen other magics, other ways. It seemed unlikely to me that calling upon the Brother would make my flames arise. After all, I'd never been a follower of the Twins, and my magic had burst free in Elfhame, not Parnese.

But if must call upon him to pass the test, I would. I briefly closed my eyes. *Flame-haired god, lend me your power. Let my flames rise. Please.*

I opened my eyes and took a deep breath.

"*Firenda des almar!*" I shouted, desperation edging my voice.

No flames.

No light.

My sorcerous power had retreated beyond my grasp.

I glanced at the priests at the table, who watched me impassively.

The candlelight flickered over the faces of Shamsan and Jenni and Lena, whose expressions held varying degrees of pity and shock.

I couldn't bear to look at my father.

One more time. I refused to give up.

"*Firenda—*"

"Enough." The woman priest stood. "Sera Celcio, you have made your three attempts. Your testing is at an end."

She glanced at my father, clearly unwilling to label me an outright failure in his presence.

Galtus Celcio paced forward. The other aspirants shrank back as he passed, until he halted before me. The flames on the altar turned his hair to molten copper, set embers in his eyes.

"Rose. I'm disappointed." His tone was mild, and I wondered if he was saving his scorn for a more private excoriation.

I dropped my gaze to the hard red floor. "I'm sorry."

"What are we to do with her?" the priest asked. "She has failed."

Failed. The word echoed hollowly through me, but hard on its heels came a spark of anger. I had fire sorcery! Even if I hadn't passed the priests' test, I knew the power was inside me.

And so did my father.

I looked back up at him. "What happens to me now?"

His lips firmed. "Usually, unsuccessful aspirants are sent home. However, your home is now with me, here in Parnese."

I nodded slowly. Much as my heart yearned to return to Raine, the test had shown I still had practically no control over my power. Not when it mattered.

I couldn't go back to Castle Raine before I'd gained a basic mastery of my fire sorcery. But how would I be able to train if I wasn't a member of the red priests?

"She's to remain at the temple?" The other priest frowned and shared a look with his companion.

"Yes." Galtus Celcio turned to face them, his expression stern. "Rose will be restricted to the warder's apartment and inner courtyard, and will be escorted whenever she leaves those areas. I trust that will be sufficient."

His words held the authority of his station, and I could tell that, though they might not like it, his subordinates would agree.

The priests nodded reluctantly, then turned their attention to the other aspirants. Initiates now, I reminded myself.

"New priests of the Twin Gods," the woman said, "follow me to your quarters."

She walked past me without a glance, and the new initiates followed. Shamsan gave me a rueful look, Jenni ignored me entirely, and Lena's brows knitted into a frown.

"I'm so sorry," she whispered as she passed.

I pressed my lips together and nodded, unable to escape the knowledge that, by helping her succeed, I'd somehow cut off my connection to my own power. It was horribly ironic—but far too late to change what had happened. Once again, my impulsiveness had worked against me.

The other priest brought up the rear, shepherding the initiates out of the room and leaving me alone with Galtus Celcio. The most powerful person in Parnese.

The man who'd come to Raine to fetch me.

The father I'd just, quite spectacularly, failed.

CHAPTER 14

"Well, Rose." My father turned to me, and I searched his slate-colored eyes for the contempt he surely must feel. Strangely, although he was clearly displeased, there was no trace of the bitter disappointment I'd expected.

"I'm sorry," I said, dropping my gaze as I forced the words out. "I failed the test."

The very reason he'd brought me to Parnese was to become a member of the red priests. What was to become of me now?

"It wasn't entirely unexpected," he said.

I jerked my head up to see a tiny, cold smile curl his lips. "It wasn't?" I blinked at him, trying to understand. The candlelight cast flickering shadows across his skin. "Why?"

"Your power is...odd. It moves in unforeseen ways." His expression hardened. "Or was I mistaken that you attempted to help one of the initiates?"

Guilt stabbed my gut. "Is that forbidden?"

"It is not—but only because it's considered impossible for fire sorcery to be channeled in such a manner."

Considered impossible. Yet my father had sensed my attempt.

"Proctor Tal said that the demonstration in the temple, the day I arrived..." I swallowed, then continued, "He said it was *your* power, not mine. Is that true?"

One of the warder's auburn brows rose slightly. "The proctors need to learn to keep their opinions to themselves. You have sorcery of your own, Rose, make no mistake."

It wasn't an adequate answer, but I wasn't in any position to press for more. Not with the shadow of my failure hanging over me.

"Yet I didn't show enough power to become an initiate." I pressed my lips together, trying to contain my disappointment. I'd given up everything to come to Parnese, and for what?

Galtus Celcio waved his hand dismissively. "The will of the Twin Gods is not always clear to those with limited vision. You will receive the necessary training to master your sorcery."

"I will?" I met his gaze. "What will the other priests think about that?"

"They know better than to question me."

Relief blunted the sharp edges of my misery. As long as I learned to control my power, agreeing to come with Galtus Celcio hadn't been a mistake. I hoped.

"Who will teach me? Will I be with the new initiates?"

"No. I'll coordinate your training, but Paulette, and perhaps Ser Naldi, will be conducting the majority of your sessions. Now, come."

He waved his hand, and the candles snuffed out, leaving only the sullen glow of the wall sconces. In the dimness, he strode out of the room. I scurried to follow him, a dry leaf scudding in his wake.

The flame-embossed door shut with a thud behind me.

Galtus Celcio led me past several arches, then through two doors in quick succession. I tried to orient myself, but even with my generally good sense of direction, it was difficult to keep track of where we were in the maze of featureless walls.

As we went, I pondered my changed situation. So, Paulette was to be my teacher. Probably because of her connection to me and her unswerving loyalty to my father. I wondered if her power was strong enough, then dismissed the notion. Galtus Celcio wouldn't give me an inept tutor. Whatever sorcery my former friend wielded, it would be sufficient to train me in the ways my father wanted.

He finally emerged onto a patio shaded by the high dome of the main temple. The gold-covered roof arched above us, covering half the sky. Unlike the open space outside the dining hall, this courtyard boasted no fountain or comfortable benches. I tried not to frown at the dry expanse of brick.

A heavy door carved from the black wood of Ypteg dominated the far wall, flanked by two armed temple guards. Galtus Celcio nodded to them, then opened the door and ushered me into a surprisingly cool and airy space. Instead of the ubiquitous blood-colored granite, the rooms were floored with pale pink marble, the walls plastered with white.

It was a welcome change, and I drew in a deep breath. All that red had been weighing upon my soul.

We stood in the main foyer, which opened to a living area straight ahead. I glimpsed blue sky through the tall windows and was glad to see a much more hospitable courtyard beyond, complete with lemon trees growing in huge clay pots and a blue-tiled fountain like the ones found all over Parnese.

"Your room is this way." My father led me past a scattering of low couches and tables and into a bright hallway, lit on one side by windows that looked onto the courtyard. He opened a door—not the flame-resistant onyxwood of Ypteg this time, I noted—and gestured for me to enter. "I trust you'll be comfortable. Let one of the servants know if there's anything you need."

I nodded and stepped over the threshold, curious to see what my new accommodations held. And very relieved that, *finally*, I'd have the privacy to contact Thorne.

I'd lived in an apartment in Parnese before, with Mama, but although my new bedroom held a similarly carved window screen and bright rugs, it was far more elegant than our old home. I felt a momentary pang for the tattered carpets, the worn spots on the windowsills. This room was unlived-in, a pristine and empty space waiting for a guest.

Unlike my suite in Castle Raine, there was no sitting room. A bed was pushed up against the right-hand wall, and on the other side of it, a curtained opening led to a washroom. Opposite the bed stood a wicker settee, and a matching table holding a pitcher of water and a glazed blue cup. My father watched from the doorway as I crossed to the wide window on the far wall and pulled back the screen to see if I had any view.

A row of bars met my gaze, dark iron against the hard red stone of the outer temple walls. I whirled, giving him an accusing look.

"Am I your prisoner now?" My throat was tight with dismay.

He shook his head. "It's for your own protection. And I must reiterate that you are not to leave this apartment without an escort. For any reason."

"What about my training?"

"Paulette will come to you."

I glanced about the room, noting the many flammable objects—including the window screen, the bedframe, the wardrobe...

As if sensing my thoughts, Galtus Celcio let out a sharp laugh. "Don't fear. There is an appropriate practice area where you will learn to master your flames."

"What about Donal? Am I allowed to see him? Or is he behind bars too?" I couldn't keep the edge from my voice as I wondered how my guard fared. They'd kept us separated since arriving at the temple, though Paulette had assured me she'd look after him.

My father frowned slightly at me. "He will accompany Paulette when she visits, so that the King of Raine is assured of your continued good health. Which reminds me"—he waved at the bedside table —"there is a letter for you."

I hurried to the table and snatched up the envelope. Even though I knew there was no way Thorne would write to me—not here, in the stronghold of the red priests—my spirits fell when I recognized my mother's elegant script. Flipping the envelope over, I frowned to see that the wax seal of the kingdom of Raine had been broken.

"You read it?" I frowned at my father.

"I prefer to make no secret of the fact," he said. "Honesty between us is the best course, Rose. You may reply to her, of course—there's paper and pen in the drawer there. But don't bother sealing the letter. I'll set my ring to it once it leaves the temple."

Wonderful—though the warder wasn't telling me anything I hadn't already suspected. He would be reading my letters, both coming and going. I'd have to be careful with anything I wrote.

"Shall I tell her I failed the test?" I asked.

"You may share anything you like. Or nothing at all—though I do remind you that she'll be expecting a reply." He gave me a faint smile. "We wouldn't want Lord Raine to do anything rash, after all. Now, I'll leave you to get settled. I'll send someone to fetch you when dinner is delivered."

He left, closing the door behind him. After a moment I went and tried the handle, relieved to find that he hadn't locked me in. I opened the door and shot a glance down the hallway, then retreated back into my room.

My trunk was set at the end of the bed. The clothing I'd brought didn't look disturbed, but I'd no doubt the priests had thoroughly searched my paltry belongings. Quickly, I checked the secret compartment, and was relieved to find my bag of coin still within. Not that I'd be able to use it if I couldn't figure out a way to leave the temple.

With a sigh, I pulled out the gold circlet that denoted my status as a princess of Raine and set it on the dressing table.

There wouldn't be much call for me to wear it—Galtus Celcio had made it clear he thought I should leave Raine behind—but at least it would be out of the way.

So. I wasn't truly a princess, and I was no longer an aspirant of the red priests.

I was back to being just Rose, though my status as the daughter of Galtus Celcio was like the weight of a sword. A double-edged one, since I'd been shown special favors without, in the priests' judgment, demonstrating that I deserved such treatment.

I didn't belong in the Temple of the Twin Gods, let alone the inner sanctum of the warder's apartment. Yet there was no place else for me to go.

With a deep sigh, I sat on the edge of the bed and pulled Thorne's stone from my pocket. Just a polished gray pebble, to carry all of my heart within. I cupped it in my hand, staring at it for a long moment, my mouth shaping the rune for light. I almost spoke it. Almost...

But it wasn't safe yet. My father had mentioned servants, and one of them could knock at the door at any moment. Best if I waited until the deep of the night to attempt to contact Thorne, though my blood burned with impatience.

I set the stone gently upon my bedside table, then changed from the drab aspirant's robe into my familiar blue gown. Its pockets were deep, and my secret stone felt safe there, slipped into that comforting darkness.

Unfortunately, the heavy fabric of the dress was more suited to the cool, damp climate of Raine than the dry heat of Parnese. Sweat prickled the back of my neck, and I wondered if I could ask my father for a few Parnesian-style garments. That had been the only good thing about the aspirant's robe—it was a lighter fabric, cool against the skin.

Not that I'd keep wearing it. I was no longer an aspirant, and by now the entire temple must know that I'd failed the test.

I wondered what they thought—if I was the whispered object of pity and scorn. Cooped up in the warder's rooms, I couldn't defend myself or prove that I belonged. Except, of course, to Paulette, when she came to train me.

As long as I could get my fire to cooperate.

Now, however, it was time to inform Mama of my failure. I suspected she'd be glad to hear it, and my mouth twisted as I opened her letter.

My Dearest Rose,

I worry for you so much, my darling. Please be careful, and write as often as you may, so that I know my fears are unfounded. Return to us soon. Only then will my mind be at ease.

Mama

I SHOOK MY HEAD. Not unexpectedly, my mother's thoughts were all for herself.

As Galtus Celcio had said, the drawer in the bedside table held pen and paper, and little else. I paused a moment before penning my reply, thinking of what to say. Setting down the words would make my situation all too real.

DEAR MAMA,

I cannot believe barely a week has passed since I left Raine. You must have sent your letter by the next ship to depart Portknowe.

A SUBTLE REBUKE that she didn't need to deluge me with correspondence. I wondered if she'd catch my meaning, or if I'd continue to receive weekly letters imploring me to respond right away.

IT IS *a little strange to be back in Parnese, and within the temple itself, of all things. Although it turns out I am not going to be admitted as a regular initiate of the red priests, my training will continue.*

I WAS SIDESTEPPING THE ISSUE, but my words were true enough. Even if I wasn't being entirely candid about the reasons behind my lack of initiation...

PLEASE LET *me know if there are any changes in Raine. I will keep you informed of my progress here.*

Rose

I COULDN'T COME RIGHT OUT and ask if there was any word of Neeve's improved health. The less Galtus Celcio could glean about events in Raine, the better.

That task done, I set the letter aside, ready for the warder's seal. Then, with nothing else to do, I left my room and went back to the living area. It was empty, but the fountain in the courtyard beckoned, the afternoon sun catching the droplets like they were made of diamonds. I perched on one of the benches set along one wall, grateful for the shade of the temple's dome, even as I disliked the way it loomed overhead.

But for now, there was nothing I could do about the oppressive presence of the Temple of the Twin Gods in my life.

CHAPTER 15

D inner, as my father had said, was delivered to us on covered trays by the temple's servants. He and I went out into the courtyard, the splash of the fountain and the smell of lemon blossoms providing a pleasant atmosphere.

We settled in wrought-iron chairs at a matching table while our meal was unveiled. I'd felt lightheaded from skipping lunch, and my mouth watered at the sight of the plates filled with food: baked fish, a salad made of mint and grains, cured olives, hard cheeses, and sliced oranges. It was far better fare than the aspirants had been served.

"Do you ever go to the refectory?" I asked Galtus Celcio.

"Seldom. In fact, I take most of my meals at my desk." He sent me a rueful look. "There's much to do, and not enough time to accomplish it. I will try to join you for dinner once a week, however, and you can update me on your progress."

I nodded and took a bite of fish, trying not to show my disappointment. My father was a busy man. I'd been foolish to think he'd have hours to devote to my training. Especially when he could delegate Paulette to do it.

"You'll also be attending services in the temple," he continued. "Though only as an observer for the time being, I'm afraid."

"That's fine," I said hastily.

I wasn't particularly interested in a repeat of the flame demonstration he'd channeled through me. Or hadn't. My lips twisted as I tried to sort out where my power ended and his began, but I didn't know enough about my own ability to make any solid guesses. Yet.

My father's auburn brows drew together with displeasure at my lack of enthusiasm, and I quickly changed the subject.

"Would it be possible to get some lighter clothing?" I asked. "The climate here is so much warmer, and I'm afraid I didn't bring many gowns suitable for living in Parnese."

No matter how temporarily.

His expression cleared. "Certainly. I'll have Paulette bring a few things for you tomorrow morning, when she comes to begin your training, and you two can consult about the rest of your wardrobe."

"Thank you," I said, as the servants came to take away our empty plates.

They were followed by a silent woman who served us iced melons in chilled silver bowls. I smiled my thanks, though my father ignored her presence entirely.

The first cold spoonful was delicious, reminding me of the *vorniquesse* the Nightshade Lord had conjured when I dined with him. Without thinking, I turned the scarlet ring about on my finger, and my father's attention shifted to my hand.

"Might I see your ring?" he asked.

My pulse spiked. "I promised never to take it off."

Would the gateway close if I removed the ring? I'd no idea what, precisely, was keeping that door between the worlds open, and I couldn't risk upsetting what might be a very delicate balance.

"Hm." Galtus Celcio didn't sound particularly pleased at having his request denied. It probably didn't happen often. "Who gave it to you, again?"

"An admirer." I summoned up a weak smile. "Once, I thought we might get married, but that was before..."

"Before your power manifested," my father finished. "I'm glad you've realized you're destined for greater things than marrying some minor lordling from a backwater kingdom."

I widened my eyes and nodded, keeping my stab of bitter amusement hidden. Lord Mornithalarion Shadrift of the Nightshade Court of Elfhame would certainly object to being described in such a manner.

There was no point in mentioning the Athraig prince, or Kian's brother, either. The time for marrying princes was past.

Thorne, my heart said with every beat.

Galtus Celcio scooped up his last bite of melon, then patted his lips with his napkin and stood. "I'm sorry I must leave you—but you're welcome to linger."

"Oh." Despite the fraught moments during our meal, I was sorry to see him go.

"I'll see you in a few days. And don't worry, Rose, there will soon be plenty to keep you busy."

He gave me an enigmatic smile, then strode back through the double doors, leaving me alone on the patio.

Glumly, I chased the last bits of melon around with my spoon, then glanced up at the sky. It was still too blue for twilight, but I'd tell the servants I was tired from the events of the day and was going to bed early. There was more than a little truth to it.

Once I gained the privacy of my bedroom, I locked the door. I was glad there was a solid latch—although my father probably had the key to every room in the temple. Still, I didn't think I'd be interrupted. I'd asked the servants not to disturb me until the morning.

The pitcher of water awaited on the low table beside the settee. I poured some into the blue cup and took a sip. Lemon flavored the water, as was customary in the wealthier homes of Parnese. I hoped the addition wouldn't impair Thorne's ability to scry me.

I carried the cup over to my bed and sat, then, hands trembling with excitement, pulled the stone from my pocket.

"*Calya,*" I whispered, bringing it up to my mouth.

For a moment nothing happened, and I pulled in a deep breath. *Please.*

A spark lit within the stone, slowly suffusing the gray rock with the bluish light of Dark Elf magic. Stone in one hand, cup in the other, I waited, staring at the surface of the water. Thorne would only be able to scry me if he were in the mortal world, and I had no idea how long I'd have to wait.

If morning came and there was still no word, I'd have to extinguish the light and try again the next evening, when it was safe for us to speak.

As I waited, I tried to imagine what Neeve might be doing in the Nightshade Court. No doubt she was learning more Elvish magic under the tutelage of the Dark Elves and becoming well versed in the intricacies of court life in Elfhame.

I hoped for her sake that she felt well enough to take up her sword work again. Which, come to think of it, I should consider doing. Well, not swords, but my smaller blade, which had been returned to me along with my other belongings in the trunk.

Did I still have my newfound skill with weapons, or had leaving Raine caused that ability to disappear?

I glanced about my room, then shook my head. There wasn't enough space to practice without risking stabbing the bed or knocking over the furniture. I'd have to figure something out. Perhaps the courtyard...

The stone flared bright blue, and I focused my attention on the surface of the cup. Hope fluttered in my belly. It had only been a week since I'd embraced Thorne in the starlit forest outside Portknowe, but it felt like an eternity.

The water shimmered, as though an invisible breeze passed over it, then cleared to reveal Thorne's sharp-planed face gazing out at me. It was all I could do to keep from exclaiming loudly with joy.

"Thorne." I kept my voice low, though my throat was tight with emotion. "I miss you."

"And I yearn for your presence like the moon craves the sun," he said with a wry smile. "Tell me how you are faring in Parnese."

"Not well. I failed the red priests' tests and am now confined to Galtus Celcio's apartment."

Thone's eyes widened. "You failed? How is that possible?"

"Well, I didn't have very long to prepare. And then..." I hesitated a moment, but there were no secrets between us. "I used my power to help one of the other aspirants, and that may have played a part. I'm not sure." I grimaced in apology.

"As impulsive as ever." He shook his head, but the words were fond. "Perhaps it's for the best."

I sighed a little and leaned back. "That's kind of you to say, but I can't imagine it's true."

"Consider." He held up an elegantly long finger. "It was never your intention to remain in Parnese. This way, it will be simpler for you to leave the temple once you've learned to control your powers."

"Galtus Celcio..." I glanced at the door, then lowered my voice to a whisper. "I don't think he'll let me go that easily."

"You are brave and clever," Thorne said. "I've no doubt you'll find your way back to Raine."

"To you." I wished I could touch him, could reach through the silvery membrane of the scrying and take his hand. Judging from the yearning in his eyes, he felt the same.

But at least we could speak with each other, and I knew I should be grateful for that much.

"How is Neeve?" I asked.

His smile broadened. "Improving, I'm glad to say. She's been working with the healers to create a more potent infusion of the *nirwen* essence. Mistress Ainya taught her well."

"And the Darkwood?"

"Quiet—for now. No dire creatures stirring out of season."

I thought of the basilisk that had come into the schoolroom, the drake that had menaced Neeve and me in the forest, the dire wolves that had pursued us to the castle wall.

"My mother wrote to me," I said.

"She is very worried." Thorne's brows drew together. "I can't believe she concealed your father's identity from you for so long."

A hot stab of anger raced through me. "Me either. But I'm here now."

"And what of your sorcery? Will you be able to glean anything more about how to use it?"

"Oh, yes—my father has decided I'm to receive further instruction from Paulette."

Thorne tilted his head slightly, the blue light of foxfire sheening off his black hair. "Will that be enough?"

I shrugged. "Who knows? But my father might help me too."

I couldn't help the nagging suspicion that the warder of the red priests wanted to use me for his own gain, despite my unpredictable powers. But if he thought to transform me into a weapon he could brandish, he was destined for disappointment. I would never let him turn me against Raine—or any other kingdom, for that matter.

"Still, you must take care," Thorne said somberly. "And I must go— I was on my way to the doorway when your summons came."

"Tell Neeve hello." I tried to keep the heaviness from my voice. "I hope I can see you again, soon."

"As do I. Be well, my beloved." He reached, as if he would caress my cheek.

The surface of the water shivered, and for a bare moment I thought I felt Thorne's touch. Then he was gone, and I was left staring at the empty reflection of my own face.

CHAPTER 16

Those next day, I was awoken from a surprisingly restful sleep by a knock at my door.

"Yes?" I called drowsily.

"Sera Celcio, your breakfast," one of the servants called.

By the time I'd donned my blue dress and opened the door, the man was gone. A covered tray sat in the hallway just outside, and I sleepily carried it out to the patio. The air held a touch of night coolness, and, judging by the angle of the sun, the morning was still young.

I wondered if I could ask the servants to wake me later, then recalled that I was to have lessons with Paulette every morning. I screwed up my face—half yawn, half stretch—wishing I could control the pattern of my days. Even though I was now of age, the independence I craved still lay out of reach.

The wrought-iron table was half in the shade, and I settled there, inhaling the sweetness of the lemon flowers. My tray contained an assortment of pastries and sliced fruit. And, I was glad to see, a cup of strong, smoky black tea.

I spent most of breakfast recalling my conversation with Thorne and trying to fix every detail of his face and voice deeply in my thoughts. Not that I'd ever forget him, but I knew how distance could change one's memories. Look at how different Parnese was, and Paulette.

Of course, most of those changes were due to the passage of time —and Galtus Celcio's influence. The city had fallen fully under the shadow of the red priests, as had Paulette. I sighed and finished my tea.

Just as I was wondering whether to leave the dishes or bring them inside, another servant came out to clear them.

"What's your name?" I asked the gray-robed woman.

"It's no matter," she said. "I am a servant of the Twin Gods."

She didn't meet my eyes, and I frowned at her as she took the tray and went back into the apartment. Had my father instructed the staff not to interact with me, or was that self-effacement a requirement of coming to serve the red priests?

I picked up a fallen leaf from beneath the lemon tree and absently shredded it with my fingernails. There was so much about the temple I didn't know. But I'd learn.

At least I had the fountain to keep me company, though its liquid murmur was incomprehensible. I smiled faintly, once again recalling the strange mud maidens I'd encountered in the Erynvorn. Magic was woven through the land of Elfhame.

But what of my own magic? It hadn't stirred at all since the testing. Had it gone into permanent hiding?

There was one way to find out. Slowly, I held out my cupped hand.

"*Firenda,*" I said, concentrating on summoning my power.

I felt the coals inside me begin to glow. After a moment, a thin orange flame flickered to life in my palm, and I smiled in triumph. Now, how did I feed that fire? Obviously, I needed to access more of my power. Perhaps that was done by speaking the full chant.

I was opening my mouth to try when Paulette stepped into the courtyard.

"Very good!" she said, her gaze going to the flame in my hand.

As if her attention was a splash of cold water, the fire immediately went out. I released a heavy breath and stood. "Good morning, Paulette."

"I'm so sorry about the test," she said. "I would have welcomed you as a true sister into the fold of the red priests. And clearly you have the power... I just don't understand." She shook her head sadly, then met my gaze. "At least you don't have to leave the temple. I suppose the Twins have other plans for you."

"Maybe so." I glanced at the high dome overhead and tried to ignore the prickle of foreboding on the back of my neck. "Galtus Celcio mentioned that I'm expected to attend services. When are those held, exactly?"

Mama and I hadn't been followers of the Twin Gods when we lived in Parnese. I had a hazy notion that the faithful came to worship once a week, though the most devout might attend a midweek service, too.

Paulette made a face, as though she couldn't imagine me being unfamiliar with the workings of the temple. "You *do* know the main worship is on SunDay?"

I nodded. The second day of the weekend allowed the working people of Parnese to attend the temple.

"First service is at dawn," she continued cheerfully, and I tried not to let out a groan. "Second is midmorning, and third begins at sunset."

"Am I expected to attend all of them?"

"You're certainly welcome to. All the initiates do."

But I wasn't an initiate.

"I suppose I'll ask the warder," I said. And hope he wouldn't insist I spend the entire day yawning in the temple.

"That gives us three days to work on your training." Paulette clasped her hands together. "I'm so lucky to be able to guide you this way. Surely the Twins have blessed us both."

I smiled weakly at her, having no other response. Her devotion made me uncomfortable, as I couldn't share it—at least not genuinely.

"Where's Donal?" I asked, glancing through the doors into the living area. "I thought, now that I'm no longer an aspirant, he'd go back to guarding me."

"Oh, don't worry! He's with the soldiers just outside. Once our morning session is over, you can say hello."

I nodded. I didn't like the fact that my guard had to wait at the door, but it made sense. Galtus Celcio certainly wouldn't welcome a Rainish soldier striding about his apartments.

"Is he faring well?" I asked.

"Very." She gave me a coy smile. "Now, let me show you the training room."

I thought she'd take me back into the temple complex, but to my surprise, Paulette led me around the courtyard and through a single door opposite the main apartment. It opened into a red stone room as featureless as the practice rooms the aspirants had used.

Unlike those rooms, however, this one bore huge black scorch marks against the walls and pitted areas where fire had eaten into the stone. I shivered at this evidence of Galtus Celcio's sorcery. It was easy—too easy—to forget that my father wielded immense power.

Remember Ser Pietro, I told myself, then swallowed back bile as the faint smell of smoke in the room echoed that long-ago day when I'd seen a man burned to death.

"Don't be afraid," Paulette said, misinterpreting my sudden hesitation. "We'll start with simple chants."

I nodded and collected myself. I was there to learn everything I could about controlling my power. Whatever the cost.

৩২৩

AN HOUR LATER, my confidence had ebbed.

While I could bring a flame into my hand, I couldn't sustain it long enough to complete the flinging movement I'd failed during the test.

At the start of the training session, I'd deliberately kept myself from using the mirror shield—which apparently made no difference, after all. Although, to be honest, it did seem as though summoning *firenda* was easier. When I called, the fire came. It was just the scorching movement that continued to frustrate me.

"*Quera quemar,*" I chanted for what felt like the thousandth time, and thrust my hand toward the far wall. The flicker of orange in my palm wavered, then went out. I let out a sigh. "I'm getting worse."

The first few times I'd tried the move, the fire trickled down my hand before disappearing. But now it faded before I could even attempt to toss it at the wall.

"It takes practice," Paulette said, but despite the cheery note in her voice, I could tell she had her doubts.

"Maybe there's something else I could try." The current chant wasn't working, that was certain. I thought of the words I'd learned from the little red book. "What does *Esfera to quera* mean?"

She stiffened and shot me a sharp look. "Where did you hear that phrase?"

"I overhead someone say it outside the refectory," I lied.

"That was careless." Her lips firmed. "That chant is sacred to the inner circle of the priesthood. Who said it? What did they look like?"

I shrugged. "I just saw a flash of scarlet robes—they were headed around the corner."

"I must inform Galtus Celcio," she said, and I felt a stab of pity for my imaginary tattling.

Revealing the red priests' secrets was clearly a greater offense than I'd thought. Which didn't bode well for my own departure from the temple.

Resolutely, I thrust that worry from my mind. The first thing, after all, was to actually learn some of those secrets for myself.

"Still, I can't unhear the words," I said, determined to pursue the matter. "What do they mean?"

"I shouldn't tell you."

"But you're my teacher." I sweetened my tone. "Where will I learn, if not from you? After all, you know so much—and I know nothing. Besides, the warder chose you, especially, to work with me."

After a moment, she drew in a breath. "I suppose that's true. And you *are* Galtus Celcio's daughter..."

I nodded, trying to look appropriately awed and humbled by the fact. "Anything you could share with me will please my father, I'm sure."

"Well, then." She straightened. "The Esfera is the sacred relic of our sect. Originally it was a perfect sphere of red crystal containing great power, but it was broken centuries ago during a battle between the gods. All that remains are a few shards, but we remember."

"The chant must be old, then."

"It's ancient. Only the strongest priests are able to use it, however.

For the rest of us, the chant is just syllables."

Like me and my failure with the fire flinging, I thought wryly.

And yet, during my last escape from Parnese, I'd been able to harness a fireball with those ancient words. Even now, they echoed inside my head. *Esfera to quera, firenda des almar.*

Not that I'd speak them aloud. Doing so would horrify Paulette, not to mention shatter my guise of innocence about all thing red-priestly.

"That's enough of a break," Paulette said briskly. "Back to work."

Obediently, I held out my hand and spoke the words to summon my fire. A little orange flame sprang up, comfortably warm in the cup of my palm. At least that part was going reliably.

"Now *quera quemar*," she said, taking a step back.

I nodded, but even as my mouth formed the words, I let the other chant ring inside my head. *Esfera to...*

"*Quera quemar!*"

With a whoosh, a fist-sized ball of bright red fire shot from my hand and hit the wall. It sizzled on impact, then faded, leaving a circle of soot behind and an acrid smell in the air.

"Oh." Paulette blinked at me, then looked at the wall a dozen feet in front of us. "That wasn't...usual."

I grinned at her, success singing through me. "But I did it!"

"Indeed."

She stepped forward and ran a finger through the blackened patch. Slowly, she brought her hand up and sniffed at the residue of soot, her nose wrinkling. Then she stared at me, her eyes wide.

"What is it?" I asked, disliking the awe in her expression.

"You summoned a fireball, instead of the regular scorching flame." There was a note of wonder in her voice.

"Are they that different?"

"Yes." She let out a breath, then wiped her hand on the inside of her sleeve and came back to where I stood. "The fireball is a concentrated fire that burns hotter and spreads very quickly when it touches a flammable surface."

I shivered, thinking of the huge, pulsating ball of flame Galtus Celcio had cast at me and my companions as we fled Parnese. Using the chant, I'd wrested control of that fire and plunged it deep beneath the surface of the sea.

Your father tried to kill you, the little voice inside me said. *Don't forget.*

I could make no reply, except that he'd been determined to stop us from fleeing. But I'd escaped, and he'd eventually pursued me across the Strait. To what purpose? Certainly not to put an end to my life. He'd wanted me to join the temple—although he hadn't seemed terribly disappointed that I failed to join the ranks of the red priests.

Perhaps he hadn't wanted you to succeed.

I blinked at the notion. It was true that I'd had very little time to prepare before Galtus Celcio decreed the aspirant test should be given. I'd thought it was because he was so confident in my abilities, but perhaps he was playing a deeper game.

Yet what could it be? How would it do the warder any good to have a failed aspirant on his hands?

"Let's see if you can control the scorch," Paulette said, pulling me out of my troubled thoughts. "No more fireballs."

She gave an uneasy laugh, and I smiled weakly, though we both knew it was not a joking matter.

Unfortunately, despite two more hours of trying, it seemed that I could either throw the potent ball of flame or nothing.

"I think that's enough for now," Paulette finally said.

"Good."

I let my arms hang limply at my sides. My throat was sore from breathing in the charred air and saying the chant over and over, and my belly had been insisting for quite a while that it must be time for lunch.

When we stepped out of the training room, we found a servant waiting for us. He bowed and told us our midday meal would be served in the courtyard, at our convenience. I took a grateful breath of the clear air and led Paulette to the little iron table.

"Don't worry," she said as we settled at the table, "tomorrow will be better. You'll be able to control *quera quemar* in no time."

I had my doubts, but there was no point in expressing them. Either I'd improve and tame my unruly sorcery, or, as it felt at the moment, I would never master it.

CHAPTER 17

A fter lunch, Paulette suggested I return to the training room and practice on my own.

"I need to tend to my other duties," she said. "But I'm sure it will be good for you to keep working. Just be careful."

"I will," I said, though I felt drained.

She departed, and I went, somewhat reluctantly, back to the red-walled room. For several long moments, I just stared at the flame-blackened walls. My mouth didn't want to form the words of the chants. I closed my eyes, trying to connect with my power, and felt only the barest flicker of flame.

However, the room was big enough to practice my blade work. There were no straw dummies for me to stab at, of course, but one year Sir Durum had taught Neeve, Kian, and me a series of dance-like fighting moves. I hadn't thought of those movements in some time, but we'd drilled the pattern of the steps so rigorously, I was sure I could recall them.

And whatever I couldn't remember, I'd make up as I went along.

I went down the hall to my room and retrieved my blade, wishing I'd packed my trousers and jerkin. It would be harder to practice in a dress, but I never thought I'd need my fighting clothes when we went to Portknowe to meet the red priests.

That seemed a lifetime ago. Once again, the course of my life had changed in a single day, in a heartbeat.

The exertion of going through the moves and trying to remember the footwork drove all other thoughts from my head. I was left with the sound of my skirts swishing as I moved, the rasp of breath in my throat. Lunge and pivot, slice and step.

In my mind's eye, Neeve and Kian worked on either side of me, moving their blades in unison, turning in time. Kian was grinning, Neeve's brows drawn together in concentration.

Oh, how I missed them.

When I finished, the reality of my solitude pierced through me. Panting, I sheathed my knife, drew my sleeve across my sweaty forehead, and then let myself cry, just a little, accepting my loneliness. My homesickness for Raine and the Darkwood. And Thorne, of course, who lay as close to my heart as my own breath.

"Enough," I told myself after some time, scrubbing my cheeks with my skirt to dry my tears.

Luckily, there were no servants lurking outside the room to see my blotchy face and perspiration-darkened gown. Tomorrow, I really had to remember to talk to Paulette about clothing.

❦

A WEEK PASSED, the pattern of my days broken only by the SunDay worship in the main temple. Thankfully, my father had just required me to attend the afternoon and evening services. I'd sat off to the side with Paulette, who prompted me when to stand and sit and what responses to make.

Donal joined us during the evening worship, and I noticed he watched my tutor more than he paid attention to Galtus Celcio and the priests leading the service. My guard seemed quite smitten with Paulette, and I wasn't happy about the fact. He was supposed to be looking after me, not courting a red priest.

My father ignored me during the ceremony too, but I didn't mind his inattention. The last thing I wanted was to be called up to demonstrate my sorcery for the congregation, especially as my days of constant training had left me quite weary.

I spent every morning working with Paulette, and every afternoon in the training room by myself. Sometimes I practiced summoning my fire—and failing to cast the scorch—but mostly I worked with my blade. As the days went by, I felt my body growing stronger and more agile, my dagger work more assured.

Paulette brought me an assortment of clothing suitable to the climate, and I thankfully folded my heavy gowns away. The Parnesian belted tunics were easier to move in as I twisted and turned, stabbing at imaginary foes. The only drawback to the lighter garments was their lack of pockets. I resorted to tying the scrying stone in my belt sash each morning and securely wrapping it around my waist.

Every night I tried to reach Thorne, and each dawn arrived without a response. His duties must have kept him in Elfhame, for I knew that if he were in the human world, he'd answer my summons. Sighing, I'd extinguish the stone and try not to dwell on how much I missed him.

Most dinners I ate alone in the courtyard with only the fountain for company. The afternoons shortened, and each day the shadow of the temple dome fell over me a few minutes earlier than the one before.

Evenings were difficult. I spent one night writing to Neeve, and another to my mother, trying to draw out the letters, though I had very little to tell them.

The monotony was finally broken one afternoon, when a servant delivered the message that Galtus Celcio would join me for dinner that evening. I'd spoken to no one but Paulette for what felt like ages, and took some extra effort to braid my hair and pick out one of the more ornate tunics from my new wardrobe.

My father was already in the courtyard when I entered. He rose to greet me, and I gladly settled across from him. The orange-tinted light of sunset Parnese made the lemons glow against their green leaves. I noted a long, fabric-wrapped bundle propped against the wall behind Galtus Celcio's chair, and wondered what it might be.

"I apologize for leaving you on your own so much," he said,

resuming his seat as the servants brought out dishes of roast chicken and vegetables. "I'd hoped to oversee more of your training. I hear it's going well."

I unfolded my napkin and draped it over my lap, conscious of the small lump of the scrying stone tucked against my belly. "I still can't control *quera quemar*," I said, hating to admit it.

He waved his hand dismissively. "Paulette tells me you are able to summon a fireball, which is far more impressive. *Esfirenda* usually takes years of training."

Tell my sorcery that, I thought wryly. My magic certainly had a mind of its own. I'd thought it might settle once I was in the temple, but it was as wayward as ever. Maybe I just needed more training...

"Can I retake the aspirant test and summon a fireball, instead?" I asked, somewhat flippantly. I didn't truly want to become an initiate of the red priests anymore.

"That is not your path," my father said, giving me an intent look. "I also understand that you are practicing your blade work."

I let out a snort of mild amusement. "A dagger hardly counts."

"I agree." He met my gaze. "That's why I'm giving you this."

He reached for the bundle behind him and carefully unwrapped it, revealing a sword sheathed in a gold-embossed leather scabbard.

"For you," he said, holding it out to me while I blinked confusedly at him.

"But I'm here to learn fire magic. Not sword work."

"Who says you can't train in both? Now take it—my arms are growing weary."

I doubted that, but gently lifted the scabbard from his grasp. Scooting my chair back to make room between me and the table, I stood and drew the blade. My breath caught as the sword was revealed, the metal gleaming darkly.

It was the black blade of the Sister.

"I don't want this," I said, slamming the sword back into its sheath.

My father watched me calmly. "It is the only blade available to you. If you agree to work with it, I'll open one of the training courtyards for you to practice in. Privately."

Half of me wanted to throw the weapon down on the table and stalk away. The other half, though, was deeply curious.

Where had the sword come from? Why had my father given it to me? And could I, indeed, become a skilled swordswoman, given the chance?

I frowned, but pulled the blade fully from the scabbard. Despite its fearsome color, it was well balanced in my hand, and not too heavy. I could tell it would be a pleasure to wield.

Accept it, my wicked voice urged.

Galtus Celcio trusted me enough to give me a weapon. That, alone, inclined me to say yes, once the shock of seeing the dark sword had worn off. Besides, if I needed to fight my way out of the temple, having a blade bigger than my dagger would prove useful.

"Very well," I said, blowing out my breath. "Thank you."

He smiled at me. "Excellent. Now, we'd best eat before our dinner grows cold."

The approval in his eyes warmed me, even though I knew it was only because I'd done as he wanted. I sheathed the blade, then sat down and took a bite of thyme-flavored chicken.

While we ate, he asked if I were comfortable in my new room. I said yes and thanked him for the new clothing Paulette had brought for me. My loneliness and boredom weren't anything I wanted to share with my father, let alone the warder of the red priests.

The servants brought a bowl of figs for our dessert. I plucked one out, glad to see it wasn't quite the end of the season. I had to admit I'd missed the fruits of Parnesia—the dates and oranges and figs—as much as I'd missed the sunshine.

"What do you know of the Sister?" my father asked, leaning back in his chair. An intensity lingered beneath his casual question.

I froze, then set my fig down, untouched. "Nothing." I glanced at the blade I'd set beside my chair. Cold tendrils of foreboding crept up my spine. "Except that she carries a sword."

And had a blaze of curling red hair exactly like my own.

"Indeed, she does." My father nodded at me, as though I'd passed a clever test. "The priesthood cleaves to the Brother—but I've often wondered if the Sister should be so overlooked."

Suddenly, I didn't want to have anything to do with blades or sword training. I grabbed my goblet of water and took a long swallow, trying to wash away the fear lodged in my throat.

"You'll help officiate the WindsDay worship tomorrow evening," he said, and suddenly it was Warder Galtus Celcio before me, stern and implacable, and not the kinder version of the man who was my father.

"I don't think—"

"Or you will be confined to your rooms for a week, only leaving them to train with Paulette."

I stared at him. With one hand, he offered me opportunities, and with the other, he took them away.

"Don't look so alarmed." His voice softened. "All you'll need to do is stand there. Paulette will help guide you."

If it was so simple, why had he threatened to shut me up in my room for a week? But despite my apprehension, I wasn't truly in a position to refuse. At least it would be the smaller midweek service.

"If you command," I finally said.

"I'll send over a ceremonial robe for you to wear," he said. "Be ready to accompany me at six o'clock. The servants will provide a light dinner for you beforehand. And don't forget your sword."

He stood, the evening shadows falling over his face, and once again I was reminded that Galtus Celcio was not my ally.

"I'm glad we could share a meal, Rose," he said. "You're making excellent progress."

I nodded weakly, then made myself thank him for joining me for dinner. Even if it had ended on a terrible note. I couldn't guess what he was up to, with his talk of swords and red-haired maidens, but it certainly didn't bode well for me.

"Ah, I almost forgot." He reached into his scarlet overtunic and brought out an envelope. "You have a letter."

I frowned as he handed it to me. How could he have nearly over-looked delivering it? I hoped he wasn't being so careless with my outgoing correspondence.

"Did you send the ones I wrote a few days ago?" I demanded.

He regarded me for a long moment, as if punishing me for doubting him. "I did. The last thing either of us wants is a deluge of frantic missives from Raine. Any letters you feel moved to write, I shall send over the Strait."

After reading them, of course.

He left the courtyard, but despite the deepening twilight, I continued to sit there, watching the last purplish light of the sunset fade against the earthen wall. Then, with a sigh, I stood, picked up the sword, and went to my room to see what my mother had written.

To my pleasant surprise, in addition to Mama's usual begging for me to be careful and to come home as soon as possible, there was a letter from Neeve tucked inside the envelope.

ROSE,

I am feeling well, and hope that Kian might come to Raine for a visit next month. It will be good to see him. You know how hard it is to be away from loved ones.

I'm thinking of you and wondering if you've burned down the city yet.

Be safe.

Neeve

I SMILED FONDLY, though my eyes were blurred with tears. My sister's voice was so clear, it was almost as if she stood beside me. The pain of missing her nearly matched my longing for Thorne.

But what good news! She was recovering, and would see Kian soon. Either he'd cross over into Elfhame or, better yet, Neeve would be able to return to the mortal world. Which would lift the burden of being the gateway's anchor point from my shoulders. I released a long, hopeful breath at the thought, then fetched paper and pen to write a reply.

DEAR NEEVE,

I'm so glad to hear that all is well for you, and that you'll see Kian in a few weeks. I'm sending my love to you both—so don't keep it all for yourself, haha.

The city of Parnese is still standing, despite the fact I've learned to summon fireballs, which is apparently an advanced technique.

I PAUSED, wondering if my father would object to my sharing the details of my training. On one hand, the red priests kept their secrets close. But on the other, everyone knew they could throw scorching balls of flame, and I suspected Galtus Celcio would approve of my boasting about my power.

I STILL HAVE much to learn, however—including a few basics that continue to elude me. Yes, just like our lessons in herbcraft, I am not always the most apt student. But! I have a sword now. I'm sure Sir Durum won't approve of me training without his supervision, but I can't practice fire sorcery every waking moment. So, who knows, maybe I'll finally become skilled with another weapon besides my dagger.

Please say hello to the Darkwood for me. I miss the forest terribly.

MEANING THORNE, of course, but I was wary of mentioning his name anywhere in my correspondence.

I DON'T KNOW when I'll be able to leave Parnesia, but my heart is there with you in Raine.

All my love,

Rose

THERE. Hopefully I hadn't revealed too much. I folded the letter, then penned a quick reassurance to my mother that I hadn't yet been burned to a crisp or turned into a fanatical follower of the Twin Gods.

Frowning, I glanced at the sword lying across the foot of my bed.

So far, I'd been surprisingly untouched by the religious aspects of living in the temple. But with my father's gift of the dark blade and his not-so-veiled hints about the Sister, I feared that was about to change.

CHAPTER 18

To my dismay, the outfit Galtus Celcio sent for me to wear to the service was an exact replica of the Sister's robes.

A servant delivered it, knocking at my door, then spreading the armfuls of scarlet cloth over my bed before taking their silent leave. I stared at the robes, stiff with their elaborate embroidery of flames, and felt my stomach twist.

I couldn't wear those.

Striding to the bed, I pushed the garments aside, then turned to my wardrobe. It wouldn't be the first time I refused to dress for the part someone else had decided I should play.

After shuffling through my clothing, I decided on the blue gown I'd brought from Raine. I donned it, then braided my hair tightly to keep the red curls from running wild. In a final act of defiance, I set my gold crown atop my head. If my father insisted I claim an identity, then I'd be a princess of Raine, not the avatar of some sword-wielding goddess.

When Galtus Celcio arrived to fetch me for the service, his expression hardened.

"Why aren't you wearing the robes?" he asked tightly. "I gave you those garments for a reason."

I lifted my chin in defiance. "I'm more comfortable like this."

"Change." He stepped back and started to close the door between us.

"No." I stared at him, refusing to be cowed, though his disapproval was a weight pressing me to the ground.

If he truly wanted me to wear the Sister's robes, he'd have to summon servants to force me into them. I'd gambled that there wouldn't be time for him to do so.

Of course, he could also decline to bring me to the service, which I wouldn't mind. Either way, I'd win.

Eyes narrowed, he looked me up and down. "You're as stubborn as I was at your age," he finally said. "At least put on the sword."

I turned, trying not to show my relief. Now that the moment was over, I could admit how afraid I'd been that Galtus Celcio would strike me down on the spot with a bolt of fire. It hadn't been likely, of course —but it was one possibility.

I didn't mind wearing the sword. In fact, I'd considered donning it anyway.

That afternoon, I'd practiced with it in the scorched training room, getting used to the weight and balance. My wrists ached a little, as did my arms, unaccustomed to bearing the larger blade. But it was a nimble weapon, and sharp enough to slash a cut at the edge of my tunic when I'd turned too carelessly at the end of a swiping maneuver. Despite what the weapon symbolized, it was comforting to have a blade at my side.

My father led us quickly through the back hallways of the complex, and I was unsurprised to see that his apartments lay only a few turnings from the main temple. We paused in the smaller, columned sanctuary, and I looked about, not bothering to hide my curiosity.

"The inner sanctum of our sect," Galtus Celcio said. "Here we acknowledge the power granted us by the Twins." He glanced at me. "Of course, only initiates may observe these ceremonies."

I frowned slightly. "You want me to impersonate the Sister, but refuse to share any knowledge with me?"

"Come." He strode to the small altar set on the far wall. "I'll show you our greatest mystery."

The Brother's flame sat on the left side of the altar, the Sister's upright sword on the right. Between them lay a scarlet cloth covering a few lumpy objects. My father pulled it aside to reveal four pieces of broken red stone, some of them blackened around the edges.

"This is what remains of the Esfera," he said. "It was an ancient artifact housing the power of the Twins, until it was broken by their avatars, sent from the heavens. When the sphere shattered, it released its power into select members of our priesthood."

"And that's how the red priests gained their fire sorcery?"

It seemed a good enough explanation as any, though I wasn't certain I believed it.

He gave me a tight smile. "I do not question the will of the Twin Gods. And neither should you."

There was a difference between the Twins and the mortal man who claimed their power, however. No matter what Galtus Celcio liked to think. But I'd seen enough of magic that the mere fact of possessing it didn't awe me the way it did the Parnesians.

Faint chanting echoed from the main temple. My father pulled the cloth back over the red shards, then gestured me to follow. It was time to make our entrance.

We went through the short hallway connecting the sanctum to the temple. The dim light glossed my father's hair to blood red, and I shivered. Maybe I should've refused to come after all. He held up his hand, signaling for me to halt behind him, then cracked the door open a scant inch.

The chanting rose and fell with a hypnotic, musical quality. We waited, the scent of rusty incense drifting into the small space, until the chant rose to a crescendo. With a flick of his fingers, Galtus Celcio pulled the door wide and stepped into the temple.

I trailed him, trying to look composed despite the apprehension fluttering through me. Though this was supposed to be the smaller service, I was sorry to see that most of the benches were filled. The roof arched high overhead, hazy with smoke from the incense braziers.

In front of us rose the large altar. Ser Naldi stood on the Brother's side, a shallow golden goblet in his hands. To my relief, Paulette was stationed on the Sister's side, though I noted with a heavy heart that the large ceremonial sword was not in its place. Its smaller version rode at my hip.

With a nod, my father indicated that I should join my tutor. Aware of the weight of the crown atop my head, I paced to Paulette's side. She shot me a sideways glance, eyes widening when she saw how I was dressed.

That's right, I thought at her. *I'm not here to play the warder's games.*

Even though I was wearing the sword.

Was that usually Paulette's role at the midweek service, to take the Sister's part? Perhaps so, judging by the tightness around her mouth as she faced the congregation.

Galtus Celcio held up his hands at the exact moment the chant ended.

"Followers of the Twin Gods," he said, his voice rich and warm, "we greet you as you come to the temple. The Brother is here to succor you with cup and flame. The Sister to defend you with blade and fire. Do you receive them into your hearts?"

"Yes," the crowd called.

"Do you accept their guidance in your lives?"

"Yes," came the response.

"Then you are welcome here." He brought his hands together, placing the two fingers of his right hand into the cupped palm of his left.

The worshippers mirrored the salute, the sign of the Twins I'd known since I was a child, though Mama and I had never been followers. Considering who my father was, her lack of piety now made complete sense. A jab of anger at her ran through me, and I pulled in a sharp breath.

Too many secrets had shadowed my life, and I was beyond ready to rip off all the veils and confront the bare truth.

Galtus Celcio paced forward to the low railing separating the congregation from the altar and halted, his gaze traveling over the crowd. I was sorry to see Donal in the front row, his expression rapt. Had he become a devout follower of the Twins, or was his attention all for Paulette? Either way, it felt like a betrayal.

"Parnesia is destined for greatness," the warder declared. A murmur of approval rippled through the temple. "And yet such things come only to those bold enough to grasp with both hands, though fire may burn them in the striving. Are you brave enough, people of Parnese?"

"We are!"

"Will you stand with me against those who would grind us back into the dirt?"

"We will!"

I firmed my mouth as I watched my father exhort the crowd. This wasn't a religious ceremony—it was a political leader consolidating his power under the guise of faith. Did the Parnesians even realize what Galtus Celcio was doing? Did they care, as long as they were given the spoils of his conquests?

"Get ready," Paulette murmured to me as the warder continued his speech.

"For what?" I whispered, trying not to move my lips.

"Sword."

I placed one hand on the pommel, aware of the hundreds of watchers facing us. The warder could have coached me a bit more, I thought sourly. Perhaps this was his punishment for my reluctance to embrace the Sister's role. Or perhaps he simply believed I would know what to do when the time came, and trusted Paulette to guide me if I hesitated.

"The Twins will always watch over you, true followers of the temple," my father said, then raised his cupped hand to the ceiling. "By flame!"

"By flame," the crowd echoed.

"*Firenda des almar,*" he said, so softly that only those of us at the altar could hear it.

To no one's surprise, bright red fire blossomed on his palm. He paused a moment, and I could feel his power focusing. The flame shot higher, coruscating golden and scarlet, and the crowd sighed in awe.

It was impressive, and my own banked fire stirred in response.

Calma, I told it. I didn't want to be used as a demonstration again—though why else would Galtus Celcio want me here, before the congregation?

Ser Naldi stepped forward, holding out the gold goblet. He bent his head reverently as my father turned and transferred the flickering flame into the cup. Another trick I hadn't known was possible.

Leaning forward, I concentrated on the fire, finally sensing the trickle of power my father still fed it. I'd no doubt he'd be able to sustain the sorcerous light until the worshippers had all left the temple.

Ser Naldi stepped back, and my father shot me a warning glance before turning to the crowd. I tightened my fingers around the pommel of the blade at my side.

"By sword!" the warder cried.

"By sword," came the response.

"Now," Paulette whispered, but I was already drawing the weapon.

It slid easily from the scabbard. I pointed it aloft, using both hands to support its weight, which was not only practical but had the added benefit of differing from the Sister's one-handed pose.

I didn't hear my father call the flame, but suddenly the sword was afire. Clenching my jaw, I held it steady. The flickering orange fire wouldn't hurt me. I hoped.

The crowd murmured, gazes focused on me, and I wondered how long I'd have to stand there with a flaming blade held over my head. It reminded me uncomfortably of the vision Neeve and I had shared—though she'd been the one holding the sword, and the fire wreathing it had been blue, not orange.

After a dramatic moment, Ser Naldi nodded at me, then paced to the altar and set the fiery cup at one end.

"Go." Paulette prodded me.

Bearing the flaming sword, I dutifully marched to my side of the altar. A holder was set there to keep the blade upright. My arms ached slightly as I lowered the pommel into its cradle.

Wisps of red hair had escaped my braid, stirring softly from the heat of the sword. Once the blade was secure, I backed hastily away to keep from setting my head ablaze.

My crown felt reassuringly heavy in that moment, and I was glad I'd worn it. I might have been constrained to bear the Sister's sword, but I'd done it as a princess of Raine. Chin high, I returned to stand beside Paulette.

The warder urged the congregation to remain pious and true, then led everyone in a chant full of devotion to the Twins. I didn't join in, or even try to mouth the unknown words. Why pretend to a loyalty I didn't feel? The priesthood had rejected me, after all.

A moment later, Paulette pulled at my sleeve, guiding me toward the door at the back of the altar. We went through, followed by Ser Naldi and my father, and the sound of the worshippers leaving the temple receded behind us.

"That went well enough," Galtus Celcio said as we stepped into the sanctum.

"I thought she would be garbed as the Sister," Ser Naldi said, as if I weren't standing right in front of him. There was an edge to his voice, as though he hadn't liked my father's plan in the first place, let alone the fact that I'd spoiled it.

"I'm not going to pretend to be some kind of avatar," I said, turning to face him. "Especially not for a sect that won't admit me into their ranks."

His gaze slid away from mine, but my father laughed.

"She makes a fair point," he said. "As I was telling you, Castin, perhaps it's time for a new priesthood. Or, should I say, priestesshood."

No. Oh, no. I took a step back.

"I can't be some kind of figurehead for you," I said, staring at my father.

Paulette, however, was nodding vigorously. "Rose, you're perfect. Look at your hair! Your flames ran up the sword, too."

"Those weren't mine," I said, though I wasn't sure of the fact. Wherever they'd come from, they had felt effortless.

"Besides," Paulette said, paying no heed to my protests, "everyone knows that you can summon the fireball."

I frowned at her—but of course she'd told the priesthood. Her loyalty was to them, not to me.

"Don't worry," Galtus Celcio said, an indulgent note in his voice. "With my guidance, you'll be able to form and direct a select circle of initiates. I know your abilities, Rose. You are more than capable of this."

Perhaps. But I'd misspoken. Whether or not I *could*, I refused to be a figurehead for the red priests. Or whatever new sect my father was trying to forge.

I opened my mouth to argue, then shut it again. My words would carry little weight, especially surrounded by the powerful symbols of the Twin Gods' power. I must bide my time.

And find some way to leave Parnese, before I became so enmeshed in Galtus Celcio's schemes that it would be impossible to escape.

CHAPTER 19

A lthough I wished no part of my father's plan to create some new splinter sect of the priesthood, I found myself nonetheless drawn into his schemes. Short of locking myself in my room and never coming out, I had little choice but to continue my training.

I'm here to hone my powers, I reminded myself, grimly blasting the walls of the practice room while trying to plot my escape. Summer was wearing into autumn, and in another month the first storms would threaten the Strait. I'd need to time my exit with the last clear sailing weather. Too bad I possessed fire sorcery and not the ability to predict the weather.

The black blade had been returned to me by an expressionless guard, who then escorted me to an outdoor training area. He'd taken up a post by the only door and told me I had an hour. I spent it whacking at training dummies, incorporating the dance-like footwork with stabs and slices. It wasn't elegant, but I supposed it was effective enough.

He brought me back to the warder's apartments and told me he'd be back every other afternoon to fetch me. I'd nodded my thanks, then went to wash off the sweat and grit from my training.

Galtus Celcio did not join me for dinner, and I was beginning to feel a bit abandoned by him. Until, nearly a week after the ceremony where he'd tried to force me into the Sister's role, I entered the training room to find I wasn't alone. Paulette had brought the initiates I'd met in the aspirants' dormitory. It seemed the red priests had decided to let me train alongside them after all.

"Rose," my erstwhile teacher said, smiling broadly, "look who's come to work with you!"

Shamsan grinned and sent me a little wave, and Jenni sniffed and stuck her chin in the air. But Lena came over and took my arm.

"I'm so glad to see you," she said.

Her pleasure seemed genuine, and I gave her a half-smile, relieved to see a friendly face besides Paulette's.

"That's because you were failing the other training," Jenni said with her usual coldness. "Though I don't think you'll do much better here."

"She just needs time," Shamsan said, but Jenni ignored him.

"I don't think *any* of us will do better, in fact." Jenni turned to look at me. "What do you know of teaching fire sorcery, Rose?"

I blinked and shot a questioning glance at Paulette.

Her smile faltered, though she kept it in place. "I'm sure Rose will be a natural instructor."

"What are you talking about?" I asked, apprehension poking cold fingers into my chest.

"You're going to teach all of us how to cast *esfirenda*," Paulette said brightly. "The warder is certain you can do it."

The suspicion coalesced, squeezing until I could scarcely breathe. This was the beginning of Galtus Celcio's attempt to start a cult of the Sister—with me at its head.

"I don't think so," I said tightly.

"Oh, please." Lena squeezed my arm. "You must."

"She's afraid she'll be expelled from the priesthood otherwise," Jenni said.

Once more, I wondered what happened to those who failed the red priests. I feared they made sure their former initiates could say nothing of the sect of the Twin Gods. But I couldn't save Lena at my own expense. Especially since the last time I'd tried to interfere on her behalf, it hadn't gone well for me.

"I'm sorry," I told her, "but I'm not an instructor. I can't teach any of you how to summon the fireball. I don't even know how I do it myself."

"One often learns by teaching," Paulette said, sounding like she was parroting back something the warder had told her.

I held up my hands and shook my head. "I can't do it. I won't, though I wish you all luck."

Before anyone could stop me, I whirled and pushed open the door of the training room. I all but ran for my room, while Paulette called for me to come back. Jenni's cold laugh followed. Gaining my bedroom, I slammed the door and then locked it.

This was terrible. Galtus Celcio expected me to teach the new initiates how to cast fireballs? I'd come to Parnese to learn to harness my own powers, not the other way around. And even if I could teach them, I certainly didn't want to. *Esfirenda* was a weapon better left unused.

Thoughts whirling, I paced back and forth. The sun cast an intricate lacework of shadows through the patterned screen, echoing the twisting complications of my life at the temple. I shouldn't have come to Parnese. Maybe Mama had been right all along, much as I hated to admit it.

I pulled the small gray stone from my pocket and stared at it a moment. Though I knew it was fruitless to try summoning Thorne, I felt I must speak to someone about this turn of events. I went to the table and poured a cup of water, then pressed the scrying stone to my lips.

"*Calya,*" I murmured, my breath warming the stone as it began to glow.

To my utter surprise, the reflection wavered. A moment later, Thorne's face appeared, his dark eyes looking intently at me.

"I'm so glad to see you." It was difficult to keep my voice low.

"Rose—what's the matter?"

I carried the cup over to the window and briefly told him of my father's attempts to mold me into a figurehead for the new sect of the

Sister.

"I won't do it," I finished.

"I fear for the consequences if you do not." Thorne frowned, the planes of his cheeks sharpening. "But help is on the way. Can you pretend to teach them until it arrives?"

I bit my lip. "Maybe. But what's happening? What kind of help?"

His expression lightened. "Good news. I'm glad to say—"

A rap at the door made me hold up my hand.

"Go away, Paulette," I called.

"It's your father," Galtus Celcio said. "Open the door. We must discuss your training."

He rattled the handle, and my heart jumped. I couldn't imagine the consequences should my father discover what I was doing.

"Rose," he called, knocking loudly. "I'd prefer not to break the door down."

"A moment," I said hastily, then stared down at Thorne's reflection.

His lips formed a kiss, and then the water went dark.

"I love you," I whispered belatedly, then set the cup down and went to open the door.

Galtus Celcio's hand was raised to pound upon it again. "Good," he said, striding into my room. "I knew you'd see reason."

He halted in the middle of the floor, brows drawing together as he turned in a slow circle. Panic stabbed through me. Could he sense Thorne's Dark Elf magic?

"What have you been doing in here?" my father asked, eyes still narrowed in suspicion.

"Thinking." I grabbed the cup and gulped down half the water, hoping that would erase any lingering residue from my scrying.

"Hm." He focused on me, his expression stern. "Paulette tells me you refuse to teach your new initiates."

"They're not mine," I said. "And I can't teach them."

"Try." His expression was more dangerous than encouraging.

"Or what?" I folded my arms and stared back at him, channeling Neeve's regal coolness. *I'm a princess of Raine,* I thought at him. *Not your puppet.*

"I'd assumed you wanted to return for a visit to that rain-sodden island at some point," my father said. "Such travel would only happen with my permission, of course. If you'd rather remain in Parnese for the rest of your days, that's up to you."

I swallowed, thinking of Thorne's words. Help was on the way, he'd said—whatever that meant. Oh, how I wished we'd been able to continue our conversation!

Despite the defiance running through me, I took a breath. Until I knew more, I'd have to pretend to agree. My father was already suspicious of me, and the last thing I needed was to be put under constant guard.

"I'm afraid I'll fail as an instructor," I said. It seemed a reasonable excuse, and there was no need to feign the tremble in my voice. "I don't know if I can show the initiates how to summon a fireball."

My father's expression eased. "Don't worry, Rose. You're my daughter—such things will come naturally to you. Now, I want your word you'll do your best."

Slowly, I nodded. "We can try again now, if you'd like."

"The initiates have already returned to the main temple. Tomorrow will be soon enough." He smiled at me, though the expression didn't quite reach his eyes. "I'm glad you saw reason. You must trust me, Rose. Great things lie ahead."

For him, maybe, but not for me. I couldn't share in his grand visions, especially when my heart was anchored to the cool shadows of the Darkwood. To the gold-flecked darkness of my beloved's eyes.

☉✹☾

"FIRE!" Pounding at my door woke me. "Sera Celcio, wake up!"

Groggily, I sat upright in my bed, blinking in the darkness. The acrid smell of smoke stung my nostrils, bringing me fully awake. I flung back the covers, grabbed the silken robe at the foot of my bed, and went to the door.

"Thank the Twins," the frightened-looking servant said. "Hurry—we must evacuate the apartment. Here."

He thrust a dampened cloth at me, then covered his nose and mouth with another one and beckoned urgently for me to follow.

Fire? I stumbled after him, eyes stinging. "What happened?"

"A bit of *esfirenda* escaped one of the training rooms," the servant said. "It smoldered for hours, then caught the roof on fire. The main temple is safe, though."

He led me into the front courtyard, eerily lit by the red and orange flames licking over the roof.

"It's tile," I said, my voice muffled by the cloth. "How can it be on fire?"

"*Esfirenda* can burn almost anything." He pulled open the door. "Hurry."

I hastened after him, glad to find that the air in the temple hallway was mostly clear of the suffocating smoke. When we reached the main sanctuary, I saw that the man had been correct—there seemed to be no trace of fire in the temple itself, and the smell of smoke had receded to a faint char in the air.

The temple was lit with lanterns and wall sconces. Despite it being crowded with servants and black-robed initiates, the majority of the red priests were noticeably absent.

"Where are the priests?" I asked, glancing about.

"Fighting the flames, along with the guards."

"Rose, there you are!" Paulette hurried up and took my hands. "I was worried. You were the last one evacuated."

"I'm all right." I glanced about the crowd, noting the general lack of panic. "Will more of the temple burn? Does this happen regularly?"

"We'll lose a ceiling or two, but it isn't out of the ordinary." She let out a small laugh. "We're fire sorcerers here, after all. But you don't need to be afraid—the priesthood will have the fire under control soon."

"You're not helping them?"

She lifted one shoulder. "The warder asked me to look after you. He says you've agreed to teach, after all."

"I'm not sure." I frowned. "It seems *esfirenda* is quite dangerous, judging by the fact the temple's on fire."

"Don't worry—as I told you, it's a common enough occurrence, and one we know how to mitigate. But I'm so glad you changed your mind.

I'm certain you'll be a wonderful teacher. Come, let's sit." She led me to a nearby bench,

"We'll see." I settled beside her, unwilling to argue, though my throat was nearly choked with words I couldn't say.

The arrival of Donal distracted her. He made me a cursory bow, then went to sit on Paulette's other side. She immediately turned to him, and I frowned at how warm their conversation was. Did she really have feelings for him, or was she simply trying to turn his loyalty toward the priests? I certainly didn't see much of the man who was supposedly guarding me, though I supposed he thought I was safe enough penned up in the warder's apartments.

A few minutes later, Galtus Celcio himself strode into the temple. The various conversations stilled as he held up his hands for silence.

"The fire is out," he announced. "We lost a section of the roof, mostly over the aspirants' dormitory, but the rest of the temple complex is safe. You may all return to your rooms."

Glad murmurs accompanied his news as people rose and began to file out of the cavernous temple. The servant who'd brought me reappeared at my elbow. I said goodbye to Paulette and Donal and let the servant escort me back to Galtus Celcio's apartments.

Now that the excitement of the night was over, weariness tugged at me. Despite the slightly smoky smell of my bed, I was glad to crawl beneath the covers. Once settled, I reached for the scrying stone, which I kept tucked beneath my pillow at night.

A stab of fear went through me when my fingers encountered nothing but the bedsheets. I felt about frantically, unable to believe the truth.

The stone was gone.

CHAPTER 20

I spent the hours until dawn searching every corner of my room for the scrying stone. The tight panic in my chest grew as I pulled apart the bedcovers, crawled under the bed and the wardrobe, and fruitlessly turned all my clothing inside out.

How could it have disappeared?

I couldn't even contact Thorne to ask if scrying stones sometimes dissolved on their own. Finally, heartbroken and exhausted, I crawled into my disheveled bed for a few hours of sleep. I swore I'd continue looking when I awoke. The stone must be in my room somewhere. It *must*.

A servant knocking on my door woke me after what felt like a scant hour of rest.

"Sera Celcio," she called, "your father is awaiting your presence at breakfast."

With a groan, I pulled a pillow over my face, but the woman continued to rap on my door, telling me I was expected to rise and join Galtus Celcio in the courtyard.

Finally, I flung the pillow to the floor.

"I'm coming," I cried. "Now go away."

The knocking ceased. "If you're not out in five minutes, I'll start up again."

Drat it.

I forced myself to get up, though it felt like my skin was coated in sand, and pull on a fresh gown. It was wrinkled, as all my clothes now were from lying in heaps on the floor all night—casualties of my desperate search. I pushed my bedraggled braid behind one shoulder, shoved my feet into my shoes, and managed to get the door open before the servant began knocking on it again.

"Sera." The woman bowed and stepped back, and I plodded to the little courtyard.

The sun was pleasant against my skin, at least, as I took the seat across from my father. I wrapped my hands around the mug of tea set at my place and took a long swallow, nearly burning my tongue in the process. Clearly, Galtus Celcio hadn't been waiting that long, no matter what the servant said.

"Good morning," he said. "I hope you slept well after the excitement of the night."

I blinked at him, then belatedly realized he was referring to the rooftop fire. "Does that happen often?" I asked.

"Once every few months. We try to be vigilant, but the *esfirenda* is dangerous."

"Yet you want me to try teaching it to brand-new initiates."

"Who better?" He smiled at me. "Their minds are unclouded by rules and expectations. I know you'll be quite successful."

"I don't think so," I said flatly, and took another drink of tea.

The same servant who'd rousted me out of bed stepped into the courtyard to deliver our breakfast, and our conversation ceased until she'd departed, leaving behind plates of pastries, fruit, and poached eggs.

Galtus Celcio leaned back, his gaze fixed on mine. "You seem tired, Rose. But, as I said, I'm certain you'll give the initiates your best efforts."

"I told you I'd do what I could." I frowned at him, then took a bite of flaky pastry.

"That won't be enough." His voice turned hard. "However, I think I can convince you."

He held his closed fist out, then uncurled his fingers to reveal my scrying stone.

I gasped and tried to snatch it out of his palm, but he pulled away too quickly.

"That's mine!" I cried.

"And it's obviously important to you." He held it up between his thumb and forefinger. "Such a little rock. I could toss it over the wall, and it would no doubt be lost in an instant."

"Don't." My voice was strangled. "Give it back. Please. As you said, it's just a stone."

"Then why do you care what becomes of it?"

Mind racing, I scrambled for an answer. "It's the exact color of my true love's eyes."

Galtus Celcio's brows went up, and he let out a dry laugh. "How very sentimental—though I'm not sure I believe you. There's something unusual about your precious stone, although I can't quite say what."

I resolutely banished all thoughts of Dark Elf magic. "I told you. It reminds me of my sweetheart."

That much was true, at least.

"Whatever the case, I'll be safeguarding it for you." He made a show of tucking the stone into his pocket. "You'll get it back when all your students can summon *esfirenda*."

"All of them?" I thought of Lena with a stab of apprehension. I didn't think she was capable of casting the fireball, which meant I'd never regain the scrying stone.

Thorne, my heart called. *I'm sorry*. I'd been careless, and we'd both paid the price.

Galtus Celcio nodded at me. "Your students will be waiting for you later this morning, in the training room. Paulette will come fetch you. Now, what about this splendid breakfast?"

I forced myself to eat, though the food held no flavor. How could I possibly accomplish the impossible task the warder had set me?

Paulette had said the fireball chant was one of the most difficult to master.

Of my trio of unwanted students, Shamsan was likely the only one who'd be able to learn the ability. Jenni might, eventually, through sheer stubbornness. But Lena... My spirits sank.

If it came to that, though, I'd plunder my own power once again to boost her abilities. I clenched my fists beneath the table, trying to give myself hope. Regaining the scrying stone was worth any sacrifice.

My father finished his meal, bade me a pleasant day, and left me with a half-eaten plate of food and a simmering sense of dread in my belly. I trudged back to my room to write to Neeve, hoping desperately that Thorne would understand and forgive me. Being unable to contact him made me feel like we were worlds apart. Which, in truth, we were.

DEAR NEEVE,

Remember the stone we found by the stream last summer, that matched my sweetheart's eyes? Well, I've gone and lost it, I'm sad to say. I hope we can find another like it sometime.

Other than that, you'll be interested to hear I've taken up sword work here in Parnese. I know I was always clumsy with weapons, but since my birthday, that seems to have changed.

PERHAPS THE SUDDEN onset of my magic had something to do with it, though I didn't want to openly speculate. Certainly not in a letter that my father would be reading.

I HOPE YOU'RE WELL, and Mama and the king, too. I don't have much more to say. Give my love to the Darkwood, and I hope to see you soon. Write back when you can.

All my love,

Rose

. . .

I FOLDED THE LETTER, suddenly more homesick for Raine than I could say. *Soon,* I told myself. I'd find some way to escape the temple and cross the Straits. I must.

Despite the tea jittering through me, I managed to nap until Paulette knocked at my door. Rubbing my eyes, I followed her to the training room, where the trio of new initiates stood.

"So, you've decided you're not too good for us after all?" Jenni asked, while Lena tried to shush her.

"Stay or go, I don't care," I said wearily. "But if you're staying, stop being so rude."

Shamsan hid a laugh in his hand, and Jenni blinked at me in affront. But at least she didn't say anything more. For the moment.

I directed them to make a line facing the far wall, then stood before them, Paulette hovering off to the side.

"What do you know of summoning *esfirenda?*" I asked.

"Not much." Shamsan grinned. "But I'm not too worried about that."

"Well, I am." Lena shot him a look. "It's supposed to be very difficult."

"For you," Jenni said in an undertone, then subsided when I frowned at her.

I sighed, then glanced at Paulette. "There's a chant to summon it."

"Yes," she said. "*Esfirenda to quera.* But, as Lena said, it's not easy to master."

"Maybe because it's not the right chant," I said, thinking of my early difficulties with summoning flame. Once I began using the correct words, it had come much more easily.

"How could the chant be wrong?" Jenni shot me a contemptuous look. "Do you actually think you know more than the red priests?"

"Do *you?*" I stared coldly at her. "Why do you think you're here? Galtus Celcio has commanded that you learn from me. Are you questioning his judgment?"

Her mouth tightened, and after a moment she looked down at the floor. "No."

"Before you begin," Paulette said, taking a step forward, "the warder wants me to make sure you all know the words to extinguish any flame."

"Any flame? Even *esfirenda?*" I frowned. Had the roof fire been only a ruse to get me out of my room, so that Galtus Celcio could search for the stone? Convenient, that the flames had damaged an empty dormitory and nothing else.

"In the confines of the training room, the chant can subdue the intensity of the fireball," Paulette said. "But we must make sure none of it escapes, or we'll have more incidents like last night. Now, repeat after me. *Calma to sacar.*"

Calma I knew already, but I spoke the rest of the words along with the initiates until Paulette was satisfied.

"Keep that chant foremost in your mind," she said. "Especially once we summon several fireballs in a row. *Esfirenda* can eat away stone and burrow into the walls, so we'll need to stop and make sure it's extinguished after every third casting."

Jenni sniffed, clearly thinking we'd have little need of the chant, but Lena nodded gravely, as did Shamsan.

"Go ahead, Rose." Paulette moved back toward the door, giving me an encouraging look.

Very well. I stiffened my back and turned toward my new students.

"I'm going to teach you a different chant to summon *esfirenda.*" I shot a glance at Jenni. "Whether it works or not, you can decide. But don't make up your mind until you've given it your best try."

I paused a moment, thinking of how I'd conjured up the fireball.

"You'll throw your hand out," I continued, "as if you're casting *quera quemar*—in fact, the last part of the chant is *quera quemar*. But you'll begin it by calling upon the power of the Esfera."

Paulette drew in a quick breath, but I remained facing the initiates. None of them looked confused by the reference, so they'd learned of the sacred relic—probably as part of their initiation.

"So, *Esfera quera quemar?*" Shamsan tilted his head, considering.

"Almost. *Esfera to quera quemar*. But"—I held up my hand—"you also need to think of the power of *esfirenda.*"

"Even though we don't speak the word?" Jenni didn't bother hiding her skepticism.

"Correct." I refused to argue with her, but couldn't resist a little dig in her direction. "Provided you're capable of it."

She wrinkled her mouth into a grimace. I looked at the three of them in turn: Shamsan, nearly quivering with eagerness, Jenni's doubtful expression, and Lena, clearly frightened by the whole endeavor. Essentially what I'd expected.

"I'll demonstrate." I motioned for them to make a space for me, then turned to face the far wall.

I couldn't contemplate failure, not with the fate of my scrying stone hanging in the balance. The reminder of what my father had stolen set a spark of anger in my belly. I harnessed it, then shot my hand forward and called out the new chant.

"Esfera to quera quemar!"

A fireball blazed from my palm and hit the stone wall with a sizzle. Lena gasped, and Jenni sent me a surprised look tinged with admiration. Shamsan let out a little whoop, and Paulette simply nodded. She already believed I was an avatar of the Sister, I realized with a sinking heart.

The flames lingered, smoldering and beginning to spread over the marble, and Paulette quickly cried the words to extinguish them.

Once they were out, an expectant silence fell over the room. No one was arguing with me now, and despite the grim circumstances, I couldn't help the satisfaction curling through me. Honestly, even though I'd spoken confidently, I hadn't been entirely sure the new chant would work. Even though I'd been using it in my head for weeks.

Whether the others would be successful, however, remained to be seen. I turned to Lena.

"I'd like you to try first," I said. "Remember—*Esfera to quera quemar.*"

It would be too demoralizing for her to watch Shamsan succeed, and potentially Jenni, and then fail herself. I'd stood in that very line and knew how soul-crushing it was to go last, without success.

Lena bit her lip. "Are you sure?"

I gave her an encouraging nod. "Imagine the blaze of a fireball—think of what you could do with it."

Uncertainly, Lena held up her hand, and I already knew she wouldn't be able to summon *esfirenda*. Still, I kept my smile in place.

"*Esfera to...quera quemar*," she said.

A dribble of flame fell from her fingers onto the floor, the fire going out the moment it hit the stone.

"Push your hand forward," I said, demonstrating the motion. "Say the chant with conviction. You can do it." Jenni let out a quiet snort of disbelief, but I ignored her and focused on Lena. "Ready?"

She pulled in a breath, then extended her palm and spoke the chant without halting. This time, the flames left her hand and traveled a few inches before sputtering and dying.

"Good try." I patted her shoulder, trying to think of how to give her the internal strength she needed to summon *esfirenda*. "You'll get there."

She *must*, for otherwise I had no way to contact Thorne except for the stilted letters I sent to Neeve. The knowledge was salt in the wound of my longing.

"I hope so." Lena glanced down at the floor. "I was doing better with the regular training."

"No, you weren't," Jenni said.

"Enough." I turned to her. "Are you ready to attempt the chant?"

"Of course." She straightened her shoulders, narrowed her eyes, then spoke the words, confidently thrusting her hand out.

Hot red flames gathered on her palm and flew forward, but they lost the intensity of *esfirenda* halfway across the room. The fire that splattered on the far wall was a normal scorch—impressive enough, but lacking the deadly force of the fireball.

"Let me try again," she said.

After three attempts with decreasing results, I stopped her.

"You'll master it," I said. "But there's no need to exhaust yourself today."

Until Lena had better success, I wouldn't push the other aspirants, even though my heart screamed at me to keep them working until they all could cast the fireball. In the past, I'd gone more than a week without speaking to Thorne, I reminded myself. There was plenty of time.

With a bit more hope, I looked at Shamsan. He grinned back at me, then turned to the far wall, cried the words, and flung a fireball across the room. The flames smoldered, clearly *esfirenda*, before finally subsiding.

"Oh, well done!" I cried, smiling. He'd exceeded my expectations.

"I knew I could summon the fireball." He grinned, then looked past me at Lena. "You can too—I just know it."

She gave him a doubtful look, but his smile didn't falter. Even Jenni nodded, for once keeping her sharp words to herself. A wash of relief went through me. Maybe the scrying stone wasn't as far out of reach as I'd thought.

"Good work, everyone," I said. "Let's go down the line once more, then stop for the day."

The last thing I wanted to do was deplete their energy by pushing them too hard. But if Lena didn't make better progress, I'd have to come up with some kind of plan to ensure her success.

Even if it meant depleting my own fire in the process.

CHAPTER 21

For the next week, my aspirants continued to make progress. Of sorts. Shamsan and I continued to refine our skills, taking turns pinpointing areas on the wall to burn. Jenni managed to call *esfirenda* more often than not, and even Paulette left her watchful post to work on summoning the fireball.

Of the five of us, only Lena was unsuccessful, though I could tell she was trying her hardest. I began to feed her some of my power, which only resulted in making me tired and ineffective and had no noticeable impact on her skill.

It took effort not to snap at her as the days went on and Thorne grew more distant. I dined twice with my father, though our conversations were stilted. I couldn't forgive him for stealing my stone.

Then, one morning, he joined me for breakfast. At the end of our meal, he pulled out a sheaf of letters from Castle Raine.

"These arrived for you," he said, handing them to me.

"I wish you wouldn't read them." I frowned at the open seals.

He raised one auburn brow. "I'm only looking out for your best interests, Rose. You know how your mother can be."

I pressed my lips together, thinking of Mama's various plans to marry me off for Raine's political advantage. Of course, she'd also claimed she was trying to protect me. I was growing weary of parents deciding the direction of my life.

The letter from her was on top, so I read it first.

My dearest daughter,

The happiest of news! I've no doubt you'll be delighted by it. We will see you soon. Certainly everyone there will agree that you must return to Raine for the occasion.

All my love,

Mama

I flipped the letter over, frowning. The back was blank. It was so like my mother to leave out the most important parts.

"What is she referring to?" I glanced up at Galtus Celcio.

"Keep reading." He nodded to the correspondence in front of me.

The next one was from Neeve.

Rose,

I received your letter. There are more stones in the world, don't worry. I am here in Raine to help you find another.

A rush of relief went through me. Neeve was back in the human world! There could be no other interpretation. My sister was out of danger. I closed my eyes in a moment of gratitude that she'd recovered enough to travel between the worlds.

Which also meant that I was no longer obliged to serve as the anchor point between Raine and Elfhame. I pulled in a deep breath and kept reading.

Kian is here, too, and we've sent along the official invitation. My father insisted we observe all the formalities.

I'll see you soon. Until then, keep the forest in your heart.
Love,
Your sister, Neeve

OFFICIAL INVITATION? My pulse speeding, I picked up the last envelope. It was a creamy parchment, heavy with the official seal of Raine. My name was calligraphed across the front in a flowing script that had certainly not been penned by either Neeve or Kian. I slipped out the equally rich paper inside, eagerly scanning the words.

To: Princess Rosaline Valrois

IT IS with the deepest delight that we announce the marriage of Princess Neeve Shadrift Mallory of Raine to Prince Kian Leifson of Fiorland this autumn: the ceremony to commence on the fifteenth day of the ninth month.

I CALCULATED QUICKLY in my head. Two weeks from now, plus a day.

I looked at my father. "I have to be there."

He gazed back at me, eyes hooded. "It's too close to when the fall storms close the Strait."

"The water will be open for another month," I said, trying to keep my annoyance at bay. "I'll be able to cross to Raine safely."

"Yes." His tone was cold. "But will you be able to return? I find the timing quite suspicious."

I bit my tongue on the arguments rising in my throat. Perhaps he was right, and Neeve and Kian had chosen that date in order to try to spirit me safely away from Parnese. However, I thought it far more likely they'd set the wedding for the soonest possible day the king and queen would allow.

"I'll return to Parnese afterward," I said, trying to sound as though I meant it.

"Maybe I ought to come with you."

Danger! my nerves screeched. *What if the Nightshade Lord attends the wedding?*

The thought turned me cold. Of course he would. His niece was getting married, and Lord Mornithalarion Shadrift would certainly be there to witness the ceremony that strengthened the binding between the worlds.

I swallowed past the dryness in my throat and glanced at my father. "I don't think you should."

If he insisted on accompanying me, I'd have to stay in Parnese. Under no circumstances could Galtus Celcio come near the heart of the Darkwood or be allowed to discover the existence of the magical Dark Elves.

What would the warder of the red priests do should he uncover the power of Elfhame?

Invade, of course, and try to take it for his own. The knowledge made me feel ill.

"Hm." My father had been watching me closely. He sat back, as if coming to a decision. "It's true I have other things to attend to at the moment. The situation in Caliss needs a firm hand."

I tried not to slump with relief.

Though I hated to admit it, a part of me loved my father. I'd so wanted him to be everything my mother wasn't, and at first he'd seemed to be. Warm, attentive, caring what I thought. His approval had meant the world.

I should have known better. Though he seemed fond of me in his own way, I was a tool for him to use. He loved power, and himself, above all else.

It was a bitter realization that both my parents had only ever seen me as a means to an end.

How can you continue to believe in love, my little voice asked, *if this is the example you're given?*

I just do, I answered stubbornly, thinking of Thorne's smile.

"So, I can go to the wedding?" I asked.

My father's mouth firmed, but he nodded. "You'll take Paulette with you."

Ah, so that was the catch. She would be his spy, and certainly do what she could to force me back to Parnese. The situation wasn't so impossible, though. Whatever she saw, the Dark Elves could tamper with her memory, erasing all knowledge of their existence. I didn't like the idea, but it was the obvious solution.

"Very well," I said.

"But..." Galtus Celcio held up one finger. "Your initiates must all be able to cast the fireball before you leave."

I stared at him, anger stirring hot coals in my belly. "You can't make that a condition!"

"I just have. So, you'd best get to work."

With a complacent smile, he rose and left the table, ignoring my glare.

I hate you, I thought at his retreating back. For a moment, my fingers twitched and I was tempted to cast *esfirenda* at him. If I did, though, I knew he'd sense it and turn the fire back on me. Challenging the warder would only result in me being burned to a cinder.

Frustrated, I finished my tea and took a bite out of the last pastry, though I wasn't hungry.

I had to return to Raine—to see Thorne, to celebrate Neeve and Kian's wedding, and to escape the net of the red priests. Despite my intentions to remain clear of the warder's entanglements, I felt the strands tightening every day.

And now he'd trapped me even more, making my departure contingent upon Lena's ability to cast *esfirenda. I never should have helped her pass the initiate's test,* I thought sourly.

But you did, my little voice said, *and now you'll have to help her with this one.*

Scowling, I rose from the table and left the sun-warmed patio for the cool shadows of my room.

A HALF-HOUR LATER, I stood before the trio of initiates in the red-walled training room. My gaze went to them one by one.

Shamsan, of course, was a gifted sorcerer, and I'd no concerns there. Jenni was well on the way, and I knew that, given two attempts at casting the fireball, she'd succeed at least once.

Lena, though...

She squirmed as I stared at her.

"Maybe I should go back to the other training," she said. "I'm not suited—"

"You *are* suited," I said forcefully. Maybe too forcefully. "I know there's fire in you, Lena. You just have to find it."

From the corner of my eye, I saw Paulette nodding. Despite being a full member of the priesthood, she'd had the same struggles. Her blind devotion to Galtus Celcio had as much to do with her advancement through the ranks as the middling amount of power she possessed.

However, Paulette could cast *esfirenda*. Not a blazing fireball, like Shamsan or I could, but adequate enough.

"Do you ever get angry?" I asked Lena.

She blinked at me. "Well, of course I do. Jenni annoys me every single day."

"I don't mean annoyed. I mean *enraged*. So full of emotion it singes you from head to toe."

"Not...not really, no." She swallowed and glanced at the floor.

"I think it's time you did." I was following my intuition, thinking about the doors that had opened my own power, even before I knew it existed.

The flames erupting at the Yule Feast. The fireball I'd seized control of, cast at me by my own father. The drake that had wounded me, blasted to a crisp.

Somehow, I had to force Lena's temper to the surface. That or spend my own power on her—but once I was gone, she'd be unable to cast *esfirenda* again. Would my father be suspicious? Would he make every effort to haul me back from Raine?

Well, yes, regardless of whether or not Lena rose to the challenge. Still, it would be better if she could do it on her own.

"She only knows how to be sad," Jenni said with a touch of scorn.

"I do not," Lena replied, far too mildly for my liking.

"Sad and placid, like a lost cow."

"Jenni, stop." I shot her a look. "You're not helping."

Indeed, Lena's gaze was still fixed on the polished marble beneath our feet. I pressed my lips together, thinking. Perhaps it would be better to proceed without interference.

"Paulette," I said, "could you take Shamsan and Jenni to another room to practice? I'd like to try working with Lena alone."

"Certainly." Paulette went to the door and beckoned the other two to follow.

Jenni let out a disdainful sniff as they left, but Shamsan sent me a nod and a grin. I wondered if he tapped his natural joy to help spark his power, then set that thought aside and turned to Lena.

"I'm sorry I'm such a failure," she said, not meeting my gaze.

"You're not a failure." I touched her shoulder. "You're an initiate of the red priests. Not all of us are able to control our sorcery right away. I certainly couldn't, if you recall."

And I still had problems with the less powerful chants, though Lena didn't need to know that. I was trying to encourage her, not give her more to fret about.

She lifted her head. "But you're the warder's daughter."

"That doesn't mean everything comes easily. Remember what happened at the testing? I couldn't summon the scorch."

"I'd almost forgotten." She lifted her head, searching my gaze.

"And yet here I am, still in the temple." Being groomed to lead a new sect, unfortunately. But I'd soon be in Raine and done with my father's machinations.

"When I asked if you've ever gotten angry, I meant it," I continued. "Think back, even to when you were a child. What made you simply furious?"

Her brow furrowed and she looked at the far wall, clearly rifling through her memories. After a moment, her jaw set and her eyes narrowed.

"My brother stole the last sweet orange of the year, the one my mother had been saving for me, and then he lied about it. I'd been dreaming about the taste of it, waiting for one more day... And then he took it and ate it himself!"

"Hold on to that feeling," I said. "Summon the *esfirenda* and throw it against the wall. Put all your temper into it. Yell the words—now!"

She blinked, then pulled in a deep breath. "*Esfera to quera quemar!*"

Her hand shot out, and I let out a cheer as a little ball of red flame flew forward to splatter softly against the far wall. The *esfirenda* wasn't strong enough to take hold against the stone, but that didn't matter. The mere fact that Lena had summoned it was cause for rejoicing.

"You did it!" I danced around to face her, grinning with relief. She'd tapped her power—and I was free to leave Parnese.

"I did." She stared down at her hand, then at the wall, then back to me. "I actually summoned a fireball."

"Cast it a few more times," I said, mindful that she'd have to demonstrate her newfound ability to Paulette, and potentially to my father, before the red priests let me go.

"I'll try." She bit her lip.

"You'll do better than that. Just hold on to that sense of power, and the knowledge that you *can* summon *esfirenda*."

I stepped back beside her and nodded for her to go ahead. The acrid scent of the fireball still hung in the air as Lena spoke the chant again.

Her fireball sputtered out partway across the room, and she glanced at me.

"Louder," I said. "Stronger. Find your voice."

She cried the words and had better success, though the fireball fluctuated from red to orange, barely potent enough to be called *esfirenda*.

The next time, however, she only managed a sputter of flame. Shoulders slumping in defeat, she turned to me. "I've lost the ability."

"Of course you haven't." I held her gaze, willing her to believe me. "You're tired, that's all. Nobody can cast fireball after fireball without their power waning a bit." Except maybe my father.

"If you say so."

"I do. Tomorrow you'll be back to full strength. Come, let's have a cup of tea together on the patio before you go."

Her downcast expression cleared as we went out to the courtyard. I hailed a passing servant and asked for mint tea and a bowl of sugared almonds.

"You're from a village to the north, is that right?" I asked as we settled in the shade of the temple dome.

Heat radiated from the bricks underfoot, and the dry air carried a whiff of grilling meat. Bells rang in the lower city, and for a moment I felt swept back to my childhood. But Parnese was no longer my home, though it would always be my past.

"Yes," Lena said. "Aldeia—it's a small fishing town. People from there hardly visit the city, let alone get chosen as aspirants to the temple."

"But you did."

Her family must be very poor, too, for a sweet orange to be such a treasure. I recalled that my mother kept a bowl of them on the counter year-round. I'd never thought much of the cost.

Lena nodded slowly. "I did—to everyone's surprise."

"See? You deserve to be here."

The servant set a tray on the table with a pitcher of cool mint tea, the bowl of almonds, and a plate of figs. I thanked them and poured out two glasses.

"To success," I said, raising my tea to Lena.

She echoed the motion, a small smile on her lips. "Success."

Now if only I could succeed in getting on a ship back to Raine...

CHAPTER 22

For two mornings in a row, I tried to find my father and speak to him about leaving Parnese, but each time the servants informed me he had already left the apartment. He might be very busy—I'd heard whispers of an uprising in Caliss, backed by the Athraig—but it still seemed he was avoiding me.

Finally, on the third day, he appeared in the courtyard as the servants were serving my breakfast.

"There you are!" I jumped up, ready to catch his arm if he made to leave again.

"Good morning, Rose." He gave me an indulgent look and seated himself at the wrought-iron table. "Were you going somewhere?"

"No." Frowning, I retook my seat. "I just wanted to ask you when I can depart for Raine. The wedding is in less than two weeks."

He raised his brow and took a bite of fresh melon. I waited impatiently until he finished chewing, trying not to drum my fingers against my mug of smoky tea.

"I've yet to hear that all your students can summon *esfirenda*," he finally said. "Paulette tells me that Lena is continuing to have difficulty."

He'd come to observe the training the day after Lena successfully called *esfirenda*, but she'd faltered, unable to cast it. Perhaps because Warder Galtus Celcio had been watching her so intently. She didn't do well under that kind of pressure.

"She can summon a fireball," I replied shortly. "I've seen her do it."

"So you say." He raised an eyebrow. "Of course, you have every reason to tell me that she's succeeded. But without proof, I'm afraid you can't leave the city."

I narrowed my eyes but slid my gaze to the guard standing inside the apartment, near the front door. It hadn't escaped my notice that one had been stationed there ever since I'd learned of Neeve's upcoming marriage. Clearly, my father didn't trust me not to try to slip away.

And he was right—I'd leave, if I could manage it. Of course, once Galtus Celcio noticed I was gone, he'd turn the city upside down to find me. Without some kind of prearranged escape route from Parnese, he'd recapture me quickly enough.

"Today," I said, daring him to contradict me. "She'll cast the fireball at our next training session. Come see for yourself."

He gave me a look of mild disbelief, but I was done arguing. Pushing my plate away, I rose and stalked back to my room. As soon as the training session started, I'd encourage Lena, reminding her to tap into the strength of her emotions.

And if that didn't work, I'd give her a boost of my own power—no matter the consequences to my own sorcery. The days were trickling past, and I *must* be back in Raine in time for my sister's wedding. Indeed, I had the sinking feeling it was my last chance to extricate myself from the red priests. There would be no better opportunity.

An hour later, Galtus Celcio strode into the training room where I was working with the initiates. We'd been doing the basic exercise of calling fire into our cupped palms as a prelude to the bigger castings.

The warder joined Paulette at her vantage point along the side wall and nodded for us to continue.

"One more *firenda*," I said to the trio. "Then a quick break before we move on to summoning fireballs."

Lena sent me a wide-eyed look, her flame wavering in her hand.

"Stay strong." I lowered my voice. "Don't let his presence intimidate you."

She nodded, swallowing, and my spirits sank. Judging by the panic in her eyes, there would be no way she could cast *esfirenda* without my help.

The initiates extinguished their flames, then Jenni went to fetch a cup of water from the pitcher the servants had left beside the door. Summoning fire was hot work, especially at the end of the summer, when the sun baked the streets and rooftops of Parnese.

Shamsan stretched, bouncing up and down on his toes, and I turned to Lena. "Remember how you felt when your brother stole the orange," I said.

Her gaze darted to my father, then back to me. "I'll try."

"You can do it." I gave her a tight smile.

One way or another.

The initiates lined up and, under the warder's watchful gaze, prepared to demonstrate their ability with *esfirenda*. I let Shamsan go first. Maybe his success would help buoy the others. Unlike Lena, he loved an audience. With a flourish, he called out the chant and sent a blazing ball of flame to splash incandescently on the back wall.

Galtus Celcio gave him a nod, and Shamsan grinned widely, teeth flashing.

Next in line, Jenni stepped forward without hesitation. Her fireball wasn't as impressive as Sham's, but it was smoothly cast. She, too, gained the warder's sign of approval.

The stone glowed with the layered fire, and Paulette murmured the chant to extinguish it. I nodded my thanks, then turned to Lena.

"Be strong," I said softly. "Say the chant out like you *mean* it."

She bobbed her head up and down, then faced the wall. I could see her fingers trembling. Drat it.

My own fire glowed in my belly, half-awake as usual. I roused it with a thought. *Firenda—be ready.*

As Lena called the chant, I echoed it in my mind and gave my power a *push.*

"*Esfirenda to quera quemar!*"

For a moment, only a pale yellow flame bloomed on Lena's outstretched palm.

Go, I thought fiercely at my magic.

It leaped up, and away, and a white-hot ball of flame careened forward from Lena's hand, sizzling when it met the stone.

"*Calma to sacar,*" Paulette said hastily, and the *esfirenda* went out, leaving a curl of acrid smoke behind.

My father gave me a long, steady look, then glanced at Lena. "Most impressive. I didn't know you had such power in you, initiate."

She smiled weakly back, confusion in her eyes, but I clapped her on the shoulder.

"I knew you could do it." My attention shifted to my father. "I told you—I've seen her summon fireballs before."

I didn't mention that none of them had possessed that white-hot power. Or that it took all my remaining strength to stand upright and keep the smile plastered on my face as exhaustion swept through me. The place inside me where my flames usually sheltered was hollow and cold.

Was my power like the Dark Elves' wellspring? How was it that I could seemingly push and pull my sorcery about when none of the other priests could? Did my father guess what I was doing?

He was suspicious, judging from his narrow-eyed gaze. He thought I'd helped Lena at the testing, though I'd never admitted to anything. And now, just like that time, there was no proof I'd done anything untoward. If Galtus Celcio had been able to pinpoint my interference, I'd no doubt he would have leaped upon it as an excuse to keep me in Parnese. The fact he said nothing meant I was free.

Folding my arms, I gave him a raw-edged smile of triumph. "My students can summon *esfirenda.* I've done as you asked."

"So you have." His gaze skipped to the trio. "Well done, initiates. Take the day off to rest and celebrate your accomplishments. You're dismissed."

Shamsan all but danced out of the room, and Jenni followed, head held high. They both should be rightly proud of their efforts. And despite her uncertainty, Lena's cheeks were flushed with success as she left. Even if the power she'd used had only been borrowed, I hoped it would bolster her confidence.

"I'm impressed," Galtus Celcio said thoughtfully. "You are truly blessed by the Sister, Rose."

Paulette nodded vigorously. "Lena's fireball—surely that was divine power! I've never seen the like."

"Even the weakest can be illuminated by the flame of the Twins," the warder said, as though quoting some holy text. Then he gave me a significant look. "As long as the vessel of the gods stands near."

"I'm not the vessel of the Sister," I said tiredly.

It seemed he'd pivoted from thinking I'd consciously interfered to believing my very presence could make the red priests more powerful. It wasn't a good change. But clearly *something* had happened, and I wasn't about to confess my part, even though it left the warder thinking I was a conduit of holy fire.

Maybe I shouldn't have helped Lena after all.

But then I would've been trapped in Parnese. There was no right answer, though I desperately hoped I hadn't just made things worse for myself.

"You promised to let me go to Raine," I reminded him.

"Of course. And you promised to return."

I pushed my lips into a smile. "As you say."

"Speaking of which, you're going to have a visitor after lunch."

"I am?" I stared at him, thoughts racing. "Who? Are they from Raine?"

Surely Thorne hadn't crossed the water—he was needed in Elfhame, and besides, the *Galadhir* couldn't travel too far from the Darkwood.

My father gave me tight-lipped look. "You'll see. But channeling the Sister's power seems to have wearied you. I'll leave you to get some rest."

He turned in a whirl of scarlet robes and strode out of the training room. I stared after him, questions burning on my lips, then glanced at Paulette. "Do you know who's come?"

She just shook her head, then took my arm as I swayed. The events of the past hour had, indeed, drained me. I'd try to regain some energy before I met...whoever it was.

Thorne's words echoed through me. *Help is on the way.*

I desperately hoped it was true.

CHAPTER 23

Despite the warder's advice to rest, I'd only lain awake atop my bed, wondering who had come to Parnese. When I rose, I'd donned my best blue dress and set the crown atop my head. Whoever had come, I intended to show them that no matter what had happened in Parnese, I was still a princess of Raine.

My father didn't join me in the courtyard, and I was glad. I ate quickly, not bothering to take seconds of the minted grain salad and spiced vegetables. As soon as the servants cleared my place, Galtus Celcio appeared.

One auburn eyebrow rose at my garb, but he said nothing, only beckoned me into the main living area of his apartments.

"Show our visitor in," he said to the guard by the door.

I went up on the balls of my feet, barely breathing.

Sunlight glinted on golden hair, and for an instant, I thought Kian had stepped over the threshold. Then I realized my mistake—though I was only slightly less glad to see his brother.

"Jenson!" I lifted my arms toward him.

"Princess Rose." He strode forward and took my outstretched hands.

That warm, steady clasp nearly brought tears to my eyes. Suddenly, I was no longer alone against the power of the red priests.

"I'm so glad to finally see you," he said, shooting a look at my father.

I frowned as his meaning sank in. "How long have you been in Parnese?"

"Four days. I brought your letters, but the warder refused to let me inside the temple, let alone visit you."

"Four days?" I dropped his hands and whirled to face my father. "How could you?"

The knowledge burned through me. Jenson had been there all along. I could have escaped and been carried safely to Raine *before* I turned the initiates into fireball-casting implements of destruction.

"I did what was necessary," Galtus Celcio said, without a trace of apology. "Everything comes out according to the Twin Gods' will."

I scowled at him, hating him for his lies. "And now I'm leaving."

"Yes," he said calmly. "You may travel with the Fiorland prince to attend your sister's wedding."

Jenson gave me an intent look. "You really can go?"

"Yes." The relief of it dampened the heat of my anger. "When will you be ready to sail?"

"We can depart tomorrow morning," he said. "Is that too soon?"

"No." Not soon enough, for my liking.

"I'll tell Paulette and your guard, Donal, to make ready," my father said, moving to the door. "You wouldn't want to depart without your escort."

He gave me a last, intent look before he left. Even though he'd gone, the guard still lingered by the inner door, no doubt tasked with reporting back every word Jenson and I spoke.

"What did he mean, escort?" Jenson asked.

"One of the priests," I explained. "And the guard who came with me from Raine."

Who hadn't protected me in the least.

Though, honestly, what could one man have done to keep me from getting caught up in the webs of the red priests? I supposed his main duty was to make sure they didn't harm me, and no doubt Paulette had

provided plenty of reassurance along those lines. I didn't like to speculate on what else she'd provided. Donal was obviously smitten with her
—and perhaps she genuinely liked him in return and wasn't only
manipulating him on behalf of her sect.

I let out a little sigh. It would be good to leave the temple, even if
some of my problems traveled with me.

"Is everything all right?" Concern shone from Jenson's blue eyes.

"Well enough," I said. "I'm looking forward to going back to
Raine."

I'd explain everything that had happened in Parnese to the king, of
course, and to Thorne, Neeve, and Kian. But while I was still within
the heart of the Temple of the Twin Gods, the best course was to hold
my tongue.

"I'll come fetch you tomorrow, after the bells ring eight."

"I can hardly wait." I glanced at the guard stationed by the door,
then back at Jenson, raising one brow in caution. "But tell me—how is
everyone in Raine? Is my sister well? And your brother?"

"Aye." He gave me a genuine smile. "They are ridiculously besotted
with each other, though anyone who doesn't know them would scarcely
be able to tell."

I nodded. Neeve had never been one for grandiose shows of
emotion. A half-smile, the brush of one finger along Kian's hand—
those would be her ways of expressing her love for him. And for his
part, he knew any overt displays of affection would send her into a
skittish retreat.

"Your brother is a good man," I said.

Jenson shot me a look. "You care for him a great deal."

"I do." I smiled softly.

Once, I'd hoped Kian was my true love—when Thorne seemed as
out of reach as the stars. Now, though, my heart was filled with the
black-haired *Galadhir* of the Darkwood.

There was room there enough for deep friendship, however, and
Kian had his place in my affections. After my sister, of course.

"Neeve is recovered from her illness?" I asked, searching Jenson's
eyes.

He nodded slowly. "She's still pale, and tires quickly. But the *nirwen* essence seems to be helping. And she insisted that she and Kian must be married as soon as possible."

"I knew it." I pressed my lips together, wishing I could ask about Thorne, but unwilling to even speak his name where the red priests could hear.

"Everyone else is in good health," Jenson said, giving me a significant look. "Though the queen seems a little distracted."

"My mother is always distracted." I blew out an annoyed breath. She was the one person in Raine I wasn't looking forward to seeing.

"I'm sure she'll be glad to have you home. They all will. And relieved, I hardly need to say."

"That I haven't turned into a wild-eyed fanatic?" I gave him a wry smile. "No need to worry."

The front door opened, and Galtus Celcio stepped back in. His gaze settled on Jenson.

"Still here?" he asked, holding the door open. "Surely you have other things to attend to if you're departing on the morrow."

It was a blatant dismissal, but Jenson was too polite to argue. Besides, we'd said everything we needed to—or safely could.

"I've got to pack, anyway," I said. "But it was so good to see you."

Somewhat to his surprise, I stepped forward and embraced him. A moment later, his arms came around me. He wasn't Thorne, or even Kian, but I let myself draw strength from his support.

My father cleared his throat, and Jenson stepped back. "I'll see you in the morning," he said.

"Yes." I couldn't help the gratitude infusing my voice.

Frowning, my father watched him go, then closed the door firmly.

"I can't forgive you for keeping him from visiting," I said, once again reminded of the warder's manipulations.

"You don't have to." He gave me a tight smile.

Speaking of manipulation...

"I'd like my stone back now," I said, holding out my hand.

"It's important to you." He pulled the small rock from his pocket and turned it thoughtfully between his fingers. "I've been studying it, you know. There's a strange residue of power here."

"I don't care." I thrust my palm toward him. "It's mine."

"Perhaps it's the mark of the Sister," he continued, ignoring my outstretched arm. "Have you ever seen the stone change in some way? Heat up, or glow with an inner fire?"

"No," I lied. "Give it back."

With a grim smile, he slid it back into his pocket. "It merits further investigation. You can have it back upon your return to Parnese."

I clenched my jaw to keep from screaming in frustration. The warder continually changed the terms of his promises to me. Well, I could do the same.

"When I return, then."

I dropped my hand back to my side, vowing that day would never come.

PART III

CHAPTER 24

The peals of the city's bells followed me across the water as the Fiorland ship left the harbor. I didn't stand at the railing, watching longingly as the shore of Parnesia receded, but set my face toward the prow and thought of Raine.

My time in Parnese hadn't been at all what I'd thought, but at least I'd learned to work with my power. I cupped my palm against my chest and murmured the flame-calling chant.

A wisp of orange fire obediently appeared in my hand, unbowed by the dash of sea spray against the hull.

With a thought, I extinguished it, then curled my fingers over my empty palm. I could summon my flame, I could toss sizzling fireballs and channel my power to another—but I still couldn't manage the in-between chants.

Nor could I flick my fingers and light the lamps, as I'd seen Galtus Celcio do, though I'd tried on several occasions.

What was I? I frowned at the blue-green waves surging to the horizon.

A half-trained fire sorceress, daughter of the warder of the red priests. Former gateway anchor to the land of Elfhame, nearly married to a Dark Elf king, but in love with the *Galadhir*. Neeve's sister, Kian's friend.

"Rose," Paulette called, beckoning me to the aft of the boat, where she and Donal stood. "Come look—you can still see the temple."

Unwilling would-be avatar of the Sister, I added to my list as I slowly went to join them.

The morning sun sprawled lavishly over the red roofs of Parnese, and the gilded dome of the Temple of the Twin Gods glowed as if it were on fire. I'd be happy never to see it again.

But what was to become of Paulette?

I hated the thought of the Dark Elves tampering with her memory, yet we couldn't imprison her in Raine indefinitely. I blew out a breath, resolving to deal with that question later. For now, I was out of Parnese.

"Don't worry." Paulette patted my arm, clearly taking my exhalation for some kind of wistful sigh. "We'll be back in a month."

"I hope no early storms close the Strait," Donal said, a bit too earnestly.

I shot him a look. "You want to return to Parnese so much?"

"I only want to be where Paulette is," he said, blushing faintly.

She went on tiptoes and kissed him on the cheek. "You're so sweet."

He blushed even more, and I stepped away from the railing. "I'll leave you two to enjoy the view." I far preferred facing forward, though I knew the shore of Raine wouldn't be in sight for at least two days.

Donal slipped his arm around Paulette, and she leaned against him. They *seemed* happy together, but would that change once they were in Raine? Perhaps I was just jealous, wishing Thorne was by my side.

Soon.

I returned to the prow of the ship, making idle conversation with the Fiorland sailors working the ropes and watching the waves slip beneath the deck. Every now and then I glanced back to see Paulette and Donal still at the railing. They lingered until the gilded dome of the Temple of the Twin Gods was a mere spark in the distance.

Prince Jenson joined me after a time. "We're well away," he said. "The lookout says there's no sign of pursuit."

"Thank the stars. I wasn't certain my father would let us go that easily."

"Does he think he can pull you back to him, like a puppy on a leash?" Jenson asked.

"Something like that." The bonds between Galtus Celcio and I were complicated, to say the least. A part of me—a very small part—grieved that things couldn't have turned out differently. I wished he was the father I'd always wanted: warm, understanding, accepting of everything I was.

But the warder of the red priests couldn't be that man, just as my mother would never be able to see past her own selfishness.

The family of my blood had orphaned me. Thankfully, I had the family of my heart. Neeve, my true sister. Kian, soon to be my brother-in-law as well as brother-in-spirit. And, always, Thorne, refuge of my heart, who would have sacrificed everything to save me. Except I'd done the same for him first. Even though it meant a future forever apart.

Now, despite everything, I was coming back to him. I was coming home.

⚜

THE CLAMOR of gulls wheeling over Portknowe sounded like pure rejoicing as we entered the harbor.

The moment dawn broke, I'd risen and gone to the railing, scanning the horizon for a glimpse of Raine. My cloak grew damp with mist, and I gnawed on a hard biscuit as I waited.

After what felt an eternity, though it was likely only an hour, the dark coastline of the island appeared. I'd stayed at my post, gaze fixed on the heavy fringe of trees covering half the shoreline. The Darkwood.

Thorne, I thought toward that carpet of cedar and pine, wishing the waves could carry my love to him, so that he might know of my arrival. Surely, though, the *Galadhir* would be aware the moment I set foot in the forest he guarded.

We tied up at the docks, and a delegation of soldiers came up the pier to meet us. They bowed to me and Prince Jenson as we descended the gangway, eyed Paulette in her scarlet robes with suspicion, and hailed the return of Donal, who nodded in greeting to his comrades.

I wanted to dash down the wooden planking and sink my fingers into the soil of Raine, but restrained myself to a walk. *I am a princess, and a sorcerer,* I reminded myself.

And a foolish girl pining for her lover, my little voice added.

Chin high, I ignored its needling and let the soft air of Raine touch my face in greeting.

Then I saw him—a tall, dark-haired figure in a green cloak waiting where the sea met the shore. His black hair glinted like ebony in the pale sunlight, and even from a distance, I could tell he was smiling.

"Thorne!" I cried, and, abandoning all decorum, raced forward.

He opened his arms, and I fetched up against him, my hands on his shoulders while he folded me into his embrace. I stared into his amber-flecked eyes and breathed deeply of the scent of him—cedar and loam, with a hint of wild magic.

"You're home," he said simply.

"I am." I blinked back the moisture heating my eyes. "I'm so sorry I couldn't scry you again. Galtus Celcio took my stone, and all I could think was how worried you'd be."

"I was, but I trust you, Rose. I knew that, even if you'd encountered trouble, you'd come out the other side." He smiled gently, his arms tightening about me. "I must admit, though, it was a great relief to see you step off that ship."

My body hummed with joy, the sharp, ever-present ache of missing him finally gone. I could breathe freely again.

"I'm so happy to see you." I leaned my cheek against his shoulder, content to stand there forever.

Thorne's lips rested on my hair, and we breathed in unison. *I'm never leaving you again.*

Footsteps sounded behind me, and Thorne lifted his head.

"Thank you for bringing her safely back," he said.

Prince Jenson let out a small, rueful laugh. "It was my pleasure to retrieve Princess Rose from Parnese. I see that you're very fond of one another."

I turned in Thorne's embrace. "We are. But I owe you a debt of gratitude, Jenson. Thank you."

He nodded, his gaze clear. "You're welcome." Whatever lingering regret he might feel to see my heart taken by another, he hid it well, like a true prince. "I believe there's a coach waiting to take us to the castle. If we depart immediately, we'll arrive by nightfall."

"I'll ride with Thorne," I said, glancing at my beloved. "There are horses?"

"Yes." Thorne's gaze met mine, and for a moment it felt as though no one else existed in the world but the two of us.

Then a pair of sailors jostled past, carrying my trunk, and I recalled myself. "A red priest is with us," I said in a low voice. "Can you make sure she travels safely through the Darkwood?"

The last thing we needed was for Paulette to be strangled on the way to Castle Raine. Still, her power wasn't nearly as intense as my father's, or Ser Naldi's. With the *Galadhir's* help, I hoped she'd be able to pass unscathed through the Darkwood's wards.

"Of course," Thorne said. "As long as she doesn't attack, I'll make sure the forest leaves her alone."

I nodded, then beckoned for Paulette to join us. Donal came with her, of course.

"Paulette," I said, "I'd like you to meet Thorne."

Her brows went up. "You never mentioned you had a lover."

It was too late to step away from Thorne's side, though I could feel a blush heating my cheeks. "He's a close friend," I said, though of course we were more than that to each other.

"A very handsome one." Paulette nodded to Thorne. "Pleased to make your acquaintance."

"Likewise." He made her a slight bow. "I hope you enjoy your time in Raine."

"I'm looking forward to it, and meeting Rose's sister. But is it always so chilly here?" She shivered and pulled her red cloak closer about her shoulders.

For my part, I welcomed the cool dampness in the air, the smell of greenery and soil. Given the dry heat Paulette was used to, though, I could see how she found it a bit cold.

"I'll lend you some warmer gowns once we reach the castle," I said, recalling how she'd helped me dress for the climate of Parnesia. "And speaking of Castle Raine, we'd best be on our way."

We made good time through the Darkwood, perhaps because of the *Galadhir's* presence. The road was clear of muddy patches and fallen branches, sunlight dappled the embankment on either side, and birds sang as if it were still dawn and the world was appearing anew.

Thorne and I rode as closely together as possible, and I told him everything that had happened in Parnese, including the fact that I still struggled with the less powerful chants of the red priests.

"There has to be an explanation," he said, when I voiced my frustration. "Your power came upon you so forcefully, perhaps it blasted away your subtler abilities."

I frowned in thought. "The fireball isn't subtle, I can tell you that."

The cedar and sycamore branches stirred overhead, as though disturbed by the fact we were discussing fire sorcery, and I changed the subject.

"Is Neeve fully recovered?"

"Nearly, though the healers would've liked for her to remain in Elfhame longer. But she insisted on crossing back between the worlds."

I shook my head fondly. "No one can tell Neeve what to do."

"You do realize she came back as soon as she could in order to free you?"

"Yes." I swallowed the painful lump of gratitude suddenly blocking my throat. "I hope it won't cause her harm."

Thorne looked at me. "You were willing to risk even more on her behalf. You nearly gave your life for her—for all of us."

I'd do it again, too, if it meant that those I loved were safe.

I shot him a wry smile. "I take it you didn't try to argue with her?"

"Neeve isn't the only one concerned for your safety. If I could have stepped off the soil of Raine to come for you, I would have."

Again, the trees rustled with distress. Thorne glanced up, murmuring softly in Elvish, and they subsided.

"The wedding, though," I said. "That's not just a ploy to get me back to Raine, is it?"

"No." Thorne's expression softened. "Both Neeve and Kian agreed it would be best if they married as soon as possible. Bringing you home from Parnese was one of the more important reasons, but not the only one."

"Eight days until the ceremony." I let out a sigh. "I wish Galtus Celcio would've let me leave without bringing a red priest along."

"Paulette." Thorne glanced over his shoulder at the coach traveling several yards behind us. "I don't suppose we can trust her to keep Raine's secrets."

"Not at all—her loyalty is to the warder. We can keep her from sending letters, but the moment she gets back to Parnese, she'll tell him everything."

"Or not." His voice darkened. "Don't fret. After the wedding, we'll take whatever precautions are necessary."

I glanced at him with a touch of alarm. "She'll need to return unharmed."

"I'm well aware that we cannot raise the warder's suspicions. The Oracles and I will discuss what needs to be done."

It wasn't a promise, but I knew Thorne would do his best to keep Paulette safe. Although she might be our enemy, she'd been my friend once, and my somewhat-ally during my time in the temple.

"There will be others at the wedding," he said with a significant look.

"Nightshade."

I wasn't particularly looking forward to seeing Lord Mornithalarion again. But Neeve was his niece, and the Nightshade Court currently presided over the gateway between the worlds.

"The king and queen of Fiorland, too," Thorne continued, "along with their war commander."

"Merkis Strond." I smiled, wondering what she would think of the haughty elven lord. "It will be interesting to meet Kian's parents. When do they arrive?"

"They're expected in another two days. The castle's in a bit of a hubbub."

"Preparing for a royal wedding isn't a simple thing. Especially since my mother will have strong ideas about how it should go." To say the least.

Thorne's lips twitched. "Neeve tells me they've disagreed a number of times."

"Oh, I've no doubt."

Mama might seem pleasantly sweet to those who didn't know her, but once she fixed her mind on something, it was nearly impossible to make her budge. And Neeve was the most stubborn person I'd ever met. The two of them would be like marble meeting granite.

"Probably a good thing that I'm back," I said, thinking of the delicate line I'd have to walk between my mother and her stepdaughter. Though Neeve held my primary loyalty. It was *her* wedding, after all.

"I'm glad you're home." Thorne flashed me a smile. "For so many reasons."

I met his gaze a moment while our horses walked side by side. It was too soon to speak of the possibility of our own marriage. I knew it, yet it was all I could do to keep from blurting out the words.

In the past, Thorne had said he didn't see how such a union between us could succeed, though he'd admitted he loved me. Whether the Oracles would ever let me set foot in Elfhame again remained to be seen, since they'd rather forcefully ejected me. But my fire sorcery was now under control. More or less.

And if I was forever banned from Elfhame?

I looked at the man I loved. No matter what, I'd fight for a future with him—even if it meant spending half of every year parted from him.

One wedding at a time, though. After Neeve and Kian were settled, Thorne and I could discuss our own future. Which didn't hold a return to Parnese, that much I was sure of. No matter what Galtus Celcio might want.

CHAPTER 25

Dusk was painting the sky with lavender when we passed through the gates of Castle Raine. To my grateful surprise, Thorne hadn't turned away into the forest, but continued to ride at my side. Though he preferred the trees, the *Galadhir* was able to spend time within stone walls, and I was glad he'd chosen to stay with me rather than slip back into the shadows of the Darkwood.

We dismounted at the foot of the steps leading to the tall double doors. Grooms were waiting to take our horses, and we were halfway up to the entrance as the coach clattered in behind us.

The castle doors opened, and Neeve was the first one to step outside.

"Rose!" She held out her hands, and I hurried up the rest of the steps to embrace her.

"Neeve," I said into her hair. "I'm so glad you're all right."

"But not completely well," she said, in her usual forthright manner.

I stepped back, noting the pallor of her face, the sharpness of her cheekbones, and the dark glitter of her eyes. "Should you be resting?"

"Not for this." She gave me a taut smile. "Welcome home, Rose."

A heartbeat later, Kian strode through the doors. His concerned gaze was fixed on Neeve, but a moment later he saw me and smiled. "There you are!" His hug of greeting was much more robust than my sister's.

Breathless, I grinned up at him. "Look at you! About to be married."

He nodded and released me, slipping his arm around Neeve's waist. "To the most wonderful, maddening woman in all the worlds."

She shot him a sidelong glance. "It's your own fault if you lose your patience. I'm always quite reasonable."

I let out a short laugh, my heart clenching with gladness to see them both. "You're perfect for each other."

Neeve's brow went up, a hint of color warming her too-white cheeks. "Your room is ready for you."

"And Trisk?" I'd missed my feline friend and hoped she'd forgive me for leaving her again.

"You might have a rival for her affections," Kian said. "Sorche's been feeding her."

I was happy to hear the cat hadn't been completely abandoned. I'd have to give her many treats and scritches behind the ears in apology, of course.

"Rose!" My mother emerged from the castle and enfolded me in her fluttery, perfumed embrace. "Oh, my darling girl—I feared I'd never see you again!"

"And yet here I am." I patted her on the back, then pulled away. I didn't think I'd ever be able to forgive her for lying about the identity of my father.

Even though it turned out he'd only wanted to use me to achieve his own ends.

"Welcome home, Princess Rose," the king said, appearing at his wife's side. "We are glad of your safe return."

"Thank you, my lord." I dropped him my best curtsey. "I couldn't miss Neeve's wedding."

"Are you back in Raine for good?" His granite-colored eyes bored into mine.

I lifted my chin. "I am. However, Warder Galtus Celcio has sent along a red priest to accompany me."

I looked to the bottom of the stairs, where Paulette and Prince Jenson had exited the coach and were being escorted to where we stood.

"I see." Lord Raine's voice was hard.

I didn't need to point out how problematic the presence of a red priest was at an event where Dark Elves would be in attendance. Somewhat relieved, I let the king take on the burden of what to do with Paulette for the time being.

Flanked by guards, Paulette bobbed a curtsey to the king and queen.

"Welcome to Castle Raine, Sera Dominas," Lord Raine said, clearly remembering her from the meeting at the harbor.

"Thank you so much. I'm delighted to be here." Her smile seemed genuine.

"And welcome back, Prince Jenson." My mother extended a hand in greeting, and the Fiorlander bent over it.

"It is a pleasure," Jenson said. "Thank you for trusting me to retrieve your daughter."

Mama gave me a pointed look. "We owe Prince Jenson a debt of gratitude for extricating you from the clutches of the red priests. He deserves *all* your thanks."

"And he has them," I said. "But nothing more." I threaded my arm through Thorne's, pulling him close.

Mama's eyes narrowed, but I was done with her schemes to wed me off to this prince or that. My heart had made its own choice long ago.

"Come inside." The king gestured to the warmly lit great hall. "A meal is prepared, and your rooms await."

We trooped inside, and I couldn't help smiling as I gazed about the hall. So many years, so many memories overlaid on its stone walls. The head table was set and waiting, and servants greeted us with bowls of warm water and towels to wash away the dust of our travels. Usually the great hall was reserved for castle-wide feasts, but I was glad we didn't have to go down to the smaller dining room. My belly had been growling with hunger since late afternoon.

Ignoring the usual protocols, I went to sit beside Neeve, pulling

Thorne with me. I didn't want to let him out of my sight, let alone release his hand. At least, not until I must.

With an indulgent look, he let me tow him to the chair next to mine.

"I'm glad you stayed for supper," I said softly.

He nodded. "I've been taking most of my meals in the castle."

"Thorne is underfoot all the time," Kian said, a smile taking the sting from his words.

The *Galadhir* looked at him. "I take my duties seriously. The Darkwood is well at the moment, but the same cannot be said of your bride-to-be."

I sent Neeve a sharp glance. "Don't you dare exhaust yourself over this wedding, sister."

She sent me a wan half-smile. "Thorne exaggerates."

I wanted to argue with her, but Paulette was watching us intently from across the table, so I held my tongue. After dinner, I'd make Neeve come to my sitting room and tell me the truth about her time in Elfhame, and her battle against the Dark Elf sickness.

Sir Durum joined our party, though he hadn't greeted us on the steps, and gave me a gruff nod of greeting. It was good to be back, to glance around the table and see so many familiar faces—though I did note one was absent.

"Where's Jarl Eiric?" I asked Kian, who'd settled on Neeve's other side. Not that I particularly missed the Fiorland nobleman's hawklike visage and too-keen eyes.

"He'll be accompanying my parents from Fiorland, then staying on as their emissary to Raine."

"So, we're not rid of him." I gave a small grimace. I'd never quite trusted the jarl, but now that Kian was of age, hopefully his advisor had little influence. "Is Master Fawkes in residence yet?"

"He's still traveling," Neeve said. "But he's due back for the wedding."

I nodded. The bard usually spent the summers on the move, performing and, more importantly, gathering information for the king. I hoped Master Fawkes had been able to steer clear of the red priests.

His ability to cast illusions with his music was a small talent, but enough to put him in danger.

The other people important to me weren't at the meal, of course. Mistress Ainya almost never came to the castle, and Miss Groves and Sorche took their meals less formally, with the staff of Castle Raine.

The servants began bringing out plates of food the moment we were all seated, along with water and ale. I let go of Thorne's hand long enough to eat, and didn't contribute much to the conversation, as my mouth was mostly occupied with chewing.

Prince Jenson was seated beside Paulette and displayed the same charming manners as his brother, drawing her into conversation without straying into hazardous territory. At least for a time.

"I'm so excited to be visiting Raine," she said, no trace of dishonesty in her eyes. "It's very different from Parnesia."

"If you'd like even more variety, I'd be glad to show you Fiorland after you depart these shores," Jenson said lightly.

She blinked at him. "That's kind of you—but I'll be returning to Parnese. The red priests have need of me."

I shot him a wry smile, quickly concealed. Jenson was well aware of the issues. It had been a good try at diverting Paulette from running to the warder the moment the wedding was over and telling him everything she'd seen. Too bad it had been unsuccessful.

"Perhaps another time, then," Jenson said, with an easy smile. "The winters are not to be missed."

"True," Kian said. "I miss being able to pelt my annoying brothers with snowballs."

We all laughed, as we were meant to, and the tense moment passed.

At the end of the meal, my mother caught my arm as we were preparing to leave the great hall. "Come to my rooms tomorrow," she said. "We must decide what you're going to wear to the wedding."

My lips flattened into a frown. "That's not necessary. I'm quite able to determine my own wardrobe."

"Please." Her fingers dug into my forearm. "I wish to see you."

While my first impulse was to continue to refuse, I was aware of the king watching me. And Thorne, too. Not wanting to seem an ungrateful child, I relented.

"Very well. I'll come after breakfast." And bring Thorne along, if he'd agree. It was difficult for me to deal with my mother when it was just the two of us, and I'd welcome the buffer of his presence.

"I'm glad." She pressed my arm and leaned over to kiss my cheek.

This close, I realized that her face was as smooth as ever. Perhaps even more youthful, for the fine lines I recalled around her eyes seemed entirely gone. Her skin was luminous, but she seemed fragile, as though her bones were made of porcelain and might shatter should she lose her footing.

Nirwen was used in cosmetics on the Continent and touted for easing the signs of aging. At one point, Neeve had hinted darkly that it was dangerous if overused—though she herself was currently taking a potent dose of its essence.

I'd have to ask my sister about that, too.

"I wish you all a good evening," Lord Raine said. "Meals tomorrow will be served in the dining room, though if you'd prefer a tray sent up for breakfast, simply let one of the servants know."

I nodded, as that was always my choice. Given the chance to sleep in, I invariably did, and then missed breakfast. Thankfully, the kitchens had always been happy to provide me a leftover roll and cup of tea.

The king and my mother left the hall, and Neeve turned to Paulette.

"You and Prince Jenson have rooms near Kian's," she said. "He'll show you up."

Kian's brows quirked, but he nodded at his brother and Paulette. "I seem to have been volunteered to be your official guide—though Jens, you probably recall the castle well enough." He turned to Paulette. "I'll explain the layout of the place to you as we go."

"Oh, thank you." She glanced about the hall. "It seems rather large and confusing."

"The temple was worse," I said dryly.

"Was it?" Sir Durum sent me a look.

"Yes."

I still had very little sense of the Temple of the Twin Gods, beyond my father's apartments, the aspirants' dormitory, and the echoing main temple beneath the dome. If Sir Durum wanted me to draw a map from memory, he'd be sorely disappointed.

The captain of the castle guard left us at the bottom of the stairs. Our party split again at the landing, Kian leading his brother and Paulette to the east wing of the castle, while Neeve, Thorne, and I continued in the other direction.

It was strange to tread the halls again. So much had changed within me, but the castle seemed exactly the same.

When we reached my door, I grazed my thumb over one of the roses carved into the wooden panel, smiling as I remembered the first time Neeve had shown me to my suite. It felt like a lifetime ago.

"Come in," I said, and opened the door.

A peat fire glowed on the small hearth of the sitting room, and I drew in a deep breath as the familiar confines of the room wrapped about me.

Trisk was napping in one of the chairs before the fire, but leaped down when she saw me.

"*Mrow*," she said, dipping up and down in her three-legged walk as she came to greet me.

"Hello, kit." I went down on my knees and reached a hand for her to sniff. "I'm home."

She butted her head against my fingers, then let me pet her. Her gray fur was a soft as ever. A rumbling purr started in her chest. I was happy to see her, and pleased that she seemed to feel the same. She wove back and forth against my dress, before finally going to the door and ducking through into the hallway.

"I've never understood that creature." Neeve moved past me to take one of the chairs before the fire. The one Trisk hadn't been occupying, I noted.

"That's because you're too alike," I said, rising and brushing cat hair off my skirt.

"Hardly." Neeve shot me a look.

"I see Rose's point," Thorne said as he brought over the low stool I kept beneath the table. "You and Trisk are both particular in your affections, a bit aloof, and most definitely go your own way, regardless of what people think."

My sister made a sound of disagreement. "I've yet to see a cat plan a wedding. What *other* people think matters a great deal, apparently."

"Don't let my mother override your wishes," I said as I settled in the chair across from my sister. "I'm sure her idea of a royal wedding involves a great deal of spectacle."

"To say the least." Neeve frowned. "We are most definitely not going to release a hundred doves, for instance."

"A hundred doves?" Thorne looked faintly horrified. "The poor birds."

"The poor spectators," I added. "There's a good chance their wedding finery would be ruined by an unfortunate rain of bird scat."

He laughed softly, and Neeve's lips twitched in amusement.

"That's almost enough to change my mind," she said. "But no."

"I'm happy to support you against my mother's schemes," I said. "Does Kian have any say?"

"He mentioned a few of the Fiorland traditions, but that's all." Neeve sighed. "I wish it were easier. I'd be content to slip away into the forest and pledge ourselves in a simple handfasting. But with the King and Queen of Fiorland coming, not to mention the Nightshade Lord, there are certain expectations."

"When is your uncle arriving?" I asked.

"When I fetch him," Thorne said, tilting his head at Neeve. "Which is entirely up to you."

"Not too early," she said. "Especially now that your red priestess is here, Rose."

"She's not mine," I replied, a touch defensively. "I couldn't keep her from coming with me."

"You could've thrown her overboard," Neeve said, and I couldn't tell if she spoke the words in jest, or meant them entirely.

"I'll cross into Elfhame when Kian's parents come," Thorne said. "That should put our return a day or two before the ceremony. If that suits you, Neeve."

She pressed her lips together a moment in thought, then nodded. "Bring more *nirwen* essence back with you, too."

"I'd like to consult the healers about your dosage," Thorne said. "You know the dangers of taking too much, especially for mortals."

"I'm only half human," she said sharply. "Trust me to know my own limits, *Galadhir.*"

I leaned forward, catching her gaze. "I'm worried about you. How are you feeling?"

"I'm well enough to plan a wedding and come out the other side," she said.

"That's not a real answer. Tell me the truth, Neeve." I took her hands, dismayed by the translucence of her skin.

She looked away, into the fire. Silence pressed upon us while I studied her face.

"It would be better if I were in Elfhame," she finally admitted, looking back at me. "But I couldn't stay."

"Why not?" Confused, I glanced at Thorne. "Is something wrong at the Nightshade Court?"

"Nothing more than the usual posturing of the courtiers," he said.

"Spoken like a true hermit of the woods." A dry smile touched Neeve's lips. "Everything in Elfhame is as it should be, Rose. It's the events of the mortal world that made it impossible for me to remain. You're not the only one capable of making a grand sacrifice, you know."

I stared at her a moment as realization dawned. "You came back for my sake?"

"And Kian's, and Thorne's, and my father's." Her expression softened. "But yes, mostly for you. I know what a burden it can be, anchoring the gateway between worlds. And even worse, you were in dangerous territory, surrounded by the red priests."

I nodded. It hadn't been easy. There had certainly been moments when I was terrified my father would discover the existence of the Dark Elves.

I gently pressed Neeve's hands, then released her. "Thank you. Though I fear you've put yourself too much at risk."

"Once the wedding's over and the guests depart, Kian and I will step across the worlds for a time. Then *he* can have the pleasure of being the anchor." She gave me a grim smile.

"I don't think it will weigh too heavily on him," I said. "As long as he's with you."

"Thus, the wedding. It's for the best—for all of us."

"As long as you don't collapse beforehand," Thorne said sternly. "You've been taking on far too much."

"Well," I said briskly, "I'm here now. Give me any tasks you don't want to take on."

"I will." Neeve smiled wearily. "I'll write you a list tomorrow."

"Please do. But right now, I think you ought to get some rest."

Her black brows arched. "And give you two lovebirds some privacy, yes?"

"That's not what I meant!" I could feel the blush heating my cheeks, even as Thorne let out a low chuckle.

I went with my sister to the door and gave her a quick embrace.

"I love you," I whispered in her ear. "Now, take care of yourself."

She nodded and went down the hall to her room. My heart ached at the sight of my strong, fiercely independent sister looking so fragile. I watched until she was safely inside, then shut my door and returned to the fire.

Thorne had risen, and gently folded me in his arms. I hadn't realized I was crying until he wiped the moisture from my cheek with the back of one finger.

"She'll be all right," he said.

"I hope so." I pulled in a wavering breath. "I don't suppose we can move the wedding forward and get her back into Elfhame sooner?"

He gave me a wry smile. "We both know how unlikely that is. But I'll return with plenty of *nirwen* essence to keep her strength up."

"I don't want you to go." I tightened my arms around his strong, slender form.

"And I don't want to leave you—but it will only be for a handful of days." He brushed a kiss over my forehead.

I lifted my face to his, and our lips met. A shimmer of sensation coursed through me, a warm glow that erased all the sorrow and difficulty of the past few months. I was home—completely.

After some time, he broke the kiss.

"Rose," he murmured, "I should go."

"One more kiss." I smiled at him. "We have to make up for lost time."

His dark eyes glittered with sparks, and he didn't argue.

For too brief a time, the world consisted of only the two of us, our hearts pressed close together, our breath tangling as we sought the stars.

CHAPTER 26

T he next morning, Sorche gently woke me with a cup of tea and a fresh scone.

"Good day, Lady Rose," she said, pulling back the curtains to show a sky half-filled with clouds. "I'm so glad you're home."

"So am I." I smiled at her. "I understand you've been tending to Trisk. Thank you."

As if hearing her name, the cat lifted her head from the nest she'd made in the covers and let out a sleepy meow.

"She's fine company." Sorche came over to pet Trisk while I sipped my tea. "So, are you a red priest now?"

"No. I'm not."

And what a relief that was. Even though I'd felt like a complete failure at the time, I wouldn't be sitting in my own bed at Castle Raine if I'd passed the aspirant test.

"Well, that's good," Sorche said, echoing my thoughts. She gave the cat a final scritch between the ears, then went to my wardrobe. "What would you like to wear today?"

"Something more formal, I think. Maybe the embroidered gold." If

I had to face my mother, I wanted to do so as a princess of Raine—though I wouldn't go so far as to don my crown.

I finished my scone, spent another moment cuddling with Trisk, then got up and let Sorche help me dress. She was braiding back my unruly hair when a knock came at the door.

"Come in," I called, unsurprised to see Thorne step into my sitting room. As I'd hoped, he'd agreed to come with me to see Mama.

"Ready?" he asked with a warm smile.

"Almost." I put on the necklace Neeve had given me, letting it sparkle against the velvet bodice. The red drops of rubies glinted within the delicate silver thorns. I laid my fingers against it and glanced at Thorne. "Should we trade back?"

"Not yet." He gently touched the necklace, an intent look in his eyes. "Maybe not ever."

I nodded. My sister and I were bound to one another, and to Elfhame, and I was happy to do anything to keep those bonds strong. Wryly, I glanced down at the Nightshade Lord's ring clasped about my finger.

"What about this?" I lifted my hand, and crimson fire sparkled in the ring's depths. "He won't think it means anything that I'm still wearing it, will he?"

The last thing I wanted was for Lord Mornithalarion to believe I had any interest in taking him up on his offer to become the Nightshade Lady.

A complex series of emotions moved over Thorne's face, but he shook his head. "Never fear. The Nightshade Lord has released all claim on you, Rose."

Then why won't you make me any promises? I thought, staring into his eyes.

I knew why, though. We'd barely confessed our love for each other when I went to Parnese. Besides, all of the complications that had existed before were still there. He was the Dark Elf *Galadhir* of the Erynvorn. I was a mortal, and a fire sorcerer at that. He must spend a portion of the year in Elfhame, and I'd been summarily ejected from that realm. How could we possibly balance ourselves, our lives, together?

I didn't know. But I was determined to try.

"After the wedding," Thorne said softly, reading the question in my eyes. "We'll plan our future then."

Sorche let out a little sigh, and I glanced over to see her watching us with a dreamy expression.

It's not as easy as it looks, I wanted to tell her. But it was still everything.

I took Thorne's arm as we went down the hallway. At the landing, we encountered Paulette and Kian coming from the west wing.

"Good morning," I said. "I hope you slept well, Paulette."

"I did," she said. "It's so cool and restful here. Prince Kian is going to show me the meadow where the wedding is to be held."

I glanced at Kian, and he nodded. Upon consideration, it made perfect sense to hold the wedding within sight of the Darkwood. Would he and Neeve also have a ceremony in Elfhame, honoring the Dark Elf traditions? I'd have to ask them later.

"Enjoy your stroll," I said. "I'll see you at lunch."

Paulette smiled at me, then she and Kian continued on.

"That's a fine idea," I said to Thorne. "To have the wedding outside. I imagine my mother was opposed to the idea." Mama had never been much for dirt and bugs and wayward breezes.

"According to Neeve, she didn't like it. Apparently, it was difficult to make her change her mind." Thorne let out a brief sigh. "I wish the queen wasn't quite so set on trying to control every aspect of the ceremony."

"I'll see what I can do. Neeve needs to conserve her energy, not spend it arguing with my mother."

"Agreed."

We halted outside Mama's door. I'd no doubt my mother had an ulterior motive in summoning me, beyond trying to dictate what I'd wear to the wedding. Since our arrival last night, she'd seemed quite intent on pushing me toward Prince Jenson. Hopefully, my bringing Thorne along would make it clear where my affections lay.

I knocked on the gilded door, and Mama pulled it open. Her gaze skipped from me to my companion, and a small frown marred her forehead.

"Thank you for escorting Rose," she said to Thorne. "No need to wait for us to finish, however. I'm certain she can manage to return safely to her rooms without you."

"He's with me." I laced my arm through Thorne's. "Mama, I love Thorne."

"And I am in love with your daughter," he said, then smiled at me.

My mother blinked with displeasure and stepped back. "Well. You needn't announce it to the entire world. Come in, I suppose. And shut the door behind you."

She stalked away into her opulent sitting room, then gracefully sank down on one of the brocade chairs set before the fire and beckoned for us to join her.

I stepped over the threshold, and my pinky stub sent a sharp, sudden jolt of pain through me. I gasped, and Thorne shot me a look. Pressing my lips together, I shook my head, then surreptitiously rubbed my left hand. It had been so long since the injury had hurt, I'd almost forgotten I had only the stub of a pinky there, not my whole finger.

How strange, that every time I entered my mother's rooms, my pinky ached.

It's not a coincidence, my little voice said. *Maybe you should find out why.*

I banished the thought. Mama had nothing to do with the accident that had maimed me.

The fire in the hearth burned brightly, heating the rooms to an uncomfortable level. Despite the fact I could feel perspiration prickling the back of my neck, my mother pulled a delicate shawl over her shoulders and had seated herself close to the flames.

"Are you well?" I asked, taking one of the chairs and looking her up and down. Thorne remained standing behind me, one hand resting on my shoulder. I covered his hand with my own, squeezing it briefly in thanks.

"I'm perfectly well," Mama said. "Other than having a daughter who insists on making terrible choices, and a stepdaughter who's doing the same."

"Loving Thorne isn't a mistake," I said fiercely. "And Neeve is entitled to plan her own wedding, without you bullying her."

"That's an uncouth accusation. And untrue. I thought I raised you better, Rose."

"You scarcely raised me at all," I retorted.

"I did what I must for a child who'd inherited—"

She broke off, turning her face toward the fire. The heat that had been smothering me suddenly receded, replaced by icy suspicion.

"Mama." I leaned forward, eyes narrowed. "Did you know I had sorcerous power, before this year?"

She let out an artificial laugh, though she wouldn't meet my gaze. "Of course not! How could I have guessed such a thing?"

"Don't lie to me." I clenched my fingers in my skirts, crushing the gold velvet. "You knew very well who my father is."

My power stirred, embers beneath my skin. Thorne's grip tightened on my shoulder, and I tried to slow my breathing, calm my rising temper. My pinky stub pulsed in time with my heartbeat.

Mama looked at me, her eyes sparkling with tears. "I only wanted to keep you safe. Everything I've done was for your protection."

I wished I could believe it.

"What kinds of things did you do?" I asked coldly.

A tear spilled down her cheek, and I scowled. My mother even cried beautifully, her complexion unmarred by red blotches, her eyes clear despite her tears. She pulled a lace-edged handkerchief from her sleeve and dabbed at her cheeks, delaying giving me an answer.

"Did you bind Rose's powers?" Thorne asked, a grim note in his voice.

My mother's lips parted, as though she would deny it. Then she closed her mouth and gave a sorrowful shake of her head. "It was for the best," she said.

Rage surged through me, and I sprang to my feet. "How could you!"

All I'd ever wanted, my whole life, was to have magic. To be special. And now, *now*, I discovered that my own mother had stolen that dream from me. She had lied, and lied, and I could never forgive her.

The fire on the hearth blazed up, and Thorne moved to stand at my side. "Rose," he cautioned.

I clenched my fists, battling my emotions back down. *Calma. Calma to sacar.* No matter the anger coursing hotly through me, I couldn't burn the castle to the ground.

You could dance in the ashes, my wicked little voice suggested, and for a moment I was sorely tempted.

But the target of my wrath was my mother. The rest of the castle was innocent. Probably.

"Does the king know?" I asked.

"No." Mama's voice was hollow. "No one knows."

"Except, presumably, the person who created the binding," Thorne said, narrowing his eyes at my mother. "I presume it was done in Parnese?"

Mama gave a quick nod. When she didn't elaborate, Thorne's frown deepened.

"And is tied to Rose's birthday," he said slowly.

It explained so much. I let out a breath and all but collapsed back into my chair. The fire simmered back down to ordinary flames. Thorne, however remained standing, anger tightening his shoulders, though he kept his voice calm.

"That is perilous magic," he said. "Rose nearly died of it—more than once, I believe."

Mama reached out to me, a beseeching look on her face. "I didn't mean to endanger you!"

Heart clenching, I shook my head at her. "But you did."

Thorne glanced from me to the queen, his expression hard. "The binding was supposed to be renewed yearly, wasn't it? But then you came to Raine."

"I had to." There was a note of defiance in my mother's voice as she looked up at him. "The red priests were gaining power in the city. If they discovered Rose, they would have taken her, forced her into the priesthood. And I would have been put to death for hiding her abilities."

"The warder might have spared you," I said flatly.

"No." Mama glanced down at the floor. "We parted on very bad terms."

"You repudiated him before he could guess you bore his child," I said.

She slid to her knees and grabbed my hands, her fingers cold over mine. "You are *my* child. I sacrificed everything for you."

"You sacrificed my future. You endangered me, over and over."

"I love you." Her voice was nearly a whisper, her luminous eyes staring into mine.

Chest tight with grief, I pulled my fingers from her grasp. "You have a poor way of showing it. What happened when I was seven years old?"

Slowly, she returned to her chair, moving like a woman twice her age. "Do you remember Ser Pietro?" she asked.

I gave a sharp nod. "How could I forget?"

"After that day, your power began to wake. I didn't realize at first, until you lit the fire on the hearth with only a gesture. Then I knew we were in danger. There was a woman in Parnese I'd heard of, a doctor of sorts..."

"Madame Caplata," I said when it seemed she would not continue. I turned to Thorne. "The woman Mama took me to, when she insisted I must be tended in Parnese after I fell so ill on my sixteenth birthday."

"What did she do?" Thorne's voice was hard.

"She said it was the only way." Another perfect tear trickled down Mama's cheek. "I refused at first. But you wouldn't stop creating fires, though I begged you to stop. And so I took nearly all our savings and brought you to Madame Caplata. And she..." Mama's lips trembled. "She took your pinky in return."

I clasped my hands, wrapping my right over my left as though I might protect my poor pinky. But it was already gone.

"*That* was the so-called accident?" My voice came out a hoarse whisper. "You let a blood magician cut off my finger?"

Thorne took two agitated steps away, then whirled to face my mother. "Where is it?"

"Does it matter?" she cried. "The binding burned away on Rose's last birthday. It's powerless now."

"Of course it matters." I stood abruptly, going to join Thorne. "It's still *my* finger."

Though certainly it was nothing but bones now. The binding had burned away when my power freed itself in Elfhame. The box was just a reminder of my past.

I turned in a slow circle, concentrating on the pain pulsing through my pinky stub. A sharp twinge went through me as I faced my mother's ornate desk. Without a word, I stalked over to it.

"Please." Mama held out one hand. "It was to save you. You must understand."

"Surely there were other ways," Thorne said. "You came to Raine, after all, far from the red priests' notice. Why not earlier?"

She let out a brittle laugh. "I had no money, no stature, and the binding seemed to have banished Rose's power. All was well for years. Then the warder seized control of Parnese and I realized we must flee —especially as she was still fascinated by anything to do with fire sorcery."

I recalled my collection of forbidden texts, painstakingly gleaned over the years of my childhood, and how Mama had flung them all into the fire. And then married the King of Raine and whisked us away from everything I'd ever known.

"Lord Raine," I said, still staring at the desk. "What did you do to make him marry you?"

"Nothing any other clever woman wouldn't have done. I know how to wield my charm." There was a bitter note to her voice. "And I promised to be a mother to his daughter."

I whirled, anger momentarily distracting me from my quest. "So you lied to him, but at least Neeve escaped your tender attentions. You are the worst mother anyone could possibly have."

Mama stood, looking as fragile and brittle as a dry leaf at summer's end. "I did my best. It might not have been what you would have liked, but I protected you!"

"You meddled in powerful magics you didn't understand," Thorne said. "No wonder Rose nearly died. She was strong indeed to survive the intensity of her flames trying to emerge."

I turned back to the desk and yanked open the uppermost drawer on the right. A bundle wrapped in red silk called to me, and I pulled it out. Carefully, I unwound the silk, letting it flutter to the floor, a scarlet stain upon Mama's carpet. It had been covering a small box made of ebony, jet-black, with a golden lock.

"Key." I held my hand out to my mother.

She crossed haltingly to where I stood and pulled a fine gold chain from beneath the neckline of her dress. A small key dangled from the chain. With a sigh, she slipped it over her head and handed it to me.

The key was warm from her body. Slowly, I set it in the lock and turned.

"Careful," Thorne murmured, coming to stand beside me.

With a click, the box opened. I lifted the lid, breath pausing in my lungs. What was I about to see?

Two fragments of bone, surrounded by ashes.

Any vague thoughts that I might regain the wholeness of my hand faded like mist under the scorching sun.

"What was the binding?" Thorne asked, his expression darker that I'd ever seen it.

"Scarlet ribbons, infused with"—Mama swallowed—"with Rose's blood."

I glanced sharply at her. "When you took me back to Madame Caplata, she renewed the blood bindings."

No wonder I'd been so weak, my recovery taken so long.

"I saved you." Mama's voice was flat. She knew I'd never forgive her.

Mouth set in a tight line, I turned away from her. "I'm taking this." I gripped the box tightly as I went to the door.

Thorne came with me. As we stepped over the threshold, my mother spoke not a word.

CHAPTER 27

I felt as though I was moving through shadowy cobwebs, the strands clinging to me, obscuring my vision. When I stumbled, Thorne took my elbow and helped guide me through the stone corridors of Castle Raine.

Finally, we reached my rooms. I sank into one of the chairs before the hearth, my thoughts whirling. At last, all the strange, jagged pieces of my life were falling into place.

Ser Pietro, burning.

My mother's abrupt marriage and our subsequent relocation to Raine.

The sickness surrounding my birthdays.

Most of all, my poor pinky, sacrificed in order to smother my sorcery.

I stared down at my left hand. In the end, that loss had been for nothing.

You should have listened to me all those years ago, my little voice said.

Are you the ghost of my bound power? I asked it. There was no reply.

"I had magic all along," I said, my voice hollow.

Throughout those years of desperate wishing, the ability to

summon fire had been buried inside me all the while. Trying to get out. Trying to speak to me.

"So much makes sense now." Thorne took my hand and gently pushed up the sleeve of my gown, revealing the vine and leaf tattoo. "It's why the forest tried to kill you when you first came to Raine, why the ceremony binding you to the Darkwood had such unexpected consequences."

"That time the nixie tried to drown me," I added. "The forest knew what I was, even when I didn't."

He nodded solemnly. "Your power was hidden well. Yet it was so strong that when it couldn't find a direct outlet, it learned to work in subtle ways. That's why you can reach out and affect the magic of others."

"And why it's so hard to control, I suppose." My throat clogged with anger, with grief. "Why did she do it?"

"She was afraid."

"She ruined everything." I bent over, curling into myself.

Thorne slipped to his knees before me and gathered me into his arms, holding me while I sobbed for what I'd lost. For what could never be.

After a time, the storm passed. I dragged my sleeve across my wet face and reminded myself of what I still had.

My life, to begin with. And Thorne.

If Mama hadn't fled to Raine, I never would've met him. Perhaps I'd be a fire sorceress of Parnese instead, an avatar of the Sister sitting at Galtus Celcio's side and flinging *esfirenda* at innocent citizens in the name of conquest. The thought made me shiver with distaste.

I couldn't say it was better this way. But I couldn't say any other future would have been preferable, either. Taking a deep breath, I sat up. This was the path my life had taken. There was no use weeping for what hadn't been.

"Better?" Thorne wiped the last tear from my cheek, his fingers soft against my face.

"For now." I leaned forward and kissed him, though I probably tasted of salt.

He kissed me warmly back, and for a few moments I forgot about the rawness deep in my heart, left by my mother's betrayal.

A knock at the door interrupted us.

"Rose?" It was Neeve's voice. "Are you there?"

Thorne scooted back into the other chair, and I called for my sister to enter. She did, pausing to give me a sharp look before she closed the door behind her.

"What happened?" she asked, her gaze intently fixed on me.

"I'll go fetch some tea," Thorne said, standing. "We could all use something warm, I think."

I could have rung for one of the maids, but he was kindly giving me the privacy to speak with Neeve, to say whatever words I needed to her, and her alone.

"Thank you." I summoned up a weak smile.

He paused, setting one hand on my shoulder in a brief gesture of support. "I love you, Rose."

I stared into his dark eyes, knowing he could read my reply. I loved him, and always had.

He leaned forward and brushed a kiss across my cheek.

"Are you going, or do I have to stand here and watch you two love-birds all day?" Neeve asked, though a smile hid behind the words, blunting their sharpness.

"It would be a just return," Thorne said. "You and Kian are almost as bad."

"Never." Neeve let out a sniff of disdain, but I could tell she didn't mean it.

As soon as Thorne left, she slid into the chair across from me, her expression concerned. "Did you meet with your mother?" she asked.

"Yes." I drew in a deep breath, then told her the whole horrifying, tragic tale.

Her gaze never left me as I spoke, and though she didn't exclaim or gasp or give much reaction at all, I could feel the sympathy radiating from her. It was like talking to a sun-warmed slab of stone—unyielding yet comforting at the same time.

When I was finished, she gave a slow nod. "This doesn't make you any lesser, you know. In fact, knowing *why* makes you even more yourself. You always want to understand the reasons for things, and now you have answers."

"More than I might have wished." I frowned and rubbed my pinky stub, but my sister was right. My past had shifted, the blurred edges sharpening into some kind of sense.

"Nothing has changed," Neeve said. "Your power was already unbound on your birthday. And the red priests found you anyway. And let you go."

"Maybe. I don't trust Galtus Celcio not to send a delegation to haul me back to Parnese."

"We won't let him." Her voice was calm. "I promise. If it comes down to that, you and Thorne can go into Elfhame. The red priests could scour the kingdom and never find you."

"They'd find the gateway," I said darkly. "What then?"

"They won't. The Darkwood protects itself."

I wished I could believe her, but she didn't know the strength of my father's power. Still, the forest wasn't without weapons. I thought of my first venture into the Darkwood, where I was attacked by boglins, freed a hobnie...

"Do the hobnies still owe us any debts?" I asked, recalling the seven rude little creatures and how Neeve and I had saved each of them from a difficult circumstance.

"One of them does." Neeve's brows drew together. "But whenever I try to find Cancrach, he disappears completely."

"You hardly need favors from the forest."

"Not any longer." A brief smile warmed her expression. "And neither do you, might I say, now that you're all but betrothed to the *Galadhir*."

"About that." I sighed heavily and leaned back in my chair. "I'm afraid Thorne still thinks I should marry some mortal prince."

"But he loves you. He just said so, out loud."

"Yes, but in his honorable Dark Elf way he's worried that, if we pledged our lives together, his duties would make things too difficult for me."

"It would be worse marrying someone you don't love," my sister pointed out. "And it's not his place to decide for you. But I'm certain the two of you will be able to come to some agreement."

"I hope so—but he's as stubborn as you are."

I almost told her of Thorne's vision, where he'd seen me on the cusp of marrying the Nightshade Lord. That knowledge had torn his heart in two. Was he trying to protect himself by attempting to let me go?

It wouldn't work—I was as tenacious as the fall burrs in the meadows that wove their way into one's clothing and were nearly impossible to remove.

"He'll see reason," Neeve said, then fell silent as Thorne pushed open the door, the promised tea tray in his hands.

"So," I said brightly, once he'd handed us our cups and settled on the little stool, "what's next?"

"Preparing for the King and Queen of Fiorland's arrival tomorrow," Neeve said.

Her voice was calm, but I saw a touch of uncertainty in her eyes. Even though she and Kian had reached the expected outcome, it would be a little unsettling to meet one's fiancé's parents only days before the wedding.

And things would become more fraught when the Fiorland monarchs were introduced to the Nightshade Lord. At least the wedding offered plenty of distraction from the bitter knowledge that my own mother had maimed me in order to protect herself.

And protect you, my voice said.

I slammed the door on it. Whether it was my own suppressed power speaking, or some wickedness buried deep inside me, I didn't care. I had enough to worry about without its constant contributions leading me into trouble.

"Here." Neeve took a folded piece of paper from the pocket of her dress and handed it to me. "You said you wanted a list."

I took it and scanned the contents, which were full of little details, like finding out what the Fiorland royals' favorite dish was and making sure it was included in the wedding feast, confirming with the local brewery on the delivery of casks of ale and cider, checking that the servants had enough flowers and ribbons to make garlands for the great hall, and the like.

"Consider it done," I said, glad to have the distraction. Especially as Thorne would be leaving to fetch the Nightshade Lord from Elfhame. I looked at him. "When do you go?"

"Tonight," he said, and my heart gave a little clutch. "But before I do, I want to visit Mistress Ainya with you. Especially in light of this morning's revelations."

I pressed my lips together and gave him a short nod. While half of me wished never to speak of Mama's betrayal again, I knew that Thorne and the herbwife were the only two people who could help me understand how the binding had affected my power.

Aside from Galtus Celcio, of course. What would the warder think if he discovered my mother had so cruelly bound my sorcerous power? He'd be enraged, I had no doubt. Better if he never learned the truth.

CHAPTER 28

That afternoon, I followed Thorne out the small wooden door in the castle wall and across the flower-spangled meadow to the Darkwood. My pulse sped as we approached the cool shadows beneath the trees. Now that I'd trained my fire sorcery in Parnese, would the forest turn against me? It hadn't during the journey up from Portknowe, but I'd been riding through it, not deliberately setting foot beneath the trees.

I was glad to be in the *Galadhir's* company. With every step, I concentrated on keeping my flames quiet—slumbering coals in my belly and nothing more.

Just before we entered the fringe of cedars, Thorne took my hand.

"Don't worry," he said. "I won't let the Darkwood harm you."

"I'm not afraid," I said, and it was mostly true.

Together, we strode into the trees. A breeze whispered through the branches and a small bird burst into startled flight from a nearby thicket. I jumped at the flutter of wings, then made myself breathe slowly. Thorne squeezed my fingers, then tilted his head, as if listening.

"Roll up your sleeve," he said, letting go of my hand.

I didn't need to ask him which one, and silently pushed up the cloth on my left arm, revealing the leaf and vine etched on my inner elbow.

"*Enyalia,*" he said, lifting his voice.

The leaf glowed bright emerald for a moment, the memory of pain making my pinky stub throb.

"What does that mean?" I asked softly.

"I reminded the Darkwood of your vow of binding." He took my arm, gently tracing the tattoo, and I caught my breath, swaying. "Does it hurt?"

I met his concerned gaze. "No."

It was his touch, his nearness, that made my senses swim—the achingly bright knowledge that I had everything I'd ever wished for. Magic. And Thorne.

At that moment, standing beneath the hushing boughs, everything seemed possible.

"Thorne Windrift," I said, before I lost my courage, "I wish to marry—"

He set his fingers to my lips, a sudden flash of anguish in his gaze. "After Neeve and Kian are wed, we will speak of it. Not before."

I kissed his fingers, then gently pushed his hand aside, and my own impatience as well. Thorne had his reasons, though in this case I was certainly entitled to know more. "Why? Have you seen another vision?"

"No, but..."

He glanced away, to the dark columns of the tree trunks rising about us. It seemed that he looked toward the center of the Dark-wood. Toward the gateway.

I bit my tongue and tried not to demand answers. I trusted he would tell me what he could.

After a long moment, he turned back to me. "The Oracles have instructed me to wait."

"I'm tired of waiting." I frowned. "Why? Is something going to happen at the wedding? What do the Oracles know?"

He shook his head, the burden of being the *Galadhir* clear in the weariness of his gaze. "They will not speak of it."

"I'm growing annoyed with their mysterious ways." I crossed my arms. "What good is it to see the strands of fate, if they can't just tell people what's going to happen?"

"If they do that, then the future changes. It's a delicate balance."

It seemed pure manipulation to me. If I ever returned to Elfhame, I planned to tell the Oracles precisely what I thought of them. Though they probably already knew that, too. Wry amusement dispelled my irritation, and I exhaled in surrender.

"Very well. After the wedding."

The instant the ceremony was over, though, I'd pull him aside and force him to have the conversation with me. Constantly pushing the question into the future was doing neither of us any good. But I'd let the matter rest for now.

In five days, though, I'd ask him to marry me, no matter what road the Oracles might try to force us upon.

Thorne led the way through the forest to Mistress Ainya's. I brushed my palms over the bushes bright with little red berries, and nodded at the old stump as we took the branching path toward the herbwife's cottage. The sapling growing from the stump was now as thick as my forearm, its new branches reaching toward the light.

The low gate creaked in welcome as we stepped into the herb garden. Bees hummed loudly in the lavender, and bright orange nasturtiums spilled from the flowerpots beside the path. The top of the green half-door was open, the entryway shaded by white and red roses. A few petals had fallen, drops of snow and blood on the front stoop.

Before we reached the door, Mistress Ainya popped her head up.

"There you are! Come in." She pulled the rest of the door wide in greeting. She looked just the same, her wizened face creased in a smile, the wisps of her white hair like thistledown atop her head. "I wondered when you'd come visit, the both of you."

"You knew I'd returned to Raine?" I asked.

"I knew you were going to," she said. "Thorne and I have spoken about you several times. Come sit, tell me everything you learned among the red priests."

Thorne and I stepped inside, while Mistress Ainya bustled to set the kettle over the fire. I sat at her worn wooden table, inhaling deeply of the scent of dried herbs and spices. The smell conjured up an echo of the longing I'd felt, summer after summer, watching Neeve study magic and wishing with all my heart I might do the same.

"Before we speak of Parnese," Thorne said, "we discovered something very important about the development of Rose's power."

"Did you?" Mistress Ainya strewed a handful of dried herbs into her glazed brown teapot, then came to join us at the table, eyes bright with interest.

Thorne glanced at me, one eyebrow up, and I nodded. I was strong enough to tell the tale.

"It turns out I've had fire sorcery all along," I said, spilling the words in a rush. "My mother had it bound when I was young, but it's been there the whole time, trying to break free."

Mistress Ainya's smile fell from her face as I spoke, her gaze sharpening to a dagger point. "Well," she said softly, "that explains a *great* deal. How was the binding done?"

I lifted my hand, turning the pinky stub toward her. "Blood magic."

She inhaled sharply, then looked at Thorne. "I thought such practitioners no longer existed, especially in the civilized world."

"There are always those who follow the darkest paths," he said. "Luckily, they are few, and such power always catches up with them. Eventually."

I shivered. Was the same true of fire sorcerers? Was I destined to immolate myself some day in a gruesome ball of flame?

"Your mother must have been desperate," the herbwife said to me.

"She feared for her life," I said.

"And yours, too."

I frowned at her. "I don't think so."

"If she truly didn't care what happened to you, she would've paid someone to toss you into the harbor, and her problem would have been solved. Instead, she went to a great deal of effort—and expense too, I'd wager—to find another way."

I pursed my mouth, not liking her words. Mama had always been selfish, and I couldn't reconcile that knowledge with the picture of a woman who'd risk everything to save her child.

"Marrying Lord Raine to get you both out of Parnese was a sacrifice, too," Mistress Ainya continued. "Though you didn't think so at the time, it surely cost your mother to abandon everything she'd ever known and flee—not to mention pledging her future to a man she hardly knew."

"Whatever her reasons," Thorne said, and I was grateful for the change of subject, "what she did nearly killed Rose, and warped her power. We should concentrate on rebuilding her abilities."

"Being able to siphon magic..." The herbwife gave me a thoughtful look. "I believe your sorcery was desperate to free itself. Since your own power was bottled up, it had to seek other sources. Especially when the binding wasn't refreshed, and its hold on your magic began to erode."

"I had no idea I was doing it," I said in protest.

"An indirect, involuntary use of power." Thorne's brows drew together. "No wonder it's hard to control. You'll have to keep coming at it sideways, Rose."

I grimaced. "I suppose that explains why I can't master the simple chants, but my magic seems all too eager to fling fireballs around."

The flaming Yule Feast tapestries, the exploded drake, the blazing throne room of the Nightshade Court—a chaos of fire lived inside me, waiting to come out.

Calma, I thought as my flames roused. I was the one in charge now. More or less.

"Magic usually is coaxed forward along small channels," Mistress Ainya said. "Then, once those paths are open, stronger power can emerge. Is it the same with your people, Thorne?"

"Very similar. Dark Elf children begin with simple magic, like calling light." He glanced at me. "Or basic scrying. Later, they grow into their abilities."

I shook my head. "If I ever had *small channels*, I fear they've been blasted away. Or maybe withered from lack of use." It was strange, discussing the convolutions of the magic inside me as if my sorcery was another organ, a physical part of me.

I wiggled the stub of my pinky. In a way, I supposed my power *had* been connected to my body. Maybe that contributed to my ongoing struggles.

"If you are left with only great power," the herbwife said, "then that is what you must work with. There's no training a huge tree to become smaller again, and no use wishing it was any different than it is. Your sorcery, Rose, is unique to you. The regular ways of learning magic will be of no use."

Though I wished her words weren't true, they made sense. I pressed my lips together, grappling with the notion. If my subtler abilities had been incinerated then I had no choice but to contend with the intensity of my full power. Frustrating and difficult as it might be.

"Can you help me?" I asked.

She shook her head. "Not a great deal, I'm afraid. My own magic runs in the smaller channels." She glanced at Thorne. "Do you have any advice for Rose?"

He regarded me thoughtfully. "Perhaps learning the greater runes of the Dark Elves would give you some way forward."

Mistress Ainya's eyes widened. "A good thought. Begin at the top. When you have time, I look forward to further exploring Rose's sorcery together. Perhaps after the wedding."

Thorne's expression shuttered, and I couldn't read what was in his eyes. Before I could ask what was wrong, the kettle let out a low whistle, and the herbwife rose to pour boiling water into the teapot.

"How is Neeve?" she asked, returning to the table. "Tell her to come visit me."

"I will," I said. "Though you'll have to wait until after the ceremony. Kian's parents arrive tomorrow, and the castle is humming like a hive of bees. You're invited to the wedding, I hope?"

"Of course." Mistress Ainya smiled, a glint in her blue eyes. "One doesn't ignore the local witch. I'm sure you've read the tales."

"I doubt you'd curse the marriage and any offspring, however," Thorne said, amused.

"Ah, no." The herbwife's smile faded. "They'll have trouble aplenty without adding such foolishness into the mix."

"Why?" I stared at her. "What do you know?"

She reached over and patted my hand. "Only that children of two worlds always have a difficult path to walk. There's no dire fate waiting to pounce upon Neeve, Kian, or their children. At least, none that I've seen."

"Good." I let out a breath. "But there will be children?"

"If the gateway is to remain open, there must," Thorne said.

"Everything in due time." Mistress Ainya poured out our tea, and then she and Thorne began discussing the distillation of *nirwen* and how the potency might be affecting Neeve.

I let their conversation wash over me, suddenly weary from the shocks of the morning. Sad, too, at the fact that Thorne would be leaving for Elfhame—though he'd promised he wouldn't depart until after dinner. We'd have the rest of the afternoon to spend in the Dark-wood, and I was determined to wring as much sweetness from it as possible.

CHAPTER 29

D usk was burnishing the sky when Thorne and I returned to the castle. We'd tarried long in the Darkwood, and I had only a short time to make myself presentable for dinner. I hurried to my room, nearly running into Neeve as I rushed down the corridor.

"Rose." She took my shoulder. "Is something the matter?"

"Only that I'm late," I said. "Has the bell rung already?"

"A few minutes ago. Whatever have you been doing?" She reached up and brushed a few pieces of fern from my hair, then plucked out a bit of moss and held it up. "Did you fall in the forest?"

A fierce blush heated my cheeks. "In a manner of speaking."

She looked at me a moment, then comprehension dawned. "Ah. You and Thorne are making the most of your time together, I see."

"I need to get ready for dinner," I said, attempting to change the subject.

"You most certainly do." My sister followed me into my room. "I'll comb your hair. It looks as though half the ferns of the Darkwood are stuck in it."

Thorne and I had made a little nest to embrace in, and he'd lined it with his cloak. Not well enough, apparently.

I sat at my dressing table while Neeve swiped a brush through my unruly curls. When she pronounced my hair presentable, I hastily changed into a fresh gown, and the two of us went down to dinner.

We were the last ones to step into the dining room. Mama sent me a beseeching look as we made our curtsies to the king and went to find our places. The white tapers in the silver candelabra shed warm light over the table, and the servants had already filled people's goblets with wine and water.

Paulette was seated near the bottom, with an empty chair between her and Thorne. I slipped into it and took his hand, hating the thought of his imminent departure. The next time he went to Elfhame, I vowed to be at his side.

On the other hand, I'd left Paulette to her own devices for the entire day. Neeve had told me she'd spent most of it with Donal, but I should be keeping a closer watch on the red priest in our midst. Even if the Dark Elves could blur her memory, it was better she didn't discover too much about Raine.

"Is everything in readiness for the King and Queen of Fiorland to join us tomorrow?" Lord Raine asked Neeve once the servants finished serving the first course.

Mama narrowed her eyes, clearly displeased at being left out of the question, but I thought it wise of the king to acknowledge his daughter's role.

"Yes," Neeve replied. "I'm certain Kian's parents will find their rooms hospitable."

"And Merkis Strond?" Sir Durum asked from across the table. "Will she want to bed down in the barracks with her soldiers?"

"Since they're only bringing an honor guard, I don't think that's necessary." Kian glanced at his fiancée.

"I've asked the servants to ready one of the guest rooms on the ground floor for her," she said.

The gruff captain gave a nod of approval, and Kian smiled.

"What of our other guests?" Mama asked, with a glance down the table at Thorne. "Will they have any...special requirements?" She made it sound as though the Dark Elves were just shy of barbarians.

Neeve's lips tightened. "My uncle and his guards are accustomed to a certain standard, it's true. But they'll make do with what we have here at Castle Raine."

I turned my head to hide my smile as my mother blinked, affronted.

"I don't suppose his soldiers will want to sleep in the barracks, either," Sir Durum said, though his tone was more respectful than my mother's had been.

"We'll give them the suite adjoining the Ivy room," Neeve said, her composure back in place.

"It's a good thing my ancestors built Castle Raine with so many rooms," Lord Raine said. "Don't forget the Lord Mayor of Meriton and his family, Portknowe's port master, and the minor nobles from the northern villages."

I made a quick tally in my head. The Fiorland royals and their honor guard plus Merkis Strond, Prince Jenson, and Jarl Eiric, who'd presumably take up residence in his old rooms. Add in the Nightshade Lord and whatever entourage he planned to bring. Paulette. And then, apparently, half the kingdom.

"We'll erect tents in the front meadows, if needed," Neeve said calmly, though I glimpsed the anxiety in her eyes.

Paulette had been following the conversation with interest, and leaned toward me. "Where is Neeve's uncle from?" she asked.

Drat—she'd been paying too much attention.

"The northeast of Raine," I said vaguely. "They keep to themselves, mostly."

"It sounds as though they're wealthy." Paulette glanced up the table, to where Lord Raine sat. "Richer than the king?"

"They control a trade route, a small one." It wasn't exactly a lie. "I believe they make the most of it."

"I look forward to meeting Princess Neeve's family, then. They sound very mysterious."

I searched Paulette's eyes, but saw no trace of suspicion that Neeve's uncle was anything other than a reclusive lord.

"The Fiorlanders are interesting too," I said, trying to redirect the conversation. "You should consider Prince Jenson's offer of a visit."

Though he was several chairs up and across the table, Jenson looked our direction, clearly having heard me say his name. He lifted his glass, meeting my eyes, and gave me a smile.

At my side, Thorne stiffened. "That princeling is still trying to woo you," he said softly.

"He's just flirting," I said, turning to my beloved. "He knows that my heart is already taken."

Thorne stared into my eyes, an edge of bleakness shadowing his gaze. "Don't close any doors just yet, Rose."

I set my fork down with a clack. "Stop it. You are the only one for me, Thorne Windrift."

Paulette had been watching our exchange with wide eyes. Recalling my manners, I sat back and gave her a bland look.

"So," she whispered loudly, "I understand why you might want to stay in Raine. He's so handsome."

Thorne heard every word, of course, but gave no reaction.

"Yes," I said flatly, trying not to encourage her.

"He should come back with you to Parnese. I'm sure the warder wouldn't mind."

"We'll see." I picked up my fork and took a bite of roasted pheasant. "Have you tried this? It's delicious."

The rest of dinner went more smoothly, without further mention of the Dark Elves or looming political pitfalls. I arranged with Paulette to go for a cart drive to Little Hazel the next morning, after she confessed she couldn't ride.

"When I first came here, I was terrible on horseback," I said. "I could barely stay atop the little pony they gave me."

"I'm sure you're a fine rider now," Paulette said, admiration shining from her eyes.

I hid a sigh. In the absence of Galtus Celcio, it seemed she'd transferred some of her hero worship to me. I wished I could convince her I wasn't some avatar of the Sister.

"I'm merely adequate on horseback," I said. "It helps to have a good mount."

I thought of Sterling down in the stables. Wedding or no, I should suggest to Neeve we go out for a ride in the next few days. She could use the distraction.

"Can Donal come with us to the village tomorrow?" Paulette asked. "I think it would be good to have a guard's protection. Especially with that frightening forest so close. I can't imagine what kind of horrible creatures live in its depths."

Thorne let out a small sound of amusement.

"It's not that dangerous," I said, then recalled that the Darkwood would count Paulette as an enemy, especially without the *Galadhir* accompanying her. "Though I agree, it's best to stay out of the forest."

"You can be sure I will." She gave a little shiver. "There's so much to explore in the castle, anyway. Have you *seen* the library?"

"I grew up here," I reminded her dryly.

"Of course." She blinked. "I think of you as living in the temple now. I can't believe it took you so long to come to us."

Paulette seemed to have conveniently forgotten that Galtus Celcio hadn't known I existed until recently, and I didn't feel like reminding her.

"The library is grand, I agree. What do you like to read?"

Paulette launched into an enthusiastic description of the seafaring tales that were her preference. I listened, nodding at appropriate intervals, but my thoughts strayed to the hidden shelf I'd discovered in the back of the library, and the three books concealed therein.

The first, the *Studie of the Dark Elves and their Wayes*, had caused its share of trouble. As had the little recipe book hiding the long-ago spy's report on the red priests.

The last one had been a leaflet of parchment, written in a language I didn't know. For the first time, it struck me that perhaps it was in Elvish, and I felt a fool for not thinking of it earlier. I'd have to retrieve the leaflet from its hiding place and show Thorne.

Except that he was leaving as soon as dinner ended.

"...and the hero finally returned home, but only his dog recognized him," Paulette said. "It was quite wonderfully tragic."

"So it seems." I returned my attention to her. "I'll certainly have to read it."

A visit to the castle's library was absolutely in order, though I knew the door was locked at night. Tomorrow afternoon, then. I'd retrieve the third book to show Thorne when he returned from Elfhame.

I squeezed his hand again, his fingers laced with mine, and reminded myself our time apart wouldn't last too long. Mere turns for him, and a handful of days for me. I'd survived worse.

CHAPTER 30

T horne and I parted at the edge of the Darkwood. The dome of the night sky was sprinkled with stars, and the single moon of the mortal world rode low, a crescent sailing behind the turrets of Castle Raine.

"I'll come back as soon as I can," he said, holding me tightly in his arms.

"I know." I brushed my lips against his. "Travel safely. And don't let your liege bring too many guards with him."

I knew Thorne's power was strong enough to transport him into Elfhame and return the same way with the Nightshade Lord. But the fewer people he had to carry between the worlds, the better.

"It will likely be just his two guards accompanying him," Thorne said. "Lord Mornithalarion understands the cost to my wellspring. He'll do what he can to help."

"He'd better." I gave Thorne one last, fierce kiss.

I wanted to stay there forever, clasped in his embrace while the forest sighed around us. But the sooner he went, the sooner he'd return. Slowly, I released my hold about his waist.

"If anything goes wrong—" I began.

"Nothing will go wrong." He brushed a stray curl from my cheek.

"We're safe, Rose. The doorway is stable, your power is under control, and Neeve is holding strong."

I wasn't as sure about the last two, but bit my tongue on my doubts, even though events always seemed to take a turn for the worse when we weren't together.

"Take care."

"I will. We should cross back the day before the wedding. Earlier, if my lord has everything in readiness for a quick passage."

I hoped the Nightshade Lord had packed his bags and had plenty of *nirwen* essence to bring along, though it was more likely that Thorne would have to spend precious time taking care of the details. I let out a sigh and stepped back.

"Then you'd best be on your way."

He nodded, making a complex gesture with his fingers and murmuring in Elvish.

Between one heartbeat and the next, he was gone.

I stood there for a time, listening to the wind in the branches, the far-distant cry of an owl, letting the cool, moist scent of the forest fold around me.

Finally, I went back into the castle. Now that Thorne was gone, I had Neeve's lengthy list of preparations to distract me. Not to mention keeping a sharper eye on Paulette, raiding the library, and avoiding my mother whenever possible.

When I opened my door, a note fluttered to the stone floor.

My rooms, it said.

Though it wasn't signed, I knew who'd left it. And to be honest, I was glad to be saved from an evening of solitude, staring alone into the fire. I tucked the note in my pocket and continued down the hall to Neeve's door.

The moment I rapped upon it, she called for me to enter. I stepped into her sitting room, unsurprised to see Kian there too. He stood in greeting, and my sister nodded for me to join them before the hearth. A chessboard was set on a table between their two chairs, and a third seat was drawn up nearby.

"You got another chair," I said, settling into it.

"The castle does have extras," Neeve said. "Though some people enjoy perching on stools, I suppose."

"Your parlor is bigger than mine," I said, quite untruthfully, as we both knew our rooms were the exact same size. "An extra chair would make my space far too crowded."

Neeve sent me a look, and Kian laughed.

"Speaking of room," he said, "once we're married, we're supposed to take one of the large suites in the east wing. Plenty of space there."

"I don't want to move," Neeve said. "At least, not right away. Maybe once we come back from Elfhame."

I nodded slowly. "How soon after the wedding do you plan to go?"

"The day after," she said. "We'll accompany my uncle when he leaves. Less work for Thorne that way."

"Still, he'll be transporting, what, six people?" I pressed my lips together in doubt.

"We'll ride to the center of the Darkwood," she said. "And then through the Erynvorn to Nightshade. That should help conserve the *Galadhir's* strength. Besides, Thorne has told me it's easier to cross between the realms with the anchors present."

"You and Kian. I suppose that's why you were able to slip through the gateway at the end of last harvest."

I'd forgiven my sister for her ill-advised escape from our world, though that action had changed all of us forever.

She and her betrothed exchanged a look, and Kian nodded.

"We think you should come with us," he said.

I blinked at him. "I should?"

"Yes." Neeve reached over, briefly setting her hand atop mine. "We know that Galtus Celcio wants you back in Parnese, and that he can sense your power in the mortal world. You'll be safe in Elfhame."

"And you'll be with Thorne," Kian said, with a wink.

"My father will still come in search of me," I said, shaking my head. Though appealing, it wasn't a true solution to my problems. "We can't let the warder of the red priests come to Raine."

"We'll tell him you died," Neeve said calmly.

"Oh?" I raised my brows at her. "What ended my life?"

"A fall from horseback. Or perhaps you tripped coming down the grand staircase and broke your neck."

"That's gruesome." I didn't want to contemplate my own death, faked or not. "What about Paulette?"

"The Nightshade Lord has the power to alter her memories," Kian said. "He'll have to erase the knowledge of the Dark Elves anyway. Might as well add the sad fact that you perished."

I sent him a look. "You don't have to sound so cheerful about it. Besides, since my father can, as Neeve said, sense my power, that means I'll never be able to come back to this world. I'll be trapped in Elfhame for the rest of my life."

"That's not such a bad thing," my sister said.

"For you, maybe. But Thorne crosses between the realms. I want to travel with him—we've spent enough time apart."

"Then it's a good thing time passes differently there," Kian said. "You won't have to wait nearly so long in Elfhame."

I let out an unhappy breath. Their arguments made sense, yet a part of me stubbornly refused the idea.

"The Oracles don't want me in Elfhame," I said. "Or have you forgotten that they cast me out?"

"That was before you could control your sorcery," Neeve said. "Thorne can make them reconsider."

"What about your uncle? I doubt he wants me to take up residence after nearly burning the Nightshade Court to cinders." Not to mention the awkwardness of living next to a Dark Elf lord whom I'd nearly married.

"I will speak with him."

"Don't." I crossed my arms. "I'm fairly certain I wouldn't want to live in the Nightshade palace anyway. Not on a permanent basis."

"One of the other courts, maybe?" Kian asked, then shook his head. "Except Thorne won't be there, so never mind."

"Hawthorne isn't too far away," Neeve said. "Or what about the Erynvorn?"

"I'll consider it," I said. "And I'll discuss it with Thorne."

Other than the fact I'd never see the sun again, it seemed an easy solution to my problem of the red priests. Maybe too easy. I'd learned that fate never took the straightforward path.

Especially not when far more treacherous options awaited. Even if I fled into Elfhame, I knew that Galtus Celcio and his plans for me wouldn't be that simply thwarted.

CHAPTER 31

The day after the King and Queen of Fiorland arrived, a welcome feast was held in the great hall. Candles in tall candelabra lit the long tables, and the sconces burned brightly, picking out glints of gold thread in the tapestries adorning the walls. Most of the tables in the hall were filled. In addition to Kian's parents and the inhabitants of the castle, guests from around the kingdom had begun to assemble at the castle.

Sadly, Thorne and the Nightshade Lord were still a day from stepping through the gateway. I tried to be patient, but found myself watching the Darkwood from my window, hoping to see the Dark Elves emerge from that wall of cedars and hemlock. The leaves were changing, the few maples and birch trees in the forest bright patches of red and gold against the evergreens.

The edge of autumn was near, and I hoped—probably in vain—that early storms would close the Strait, keeping my father at bay. I would not return to Parnese, though I was wary of escaping into Elfhame. The ruse of my death might work...or it might not, which would guarantee a return of Galtus Celcio and his priests to Raine.

First, though, came the wedding. I resolved to put off thinking about the rest of my future until my sister and Kian were married.

They sat at the middle of the head table, surrounded by the older royals. I was relegated to the next table down, along with Prince Jenson. I suspected my mother had drawn up the seating arrangements, as we were placed next to each other.

Merkis Strond was across from us, as joyful and outspoken as ever. While she and Sir Durum engaged in a lively argument over the merits of wielding two swords as opposed to using one plus a shield, Jenson turned to me.

"I want you to know that I respect your bond with Thorne," he said softly. "My parents thought I should court you, but I've told them it's not possible—that your heart belongs to another."

"Thank you." I gave him a gentle smile.

I'd briefly met the Fiorland monarchs the night before, as part of the welcoming party on the steps of Castle Raine. They seemed kind enough, the king smiling, his wife more reserved, though they'd both embraced Kian, and Neeve as well.

She'd held herself stiffly during their greetings, and I suddenly realized that Lord Raine had never shown her much physical affection. Marrying Kian would be good for her, I thought, noting how she relaxed as he wove her arm through his and pulled her closer to him.

Jarl Eiric had followed his king and queen into the castle, but not before pausing and giving me a searching look.

"Princess Rose. I see you've returned in time for the wedding."

"Of course." I gave him an insincere smile.

"How was your time in Parnese?" His gaze sharpened with distrust, and I had to admit the feeling was mutual. "Do you plan to return there after your sister and Prince Kian are wed?"

I gave an airy wave. "Perhaps."

My plans were none of the jarl's business. Though I'd no intention of leaving Raine, I liked to keep him off balance.

He let out a sniff, then stalked past me. Merkis Strond was right behind him, and she gave me a smile and wink.

"Always a bit puffed up, isn't he?" she whispered, loud enough for him to overhear.

I smothered a laugh, and my mother sent me a glare. I ignored it, the way I'd been pretending she didn't exist for the past several days.

If you're staying in Raine, my little voice pointed out, *you'll have to speak with her eventually.*

Eventually, however, could last a long time.

The servants tended to the head table, then made the rounds, serving venison and vegetables baked with rosemary. The herb smelled delicious, and was also a sign of fidelity and honesty in marriage. I wondered if Neeve had chosen the menu. It would be like her to make subtle statements with the use of aromatic plants, though I might be the only person in the room who understood the significance of her choices.

I took a sip of wine, then turned back to Jenson. "Will you return to Fiorland after the wedding?"

"I'd originally planned to, especially if I could entice your red priest friend to come with me."

I glanced at Paulette, seated further down the table near Jarl Eiric. I wondered if he was trying to pull the secrets of the Twin Gods from her. Despite her seeming naivete, however, Paulette would never tell the Fiorlander anything important.

"Thank you for trying," I said to Jenson. "But she'd never go so far from Parnese without Galtus Celcio's permission. But it sounds as though your plans have changed?"

His expression sobered. "My parents would like me to go to the Athraig, as the official Fiorland emissary."

"Isn't that dangerous?" The Athraig were our common enemy. Despite the fact that Lord Raine had spoken of marrying me off to their prince, I knew he'd never seriously considered it.

Jenson grimaced. "With the threat of the red priests growing, my parents believe that those of us in the north need to rally together, no matter our past enmity. Apparently, the prince's cousin is of marriageable age."

I tilted my head in sympathy. "I'm almost sorry I can't save you from that fate."

"So am I." He gave me a hollow smile. "Unfortunately, all my other brothers are paired off. I'm the last pawn on the board."

"My sympathies." I set my hand on his arm, then pulled it quickly away when I saw my mother watching us.

"Ah, well." Jenson took a swallow from his goblet. "It keeps my life interesting, at any rate."

"Interesting is just another word for trouble." *Something I knew all too well.*

"I don't know about that." He shot me a look. "Your Thorne seems rather mysteriously interesting, as does Neeve's uncle. I look forward to meeting this Nightshade Lord."

"As do I," Merkis Strond said from across the table. "Fiorland has a vested interest in understanding the military capacities of our neighbors."

I squirmed, though it wasn't my fault the monarchs of Raine had chosen to keep Fiorland ignorant of the existence of the Dark Elves.

"No need to worry," Sir Durum said. "They aren't a conquering kind of people."

Merkis Strond's brows went up. "I'll make that determination for myself, thank you."

I studied her in the warm candlelight. With her honey-colored hair and rosy complexion, not to mention her outspoken, cheerful ways, she was the very opposite of Lord Mornithalarion. I looked forward to seeing the sparks fly when they met.

At the end of the feast, which went on until everyone had more than enough to eat, Lord Raine stood.

"It is my pleasure to welcome you all to Castle Raine," he said. "Before you go, I'd like to entertain you with a performance from our royal bard, Master Fawkes."

He gestured to the musicians' gallery, where a handful of players had been strumming pleasant instrumental accompaniment all evening. I glanced up, glad to see my old teacher had returned, and guilty that I hadn't noticed him before. In my defense, my back had been to the musicians all night, but I should have recognized the sound of his harp.

Master Fawkes stood and bowed, then turned to the other musicians with a nod. The vielle struck up a lilting melody, and the others joined in. I thought I recognized the strains of a Dark Elf melody weaving through the music.

As the candlelight dimmed, people looked up at the ceiling,

murmuring in wonder. Instead of the stolid beams and stones, the roof was now a night sky brimming with stars. After a few moments, Master Fawkes played a glissando of descending notes. The stars began to stream down, leaving bright streaks of light in their wake.

"That's a lovely trick," Merkis Strond remarked, smiling up at the rain of light. "It's been a long time since I've seen a bard at their work."

"You have bards in Fiorland?" I asked.

"We did." She looked over at me. "It seems Raine has been more successful at retaining its magic than my kingdom."

Magic. I shot a look down the table at Paulette, who was watching the illusion with wide eyes. This would have to be the first of her memories to be erased, I realized with a pang. That knowledge stole the beauty of the illusion from me, leaving regret in its wake.

When the last star was gone, the candles brightened once more. The room broke out in applause, and Master Fawkes bowed again, then left the musicians' gallery. Chairs and benches scraped back as the guests rose and began making their various ways from the great hall. The feast was over.

I stood and smiled at Prince Jenson. "Thank you for your company."

"The pleasure was mine." He took my hand and bowed over it, wise enough not to try brushing a kiss over my knuckles. "Good evening, Princess Rose."

I nodded and left the hall, aware of my mother's gaze following me. *No,* I thought at her. *I won't be marrying any prince of Fiorland.*

The time when she had any say in my life was now gone, forever.

FINALLY, the day before the wedding, Thorne and Lord Mornithalarion strode out of the Darkwood. I saw them from my window, where I'd been obsessively keeping watch. As they crossed the stretch of meadow outside the castle wall, the morning sunlight struck obsidian highlights from their dark hair. Not for the first time, I noted their family resemblance, though Thorne was a distant cousin to the Nightshade Lord.

The two guards followed, one silver-haired, the other with ornate black warrior's braids framing her lean face. They carried large packs filled with what were probably the Nightshade Lord's outfits and accoutrements. And, hopefully, plenty of *nirwen* essence for Neeve.

I flew out of my rooms, making a quick detour to knock at Neeve's door.

"They're here," I said, already turning away.

"Have you really spent every waking hour watching for them?" she called after me.

"No," I answered, heading for the stairs.

I'd done a few other things: taken Paulette to Little Hazel, spent time in the library—though unfortunately there had been too many people present to risk opening the secret shelf—and even gone one afternoon to practice my blade work under Sir Durum's gruff tutelage. And, of course, Neeve's wedding list.

But I had also spent hours at my window. Not that I was going to admit it.

My sister caught up with me at the landing, not a bit out of breath, her hair smooth and perfect, and together we went to the great hall.

Lord Raine was already there, along with Sir Durum. I belatedly realized he must have had a servant on the lookout, too. He nodded to me and Neeve, seeming unsurprised at our presence, then gestured for the tall main doors to be opened.

Servants pushed them wide, and sunlight spilled into the hall. I wondered if the Nightshade Lord would find it unbearably bright, then remembered Thorne telling me that Dark Elves could adjust their vision according to the amount of light present.

Neeve and I followed the king out onto the flagstones just as the *Galadhir* and Lord Mornithalarion strode through the gate. They could have come through the door in the castle wall and then around, but the formal arrival suited the Nightshade Lord's station. He was a visiting royal, after all.

My gaze met Thorne's across the expanse of courtyard, and it was all I could do not to run down the stairs and embrace him.

"You haven't been apart even a week," Neeve whispered, noticing my reaction. "Do show some self-control."

I wrinkled my nose at her, but didn't argue. My sister knew what it was to be separated from one's beloved, even if she preferred to tease me about it.

The Nightshade Lord paced up the stairs and nodded to Lord Raine, sunlight sparking off his ornate silver crown.

"Greetings, mortal king," he said in his midnight-tinged voice.

I tried not to shiver at the sound, at the memory of our near-marriage. Thorne shot me a look, and Neeve poked me in the ribs, bringing me back to the present.

"Welcome, Dark Elf lord," the king said. "We are pleased you've arrived, and extend to you our utmost hospitality. Please, do not hesitate to ask for whatever you need."

"Thank you." Lord Mornithalarion inclined his head. "I'm sure whatever you've prepared will suffice."

Faint praise, but then again, the Nightshade Lord was accustomed to his lavish, magic-filled palace. In the Nightshade Court, lights could be summoned with a single word and hot water flowed from the faucets instead of having to be heated and delivered by the servants.

"I'm glad you've come, Uncle," Neeve said, stepping forward.

He took her hands. "It is an important wedding, for all of us. I would not miss the chance to stand at your side."

And further strengthen Nightshade's hold on the gateway, I thought, a touch sourly. It seemed my time among the red priests had made me cynical—or at least wary of the words of powerful men.

As if hearing my thoughts, Lord Mornithalarion released Neeve and turned to me. "Greetings, Princess Rose. I am glad to see you've safely harnessed your power."

"Thank you." I gave him a faint smile.

Though my sorcery was under control, it still had the potential to flare up and escape my grasp. I could feel it stirring in my belly, waking at the shimmer of the Dark Elves' magic.

The Nightshade Lord's gaze went to the red ring I still wore on my right hand, and he nodded. "It's good that you keep your memories close."

I'd been afraid to take it off, even with Neeve's return to the mortal world.

Thorne unexpectedly came to my side and took my hand. "You needn't fear," he said quietly to his liege. "Rose's connection to Elfhame is as strong as ever."

I glanced at him, my heartbeat fluttering. It was the closest he'd come to declaring that we had a future together. Our gazes met, and I saw a promise, still unspoken, in the gold-flecked darkness of his eyes.

"Thorne will show you and your escorts to your suite," Lord Raine said, then looked behind him, frowning as Merkis Strond stepped through the doors.

The Fiorland commander dipped her head to the king, then turned to the Dark Elf monarch. "The infamous Nightshade Lord, I presume? I've been looking forward to meeting you."

She made him a bow, graceful despite the hardened leather armor she wore. Her long golden braid swung forward, and she tossed it back behind one shoulder as she rose.

One of Lord Mornithalarion's brows rose in a sharp slash. "And you are...?" His voice was cold.

"Merkis Inga Strond, commander of the Fiorland Army," Lord Raine said, glancing at her. "Are your king and queen coming down, too?"

"No," she said lightly. "I prefer to assess potential danger on my own."

"Lord Mornithalarion is our ally," the king said with a stern look.

"He is Raine's ally, certainly," Merkis Strond said. "But Fiorland has yet to determine our relationship with the Dark Elves."

"I am not a threat to your people," the Nightshade Lord said.

"Well." Merkis Strond gave him a slow look up and down, a smile drifting across her lips. "You certainly *look* dangerous."

Was she flirting with Lord Mornithalarion? I exchanged a quick, bemused look with Neeve.

"I commend your soldierly instincts," the Dark Elf lord said. "Though I cannot say the same of your manners."

Instead of being insulted, Merkis Strond laughed. "I look forward to deepening our acquaintance, Lord Mornithalarion."

She stepped back, and Thorne released my hand, then nodded for the Nightshade Lord and his two guards to follow him into the castle.

Neeve and I followed, out of the autumn-tinged sunlight into the clammier air of the great hall. Behind us, I could hear the king attempting to scold Merkis Strond.

She merely laughed again. "While I comprehend the finer points of courtly etiquette, your highness, such things must be put aside in the face of potential danger. I'm sure you understand. Your Sir Durum would do the same."

It was true, and Lord Raine knew it, for he subsided. A moment later, the Fiorland commander strode past us, her boot heels ringing over the flagstones. She winked at me and Neeve as she passed, and I grinned back.

"Don't encourage her," Neeve said quietly.

"I like her," I said. "She's not afraid to say what she thinks—a lot like you, actually. Are you feeling protective of your uncle?"

She blinked at me. "Of course not. He can look after himself. But he's an honored guest in this castle, and should be treated as such."

In my opinion, Lord Mornithalarion was entirely too accustomed to being fawned over. Having an outspoken Fiorland warrior woman challenge him was all to the good.

"It will be entertaining to see how they get along," I said.

"Or don't." Neeve let out a sigh, sounding suddenly quite weary. "I just wish the ceremony was over so we could get on with our lives."

Her pace slowed as we began climbing the grand staircase, and I gave her a concerned look. "And get you back into Elfhame. Don't push yourself too hard. Nobody wants the bride to collapse on her wedding day. You're almost there."

"One more day. But what will you do afterwards, Rose?"

I shook my head. "I suppose I'll find out when we get there."

As ever, the answers lay just out of reach. But I thought of the promise in Thorne's eyes and smiled.

PART IV

CHAPTER 32

The wedding day dawned warm, as though summer had decided to linger a bit longer in honor of my sister's nuptials. I rose earlier than usual, earning a sleepy meow of protest from Trisk as the covers around her were dislodged, and pulled the curtains wide.

Sunlight lay over the deep green of the Darkwood, the trees moving in the breeze as though they were engaged in a slow, stately dance. In the center of the forest, the gateway waited. Anchored now, and even more securely as soon as Neeve and Kian said their vows.

"Lady Rose!" Sorche said as she stepped into my rooms carrying a breakfast tray. "You're awake."

"It's a busy day." With a smile of thanks, I took the mug of tea and a freshly baked bun from the tray.

My first task was to make sure all the flowers were still fresh, though the servants had gathered them only the day before. I had a special assortment of white blooms set aside for my sister to weave into her hair, in what was apparently a Dark Elf wedding tradition. Although we didn't have the exact blossom that grew in Elfhame, Neeve had told me that sweet woodruff would make an acceptable substitute.

Thorne and I had gone together into the Darkwood in search of that flower, which preferred to bloom in the dappled shade of the forest as opposed to the bright meadows. Somewhat like Neeve herself.

We'd gathered a brimming basket of the sweetly scented white blossoms, then lingered, trading kisses and savoring the warmth of the afternoon. The day felt suspended in honey—a slow, golden distillation where everything was right with the world.

That languid sweetness was soon gone, however, swept away by the flurry of preparing for Neeve and Kian's marriage.

It was to be held in the early afternoon, in the meadow between Castle Raine and the Darkwood. A fitting place, but not an easy one to prepare for a grand wedding. Workers had erected tables and trellises, and the gardeners had scythed paths and a wide circle for the ceremony's participants, then brought in planters filled with greenery and more flowers.

Out my bedroom window, I glimpsed servants carrying heavy benches from the great hall toward the meadow. I gulped my tea, let Sorche lace me into a serviceable gray dress, then hurried to join the flurry of activity humming through the castle. My wedding finery would come later, after I'd tended to the myriad details awaiting my attention.

I joined the maids in sorting through flowers, making sure the proper blooms were sent up to Neeve. Next, I paid a visit to the kitchens to make sure the food preparation was going well. There would be two meals: a light refreshment laid out prior to the ceremony, and then the feast afterward, which would be held in the great hall.

While I was in the kitchens, one of the maids rushed in to tell me that mice had ruined several of the tablecloths stored in the castle's cupboards, and there weren't enough to cover the extra feasting tables.

"Use sheets," I advised her, and turned to the cook's assistant who was tapping me urgently on the arm.

"Milady," she said, "we're out of spicebark for the pies! Cook says they'll be ruined if we can't get more in the next quarter-hour."

I nodded. "I'll find someone to ride to Little Hazel and scavenge some up. Tell Cook not to worry."

I hoped Geary's Alehouse had a store of extra spices. And maybe a few tablecloths we could borrow, as well.

The morning went on in that same vein, filled with minor catastrophes. I could feel my curls escaping into a frizz around my head, and before I knew it, Sorche was pulling me away from where I was helping to hang garlands in the great hall.

"Time to get ready, Lady Rose," she said.

"A bit more to the right!" I called over my shoulder, then let my maid lead me out of the hall. "How is Neeve doing?" I asked as we climbed the stairs.

"She's been very quiet all morning. More so than usual, I mean." Sorche glanced at me. "I think she's nervous."

"Well, it's a big day for her."

We reached the landing, and I halted at the sight of Merkis Strond and the Nightshade Lord engaged in a heated argument midway down the hall. She wore an embossed jerkin over dark leggings, her high boots polished to a shine and her sword at her side. In contrast to her practical garb, Lord Mornithalarion wore a flowing Dark Elf robe of deepest purple, cinched at his waist and around his arms with glittering amethysts. They stood face to face, expressions fierce, all their attention upon each other.

"How dare you," he was saying, with all the icy demeanor of an enraged Dark Elf. "To imply that I'm an ignorant—"

"I said nothing of the sort." Merkis Strond took a step forward, her face flushed with temper. "You have some peculiar ideas about how things work in the mortal world. We're not inferior, you know."

One of the Nightshade Lord's brows rose, a sharp slash of skepticism that betrayed his thoughts. "Any of our swordsmen could easily defeat— Ah!"

He ended in a yelp as Merkis Strond hooked her leg around his and gave him a none-too-gentle push that sent him staggering against the wall.

"Barbarian!" He regained his balance and stared at her.

I'd never seen Lord Mornithalarion's mask of composure crack before, and had to stifle my amusement at the look of incredulity on his face.

"I could have put you on the floor instead," Merkis Strond said, calmly straightening her silver-embossed jerkin. "But that didn't seem...polite."

I burst into outright laughter, then grabbed Sorche's arm and pulled her into the west wing corridor before Merkis Strond and the Nightshade Lord could do more than glimpse us.

"Oh, my." Sorche blinked as I hurried her along. "That was —unexpected."

"But glorious to behold." We rounded the corner and I slowed my pace. "I'd say Lord Mornithalarion has met his match."

And an unexpected one it was, too. Yet I could see how the cheerful, fierce leader of Fiorland's army and the haughty Dark Elf lord complemented one another. They might do very well together—if they didn't kill each other first.

Even so, there were plenty of obstacles ahead for a human/Dark Elf couple, as I knew all too well. My amusement faded as we reached my rooms.

"Go in," I said to Sorche. "Lay out my dress. I'll be right back after I look in on Neeve."

My maid nodded and left me to continue down the hall to my sister's door. I knocked, then went in without waiting for an answer.

"Neeve?" I called, stepping past a bucket of mostly beheaded flowers and a length of purple fabric tossed over one of her chairs.

"In here," she called from her bedroom. "Briddy is putting flowers in my hair."

My mother had insisted on sending over her lady's maid, and I'd advised Neeve to accept, pointing out that otherwise she might have to contend with my actual mother. She'd reluctantly agreed, and now stood in the center of her room, still as a statue, while Briddy wove white flowers through her elegantly braided coiffure.

I halted, taking in the sight of my sister. She wore a breathtaking dress that was clearly inspired by the gowns of the Nightshade Court, though with mortal touches like a fitted bodice and a sleek waist that dropped to a point. The material was palest lavender silk, shading at the hem and sleeves to a purple hue the deep color of ripe blackberries.

Ice-white diamonds sparkled along her neckline and waist and trimmed the edges of the gossamer scarf fastened about her throat. The scarf flowed down like wings, trailing gracefully along her back all the way to the ground.

More gems shone from her hair, along with the white blossoms Briddy was twining among the dark tresses. Instead of her golden crown, Neeve wore a circlet of jewels and flowers that flashed as it caught the light.

A princess of the Dark Elves indeed.

"You look splendid," I said.

"You don't." She frowned at me. "Please don't tell me you're wearing *that* to my wedding?"

I glanced down at my gray skirts, decorated with bits of leaves and some flour that must have come from the kitchens. My hair was an unkempt riot, and I probably had mud on my cheek.

"Well." I grinned. "I wouldn't want to outshine you today."

She let out a small laugh, the tightness about her eyes easing. "I'm serious, though. You ought to go change—the guests are beginning to gather."

I nearly told her about Nightshade and Merkis Strond, but didn't want to share such juicy gossip where my mother's maid could overhear. Instead, I came forward and gave her a careful embrace.

"I'll be back to collect you as soon as I'm ready," I said.

"Try not to take too long." The tension was back in her face. "The waiting is the worst part."

"You'll be an old married woman soon." I pressed her hands. "Don't worry, Neeve. I'm sure the ceremony will go quite well."

She nodded mutely, and I went to my rooms to change into my pale green gown. Sorche had suggested the ornate Dark Elf dress I'd been wearing when the Oracles expelled me from Elfhame, but I quickly refused. That had been my own wedding gown, when I nearly wed Lord Mornithalarion, and I didn't want any reminders of that day.

In all honesty, he probably didn't either.

It didn't take long to prepare. I even let Sorche stick a few blossoms in my hair, once she'd combed and twisted it up. Nothing as elegant as Neeve's flower-bedecked braids, of course, just a simple array of daisies.

"Now go find your escort," I said to my maid. "I'm sure Liam is looking forward to dancing with you after the ceremony."

She'd confided in me just the day before that the object of her affections was one of the villagers, and he'd promised to spend the afternoon whirling her in his arms.

She blushed, then smiled. "That he is."

We parted outside my door, and I went back to Neeve's rooms to escort the bride to her wedding. Or at least to her bridegroom. It was Fiorland tradition that the two of them walk up the aisle together, though he wasn't supposed to see her in all her splendor until that moment.

It had been a balancing act, weaving together the wedding customs of Fiorland, Raine, and Elfhame so that everyone would be satisfied with the ceremony. Of course, the only two people who really mattered were Neeve and Kian, but they were very conscious of their duties to their people.

That would make them excellent rulers, but it had also made for a complicated ceremony. As Neeve and I went down the hall together, I crossed my fingers that everything would go as smoothly as possible.

At least the day was beautiful, one of those early-autumn blessings that echoed the warmth of midsummer. Neeve and I stepped out of the great hall, and I pulled in a deep breath, inhaling the scent of sun-warmed stone underlaid with the mossy depths of the forest, the smell of spices and sizzling meat from the refreshments the kitchens had prepared.

Thorne was waiting for us at the bottom of the castle steps, and my heart glowed at the sight. He was dressed in a formal Dark Elf tunic the deep violet hue of the Nightshade Court, with a matching short cape fastened at his shoulders with silver brooches.

The tip of one pointed ear showed through the fall of his silken hair. When our gazes met, bright sparks danced in his eyes and his expression softened. I'd never seen anyone more handsome. My breath caught and I nearly tripped over my skirts.

"Pay attention," Neeve said, gripping my arm to steady me. "I'm supposed to be the distracted one, not you."

"Sorry." I shot her an apologetic glance and tried to focus on my feet as we went down the stairs, but Thorne blazed in my senses.

"The two of you need to set a wedding date," my sister murmured.

"We will." I sent her a sidelong smile. "But your marriage is the only one of importance at the moment."

When we reached the bottom of the granite steps, Thorne made Neeve one of the most elegant bows I'd ever seen. "Lady Neeve Shadrift Mallory," he said. "I hope you know that you may call upon me as *Galadhir* whenever you have need."

"Thank you," my sister said regally, then shot him a quick grin. "Don't think you'll have any less work just because I'm getting married. In fact, you might have even more."

I turned to look at her. "What do you mean?"

Thorne let out a low chuckle. "Only that she wants to foist her potential offspring onto me. Let me remind you that the *Galadhir* of the Darkwood and Erynvorn isn't a common nanny."

"Children?" I took Neeve's hands, nearly jumping up and down with excitement. "You and Kian have decided to have children?"

She regarded me calmly. "How else will the gateway remain open throughout the years?"

It was quite a change from the girl who was terrified of dying in childbirth, as her mother had. Though, if I looked closely, I could see the shadow of fear in her eyes.

"I'm glad." I squeezed her hands. "And don't worry. I'll be here for you too."

"You'd better be," she said fiercely, then sent a pointed look toward Thorne.

"First things first," I said. "I believe your bridegroom awaits."

Neeve lifted her chin, and, arms linked, the three of us strode toward the castle wall. I couldn't help but be reminded of all the times we'd spent in the Darkwood, Neeve, Thorne, and I. Our lives were intertwined, like the vine and leaf tattoo on my arm.

As we approached the door set in the outer wall, I heard the murmur of conversation, underscored by the lively sound of Master Fawkes' harp.

"Wait here," I told my sister as we halted by the arched door. "I'll go out and make sure Kian is ready, then give the signal to Master Fawkes and your father."

It was the custom in Raine that the parents make an announcement at the beginning of the ceremony. As soon as the king finished, the bard would begin the Dark Elf tune that Neeve had chosen for her entrance.

She nodded at me, her expression tightening.

"Don't worry." I brushed a kiss across her cheek. "I'll be right in the front row."

"And I'll stay until Kian fetches you," Thorne said.

"Thank you. Both of you." Neeve reached and took our hands. For a moment, the three of us stood there, bound by all the ties of kinship and love.

A burst of laughter floated over the wall. I drew in a breath and released Neeve's hand. It was time.

Thorne nodded at me, signaling that he'd join me when he could. I smiled at both of them, then tucked a wayward curl behind my ear and slipped through the door.

CHAPTER 33

K ian was waiting on the other side of the wall, dressed in his wedding finery. The blue velvet tunic made his eyes seem the color of the summer sky, and a bright gold crown encircled his head. He grinned nervously as I stepped through the door.

"Did you bring Neeve?" he asked. "Is she ready?"

"Don't worry." I patted his shoulder. "Your bride didn't decide to run away into the Darkwood."

He heaved a sigh. "I knew she wouldn't, but still...this is a big occasion for her."

"For both of you." I glanced over the seated crowd, spotting the golden-haired Fiorland delegation up front. "I'm glad your parents came."

The King and Queen of Fiorland seemed kind enough, though, other than the welcome feast, I hadn't had much interaction with them.

"They're not quite sure what to make of Neeve. Or her uncle."

I lifted a brow. "Merkis Strond seems to have the Nightshade Lord well in hand, from what I gather."

Kian laughed. "So, you've seen them, too? What an odd pairing they make—like summer and winter."

"Two sides of the same coin. Anyway, I'm going to tell Lord Raine it's time. Are you ready?"

"I think so." He tugged at his dark blue cloak, and I adjusted the gold brooch pinning it at his shoulder.

"You look splendid," I said, then kissed him on the cheek and went to alert the king.

Lord Raine was standing at the edge of the semicircle of flowering planters where Neeve and Kian would speak their vows. As I skirted the crowd, the audience quieted. I saw all my friends in attendance: Mistress Ainya seated next to Miss Groves, Sorche with her Liam. Sir Durum gave me a short nod as I passed the second row, and Prince Jenson winked at me from where the Fiorlanders were seated.

Paulette, with Donal next to her, was near the front. She'd shown some discretion in leaving off her scarlet cloak, I was glad to see. No one wanted a reminder of the red priests overshadowing the wedding. Once again, regret stabbed through me at the knowledge that all her memories of her time in Raine would be blurred, all hint of the Dark Elves' existence erased.

As I stepped to the front, the Nightshade Lord inclined his head to me in a gesture of respect. We hadn't really spoken since his arrival— I'd been too busy attending to the details of the ceremony—but he didn't seem nearly as fearsome as I'd recalled.

Master Fawkes brought his tune to a close. By the time I reached the king, everyone knew that the ceremony was about to begin.

I nodded to Lord Raine. He returned the gesture, then waited until I slipped into one of the two empty places in the front row of benches. The other place, of course, was for Thorne. I had the momentary, uncharitable, impulse to make him sit beside my mother, but gritted my teeth and scooted next to her.

It was important to show no cracks in the façade of the royal family this day, despite the fact I was still furious about what she'd done. I gave her a tight, insincere smile then turned my attention to Lord Raine as he stepped forward.

"People of Raine," he said, his voice carrying, "honored guests, thank you for coming to witness the wedding of my daughter, Princess Neeve Shadrift Mallory, to Prince Kian Leifson of Fiorland. It is an auspicious day, and we welcome the strengthened bonds between all our realms."

It was a clever way of including Elfhame, and the Nightshade Lord, without drawing overt attention to the enchanted land hidden beside our own.

Thorne slipped, quiet as a shadow, into the spot next to me and folded his hand around mine. I squeezed his fingers, my heart suddenly full to overflowing. A momentary pause fell over the gathering, the scent of flowers sweet in the air, the sound of birds chirping in the forest clear.

Then Master Fawkes began to play, the sweet and serene notes lilting from his harp. The crowd stood, and everyone turned to watch Neeve and Kian come up the aisle between the benches.

Sunlight glittered on the diamonds edging Neeve's gown and scarf and struck gold sparks from Kian's crown. As they paced regally forward, they looked as if they'd just stepped from the pages of legend: a beautiful Dark Elf princess and her handsome prince.

The two of them had overcome so much, and had found their match in each other. No matter how much they might have resisted the outcome at first, this moment felt entirely fated.

As they passed the front row, Neeve looked over at me. I grinned at her, and the corner of her mouth lifted in a slight smile. My vision blurred with happy tears, and I hastily swiped them away as she and Kian came to a halt before Lord Raine.

The king began the ceremony with a traditional decree to the bride and groom to respect and honor one another. The couple spoke their vows, and I started crying again as Neeve pledged her heart to Kian, and he did the same.

Then, as arranged, the Nightshade Lord stepped forward, and the king moved aside. With Lord Mornithalarion presiding, Neeve and Kian gave each other rings—a simple gold band for him, a diamond set in an intricate Dark Elf setting for her.

They clasped wrists in an echo of the Dark Elf binding, and I tried not to look at the Nightshade Lord. Beside me, Thorne squeezed my hand gently, as if he knew I was thinking of my disastrous near-marriage.

"Will you speak the words of binding known to our people?" Nightshade asked, turning to Neeve.

"I will," she said.

The Dark Elf lord asked the same of Kian.

"I will," he said, his gaze never leaving Neeve.

I bit my lip, recalling that the Dark Elf rune was very complicated. Would Kian be able to say it correctly? What happened if he didn't?

Lord Mornithalarion raised his hand to hover over the bride and groom's clasped wrists.

"Speak it now, together," he said.

"*Gwedhyocuilvorn,*" they said in perfect unison.

The blue light of Elvish magic shone from the Nightshade Lord's hand, encircling Neeve and Kian's wrists. I felt a resonance, a vibration, as if a bell had rung, deeper than mortal hearing.

Startled, I glanced around me, but none of the other humans seemed to have felt it.

Thorne leaned close, his breath tickling my ear.

"Elfhame approves," he whispered, so softly I barely heard.

So, it seemed I was still bound to that land. In fact, I could feel the leaf and vine on my left elbow itching slightly, as if to remind me it was there.

Calma, I thought at it, little caring that I used the red priest's word. I was a mix of two worlds, two magics, and as long as I could control my power, it didn't matter what rune or chant I used.

Lord Raine stepped forward to stand beside the Nightshade Lord.

"The vows have been spoken," the king said.

"The promises made." Lord Mornithalarion inclined his head ever so slightly, a reminder that more than just Neeve and Kian were bound together.

"We stand as witness to this joining." Lord Raine smiled, a rare expression. "May it be long and prosperous!"

The crowd stood, cheering and clapping, and Kian pulled Neeve into his arms and kissed her. Thorne slipped his arm around me, and I leaned against him, nearly sagging with relief. It was done. My sister had wed Prince Kian of Fiorland, and the gateway between the realms was secure.

Jaunty music struck up, Master Fawkes now joined by flute and drum and vielle. The crowd began clapping in time as Neeve and Kian finally stopped kissing. He grinned at her, then, taking hands, they began a whirling dance back down the aisle that was apparently a long-standing Fiorland tradition.

Neeve had confessed to me that it made her dizzy, but I'd advised her to just look into Kian's eyes and all would be well.

"As long as I don't fall over," she'd said.

"Don't worry. The guests will think you're giddy with happiness. Or maybe drunk."

She'd made a face at me, and we both laughed—but as the couple spun past, I saw that her gaze was locked with Kian's. I held my breath, worried they'd crash into the guests, but he knew what he was doing, and navigated them safely past the benches.

The King and Queen of Fiorland followed, holding hands and merely skipping a little rather than whirling. Lord Raine waltzed Mama elegantly after them. The Nightshade Lord glanced at me, but I rather desperately clung to Thorne's arm. With a faint smile, he turned away and instead held his hand out to Merkis Strond.

She grinned and then pulled the Dark Elf lord close, whirling him around with as much enthusiasm as Kian had danced with Neeve. I glimpsed an instant of startled surprise in his dark eyes. Then he threw his head back and laughed, a full-throated sound that left both Thorne and me blinking in surprise.

Once the royals cleared the aisle, the crowd dispersed—some dancing, some twirling about with their friends and families, and the rest content to simply stroll back toward the castle.

"We did it," I said, leaning into Thorne's embrace.

"In all honesty, *they* did," he said, his voice warm. "But I know what you mean. It's been quite a journey."

It had. But we'd nearly reached the end.

"Thorne..." I turned to look at him, ready to speak all the hope in my heart.

My happiness was shattered by the clang of a bell ringing from the high tower, stridently sounding the alarm.

Castle Raine was under attack.

CHAPTER 34

T he wedding crowd surged for the castle walls. Benches overturned and the planters filled with flowers were knocked over, spilling their blossoms and dirt. Parents grabbed their children, amidst the commotion of cries and shouting.

"Soldiers, to your weapons!" Sir Durum bellowed, waving for his warriors to make haste.

The Nightshade Lord, Merkis Strond at his side, dashed for the main gates, trailed by his two guards. I looked wildly around for Paulette, but without her red cloak, I couldn't spot her in the crowd.

"We must secure the hidden door," Thorne said, grabbing my hand.

I nodded, and we ran the opposite direction, away from the panicked crush of people and toward the tiny door tucked into a nook in the granite wall.

It was a secret entrance, known to only a few. Neeve and I had used it for years to get to the Darkwood. Heart pounding, Thorne and I tumbled through it into the little garden shed on the other side.

We secured the stout wooden bar across the door. Raising his hand, Thorne spoke an Elvish rune. A flash of blue light made me blink, and I glanced at him.

"The door will remain hidden and sealed until I unbind it," he said. "No enemies will enter the castle this way."

"It has to be the red priests," I gasped, wiping cobwebs from my skirts. "But how?"

"I don't know." Thorne's voice was tight, his expression forbidding. "The Darkwood should have attacked them the moment they set foot in the forest. Somehow—though it seems impossible—they must have nullified the wards of protection."

"You didn't feel anything?"

"Not particularly. I didn't sleep well and have been uneasy all day— but I thought it was simply worry for Neeve, and hope that all would go well for her wedding."

Instead, disaster had struck.

We gained the castle, slipping in through the door near the kitchens, then hurried to the great hall. The clamor of fear-filled voices filled the room. At least the harsh clang of the bell had stopped.

The hall was packed, but Thorne and I sidled around until we were near the head table's dais. All the royals were clustered there: Lord Raine and Mama, the Fiorlanders, Nightshade, and—I was relieved to see—Kian and Neeve. Off to the side, Sir Durum and Merkis Strond spoke together, expressions grave.

"Quiet!" Lord Raine held up his hands.

Slowly, the crowd subsided.

"As some of you may have guessed," the king said, "Raine has been invaded by a force of red priests."

People gasped, and cries of disbelief rippled through the hall. Thorne and I exchanged looks of dismay.

"This should not have happened," Sir Durum said, in a low enough voice his words didn't carry. "Portknowe is well guarded."

"They didn't come through Portknowe," Lord Raine said tersely, then lifted his voice again. "Word has come from a farm to the west that was burned by the red priests. Their forces are approaching. We have little time. Gather your families and make sure everyone is safely within the walls. Those of you who can fight, meet Sir Durum in the courtyard in ten minutes."

"A force of fire-wielding priests," I whispered.

My heart turned to ice as I guessed who it might be: my father, Ser Naldi, and the senior priests skilled in casting battle magics. The granite walls of Castle Raine would hold them at bay...for a time. But I'd seen fireballs eat through stone, and my heart sank. The battle ahead would be hard-fought.

As the great hall emptied, Lord Raine beckoned for us to join him on the dais. With heavy steps, I did, Thorne at my side. Behind the king, nearly hidden by the wide skirts of Mama's satin gown, stood a boy and a girl. Their hands were clasped tightly together, their faces and clothing streaked with ash.

The acrid stench of *esfirenda* stung my nose, and I drew in a shaky breath.

"These brave children escaped the conflagration at their farm, freed the horses, and rode to Castle Raine to give us warning," Lord Raine said. "All of Raine owes them a great debt. Otherwise, I fear the red priests would have taken us by surprise."

"From the west, you say?" Jarl Eiric asked.

The boy nodded, his eyes wide with the aftermath of terror.

"There's nowhere on the coast they could have landed," Sir Durum said. "It's all cliffs."

"If a ship could land one of their boats, though?" Merkis Strond asked. "A small group could come ashore."

The king shook his head. "My captain is correct—the cliffs are sheer. Not even a small force could invade from the west."

"And yet they did," the King of Fiorland said. "How? I believed us safe here in your kingdom."

Lord Raine's expression grew hard. "We can argue over the details later. Right now, we have a battle on our hands."

"My lord." Jarl Eiric turned to his king. "You and the queen must flee. If the priests truly are coming from the west, then the road to Portknowe should be clear. You can reach your ship and return safely to Fiorland."

"No." Merkis Strond shook her head. "If even a single fire priest has circled to the south, it would put our monarchs in grave danger. It's safer for them to stay here, in the castle."

Jarl Eiric scowled at her, but didn't argue.

"I'll go rouse the Darkwood," Thorne said. "It will help us fight the red priests."

I clutched his arm, wishing I could beg him to stay at my side. But he was the *Galadhir*, and must do what he could to aid the kingdom.

The Nightshade Lord nodded. "I will come with you. Perhaps there is enough time to bring back reinforcements from our own people."

"I fear not." Thorne's voice was strained. "I cannot raise the Darkwood's defenses and also open the gateway. I am sorry, my lord."

"Don't you think the Dark Elves will be better allies than a bunch of trees?" Jarl Eiric asked scornfully.

"The Darkwood is more than trees," Thorne replied. "Drakes and basilisks and wolves will come to my call."

"Still, I hardly think—"

"There's no time." I stepped forward. "When the red priests attack, the battle could be over in minutes. We need the Nightshade Lord's power *here* if we're to have any chance against Galtus Celcio."

"Rose is right," my sister said, sounding far too calm. "With the time slip between the realms, reinforcements from Elfhame wouldn't arrive soon enough to save us. Those of us here with magic will bring what power we can to the battle."

I nodded, my mind shying from the thought of attacking my own father.

And where was Paulette? I glanced about the empty hall, realizing I hadn't seen her since the wedding. She'd need to be put under guard. Though Donal wouldn't go so far as to arrest her, I hoped he had the presence of mind to keep a close eye upon her.

"We must all prepare for the battle to come," Lord Raine said. "Sir Durum, I'll see you in the courtyard momentarily."

Lord Mornithalarion turned to Merkis Strond with a tight smile. "It seems I will have the honor of fighting by your side, lady."

"Indeed," she said, meeting his gaze with no trace of her usual boisterous humor.

The people on the dais began to disperse. I turned to Thorne and clasped him tightly about the waist.

"Be careful," I said, inhaling the scent of him—moss and cedar and Dark Elf magic.

"I beg the same of you." He held me close, shadows of anguish in his eyes. "After I rouse the Darkwood, I'll come find you."

I blinked back tears, my throat tight. It would be difficult to defeat a cohort of *esfirenda*-wielding priests. But in addition to Thorne and the Darkwood, we had magic of our own: Neeve, her uncle and his guards, and my fire sorcery.

"If it's too dangerous to approach the castle, wait for me in the forest," I said.

"I cannot promise to let you fight alone." He stared down into my eyes.

After a moment, I gave a nod. Were our positions reversed, I knew I'd do whatever it took to reach his side.

He dipped his head, our lips meeting in a fierce, desperate kiss that was over all too soon.

"I love you," I whispered as he stepped back.

"And I love you, Rose." He squeezed my hand.

Then he was gone, and Sir Durum stood before me, full of questions about the range of the fireballs, their intensity, and what other attacks the red priests might cast. I answered as best I could, and he gave me a gruff pat on the shoulder.

"We'll put you and the other magic-wielders atop the walls, near the archers," he said. "Best go put on some armor."

I glanced down at my elegant green gown. From wedding to battle in what felt like an instant. It was hard to believe we'd been standing in the meadow a scant fifteen minutes ago, clapping as Neeve and Kian danced down the aisle.

"I'm sorry," I said to my sister as we hurried out of the great hall together. "You deserved a celebration. Not this."

"At least Kian and I are married," she said, her voice strained. "That's all that really matters."

"If everything goes wrong..." I glanced at her. "Get Thorne to transport you to Elfhame. You should be safe there."

"And what of you?" She gave me a cool look, though I could see the edge of panic in her eyes. "You deserve a long and happy life too, Rose."

I wasn't so sure.

"It's my fault the priests are here." And I couldn't help thinking that the only way to defeat my father was to put myself directly in harm's way.

Would Galtus Celcio cast *esfirenda* at his own daughter? If he hesitated for even a moment, I might be able to blast him first. It was a dreadful thought, but then, we were in a dreadful situation. By marching on Castle Raine, the warder of the red priests had made himself my enemy—no matter our shared blood.

"Will you help me change out of this?" Neeve shook her gauzy, glittering skirts at me as we neared our rooms.

"Of course."

I followed her into her suite, my fingers cold and clumsy as I assisted her. No sooner was her gown off, than she began pulling on her leather armor.

"I'll meet you on the walls," I said, turning to go make my own transformation from princess to warrior.

"Rose..."

I halted at the doorway and looked back at her, the pale, reserved sister I'd come to cherish. Her eyes were filled with determination. And fear.

"You're thinking of the vision," I said.

I knew it, because I was too. How could we not, when a battle full of fire and magic was nearly upon us?

She gave me a tight nod. "Whatever happens, I hope you know I'd never attack you."

"Or I you."

Our gazes locked, as if our bond could erase the image of us facing one another in combat, flame and blue-lit sword at the ready.

Maybe the vision hadn't meant what it seemed. Fate didn't always make sense, but I knew one thing: there was no way Neeve and I would end up on opposite sides of this battle.

Back in my rooms, I shucked my gown and quickly donned the old training clothes I kept in the back of my wardrobe. The leather jerkin and trousers fit comfortably, and I was glad to have them. There was a weapons case under my bed, and I pulled it out. It contained my throwing knives—a grudging gift from Sir Durum—and my trusty old dagger.

The black sword my father gave me had stayed in Parnese. Although I'd worn it in the temple, I hadn't wanted to bring anything that smacked of the Twin Gods back with me to Raine. I'd been thinking to ask Sir Durum for a sword after we got through the wedding. Too late now. My smaller blades would have to suffice.

I strapped the knives to my forearms and belted the dagger at my waist, then pulled the last flowers out of my hair and tied my curls back. I was ready to face the red priests.

The upper corridors were eerily quiet as I left my rooms. The heels of my boots rapped against the granite floor as I picked up my pace, echoing the rapid beating of my heart. Galtus Celcio could attack at any moment.

At the landing, I nearly collided with Donal, who was pelting up the stairs.

"Rose!" He grabbed my elbows to steady me, his eyes wide with fear. "You must come—it's Paulette!"

"What happened?" My breath caught as I thought of any number of scenarios, none of them good.

"I tried to stop her, but she took a horse from the stables. It threw her in the meadow, though, and I'm afraid..." His voice was jagged with panic. "Please, come help her. No one else will."

They wouldn't; she was a red priest. The enemy. And she'd tried to flee the castle.

"Take me to her," I said, praying I'd have time to get Paulette back inside the walls before Galtus Celcio attacked.

Donal pivoted and ran down the stairs. I was right behind him as we raced through the back hallways of Castle Raine. We burst out one of the side doors. I followed him through the gardens, gasping for breath, then through the door in the walls and out into the meadow.

Some distance away, a horse stood. Beyond it, a figure lay on the ground, her scarlet cloak puddled around her like blood.

"Paulette!" I cried, forcing myself to go faster.

I dropped to my knees beside her and grabbed her hand. She opened her eyes.

"Rose..." she said. "I'm sorry."

I felt a horrible, sharp pain at the back of my skull, and then everything went black.

CHAPTER 35

My head pounded terribly, and for a confused moment I thought I heard my father's voice. Then memory returned in an icy blast of fear, and I opened my eyes.

I was in a small tent, the canvas ceiling sloping up a few inches above my face. When I tried to sit, I discovered my hands were bound in front of me. My ankles were tied together too, and I thrashed for a moment in panic.

"Calm down, Rose," Paulette said.

I turned my head sharply, causing a stab of pain, and saw her sitting cross-legged at the door of the tent.

With a deep breath, I managed to roll onto my side then awkwardly rock myself into a seated position. Judging by the angle of the afternoon light, perhaps an hour had passed. I had to get back to the castle.

"Let me go this instant," I demanded, thrusting my bound hands toward her.

She pressed her lips together and gave a shake of her head. "If I do that, I'm afraid you'll try escaping back to Castle Raine. The warder wants you here, with us, where you'll be safe."

Safe? My lips twisted bitterly. The last place I wanted to be was among the red priests.

Despite my nerves screaming at me to *run, fight, hide*, I took two breaths to steady myself.

"Did you know that Galtus Celcio would follow us to Raine?" I asked tightly.

"Not...precisely." Her gaze skittered away from mine. "He didn't think it wise to tell me much about his plan. Only that I should be at the ready to do my duty to the priesthood, and make sure you were on the correct side when the time came."

"So, you kidnapped me." With Donal's cooperation, of course.

He was a traitor to his kingdom—had turned against Raine right under my nose—and I hadn't had the wisdom to see it, let alone do anything about it. I inwardly cursed myself for my blindness. Despite everything, I'd still been too trusting.

"You betrayed me," I said tightly.

"I saved you." Paulette stood. "I'm going to tell the warder you're awake. Don't even think about leaving this tent. Ser Naldi is right outside."

She ducked out, and I wanted to scream. The flames in my belly glowed hot. I glanced down at my waist, unsurprised to see they'd taken my dagger. Thankfully, I could feel that my throwing knives were still strapped to my forearms. Given enough time, I could probably wriggle one down into my hands. Time, unfortunately, was something I feared I didn't have.

Could I cast a fireball, despite my bound hands? It would be much harder to control, but maybe I could blast a hole in the canvas wall.

And then what? I was hobbled, hands and feet. Even if I got out of the tent, I couldn't flee.

No, I'd have to wait until my father untied me. Then I'd try to fling fire everywhere and run. We couldn't be that far from the forest. Maybe Lord Raine had even sent a search party to find me!

Even as hope flared in my chest, it was doused by cold reality. It would be far too dangerous for anyone to venture beyond the castle walls. Armor and swords were no match for a blast of *esfirenda*.

"Hello, Rose," my father said, pulling aside the tent flap.

Ser Naldi, hovering at his shoulder, gave me a narrow-eyed look.

My father appeared as self-assured as ever, showing no sign he'd undertaken a recent sea journey, somehow breached the western coast of Raine, and marched partway across the country. Once, I'd taken the arrogant look in his eyes for calm strength. I'd thought his warmth toward me had been genuine. I knew better now.

"How did you do it?" I asked, dispensing with the formalities. Galtus Celcio deserved no politeness from me. "How did you manage to get this far into Raine undetected?"

"Always so forthright." He let out a low chuckle. "It's refreshing."

Ser Naldi frowned. "She doesn't need to know anything."

"Why not? The Twin Gods favor us." My father smiled at me. "We melted a ramp into the cliffs."

My eyes widened. Such a thing would have taken an immense amount of power, yet my father seemed unaffected.

"How?" I asked, my mouth dry.

"As I said, the gods are pleased to aid us. Your initiates have proven quite helpful in that regard, though young Shamsan might need some time to recover."

I recoiled. "You brought them to Raine?"

The students I'd taught to cast *esfirenda* were now a weapon at my throat, threatening everything I loved. I shuddered in horror at what I'd unwittingly done.

"Of course I did. Along with everyone else able to summon the cleansing fire. Your new chant is quite effective, my dear."

"How many?" I whispered.

"Eighteen. The ship was quite uncomfortably cramped, but they endured in the name of the Twins."

Eighteen *esfirenda*-wielding red priests, pointed at the walls of Castle Raine. I bit the side of my cheek to keep from moaning and stiffened my spine to keep from crumpling into a ball. I felt sick with despair.

My thoughts desperately battered the insides of my skull. *Do something, do something,* they shrilled. The flames churned in my belly.

"I won't help you attack Raine," I said grimly.

With a gentle smile, the warder shook his head. "I don't need your cooperation. Your presence is all that's required. Though it would be better if you'd come under your own power instead of being carried like a sack of grain."

"Why?" I asked. He must know I wouldn't join the assault upon my home.

What reason could he have had to kidnap me? I certainly didn't believe Paulette's claim I'd be safer with the priests. She might trust Galtus Celcio, but I knew that he always had an ulterior motive.

"You will amplify our efforts, lending even more divine power to our conquest." His voice rang with sincerity. "You are the conduit of the Sister's power."

I shook my head violently, my headache roaring back in full force. Surely he didn't believe that. "I'm not."

"You needn't be afraid," he said, his tone softening as if he were speaking to a child. "I know it's a heavy burden, but Her power won't harm you."

"That's because I'm not her avatar!"

He gave me a pitying look. "I was there both times the divine power moved through you and gifted your student, Sera Pecheur, with newfound ability. The Sister's fire burns in her now, though not as strongly as it does within your other initiates."

I stared at him. Even if I insisted it had been *me* helping Lena, not some red-haired goddess, he wouldn't believe me. I desperately cast about for something that might change his mind.

"I failed the test. Surely that's not a sign of the Twin Gods' favor."

"That was the Sister claiming you for her own. If she hadn't, you'd be bound to her Twin instead." He smiled. "Everything has come out according to divine plan. Even now, Castle Raine is filled with those who would oppose me. All in one place. It will not take us long to subdue them."

Another wave of despair washed over me. The King of Raine, and Neeve, his only heir. The Fiorland monarchs and two of their sons. The Nightshade Lord, though that was an enemy Galtus Celcio wasn't even aware of. All gathered together for the wedding.

If I were inclined to believe in the power of the Twin Gods, it would seem fated.

"How far are we from the castle?" I braced myself for the answer.

"Half a mile, perhaps less." His expression hardened. "I expect you to help negotiate the terms of surrender, of course."

I stared defiantly at him. "They won't surrender."

"Oh, they will. They always do. But we're wasting time." He glanced at his lieutenant. "Free her feet, but not her hands. And keep a close watch on her at all times."

Ser Naldi gave the warder a sharp nod. Without another word, my father straightened and strode away.

"Don't try anything," Ser Naldi said as he untied the rope binding my ankles.

"What can I do?" I held out my bound hands and tried to project helplessness. It wasn't hard, though the beginnings of a plan sparked through me.

His lips thinned and he gestured for me to exit the tent. I scooted forward, squinting as I emerged into an afternoon that had no right to be so warm and lovely.

I'm sorry, Neeve, I thought, berating myself for ever trusting Donal. My sister must be worried; they all must be. At least Thorne didn't know I'd been taken hostage by the red priests. Yet.

As soon as I was out of the tent, a harried-looking servant began dismantling it. I glanced around, dismayed to see so many red-robed figures. Eighteen, Galtus Celcio had said, plus himself and Paulette, so twenty *esfirenda*-casting priests, against Neeve, Thorne, and the Nightshade Lord.

Dread churned in my belly.

Even with the Darkwood's help, the red priests held the clear advantage.

Not if you incinerate them all on the spot, my little voice said.

Even if I could stomach the idea—which I couldn't—I simply didn't have that kind of power. The only time such raw force had run through me was when my fire sorcery finally burst free in the Nightshade Court.

Besides, I couldn't heartlessly destroy so many human lives. The memory of Ser Pietro burning to death made bile rise in my throat.

It's not wanton destruction if you're saving Raine, my little voice argued. *You've made sacrifices before.*

I had—but it was one thing to risk my own life for the people I loved, and another thing entirely to murder a dozen people.

There must be another way to deflect the priests. My head pounded as my thoughts whirled, trying to find some answer.

One of the red-shrouded figures came over to me, then lowered the hood of her cloak. It was Jenni.

"Look at you." Her lip curled in scorn. "Bound like some kind of petty criminal. You owe us better than that, Sera Celcio."

"That name was never mine." I met her gaze. "I owe you nothing."

With a sniff, she turned away, even as Lena came hurrying up.

"Rose! You're here." Then her gaze went to my bound hands, and her expression fell.

I gave her a small, bitter smile. "Not willingly, as you can see."

"But..." She glanced about the small camp, now mostly packed up, then back to me. "You're the warder's daughter. Don't you want to help him?"

"Help him destroy my family and home? I don't think so."

"Oh." She looked down at the ground. "I didn't realize... On the journey over, he made it sound as though you were just waiting for us to arrive so you could join us in our glorious victory."

Galtus Celcio had spun so many lies that it seemed he was starting to believe them himself.

"Enough talk," Ser Naldi said. "The carts are waiting."

"I'd like to ride with Sera Celcio, please," Lena said.

He studied her a moment, then gave a short nod. "I'll escort you both."

So much for escaping the lieutenant's watchful gaze.

I stumbled, my head still pounding, over to where two ox-drawn carts waited. They were simple farm vehicles, lacking seating. Ten priests, two servants, and assorted supplies in the back of each would be crowded, but as the carts filled with red-robed figures, no one complained.

I thought briefly of the two children who'd brought word of the invasion to the castle. Clearly the priests had stolen what they wanted from the farms along the way. My breath tightened as I desperately hoped they hadn't left a charred path of death and destruction in their wake.

Galtus Celcio and his followers must be stopped.

Paulette waved from the back of the nearest cart, and Lena veered to meet her. The two of them helped me awkwardly clamber in—not an easy task without the use of my hands. The priests grudgingly made room for me, shooting me cold looks. All except one, whose smile was a mere shadow of his once-brilliant joy.

"Hello," Shamsan said. His voice was hoarse, as though he'd been shouting for hours.

"Shamsan." I gave him a closer look, noting the ashen hue of his skin, the dullness in his eyes. "Are you well?"

You shouldn't care about any of them, my wicked voice said. *They are your enemies.*

Except I couldn't forget that they'd been my friends, my peers, my students.

My gaze went to the tall figure stepping up to the driver's bench seat. The sun struck red sparks from his auburn hair. Galtus Celcio, warder of the red priests, man who had fathered me.

That was my enemy.

As the cart lurched into motion, I braced myself against the wooden side and prepared to summon my fire. The heat in my belly sparked, but could I contain and direct it without using my hands? In the past I'd been able to call down flames without using gestures, or the proper chants, but they hadn't been the least bit under my control.

Firenda, I thought, twisting my body so the other priests couldn't see my bound hands. *Come, fire.*

A faint flicker or orange shone between my hands, and my heart leaped. Maybe I could simply burn my bonds away. Frowning with concentration, I tried to coax the little flame up to perch on the rope knotted about my wrists.

The flame snuffed out. I tried again, but the weak flame refused to do more than glow slightly between my fingers.

Subtlety has never been your strength, my little voice reminded me.

Very well. I'd have to try something more dramatic. I glanced about, trying to keep my expression innocent. Not much wood showed in the crowded cart, except for the back gate. If I set it on fire, maybe it would distract the priests long enough for me to get away.

I glanced at the dark line of the forest. Still too far away, but as soon as I saw my chance, I'd take it. The cart jolted up and down, dipping between the low hills, then rising again. Each time, the turrets of Castle Raine loomed closer, silhouetted against the sky. I stared at the Darkwood, wondering if Thorne had been able to summon the creatures that dwelt within, and when they'd attack.

I was under no illusion I'd be safe from them. Despite the oaths I'd sworn to the forest, I'd been menaced by boglins and basilisks, drakes and dire wolves. I only hoped they'd be able to thin the ranks of the priests and help turn the battle to Raine's advantage.

With a pang, I glanced at Paulette and Lena beside me, Shamsan slumped wearily in the corner. I didn't want them to die. Nor Jenni, as unpleasant as she might be, who'd chosen to ride in the other cart.

Under cover of the swaying vehicle, I flexed and wiggled my hands. I could feel my right knife loosening where it was strapped to my forearm. If my fire distraction didn't succeed, my throwing blades would be my next line of attack.

When I judged we were close enough to the forest, I took a deep breath and reached for my fire.

Esfera to quera quemar, I thought fiercely, thrusting my tied hands toward the gate of the cart.

To my relief, the hot fire of *esfirenda* shot from my splayed fingers. The nearest priests shouted in alarm as flames splattered against the wood. The edge of Ser Naldi's scarlet cloak caught fire. With a lurch, Galtus Celcio stopped the cart.

I'd been waiting for that moment. I tumbled over the edge and began running for the shelter of the trees.

CHAPTER 36

I staggered over hummocks of grass, my tied hands affecting my balance as I pushed myself toward the dark fringe of trees ahead.

"Catch her!" Galtus Celcio cried.

A heartbeat later, I heard him call the chant to extinguish fire, but I couldn't risk glancing back. *I must press forward, I must—*

Someone collided with me from behind. I fell heavily, unable to break my fall, the breath knocked from my lungs. Gasping, I rolled over to see Ser Naldi standing over me. His eyes snapped with fury.

"Get up." He caught my arm and dragged me to standing, then pulled me back toward the carts.

The one I'd been riding in was smoking slightly in back, but the *esfirenda* was gone, snuffed out by the warder, leaving a few blackened boards behind.

"Rose." Galtus Celcio strode over to me. "Must I tie your feet again? Or knock you unconscious?"

I shook my head. I'd misjudged my own strength, and that of the warder. There was no escape. Hopelessness washed over me, but I fought it back. Whatever happened when we reached the castle walls, I needed to be as mobile and aware as possible.

"Then behave." He nodded to his lieutenant. "Put her back in the cart. But any more signs of rebellion, and you have my permission to hit her over the head."

So much for having a loving father. I dropped my gaze to the dry yellow grasses beneath our feet, hiding my desperation. When Ser Naldi shoved me back into the cart, I meekly obeyed. I couldn't help the defenders of Castle Raine if I were trussed up and lying insensible in the cart.

The warder climbed back onto the driver's seat, and the two carts creaked into motion again.

"You shouldn't have," Paulette whispered to me.

I turned my face away and gave no answer. The castle loomed ahead, and with it my despair.

When we'd nearly reached the granite walls, Galtus Celcio directed the second cart to circle to the north, while we veered south toward the main gates. Clearly, he planned to surround the castle with his forces. Even as he discussed terms of surrender at the front, the red priests would be trying to breach the castle through the back.

I had to warn them—though surely Sir Durum had set a watch all around the castle, plus warriors at the small door in the wall. That was on the Darkwood side, which, if Thorne had successfully roused the forest, would prove dangerous territory for the red priests.

I thought briefly of the secret tunnel leading from the castle cellar out to the Darkwood. If Castle Raine fell, I hoped my loved ones could escape and flee into Elfhame.

My heart twisted at the realization that I might never see them again.

Don't forget your vision, my little voice said. *You'll face Neeve in battle soon enough.*

I clenched my hands, nearly numb from being bound, fearing the voice was right. Although I'd never attack my sister. No matter what Galtus Celcio might demand.

All too soon, the front gates of Castle Raine came into view. The breath caught in my throat. It seemed foolish, that two carts full of red-robed priests could pose such a dire threat to the fortress of Castle Raine. And yet the power of *esfrenda* could take down entire armies.

According to the whispers, Galtus Celcio had conquered Caliss with fewer than a dozen priests.

The portcullis was down, iron spikes biting into the road. Behind it, the heavy battle doors were closed, which I'd never seen shut in all my time at the castle. Iron and thick wood would slow the priests— but not stop them.

Atop the walls, the defenders of Castle Raine were gathered. I squinted, picking out the figures of Neeve and the Nightshade Lord among the archers, along with Kian, Prince Jenson, and Merkis Strond. The king and the Fiorland monarchs were safely out of sight, and Sir Durum was doubtless down in the courtyard with his foot soldiers.

Galtus Celcio halted the cart, well out of arrow range, and directed everyone except the servants to climb out. Even Shamsan, despite his obvious exhaustion, moved to do the warder's bidding.

Ten priests, their scarlet robes shining in the afternoon sun. And me, their unwilling captive.

I nearly lost my balance as my feet hit the ground, but Lena and Paulette steadied me, one on either side. Emotions tangled in my chest, gratitude and fear and anguish, making it hard to breathe.

My father strode around the side of the cart, carrying a belt and ornate scabbard.

"You left this behind," he said, holding it out.

Ice went through me as I recognized the black sword of the Sister. I shook my head and tried to back away, but Paulette dug her fingers into my arm.

"I don't want it," I said hoarsely.

Ser Naldi glanced at the warder. "It's unwise to give her a blade."

"Her hands are bound," Galtus Celcio said. "Never fear, Castin— the Sister is on our side."

"But I'm not." I glared at my father and held my arms tightly against my body to prevent him from belting the sword on.

"It doesn't matter." He forced my hands up and, with Ser Naldi's help, cinched the belt around my waist. The blade dragged at my side, pulling me off balance. I hadn't recalled it being so heavy.

"Paulette, come with us," the warder commanded. "The rest of you, stay back. But be ready to cast *esfirenda* at my command."

I glanced at the defenders on the wall and swallowed my panic. *They won't die,* I tried to reassure myself.

My father prodded me forward. With him and Paulette on either side, I reluctantly stepped toward the gates.

"Stop here," Galtus Celcio said, when we were still several paces from the portcullis.

The moment we halted, an arrow came whizzing at us. The warder flicked his fingers, and it burst into flame before it reached us. The ashes drifted away on the wind.

"Another arrow, and Princess Rose will pay the price," he called.

I could see Kian gesture sharply, and the nocked bows trained upon us lowered. I glanced over at my father, wondering if he truly meant to make a show of hurting me in front of my true family. I knew that the warder of the red priests was capable of terrible things, but I must give them warning.

"Beware, at the back of the castle!" I shouted.

Galtus Celcio turned to me and took my chin in a hard grip. His eyes met mine, and I stared back defiantly.

"Another word, and I'll have you gagged," he said, his voice soft with menace, then let me go.

I pulled in a wavering breath, trying not to show my fear.

"Release Rose to us," my sister called, her voice carrying sharply. "Do so, and depart Raine, and we will let you leave unharmed."

Galtus Celcio threw his head back and laughed. "You're in no position to bargain," he said, once his amusement faded. "Open the gates, and I'll let you live."

I shook my head in warning, but Neeve was too wise to take him at his word.

"We will not surrender," she said, then exchanged a quick look with her uncle.

In unison, they called out an Elvish rune. Bright blue light arced forward, two bolts of magic speeding toward Galtus Celcio's chest. I caught my breath, halfway between a cheer and a gasp.

"*Arder a sacar!*" the warder cried, stumbling back and flinging up his hands. I could hear the surprise in his voice.

Despite his being caught unaware, his red flames bloomed, intersecting the Elvish attack. Scarlet and blue met in a crackle of power. The opposing magics flared, then were all extinguished in a plume of acrid smoke. I slumped in disappointment.

His expression dark with anger, Galtus Celcio closed his fingers around my arm and hauled me back to where the other priests waited. Paulette scurried beside us, taking her place in the line of attackers.

"You lied to me, Rose." His voice was hard. "What magic is this?"

When I didn't answer, he leaned close, eyes boring into mine.

"It's from the forest, isn't it? I thought I sensed a strangeness here before. As soon as Castle Raine falls, I'll burn your Darkwood down, tree by tree, until I discover everything. *Everything*."

I winced and looked away. The red priests must be stopped, at all costs.

With a disgusted sound, the warder released me and turned to his followers.

"Make ready," he cried. "Concentrate your *esfirenda* in the middle of the gates."

"No," I whispered.

The eight of them, led by Ser Naldi, stepped forward. Lena shot me a glance, then looked away.

"Now," Galtus Celcio said.

"*Esfera to quera quemar!*" the priests cried, hands thrusting forward.

The red-hot fire of *esfirenda* shot toward the walls, to be met with a shield of blue magic. I swallowed back a shout of triumph. With a sizzle, the flames dripped down, leaving the gates untouched but igniting the dry grasses beside the road.

Although the attack hadn't succeeded, I was dismayed to see that Lena's casting was strong enough to cause damage. The only one who faltered was Shamsan, whose fire fluctuated from orange to yellow before spattering a few feet short of the gates.

Arrows flew at us, but any that were carried close enough by the wind, my father turned to cinders. Atop the walls, I saw Nightshade and my sister, hands outlined in blue magic as they continued to protect the gates.

"Again," my father said tightly. "Join them, Paulette. Shamsan, set firebreaks."

I glanced at the patches of *esfirenda* on the ground. Already the road was lined with fire. Shamsan cast a simple scorch, burning the grasses around us, then sending the flames outward. We stood in a blackened circle, while the field burned.

More searing fireballs rained toward the castle to be deflected by the Dark Elves' magic, and Galtus Celcio turned to me. I shrank from the look of rage in his eyes—but there was nowhere to run.

"There will be a reckoning for your treachery."

I lifted my chin. "You won't win."

Despite my brave words, I feared they would prove untrue. The walls couldn't hold indefinitely. Eventually, Neeve's and the Nightshade Lord's wellsprings would run dry. When they did, the gates would be vulnerable to the red priests' attack. The castle would fall. I shoved the knowledge away.

"Of course we'll be victorious. Watch."

He held up his hand, called the chant to summon a pulsing ball of *esfirenda*, and then flung it at the portcullis.

The Dark Elf shield flared blue and faltered for a moment. Three other fireballs hit the gates, the fire clinging, burrowing into the wood. I caught my breath, then let it out as Neeve shouted in Elvish and the blue sheen of protection sprang to life again.

A few sullen flames glowed between the portcullis and the battle doors, however. They'd eat through, and then only the thin protection of the Dark Elves' magic would keep the castle safe.

I desperately clenched and unclenched my right hand, feeling the throwing knife slip free another quarter inch.

Movement on my right, near the black wall of the forest. Red cloaks fluttered as four priests rounded the castle, running for their lives. I grinned savagely to see a half-dozen wolves in pursuit. The small, sticklike forms of boglins clung to the priests' cloaks, biting with their triangular mouths at any exposed flesh. With a shriek, a black-winged drake dove after the priests, breathing sulfurous fire.

Cheering broke out atop the walls, and a new flight of arrows sped toward us. One managed to strike a priest in the shoulder before Galtus Celcio turned the shafts to ash.

One of the fleeing priests pivoted, flinging countering flames at the drake. It veered off, the yellow fire of its attack spraying wide. The meadow ignited, the starry flowers shriveling and charring. The last of traces of Neeve and Kian's wedding burst into flame.

"Help them," the warder called, already sending a pulsing ball of *esfirenda* at the flying drake. "Castin, Rilla, continue with the gates."

The other priests turned to fight the creatures of the Darkwood, flinging fire at the wolves as their compatriots arrived, gasping, into our midst.

"Get them off," Jenni said shrilly, brushing at the boglins caught in her cloak.

Their serrated mouths tore jagged bites from the scarlet fabric as they clambered toward her face. She managed to dislodge them, then stomped them into the ground until they were nothing but piles of twigs and leaves.

"More are coming," one of the other priests called, sending fire at the rustling wave of sticklike figures emerging from the forest.

I shook my arms and felt the knife slip down into my hand. Thank the stars! Moving my fingers awkwardly up and down, I began to saw the blade against the rope binding my wrists. With the Darkwood's help, the red priests would be defeated. And soon I'd be free to help.

To my dismay, the surge of boglins caught fire before they could reach us. The flames licked back, reaching beneath the trees. A hot, heavy wind sprang up, and I smelled charring cedar as the forest thrashed in the grip of its oldest enemy. Fire.

Under the assault of *esfirenda*, the wolves fled, yelping, back into the Darkwood. Only the drake was left, continuing to swoop and strike. It came close enough to rake one of the priests across the back with its wicked claws.

She shrieked, and two fireballs hit it simultaneously. I cringed, then ducked as the creature exploded. Pieces of stinking, charred flesh fell around us.

"What happened to the other priests?" Galtus Celcio demanded, turning to Jenni.

"The attack caught us by surprise," she said. "Half our people were turned to stone by some lizard creatures—or taken by the wolves—before we could defend ourselves. Another went down to the flying thing, and we lost Ser Bentic to a crossbow quarrel from the defenders at the door."

"Careless." The warder seemed unmoved to hear that seven of his followers were dead. "Did you at least manage to bring down the walls?"

She glanced away. "We tried. Two more of those blue-magic casters are there—though some *esfirenda* managed to escape their shields and reach the stone."

He frowned. "Let it take its course. Go help the wounded to the carts, then rejoin us here."

"Yes, Warder." She bowed her head and turned to help her injured comrades.

Her gaze slid past me, and I saw the dazed look in her eyes. This battle would leave none of us untouched.

Galtus Celcio strode in front of his followers. "Attack all together, on my mark!"

The remaining priests turned to face the gates of Castle Raine. They raised their arms, poised to cast their searing fireballs.

The warder brought his hand down in a slashing gesture, and in unison the followers of the Twin Gods yelled the chant to summon *esfirenda*.

The one I'd discovered in the little red book.

The one I'd taught them.

The one that now blasted through the blue magic of the Dark Elves' protection, turning the portcullis to molten metal and consuming the battle doors in a fury of relentless fire.

CHAPTER 37

"No!" I cried, my vision blurred with tears.

Smoke darkened the sky, choked the air. Atop the walls, soldiers ran to dump buckets of water over the blazing gates. Plumes of steam joined the smoke but did little to douse the flames. *Esfirenda* wasn't so easily extinguished.

My hands cramped with effort as I sawed desperately at my bonds. I thought I could feel the rope beginning to part.

The dozen priests advanced, their red cloaks whipping in the searing wind blowing from the Darkwood. I watched, aghast, as the fire in the forest spread, turning the trees to torches.

Thorne, where are you?

"Bring her." Galtus Celcio gestured at me.

Ser Naldi strode over and roughly grabbed my shoulder, dragging me toward the warder. The movement dislodged the throwing knife balanced between my bound hands. I felt a sharp cut, the slickness of blood against my fingers. The blade slipped out of my grasp.

I gasped and forced myself not to look down as the lieutenant dragged me to the line of priests. Ser Naldi didn't seem to notice my dropped knife, or the blood dripping down my hands.

Blue light flared as Neeve and the Nightshade Lord sent bolts of

Elvish magic at the priests. Two of them stumbled and went down. I was glad to see neither of them were Lena or Shamsan. Or Jenni.

Or, unfortunately, my father.

The heat from the inferno at the gates had driven the defenders further down the walls. Archers still sent arrows speeding toward us, and the warder still turned them to ash with a gesture. One of the battle doors crashed to the ground. The portcullis gaped, a melted slag of iron.

Beyond the ruined gate, I glimpsed Sir Durum at the head of a formation of guards. Merkis Strond was at his side, her expression set. They stood directly in the path of the oncoming priests. I choked back bile at the thought of them burning.

A commotion on the walls. I looked up, realizing my sister and Kian were no longer there, though the Nightshade Lord still flung blue bolts at the priests. Galtus Celcio deflected most of those, too. The Dark Elf light seemed weaker, the magic fading.

As I watched, one of Nightshade's attacks struck Jenni. I gasped as she went down, then didn't know whether to weep with gratitude or despair when she unsteadily got to her feet.

Galtus Celcio halted before the destroyed portcullis, hands outstretched.

"*Calma to sacar,*" he said, and the *esfirenda* faded to a sullen glow.

As the flames died, my sister stepped to the fore, a determined expression on her pale face. She held a sword outlined in blue flame.

"I challenge you, Galtus Celcio!" she cried. "A battle of single combat. If you defeat me, Castle Raine will surrender. If I defeat you, the red priests will leave this kingdom. Forever."

The warder held his hand up, checking his priests' advance.

"I accept," he called. "But I will choose my champion."

He turned to look at me, a wild light in his eyes. The breath froze in my throat.

"My daughter Rose Celcio, avatar of the Sister, will be your adversary." There was a gloating note in his voice.

No. I shook my head. This couldn't be happening.

Ser Naldi shoved me up to stand beside my father.

"Free her hands," Galtus Celcio said.

The lieutenant pulled a small knife from his belt and slashed through the remainder of the rope binding my wrists. He frowned at the blood coating my fingers. "Warder," he said, holding up one of my red hands.

My father smiled. "The mark of the Sister. Good. Rose, draw your sword. Prepare to summon *esfirenda*."

"Neeve, no!" I cried, finally finding my voice.

I met my sister's gaze across the smoking rubble of the gates. The blue flames from her sword flickered eerily in the ash-choked air.

It was our vision come true.

Yet I couldn't attack her. I wouldn't.

Kian hovered nearby, his own sword at the ready, a smudge of soot across one cheek. There was no sign of Thorne, who must be fighting his own terrible battle against the flames in the Darkwood. My heart clenched.

I looked at Galtus Celcio. "I refuse."

He gave me a grim smile, as though he'd expected my answer. "You cannot refuse the power of the gods. If you won't use it, then I will, blood of my blood."

I turned to run, but Ser Naldi grabbed my shoulders, holding me in place. Galtus Celcio took my blood-slickened hand in his, gripping so tightly I couldn't pull free.

Panic pounded through me. I had to stop him. Somehow.

The flames leaped in my belly, demanding release.

The warder of the red priests raised his other hand. I could feel his power gathering as he prepared to summon the fireball that would incinerate my sister and bring the kingdom of Raine to its knees. My mind raced, a chaos of thoughts.

Ser Pietro, burning. My pinky pulsed with remembered pain.

Fire ravaging the Nightshade throne room. The red ring on my hand flared.

Invisible flames consuming me on the night of my sixteenth birthday. My left arm itched where the leaf and vine were tattooed, a vow to the Darkwood, and to the Erynvorn.

The black sword at my side. But if I was bound to a sister, it was not to the Sister of the Twin Gods.

I stared at Neeve, her necklace clasped about my throat, and saw the glint of gold and sapphires at hers. She met my gaze steadily and gave a slow nod.

I flung up my hand, a mirror of father's gesture, ready to call the raging power of my fire.

Galtus Celcio bared his teeth in a grin. He thought I'd finally seen reason.

And I had. But my allegiance was not to him.

"*Esfera to quera, firenda des almar!*" I shot my palm up to the sky.

A fireball formed there, sizzling overhead.

"Cast it," my father said exultantly.

Our gazes locked, and shocked realization flashed across his expression as he read the intention in my eyes. I would cast fiery death, yes. But not where he wanted me to.

Thorne. Neeve. I love you.

I brought my hand down.

The fireball fell, a fury of crackling heat.

Only to be stopped by Galtus Celcio's flame. He stretched his clawed fingers out, his face twisting with effort as his fire engulfed mine. I could feel the *esfirenda* bending to his will, turning toward the courtyard...

No.

Sweat slicked my skin as my father and I struggled, the intense heat of the fireball crackling over us. The ruddy light turned his hair scarlet, pricked fire from his eyes. Slowly, inexorably, I felt my grasp on the fireball slip.

My hand began to shake. I gulped back tears of anguish.

Rose. It was a whisper on the wind. A brief scent of moss and cedar.

The cool blue light of Dark Elf magic flowed into me. Behind its power, I felt the rustle of the Darkwood, the light of strange stars.

With a deep breath, I wrested the *esfirenda* back under control. The air burned my lungs. Gasping, I met my father's gaze and held the fireball steady.

I was not strong enough to bring it down upon us.

Not alone. But Thorne's magic buoyed me up. And other power lay all around me.

Closing my eyes, I let desperation flood me, and I *pulled*.

Behind me, Ser Naldi lost his grip on my shoulders and crumpled to the ground. Through my closed lids I could see the fireball glowing incandescently. Magic flowed through me—sparks of flame from the priests, a wisp of blue that was Nightshade's power. I leaned forward, pouring all my heart into the fire.

Finally, I touched an inferno. The warder's sorcery.

Mine, I thought fiercely.

"Rose!" Galtus Celcio shouted. "Stop."

I opened my eyes, seeing the edge of terror in my father's eyes.

I had no room for fear. Only this single purpose. I jerked my bloodied hand from his and held my arms overhead. Then I took his power, yanking it to me in a rush. I was nothing but flame. The esfirenda turned white-hot.

"*Esfera to quera quemar!*" I screamed, thrusting my hands down.

The fireball plummeted, engulfing me and Galtus Celcio, warder of the red priests.

This time, nothing could stop it.

CHAPTER 38

S earing heat took me in its arms, so tenderly welcoming me
home. The hottest day in sunbaked Parnese was nothing
compared to its intensity. *Esfirenda* stole the breath from my
lungs, parched my mouth, sent my dreams up in a conflagration of lost
hopes.

My entire life had been destined for this moment—to die
consumed by flames, in a cleansing inferno that would save not only
those I loved, but kingdoms. Entire worlds. Was the immense fireball
proof of a divine power, or just the natural result of combining the
magics of two realms? I didn't know, and ultimately it didn't matter.

The cataclysm raged.

I welcomed the fire, even as it blazed against my skin, bit fiercely
into my bones. The red curls around my face turned to flickering
flames.

Galtus Celcio was screaming, his hair afire. I looked away, through
the heat-rippled air and toward the ruined gates of Castle Raine.

My sister was running toward me, one hand outstretched, the other
holding her blue-lit sword.

"Stay back!" I tried to cry, but the words evaporated to steam on
my lips.

The black sword of the Sister fell from about my waist—the scabbard nothing but cinders—to lie abandoned on the ground beside me.

With a shriek, my father collapsed. His scarlet cloak scorched to ashes, his skin reddened and blistered.

I glanced down at my hands. The blood had caked onto my fingers like dried mud, the cut on my wrist sealed closed. My arms were bare, and my legs too, where my woven clothing had burned away, though my leather jerkin remained, as brittle as a fallen leaf. My long hair was gone, eaten by flames.

Yet my skin was untouched by the fire.

Wondering, I stared at the tattoo on my left arm, the leaf and vine glowing a brilliant emerald. A faint blue light covered me, I realized, a tracery of Dark Elf magic. It hummed over my body, flaring from Nightshade's ring on my right hand to the necklace I still wore. But it was coming from another source...

My sister's outflung hand, her blade, outlined in blue power.

She fell to her knees at the edge of the fireball, her tear-streaked face reflecting the ruddy light. Still, she channeled her power to me. Protecting me.

My father moaned. Then twitched, once.

Then lay as still and lifeless as a piece of charred wood.

Calma, I thought at the fire, my whole body beginning to shake.

Calma to sacar.

Slowly, the heat faded. I crumpled, my palms flat against the hot circle of baked earth surrounding me and the body of Galtus Celcio.

Impossibly, I was still alive.

"Rose." Neeve's voice was choked with emotion.

I looked up at her, the last flickers of blue magic outlining her hands.

Not so impossibly after all.

"You saved me," I whispered, my throat scorched raw.

"We saved each other," she said softly.

I crawled forward, to where she knelt at the edge of the charred grasses.

"Are you..." She regarded me gravely. "Can I touch you?"

In answer, I opened my arms.

With a sob, she set down her sword and embraced me. My jerkin crumbled away, and I didn't care. The air was cool against my bare skin, my fire-shorn head. A moment later, a cloak settled on my shoulders.

Thorne! I glanced up, my heart leaping.

But no, it was Kian. He crouched down, putting his arms about me and Neeve. He leaned his head toward hers, and with a sigh she rested her forehead against his cheek.

"Where's Thorne?" I asked.

Neeve frowned, a line of worry creasing her brow. "I haven't seen him since the battle started."

"But..." I'd felt his magic. It carried me when I'd thought all hope was lost.

"The Darkwood," Kian said, glancing at the forest.

I turned, then gasped in horror at the blackened line of trees. "We have to find him."

Unsteadily, with Neeve and Kian's help, I got to my feet. Sir Durum's soldiers hurried around us, rounding up the remaining red priests. The followers of the Twin Gods seemed dazed, stumbling over the blackened meadow as the forces of Castle Raine took them into custody.

I'd stolen the red priests' power, I realized. Taken it and then killed their leader, the most powerful fire sorcerer in the world. Warder Galtus Celcio.

My father.

I looked at his lifeless body, sorrow flowing over me. Not for him, but for the loss of what might have been, had he been a better man. One not driven by power and his own self-importance.

Too late now. Instead, the story of his conquest ended here, in a burned field outside the gates of Castle Raine.

"Well," an irritated voice said from the level of my knees. "Hurry it up, you whey-faced fools!"

I blinked down at a hobnie wearing a soiled tunic and dirty brown cap. His long beard was looped around his shoulders, and a scowl creased his ugly face.

"Cancrach," Neeve said. "What is it?"

"Stop wasting time in questions, you nim-witted lump." He stamped his foot. "The *Galadhir* is dying."

"What?" The breath halted in my lungs, and I clutched Kian's cloak around me. "Take us to him. Immediately."

"I would have if you'd shaken the rocks out of your heads and followed me in the first place." Cancrach turned, making for the ruin of the forest.

I hobbled after him, belatedly realizing my feet were bare.

"Soldier." Kian beckoned to a man taking one of the captive priests to the castle. "Princess Rose has need of your boots."

"Your highness." The man halted and bent to do the prince's bidding.

The priest he'd been escorting stepped forward. "Take mine."

It was Paulette, I realized with a pang. She looked weary beyond words, her hair tangled, her eyes bleak. She sat heavily on the ground and removed her boots.

"Here," she said, holding them out.

Without a word, I accepted them and laced them up. Beside me, the hobnie hopped up and down with impatience. The soldier pulled Paulette to her feet, and my gaze met hers.

"Donal's dead," she said, her voice choked with grief.

I didn't ask how, and I couldn't say I was sorry. Not after what he'd done.

"The others?" I asked. "My students?"

"Alive, though Shamsan is not well."

My fault for pulling so much power. Yet I could not regret the price of that victory.

I stared at her a moment longer, the girl who'd been my childhood companion. Who'd followed my father so blindly. The faint echo of friendship wasn't enough to overcome everything that lay between us —betrayal, and death, and the acrid scorch of *esfirenda*.

"Goodbye, Paulette," I said, then turned away.

I had my own beloved to save.

"Make haste!" Cancrach screeched, dashing in front of us.

We followed as best we could, though Neeve and I were both teetering on the edge of collapse. Kian took our arms, half supporting us, half dragging us through the charred bushes and blackened trees.

The air stank of smoke. I blinked back tears, appalled at the ruin of the Darkwood. Only a few trees stood untouched, brave green spears against a field of black. The ground crackled under our feet. Burned sticks and brittle fern stalks scraped my bare calves as we raced by. My side ached, as though a blade had been stuck between my ribs, twisting with every step.

Gasping, I kept going, Kian's grip on my elbow steadying me.

Neeve stumbled, almost bringing us all down.

The hobnie whirled around to glare at us with his red eyes. "Hurry, hurry, you lumbering dolts!"

"How far?" Kian asked, slipping an arm around Neeve as she swayed, her complexion as white as flour.

"Close," the little creature said. "An owl's screech, a deer's leap. Come!"

We went two more paces, and, gasping, Neeve fell to her knees.

"I can't," she said hoarsely.

Her eyes were dark, fathomless. She'd spent her entire wellspring to shield me and had nothing more to give.

But I refused to leave her behind, despite the hobnie's gnashing of teeth.

Between us, Kian and I got her on her feet, though I was sobbing with effort.

A flicker of white shone in the charcoal columns of the fire-blasted trees, coming closer with every breath, until it halted before us. The White Hart, its coat shining like moonlight, its antlers regal points against the ash-driven sky.

It nodded at Neeve, then bowed down, front legs extended.

"Get on, get on," Cancrach said, pushing me toward the glowing creature.

Kian boosted Neeve onto its surprisingly wide back, then helped me. The moment I was settled behind my sister, the deer rose and leaped forward.

"Make speed, oafish mortal," the hobnie said to Kian, his voice already fading behind us. "Your ungainly legs are next to worthless."

Riding the White Hart was like flying. It bounded over the silver trickle of a stream, and suddenly we were in an unburned section of the forest. I pulled in a gulping breath of cool, moss-scented air. In front of me, Neeve shuddered with weariness. I slipped my arms around her and held my sister close to keep her from toppling over.

Our graceful mount halted in a small clearing ringed with untouched birch and hemlock trees. There, in the center, Thorne lay. Unmoving.

I slid off the White Hart and steadied Neeve as she did the same, and together we stumbled to the *Galadhir*.

"Thorne," I whispered, going to my knees beside him and clutching his hand. "Don't you dare leave me."

Wind rustled the branches around us. I leaned over, trying to feel his heartbeat. Anguish twisted through me. I couldn't bear the thought of him dying. Not after everything we'd faced.

"Is he still breathing?" Neeve asked, fumbling at her armor.

"Yes...barely."

"Hold his head up," she said, pulling a vial of golden liquid from some hidden pocket.

"*Nirwen* essence?" I guessed.

She nodded. "I always carry some with me. Just in case."

I slid my hands under Thorne's shoulders and did my best to hold him up. My arms shook with effort.

"Hurry," I said through gritted teeth as Neeve unstoppered the bottle.

Thorne's head lolled, and I could feel my strength waning. Then Kian sprinted into the clearing. He dove to help me, and between the three of us, we managed to hold Thorne steady and coax a few drops of *nirwen* between his lips.

Heart pounding, I stared at him. Nothing happened.

"How long before it takes effect?" I asked.

Neeve pressed her lips together. "I don't know. He's much depleted."

"As are you," Kian said gently. "Drink some yourself, please."

She glanced at the bottle, as if she'd forgotten she was holding it, then took a small sip.

"Give him a little more?" I asked, hating how still Thorne lay. I pulled in a ragged breath. *Don't die. Don't die.*

Neeve tipped another two droplets into his mouth, and then I put my arms around him, holding him close.

"Thorne Windrift," I said in a low, fierce voice, "I didn't sacrifice everything just to lose you in the end."

"We need to anchor his spirit before it drifts away," Neeve said.

Anchor his spirit? I stared at her a moment, and then inspiration struck.

"Our necklaces." I touched the silver and ruby pendant about my neck: Neeve's necklace, exchanged with her when I'd been forced to leave Elfhame.

Thorne had gifted each of us the Dark Elf-crafted necklaces when we turned fourteen. We'd worn them ever since, except for that one trade. Fingers fumbling, I undid the clasp. The silver chain pooled in my hand, the rubies winking like drops of blood.

Neeve unclasped hers, her movements a little stronger than before. I was glad to see the *nirwen* was working on her, at least.

"Put one in each of his hands," she said, then set my gold and blue pendant in Thorne's unresponsive palm and closed her fingers over his.

I echoed her motion, clinging to my beloved's cold hand.

"Lord Thornelithiel Windrift," Neeve said, her voice steady, "*Galadhir* of the Darkwood and Erynvorn, we call to you. By the power of Dark Elf magic and our shared blood, I, Neeve Shadrift Mallory, Princess of Raine, summon you."

She looked at me.

"Thorne, beloved," I said, swallowing back tears, "I, Rose Celcio Valrois, call you back, by the power of fire and love. By the magic of the Darkwood, and the promises binding us together."

I glanced at Kian. He gave me a somber nod, then looked down at Thorne.

"I, Prince Kian Leifson of Fiorland, ask you to return. For the sake of Neeve and Rose, and for the forest you've sworn to protect and the realms you're charged with guarding. By the power of friendship and duty, I call to you."

The White Hart paced forward from where it had lingered in the trees. It lowered its majestic antlered head, touching Thorne lightly upon the chest.

As it did so, the seven hobnies suddenly surrounded us. They each laid a hand on Thorne, some at his feet, some at his shoulders and head. An owl hooted, and the wind sprang up again, stirring the trees around us.

I leaned forward and pressed my lips to Thorne's, infusing the kiss with all my hope, all my yearning, all the promise of our lives to come.

"Awake, love," I whispered. "We're waiting for you."

CHAPTER 39

S ilence fell over the clearing as every living thing in the Darkwood waited, unmoving, to see if their *Galadhir* was lost forever.

I clung to my beloved's hand, hope and anguish tangling in my heart.

Then Thorne's eyelids fluttered. He pulled in a wavering breath and, finally, opened his eyes. For a moment he lay there, blinking, as if amazed to be alive. The White Hart lifted its head, gently touched its nose to his, then bounded away in a single quicksilver leap, back into the forest.

The hobnies, grumbling and swearing, likewise scurried off, as if shy about their part in bringing the *Galadhir* home. All except Cancrach, who gave me a beady glare.

"Nearly didn't save him, no thanks to you clumsy curds. Our debt is now done." Tossing his beard over his shoulder, he followed his brethren into the shadows beneath the trees.

Thorne inhaled again, then looked from Neeve to Kian, and then to me.

"Rose." His gaze locked with mine and his lips curved in a faint, tender smile. "You survived the fireball."

I stared at him a moment, the meaning of his words sinking in. Then I gripped his tunic and began to cry, hot tears of agonized relief. "Are you telling me you foresaw the battle with Galtus Celcio? And you didn't tell us?"

"Yes." His voice was low. "I didn't think any of us would live through that inferno, though I tried my best to save you, and the Darkwood."

"So you used up your wellspring trying to avert that fate?" I bent forward, my forehead against his silken tunic, and gulped back more sobs. He hadn't even changed out of his wedding finery.

"I did." He gently stroked my hair. "I would give everything for you, Rose."

The sound of crystalline bells chimed through the clearing, and I felt the worlds shift. I sat up in time to see three white-robed Oracles step through the air. Hastily, I pulled Kian's cloak closer around me.

"*Galadhir*," the first Oracle said. "You have performed your duty well."

Thorne levered himself up to sitting, then turned his head toward the forest, his gaze unfocused.

"No," he said after a long moment, his voice heavy. "Nearly a quarter of the Darkwood burned. I failed."

"Do you think destruction is only evil?" The Oracle shook their head, white veils fluttering. "Fire clears the way for something new. The forest will flourish again, sooner than you might think."

Thorne didn't look convinced, but bowed his head in silent acceptance of their words.

"Neeve Shadrift." The second Oracle stepped forward and set their pale, long-fingered hand on Neeve's head. "You are a worthy ruler of realms, strong and true. As is your chosen husband. The mortal realm of Raine is lucky to have you as their queen."

My sister's eyes widened. "My father...does he still live?"

"He does," the Oracle said. "And he will for years yet, but time weaves back and forth. The web of tomorrow is as close as the threads of yesterday. Tend to your duties well, and the path will open before your feet."

The third Oracle, the tallest of the trio, paced forward to stand before me. I stared defiantly up at them.

"Rose Valrois, daughter of fire. Your destiny has run a twisted path."

Indeed it had, and I didn't need some mystical figure to tell me so.

"Now what?" I asked, clinging to my beloved's hand. "I refuse to leave Thorne."

"Troublesome," the first Oracle said softly.

The one standing before me shook their head. "Unpredictable. Powerful. Like a flame. We will not part you from the *Galadhir*."

I let out a heavy breath of relief. Standing against the Oracles hadn't been something I wanted to do. But I would have.

Thorne looked up at the veiled figure. "I'd set aside the mantle of *Galadhir* before I'd let Rose go."

The first Oracle made a sound of distress, but the taller one nodded slowly. "As fate wills. She is welcome in Elfhame, as long as she travels by your side."

Joy bubbled up inside me, battling through my utter exhaustion, and I grinned. Neeve looked at me, eyes crinkling at the corners, and Kian set one hand on my shoulder.

We'd won. Despite all the hardship in our way, the four of us had prevailed.

"Hold fast," the second Oracle said with a gesture. "We will take you back to the castle."

I scarcely had time to draw a breath before the clearing twisted away. My stomach lurched, and a moment later we arrived at the ruined gates of Castle Raine.

A great commotion sprang up at our appearance. I heard Sir Durum bellowing for his soldiers to bring us aid. Moments later, a stretcher arrived for Thorne. Kian swung Neeve into his arms. She made no protest, only wound her arms around his neck as he carried her up the steps into the castle.

To my surprise, the Oracles remained in the courtyard.

"Why are they staying?" I whispered to Thorne as two soldiers carried his stretcher into the hall.

He looked at me with sorrowful eyes. "They will alter the memories of the remaining red priests, erasing all knowledge of Dark Elves and our magic, before sending them home to Parnese."

I thought of Lena, and Shamsan, and Jenni. And of Paulette.

"Will they know what happened? Will they remember me?"

"You are too deeply woven into the fabric of their pasts to be removed. They will know you. And know that you defeated your father, turning the tide of battle against them."

"I won't see them again." It wasn't a question. I'd never return to Parnesia. Whatever tales the followers of the Twin Gods told of me after this, I was certain to be the villain. So be it.

Thorne gave a nod. "I'm sorry. There's much to grieve."

A dark ache twisted inside me. The death of my father, and the part I'd played in it, was a wound that went deep. It would take me time to fully come to terms with the events of the battle.

"But there is much to celebrate, too." Thorne lifted his hand, lightly cupping my cheek.

I met his gaze. "Yes."

Things could have been much, much worse. Thorne had seen a vision of fiery death for all of us. I wondered if, in an alternate future, it had come true. The thought sent a shiver through me.

"Beg pardon, milady," the soldier at the front of the stretcher said. "Where are we taking him?"

"My rooms." I released Thorne's hand. Then, securing Kian's cloak more closely around my nakedness, I trailed the soldiers up the stairs, grateful for the support of the railing.

Sorche met us at my door. With a cry of relief, she threw her arms around me. "Lady Rose! You're not dead!"

I returned her embrace and gave her a crooked smile. "No. Though it was a near thing. Neeve saved me. And Thorne."

"And bless them for it." My maid stepped back, then her eyes widened. "Your hair!"

I'd all but forgotten that the *esfirenda* had burned it away. Reaching up, I discovered my head was as smooth as an egg.

"It will grow back," I said, hoping it was true.

Though, on balance, I'd rather lose my hair than my life and those of my loved ones.

Once we were all recovered, though, I had plenty of questions—for Neeve, for Thorne, for the Oracles. Though they, of course, would only give me riddles in return.

With Sorche's help, the soldiers tucked Thorne into my bed. As soon as they departed, I drank half a pitcher of water to replenish my parched body, then lay down next to him.

"Is this all right?" I murmured, slipping one arm over his chest.

He caught my hand, lacing his fingers through mine. "Always."

Exhaustion tugged at me, but every time I closed my eyes, I was surrounded by the searing memory of *esfirenda*.

"That's why you wouldn't make me any promises," I said softly. "The future you saw ended in fire and despair."

"Yes." Thorne's voice was somber. "I wanted to tell you, to pledge myself to you despite what I knew. But every time I tried, the words turned to ashes in my throat."

"Even if we'd only had a few days of happiness, wouldn't it have been worth it?" My voice wavered.

His chest rose and fell in a deep sigh. "I could not give you false assurances, Rose. It is not who I am."

"Stupidly noble *Galadhir*." I squeezed his hand, blunting the words. "I suppose I'll have to forgive you."

"Will you?" He turned on his side to face me, his dark eyes full of anguished hope. "Despite all my flaws, I love you. I have since the moment you blazed into the Darkwood, full of questions and life and impatience."

"I know." I smiled at him. "And yes, Thorne Windrift, I forgive you. But if we're to share a future, you must always be honest with me. Even if the Oracles don't agree."

He nodded slowly. "I can make you that promise. Rose Valrois, are you willing to pledge our lives together, no matter what fate might bring? Will you marry me?"

"Of course, you foolish man. I thought you'd never ask."

Our lips brushed together, a kiss of absolution and acceptance that deepened as yearning blossomed to desire. Bright sparks scattered through me—not the fire of flames, but golden pinpricks of light, like a fall of stars in a moonless sky. The touch of skin against skin. My heartbeat settled into a new rhythm, full of wanting, and hope, and, finally, utter joy.

Thorne and I were going to be married. There was nothing else I needed in the whole world.

⚜

I WOKE IN THE DARKNESS, felt Thorne's warmth against me, and fell back into dreamless sleep.

The next time my eyes opened, I was alone in my bed. Sunlight slanted through the curtains, sending a golden bar of light across my green carpet. I stretched, amazed to be alive and unharmed, despite the odd fact of my baldness.

I ran a tentative hand over my head, relieved to feel the faint brush of new stubble against my palm.

A soft tap came at my door. I sat up, pulling the sheets around me, and called for whoever it was to come in.

Sorche entered, carrying a tray with a mug of tea and a fresh bun. The normalcy of it made tears spring to my eyes. Trisk hopped at her side and, seeing I was awake, clawed her way up onto the bed.

"Good morning." I smiled.

"Afternoon, more like," Sorche said. "You have a visitor."

She set the tray down and helped me into my dressing gown. Once clothed, I scooped up my mug of tea and went out to my sitting room. There, in one of the chairs before the hearth, sat Mistress Ainya.

"There you are." She nodded, eyes bright as she looked me up and down. "And not much worse for the wear. How are you feeling?"

I sat across from her and took a sip of tea, assessing. The flames in my belly were dark, but I sensed the bare flicker of embers among the cinders of my sorcery.

"Tired," I said. "But I think my fire survived."

"Of course it did. Your magic is a part of you." The herbwife looked up as my maid stepped out of the bedroom. "Ah, Sorche. Be a kind girl and fetch Neeve, if you would."

"Of course." Sorche dipped a bow and slipped out.

I wondered if my sister was awake. She'd spent her wellspring down to the dregs, plus she'd been fighting the Dark Elf sickness ever since returning to Raine.

"Maybe we should go to her," I said.

Mistress Ainya smiled. "Nay. Neeve is stronger than you might think."

A moment later, she was proven right as my sister, accompanied by Kian, entered my rooms. He was carrying a chair, and I nearly laughed at the sight.

"I told you," Neeve said as he positioned it between Mistress Ainya and me. "You should have gotten an extra one long ago."

"I suppose you're right." I grinned at her as she settled into the chair, noting that the shadows had lifted from her eyes. "Maybe I'll just keep this one."

She raised a brow at me, while Kian pulled over the low stool I kept beneath my side table and perched upon it.

"Where's Thorne?" I asked them, trying not to feel a touch abandoned.

"Helping the Oracles," Neeve said. "Along with Nightshade. They're almost done, and my father has coaches readied to take the red priests to Portknowe."

"What about the ramp Galtus Celcio melted into the western cliffs?"

"Sir Durum has sent messages to the garrison at Meriton," Kian said. "Once he finishes seeing the priests off, he'll go arrange for the ramp to be blasted away."

"Are your parents safe?" I asked him.

"Yes. Everyone inside the castle itself was unharmed. Although..." He trailed off, glancing at Neeve.

"Your mother has collapsed," she said.

"What?" I half stood, and my sister set a hand on my arm.

"Don't worry. She's not at the edge of death."

"What happened?" I settled back in my chair, feeling cold.

"Her long misuse of *nirwen* finally caught up with her," Neeve said grimly.

Mistress Ainya nodded. "I've been tending her. She will recover, somewhat. But I'm afraid from now on, your mother will always be an invalid."

A lovely, frail butterfly. She'd brought that fate on herself.

"I'll go visit her later." I looked back at Neeve. "But if *nirwen* is that dangerous, what will happen to you?"

My sister's expression softened, and she glanced at Kian. "We'll keep going back into Elfhame. Even a few turns there will give me the strength to return to the mortal world for several months."

"I've some ideas along those lines, too," the herbwife said. "Rose's mother will be a useful subject to test remedies upon."

I looked at Mistress Ainya in some alarm, and she patted my hand.

"Never fear," she said. "My calling is to do no harm. I aid my patients by whatever means I can. Some good will come of the queen's unfortunate addiction to remaining beautiful at all costs."

I hoped so. Unwilling sympathy moved through me as I thought of what had driven my mother. The only thing she'd possessed, once she left Parnese, was her beauty. No wonder she'd tried to keep it at all costs.

"Now, Neeve." Mistress Ainya turned to my sister. "I understand you managed to shield Rose from the worst of the fire. How?"

My sister let out a low breath. "It was the vision, really."

"Remind me of what you saw," Mistress Ainya said gently.

Neeve's gaze met mine, and I nodded, taking up the tale. "Neeve and I faced each other in battle, or so it seemed. She held a sword flickering with Dark Elf magic, while I had flames at my fingertips. I never thought—" My voice caught. I took a ragged breath and continued. "I never thought I'd actually be forced to attack her."

"I thought you probably would," my sister said calmly.

"How could you?" I stared at her. "I'd never hurt you."

"Not willingly." She shrugged one shoulder. "But visions usually come true, in some way. During my time at the Nightshade Court, I worked out a way to shield myself from fire. I never thought I'd cast it on someone else."

Our eyes met, and I saw the echo of flame. She'd given all her power to protect me.

I grabbed her hands, squeezing them tightly. "Thank you."

There was no need to count the many, many times we'd saved each other. In the scales of the heart, we were equal.

"Back to bed, the both of you." Mistress Ainya set her wizened hand over ours. "I prescribe rest, and plenty of it. I'll be checking on you regularly. Especially you, Neeve."

Kian smiled. "I promise to keep her from doing too much. Maybe I'll even let her win at chess."

Neeve snorted. "As if you are a match for me."

"Oh, I am." He stood and helped her from her chair.

She gave a half-smile and her eyes met his. "I know. I wouldn't have married you otherwise."

They gazed at each other for a long moment, until I cleared my throat. "Well, off you go."

With a laugh, Kian took a step back.

"Speaking of marriage," Neeve said, turning to me, "what of you and Thorne?"

I nodded, and her smile blazed into fullness. Kian hauled me up, and the three of us embraced. When we pulled back, I was crying— and was shocked to see that my sister was, too.

"Finally," she said, brushing the tears from her cheeks. "Don't take too long to plan the ceremony."

"It's not the wedding of queens and kings," I said. "We'll just have something simple in the forest."

Then I recalled the ruin of the Darkwood outside my window, and sorrow dampened my joy. Maybe we'd marry in the castle after all.

And then we'd cross between the worlds and say our pledges within the Erynvorn, that immense wild forest standing as witness to all our promises.

CHAPTER 40

T horne and I were, indeed, married in the great hall of Castle Raine. Despite the fact I'd anticipated a small ceremony, we ended up with nearly two dozen people attending. Kian and Neeve were there, of course, and the king and Mama, who was carefully installed in a cushioned chair. The Nightshade Lord had to be included, as Thorne's liege, though I was relieved he didn't insist on presiding over any runes of binding.

The nobles of Fiorland couldn't be left out either, and I certainly wanted my friends from the castle to be there, foremost among them Sorche and Miss Groves. Master Fawkes was happy to provide the music, and Mistress Ainya made us sweetly scented sachets to carry, filled with herbs for health and happiness.

I wore my crown, with a scarf covering the red stubble of my hair, and my favorite blue dress. I'd no need for glittering gowns or elaborate gems—not when I finally had my heart's desire. I had my own necklace back, though, and wore it gladly, the gold and sapphire pendant glinting at my throat.

Thorne was dressed simply, in the dark purple silks of the Nightshade Court. He looked stunningly elegant, of course. When he gazed at me with all the love in his eyes, I felt as beautiful as any queen.

Lord Raine said the official words, Mama cried, and Thorne and I pledged our lives to each other. During the ceremony, Merkis Strond stood next to the Nightshade Lord, and I thought I glimpsed them discreetly touching hands.

Afterward, there was a huge feast, mostly to make up for the one Neeve and Kian were supposed to have had. Thorne and I were seated at the head table, next to my sister and her husband. Many toasts were made, and the kitchens outdid themselves with course after course of delicious food—fish in cream sauce, savory corn cakes, braised vegetables, duck cooked in wine, and an array of desserts to satisfy any sweet tooth.

Finally, the feast ended, and Thorne and I were able to slip away.

"Come," he said, linking his arm through mine. "I want to show you something."

He led me out the side door of Castle Raine. Twilight smoothed velvety shadows over the land, and a partial moon skimmed across the lavender sky. By its pale light we went through the gardens and to the arched door leading out to the scorched meadow.

"Where are we going?" I asked, though the answer was obvious.

"The Darkwood."

For the past several afternoons, while I rested, he'd gone out to the forest. Each time he returned, I asked him how it fared, and he'd shaken his head in answer. Now, it seemed, I was about to find out.

The smell of char still hung in the air, a bitter reminder of the battle we'd fought. Eventually, the grim scent would fade, as would the memories of that day. I was relieved we were going out to the ruined forest under the cover of evening, when the burned trees wouldn't show so starkly against the sky.

The fight against the red priests had left more casualties than the cedars and creatures of the Darkwood. Castle Raine had lost a handful of soldiers to *esfirenda*, Donal included. I didn't know if he'd been trying to defend Raine in the end, but he was given a hero's burial along with his fallen comrades.

Jarl Eiric had also been wounded. He'd led his small group of Fiorland soldiers to the same arched door Thorne and I now stepped through. They'd made a brave stand, holding off the red priests until the beasts Thorne had summoned from the Darkwood arrived. None of the Fiorlanders had died, but several bore grievous burns, the jarl included.

As my husband and I passed through the blackened and branchless remainder of the forest, I wanted to weep at the loss. So much destruction in the name of conquest. The huge cedar we'd used to meet under was gone, as were the hushing hemlocks and bright birches.

"They will return," Thorne said softly, as if reading my thoughts. "Look."

He halted and spoke the Elvish rune for light. A small ball of foxfire kindled in his palm, and he sent it to hover overhead.

Its bluish light illuminated a hollow filled with glimmering gold, until I blinked and realized the light was cast from dozens of tiny *nirwen* flowers, their petals open to the sky. Their sweet scent perfumed the air, banishing the acrid smell of fire.

"Nirwen, blooming now?" I glanced at Thorne. "But it's not their season."

"They're healing the forest." He smiled at me. "These ones won't grow big enough to harvest, though."

I sighed and leaned against him. "In any case, they're beautiful. Like stars fallen to earth."

He slipped his arm around my shoulders. "It's just the beginning. The Darkwood will recover."

As would we all, though the healing might be slow.

We stood there a long time, letting the peace of the deepening night fall over us, breathing the delicate, miraculous smell of the blossoms.

"We ought to return," Thorne finally said. "The Fiorlanders depart tomorrow."

I could have happily stayed out there all night, but I nodded.

"I don't think the Nightshade Lord will be happy to see Merkis Strond go," I said. "Did you notice he called her Inga at dinner?"

"I'm not surprised." I could hear the smile in Thorne's voice. "I saw them riding out together yesterday, and the day before."

"I wonder if, someday, we might see her in Elfhame," I said.

"Stranger things have happened." He kissed the tip of my nose. "And speaking of Elfhame, we have our own farewells to make."

It was true. In two days, Thorne and I would accompany Nightshade back to the land of the Dark Elves. Neeve and Kian would come too, of course. This time, I anticipated that our stay in the Nightshade Court would be far more pleasant than the last.

"Are you sure you're strong enough to transport everyone between the worlds?" I asked. "Especially with all the work you've been doing to restore the Darkwood?"

"The Oracles will help open the gateway and take us into Elfhame."

I looked at him in surprise. "They're still here?"

His teeth flashed in a smile. "I might be the *Galadhir*, but even I couldn't heal the forest this quickly. The Oracles have chosen not to make their presence obvious, but yes, they remained in the mortal world."

It made sense. The two realms were intertwined, and the *nirwen* flowers so essential to the Dark Elves must be coaxed to bloom at their appointed time.

"I suppose I'll have to see Mama before I go." I sighed at the thought. Now that she was so frail, it was difficult to sustain my old anger at her.

Thorne brushed a kiss over my hair. "Would you like me to come with you?"

"Not this time."

I must meet my mother on my own terms.

Not that anything will change between you, my little voice said.

Hush, I thought back at it.

And it did.

⚜

THE NEXT MORNING, we gathered on the castle steps to bid the Fiorlanders farewell. Kian embraced his parents, and Prince Jenson bowed low over my hand.

"Now that the red priests are defeated, are you still bound for Athraig?" I asked.

"I am," he said somberly. "Perhaps the long enmity between our kingdoms can be mended at last."

I clasped his fingers. "Be careful."

"I will." He gave me a slightly crooked smile, then glanced to where Thorne stood at my shoulder. "Fare well, the both of you. I'm glad of your happiness."

Thorne nodded, and the prince turned and strode down the stairs, his bright hair golden in the sunlight. Whatever adventures lay along his path, I hoped he would ultimately find his own joy.

We stood there until the last rider clattered out of the courtyard. The slag of the ruined portcullis and cinders of the battle doors had been cleared away, and the empty gates looked out on the blackened field. Not entirely black, though. The faintest hint of green showed in patches beside the road, and a recent rain had cleaned the air, dampening the ashes and washing the soot from the walls.

My mother looked exhausted from seeing the Fiorlanders off. With a twinge of guilty relief, I decided to let her rest, and go visit the library first.

The smell of old paper surrounded me with familiar warmth as I stepped into Castle Raine's grand library. The ceiling soared two stories overhead, where windows let in filtered sunlight. In a way, I realized with a jolt, it was similar to the Temple of the Twin Gods—a hushed expanse of air, promising mysteries.

I far preferred books over the sect of the red priests, but I couldn't help wondering what would become of them, now that the warder was dead. A new leader would arise, I supposed. Hopefully not as power-hungry as Galtus Celcio had been.

A last pang went through me for the father I'd never had. But that had been a child's dream, one I had finally let go.

After the battle, I'd asked Sir Durum if anyone recovered a black sword from the battlefield. No such weapon had been found. Either it had been incinerated by the *esfirenda*, or one of the priests had managed to smuggle it out of Raine. Either way, it was no longer mine to worry about.

I made my way to the last bank of shelves, and habit made me glance about to make sure I was unobserved. Jarl Eiric had almost caught me opening the hidden shelf once. He'd been tucked away in a corner of the library, looking over maps of the castle.

For years, I'd held him in suspicion. His interest in Castle Raine's defenses couldn't mean anything good, I'd reasoned. But it turned out he'd been informing himself in case the castle ever came under attack. To save his own skin, perhaps, or that of his king and queen, but he'd still stepped to the fore when needed. He'd been the one to suggest to Sir Durum that the Fiorlanders defend the side doors, little realizing the danger Galtus Celcio was sending his way.

During the battle, I'd also wondered, briefly, where the Nightshade Lord's guards were. Instead of helping at the front gates, they'd gone to defend the back of the castle, using their Dark Elf magic to keep the priests' *esfirenda* from taking hold. Like their liege, they'd drained their wellsprings nearly dry.

Unlike Lord Mornithalarion, however, they were slow to recover, even with the aid of Neeve's concentrated *nirwen* essence. Once they were back in Elfhame, however, the healers would be able to speed their recovery.

I paused before the tall bookcase concealing the secret compartment, trying to recall which tome unlocked the hidden shelf. Bottom right—that was it. I bent and pulled the lowest book out, then gently pressed it back in.

With a soft click, the middle shelf swung open to reveal the hidden compartment behind.

"What are you doing?" Neeve's voice at my shoulder made me jump. She'd approached me so quietly, I hadn't noticed.

"Um." I turned to face her. "Opening the hidden bookshelf."

One of Neeve's brows rose. "You didn't think to inform the future Queen of Raine about the secrets contained in her own library?"

Heat rushed to my cheeks. I'd told my sister where the Dark Elf *Studie* had come from, of course, but I'd never thought to actually show her the secret shelf.

"I'm sorry. Of course you should know where it is. Although there's nothing inside, except for this."

I gently took the leaflet from the middle cubby. There used to be three books there: *Elfhame: A Studie of the Dark Elves and Their Wayes,* the little red recipe book containing the hidden history of a Rainish spy who'd infiltrated the red priests, and this small sheaf written in a language I didn't recognize.

I handed it to my sister, then closed the empty compartment. Castle Raine had given me the last of its secrets.

"Is it in Elvish?" I asked as Neeve gently turned the parchment pages.

"I think so—though I'm not very familiar with the written language."

"We'll show it to Thorne when he returns from the Darkwood this evening," I said.

Neeve nodded thoughtfully. "Or my uncle—if you don't mind."

Since we were bound for his court on the morrow, I supposed I should put to rest the last vestiges of my discomfort whenever I was in his presence. I was married to Thorne now, after all, safely beyond Nightshade's grasp.

"Very well," I said, then followed my sister out of the library and to the east wing of the castle.

She knocked at her uncle's door, and he called for us to enter. We did, and he set aside the note he'd been reading, welcoming us in and ushering us to his sitting area. As we passed his desk, I glanced sideways at the paper he'd been holding and managed to make out the signature at the bottom. *Inga.*

I smiled at this evidence that Lord Mornithalarion's romantic interest was firmly turned elsewhere. How he and Merkis Strond would manage a courtship across worlds and kingdoms, I didn't know —but given the strength of both their personalities, I imagined they'd find some way.

"Greetings," the Nightshade Lord said as we settled in his parlor. "What brings you to visit me this morning?"

"This." Neeve held out the leaflet.

Her uncle took it, his eyes widening as he paged through. The parchment rustled softly, and I leaned forward, holding my breath.

"What is it?" I asked.

"The lost poems of Lady Gwynelleth of the Cereus Court." His voice was reverent. "Wherever did you find this?"

"Hidden in the castle library," I said.

"How old is it?" Neeve asked, leaning forward.

"Centuries." The Nightshade Lord placed one hand over the cover. "This is a treasure of our people. I would like to return it to Elfhame."

My sister nodded. "That shouldn't be a problem. My father has no idea it was even here."

"Thank you." He inclined his head. "Would you like to hear one of the poems?"

"Very much," Neeve said, and I nodded.

Lord Mornithalarion carefully turned the pages again, pausing midway through the leaflet. "I'll translate as I read," he said. "I beg your patience. This one is called 'Harvest.'"

He drew in a breath and began to read.

"The light slips
Through the cracks between the worlds, glowing
Like a maiden's joy, like tears
Shed for the beloved. Listen,
The trees sing for you. Watch,
The moons' blossoms fall,
Gold and white
Upon the dark waters."

It was beautiful, though I had no idea what it meant.

"Thank you," Neeve said. "Perhaps you can teach me to read them, Uncle."

He smiled. "I would like that very much. Are you ready to travel tomorrow?"

"Of course," my sister said, then glanced at me.

"I still need to pack," I confessed, though there wasn't much I planned to take.

A few mortal gowns, my toiletries, my crown and dagger. I wished I could bring Trisk, but she belonged to Castle Raine. And now to Sorche more than me.

I took my leave, pausing in the hallway. Then, with a sigh, I turned toward the queen's rooms. It was time to bid farewell to Mama.

CHAPTER 41

"Come in," my mother called weakly when I rapped upon her door.

I rubbed my thumb over one of the gilt stags beside the latch, then entered.

She was reclining before the hearth on a low sofa. Her maid, Briddy, sat nearby, ready to tend to her needs.

"Hello, Mama." I came forward and knelt before her, taking her hand. Her fingers felt like brittle twigs, fragile under my grasp. "How are you feeling?"

"Well enough." She gave me a tremulous smile.

Even as frail as she now was, my mother remained luminously beautiful. My heart twisted, grieving for what we'd never had.

I'd thought that my father would give me the warmth and approval that Mama seemed incapable of. And for a time, he had—but that turned out to be a lie. Maybe an even worse one than Mama's cool distance.

"You're going away tomorrow," she said softly.

I nodded. "I won't be gone too long. Thorne will need to return to Raine soon, to nurture the Darkwood through the winter months."

Tears sparkled in her eyes and she reached forward, gently touching my cheek. "I wish you'd forgive me. I only ever wanted to protect you."

I thought of Mistress Ainya's argument that if my mother truly hadn't cared, she would have done away with me the moment I displayed any sign of fire sorcery.

Either that, or marched me straight to the temple and given me to the red priests. Both those options would certainly have been safer for her than keeping Galtus Celcio's child hidden from him, under his very nose.

Yet she'd chosen to take that risk, saving me from falling under the sway of the red priests at an early age. My mouth twisted at the bitter realization that I would have become my father's tool, not knowing any better than to embrace the path of the Sister.

My mother loved me—I could see that now. She had protected me as best she could. Even to the point of turning to dark sorcery so that we both could live free.

"I know." I swallowed and held her gaze. "I forgive you."

The words felt like bright petals, too long left unspoken. I let out a sigh.

Perhaps she'd taken the best path all along. Without Mama's choices, I would never have come to Raine. Galtus Celcio would be emperor over all the Continent, and probably Raine and the North-lands as well.

"I'm sorry you didn't marry Prince Jenson," she said, and my swelling affection for her receded.

Even if she'd made the right choices, they'd caused a great deal of pain—as had her lies. She was still the same self-centered woman I'd grown up with.

"Thorne is my true love," I said. "Best if you accept the fact, for there's no changing it."

She let out a disappointed breath that turned to a delicate cough. Briddy hurried over, shooting me a glare and offering my mother a glass of honey-water.

After Mama had taken a few sips and her coughing had subsided, she caught my gaze. Her eyes were like sapphires, her face as unlined as a young maiden's. "I hope I live long enough to see you again," she said.

Whether it was exaggeration or truth, I didn't know. All I could do was accept her as she was.

"I hope you do too." I leaned forward and brushed a kiss across her perfect cheek. "I love you, Mama."

She smiled at me, the corners of her lips trembling. "I love you. Don't stay away too long."

"I'll try not to. Take care of yourself, please."

"Safe travels," she said, then laid her head back and closed her eyes, clearly at the end of her strength.

Briddy motioned me toward the door. Quietly, I rose and let myself out of the suite. My emotions whirled, tinged with sorrow, but I was glad that I'd been able to forgive her. To speak the words out loud, and mean them in my heart.

Kian was just stepping out of his rooms down the hall. He took one look at my face, and held his arms out. With a little sob, I stepped into his embrace.

"It's not always easy, having a queen for a mother," he said, giving me a comforting squeeze and holding me while I shed a few tears.

After a short time, I stopped crying and wiped my face on my sleeve. He let me go.

"Will you be all right, Rose?"

"Yes." I met his gaze. "Do you miss your parents?"

"A little." He shrugged. "But it's our duty as children to move on. To take the work of the world onto our shoulders, when we're ready."

I *was* ready, I realized. Though I'd been carrying that weight for what felt like an awfully long time, at last I could welcome it. I could smile as I bore the burden of my own choices, forged my own path forward into the future.

⊗⊗⊗

WITH THE ORACLES' help, we departed Raine from the castle courtyard, though we wouldn't arrive on the Nightshade Court steps. Even the white-veiled figures were depleted, having spent much of their wellsprings to help heal the Darkwood. They would take us to the gateway in the Erynvorn, where a small encampment of Dark Elves awaited to escort us to the palace.

We gathered, Neeve and Kian, Thorne and I, Lord Mornithalarion and his two hollow-eyed guards, and the trio of Oracles.

Lord Raine embraced his daughter and then me, to my surprise. Mama lifted a hand in farewell from her cushioned chair at the top of the stairs. Sir Durum, newly returned from the west, lifted his clenched fist in a warrior's salute. Even Jarl Eiric had managed to rise from his sickbed, though bandages covered half his body.

According to Mistress Ainya, he was healing well, as was his brave cohort of soldiers. They would bear scars, but that was the worst of it. He saluted Kian then watched, as sharp-eyed as ever, as we prepared to cross between the worlds.

"Ready?" the tallest Oracle cried. Then, barely waiting for our assent, they lifted their hands and called out the rune of opening.

Blue light flashed. I clung to Thorne's hand, remembering how we'd been separated the last time I made the passage into Elfhame.

A rippling moment later, the light faded. I breathed a sigh of relief to feel my husband's fingers still laced with mine. As my eyes adjusted to the dimness, I saw two standing stones inscribed with glowing symbols. We'd arrived in the gateway clearing of the Erynvorn.

A quartet of glimglows streaked into the clearing and began dancing above our heads. Their golden light illuminated the vast columns of the trees surrounding us, the trunks stretching up smoothly for nearly a hundred feet before branching out to canopy the sky.

Beneath my feet, the emerald moss shone with a dusting of sparkling pollen, drifted from the nodding bells of *quille* blossoms. The air was rich with the scent of loam and cedar and the heady perfume of the glowing flowers. Craning my neck, I peered between the branches high overhead, glimpsing that same light echoed in the unfamiliar constellations of Elfhame.

"Home," Neeve murmured.

I glanced at her, amazed to see how much better she looked, even in the few moments since we'd arrived in the realm of the Dark Elves. Her eyes were no longer ringed with bruised shadows, and her pallor was smooth ivory, not the bleached flatness of salt. The redness of her lips were ripe berries instead of dried rosehips, and the night-black of her hair shone as glossy as a raven's wing.

She'd driven herself nearly to death, I realized with a stab of alarm.

Kian, too, was regarding his wife, and I could see the same realization in his eyes. Along with a determination that they would not leave Elfhame until she'd regained her full strength. I was glad to see it. If my sister wouldn't take proper care of herself, then at least my brother-in-law would.

A group of Dark Elves approached, blue foxfire bobbing at their shoulders and words of greeting on their lips. They urged us toward the camp, where a feast would soon be ready. Carrying our bags, we followed. Only as we stepped into the ring of tents did I realize that some of our company was missing.

"Where did the Oracles go?" I asked Thorne.

"Into the hidden ways," he said.

My eyebrows rose. "I've never heard of such a thing."

"It's one of their mysteries," Thorne said, then winced.

"What's wrong?" I set my hand on his arm.

"This." He reached beneath his tunic and pulled out a mewing ball of white fluff. "Its claws are like needles."

"A kitten!" I reached forward, and he gently handed me the little creature. I cradled it under my chin, smiling at the softness of its fur. "Where did it come from?"

"Trisk had kittens, apparently, two months ago. Sorche was saving this one for you."

"Why didn't she tell me?" I looked down at the kitten, who blinked up at me with sleepy green eyes. It was like bringing a part of Raine along with me, and even better that the kitten was Trisk's offspring.

"She wanted it to be a surprise." Thorne smiled. "Are you surprised?"

"Very." I grinned back at him. "Do you have cats in Elfhame?"

"A few, but they are not common."

The glimglows seemed very interested in the little animal I was holding. One by one, they descended to hover in front of its face. The kitten batted at them, and the glimglows zipped away in a swirl of what looked like amusement.

"What do you want to name it?" I asked, then held the kitten up for a quick inspection. "Him, that is."

Thorne tilted his head in thought. "What do you think about Isil? It means moon in Elvish."

"His coat is certainly the right color." I gave the kitten a scritch between the ears, and he started to purr. "I think he approves. Isil it is."

I held the kitten all through the meal, its sharp claws a counterpoint to the lush magic of the Erynvorn. Afterward, I deposited Isil in the tent Thorne and I had been given. He curled into a contented ball and went to sleep.

"Come." My husband held out his hand.

I took it and let him lead me away from the blue fires of the camp. Our glimglows returned, weaving patterns overhead. The light of the palemoon filtered through the interlaced evergreens high above, sending dapples of silver over the moss and ferns.

There was no need to ask him where we were going, or why. Though we hadn't spoken of it, I knew that we must say our vows in the Erynvorn, under the stars of Elfhame.

A glimmer of light shone ahead, as if the moon had descended to shelter beneath the trees. As we approached, I realized it was a small, still pool, reflecting back the moonlight. Violet flowers bloomed at its edges, shedding a soft radiance.

Thorne halted at the water's edge and held my hands.

"Will you speak the rune of binding with me, beloved?" he asked.

"I will. But what will we use for a ribbon?"

In response, the glimglows descended and began weaving around our wrists, a strand of light purer than any piece of fabric could hope to be.

I slid my hands up until they clasped his wrists. Though my nails were weak and mortal, I clawed my fingers against his skin, filled with a fierce possessiveness.

"Thorne Windrift, *Galadhir* of the forests, I claim you as my own,"

I said. "I pledge my heart and life to you, no matter which world we dwell in. You are mine, and I am yours. Always."

Our gazes met, his dark eyes flecked with golden sparks. I felt the prick of his claws against my wrists.

"Rose, you are the sun to my moon, the day to my night, the air to my lungs, the water to my thirst. I pledge myself to you in this world, and the next, and any other that we might travel through. I am yours, and you are mine. Forever."

Together, we inhaled, then spoke the rune of binding. "*Gwedhy-ocuilvorn!*"

A thunder clap, a bell, a sudden wind before the storm. The scarf covering my bare head blew away. The glimglows whirled about our clasped arms, about our heads. Suddenly we were surrounded by a flurry of golden light. A dozen, a hundred glimglows, so bright that I had to close my eyes.

"The Erynvorn approves," Thorne said, and I heard the gladness in his voice.

I opened my eyes in time to see the whirling sparks of the glimglows twist off into the night, flying upward until they blended with the constellations. I sighed, and Thorne pulled me into his arms.

"Welcome home, love," he whispered.

My heart pulsed as tears heated my eyes. Wherever Thorne was, that was my home.

Above us, the brightmoon began to climb, soaring above the trees. The dark loam of Elfhame lay beneath our feet. In the heart of the Erynvorn, the gateway shone, and beyond it lay Raine, the stars whirling about in the mortal sky.

My life had opened, petal by petal, blossoming like a *nirwen* flower, until I stood at its bright and shining heart.

It was all I'd ever wanted.

It was enough.

ACKNOWLEDGMENTS

The end of a trilogy is always bittersweet. I want to thank all the readers who let me know via email or in reviews that they could hardly wait for *Red as Flame* to be released. You kept this writer's mojo going!

Special thanks to Mulan Jiang for the extraordinarily beautiful symbol covers (and hardbacks!) and to Whendell Souza for the lovely depictions of Rose and Neeve on the "people" covers. It was a treat getting to work with two such talented designers. You're appreciated!

Particular thanks to my early readers on this book: Laurie Temple, Cathi Killian, Kimberly Belden, and Nic Page. Your feedback is, as always, incredibly helpful and keeps me out of all kinds of authorial trouble. Thank you.

A sweeping bow to the copy editing of Arran - ever dependable - and Ginger the typo-catcher extraordinaire.

Finally, I'd like to acknowledge the work of Leonard and the wonderful folks who compiled Parf Edhellen, a free online dictionary of Tolkien's languages. The Dark Elf language is deeply inspired by Sindarin, with many thanks to this excellent resource. www.elfdict.com

ABOUT THE AUTHOR

-USA Today bestselling, award-winning author of fantasy-flavored
fiction -

Growing up on fairy tales and computer games, Anthea Sharp has
melded the two in her award-winning, bestselling Feyland series, which
has sold over 150k copies worldwide.

In addition to the fae fantasy/cyberpunk mashup of Feyland, she
also writes Victorian Spacepunk, and fantasy romance featuring Dark
Elves. Her books have won awards and topped bestseller lists, and
garnered over 1.2 million reads at Wattpad. Her short fiction has
appeared in Fiction River, DAW anthologies, The Future Chronicles,
and Beyond The Stars: At Galaxy's edge, as well as many other publi-
cations.

Anthea lives in Southern California, where she writes, hangs out in
virtual worlds, plays the fiddle with her Celtic band Fiddlehead, and
spends time with her small-but-good family.

Contact her at antheasharp@hotmail.com or visit her website –
www.antheasharp.com where you can sign up for her newsletter, Sharp
Tales, and be among the first to hear about new releases and reader
perks.

Anthea also writes historical romance under the pen name Anthea
Lawson. Find out about her acclaimed Victorian romantic adventure
novels at www.anthealawson.com.

OTHER WORKS

~ THE DARKWOOD TRILOGY ~

WHITE AS FROST

BLACK AS NIGHT

RED AS FLAME

~ THE FEYLAND SERIES ~

What if a high-tech game was a gateway to the treacherous Realm of Faerie?

THE FIRST ADVENTURE - Book 0 (prequel)

THE DARK REALM – Book 1

THE BRIGHT COURT – Book 2

THE TWILIGHT KINGDOM – Book 3

FAERIE SWAP - Book 3.5

TRINKET (short story)

SPARK - Book 4

BREA'S TALE - Book 4.5

ROYAL - Book 5

MARNY - Book 6

CHRONICLE WORLDS: FEYLAND

FEYLAND TALES: Volume 1

~ THE DARKWOOD CHRONICLES ~

Deep in the Darkwood, a magical doorway leads to the enchanted and dangerous land of the Dark Elves~

ELFHAME

HAWTHORNE

RAINE

HEART of the FOREST (A Novella)